The Iron Hotel

The Iron Hotel

SAM LLEWELLYN

MICHAEL JOSEPH
LONDON

MICHAEL JOSEPH LTD

Published by the Penguin Group
27 Wrights Lane, London W8 5TZ
Viking Penguin Inc., 375 Hudson Street, New York, New York 10014, USA
Penguin Books Australia Ltd, Ringwood, Victoria, Australia
Penguin Books Canada Ltd, 10 Alcorn Avenue, Toronto, Ontario, Canada M4V 3B2
Penguin Books (NZ) Ltd, 182–190 Wairau Road, Auckland 10, New Zealand

Penguin Books Ltd, Registered Offices: Harmondsworth, Middlesex, England

First published 1996
1 3 5 7 9 10 8 6 4 2

Typeset in 11/12.75 pt Monophoto Plantin by
Datix International Limited, Bungay, Suffolk
Printed in England by Clays Ltd, St Ives plc

A CIP catalogue record for this book is available from the British Library

ISBN 0 7181 3790 6

The moral right of the author has been asserted

For Karen

'Cargo,' he said tonelessly. 'They were cargo.'

Fritz Stangl, Commandant of Treblinka,
quoted by Gitta Sereny in *Into that Darkness*

Author's Note

This story could not have been written without the kind help of the China Navigation Company. I also owe a huge debt of gratitude to Captains Jim Bird, Mike Allison and Geoff Garrett, Chief Engineer Brian Ingleson, and the other officers and crew of MS *Micronesian Pride*. If any of these kind people think they recognize themselves, their ships, or their company in this narrative, they are quite wrong.

All day the rain had hissed down on the flat fields by the estuary, blurring the maze of creek and island into a wet grey haze, soaking the three hundred and seventy people waiting nervously on the concrete to see if the promises were to be kept.

At first, the people had tried to cover up the boxes and sacks, the old suitcases done up with string. But rain like this soused hessian and melted paper and ran round plastic until it found a puncture or a tear where it could creep in. There were plenty of punctures and tears, because most of the people had travelled hundreds of miles to be here. They had travelled rough, by roundabout routes; that had been part of the instructions. The organizers had made good plans, and they did not want them messed up by a curious militiaman in a station jammed with anxious families carrying all their possessions. Three hundred and seventy people and their families was a big crowd to be converging on a small village by the Pearl River in February, even at Chinese New Year, when families assemble and debts are paid.

Night fell. Floodlights made glittering silver Chinese lanterns in the rain and turned the faces of the people the colour of stone.

The people no longer spoke. There was only the hiss of the rain on the quay, and the chewing-gum-coloured water of the river, wrung with eddies, rushing towards the South China Sea.

At seven o'clock, a voice came from the loudspeakers on the building behind the quay. The people stirred and began to form an incoherent straggle focused on the entrance to a double line of crowd-control barriers, like the entrance to a cattle market. The way led through a small shed. Inside the shed, a man with spectacles was sitting behind a table, smoking a cigarette. From time to time he spat into a porcelain spittoon and ticked off an entry on *the paper in front of him. The people passed on, out of the shed's second door and into another double line of barriers. At the end of this line was a gangway, leading to an entry port in the side of a ship, full of windows, with the rusty remains of rails and supports for awning stanchions; a ferry, streaming with water alongside the quay.*

By nine o'clock, the serpent of people had crawled through the shed and into the entry port in the ship's side. The last to go in was a man balancing a ten-foot plank on his shoulder. Held to the plank by staples, one over each toe, were ten chickens, drenched by the rain until they looked like melted candles.

The entry port ate the plank and the chickens. Someone rolled away the gangway and closed the port. A pair of stevedores splashed through the puddles, casting off. The current plucked the ferry from the quay. Its rain-varnished side gleamed for a moment in the lights. Then the black rushed in behind it, and it was gone.

The stevedores climbed into a van. The van coughed away, trailing cigarette smoke from its windows, its headlights a cheerful orange in the blackness. On the quay and downstream among the mudbanks and channels and creeks the night became empty, except for the rain.

BOOK I

Chapter One

On the day it really began, Jenkins was playing tennis.

It was Diana's serve. Jenkins watched her long, suntanned legs, her short white skirt, the patch of sweat at her armpit as she tossed the lime-green ball into the steamy February air. He watched the mettlesome stamp of her new Reebok, the lift of her breast under the Aertex blouse, the working of the muscles at the corner of her still-clean jawline. Looking at her, it was possible to believe that nothing had changed since they had married. Except that, then, behind the wire mesh of the tennis court had been the green trees of Dorset. Now, her racket framed the distant towers of Hong Kong, jutting into their sulphurous haze.

Dorset had been twenty years ago. Everything had changed beyond recognition. And who the hell, thought Jenkins, could tell where it would all end?

Diana caught the ball and tossed it up again. It seemed to Jenkins to be moving with abnormal slowness. Perhaps it was just that, for him, life had recently started moving horribly fast. He knew her serve by heart. Get on with it, he thought: the famous in-swing off-break, a serve packed with guile, but the same serve every time.

Alongside her Jeremy Selmes was crouched, grinning, passing his brown left hand over his crinkly black hair with the obsessive neatness of an ape in a cage. He was wearing white shorts and one of those shirts with an alligator. Until recently, Jeremy had been an inspector in the Hong Kong Police, so Jeremy knew how to dress for formal occasions, including tennis. So did Jenkins' partner, Rachel, his daughter, a browner and fresher and brighter version of her mother. Jenkins was aware that he himself was wearing cutoff jeans and plimsolls of doubtful cleanliness, in whose uppers his toenails were steadily drilling holes. The faint, rancid whiff of his Dan Dare T-shirt rose to his nostrils.

Jenkins glanced at his watch, feeling the flutter of panic under his sternum. The grip of his racket became suddenly slimy.

Rachel's voice said, 'Dad?'

Diana's arm came over. She grunted, the way her coach had told her. The ball swung, hit the ground well inside Jenkins' court, broke away and whirred past to starboard.

'*Played*,' said Jeremy.

Jenkins stood as if poured from concrete, unable to associate the whizzing lime-green sphere with the racket in his hand. 'Out,' he said.

Jeremy said, with the thin violence of a friend minding his manners, 'Are you sure?'

Diana said in her sharp Home Counties voice, 'It was in. I could absolutely *see* it was in.'

Jenkins shifted his gaze across the court to Rachel. Rachel's face was smooth and heart-shaped, the skin naturally brown. Her eyes were brown too, and amused, like an intelligent version of her mother's. She knew that tennis made Jenkins desperate. She knew he was cheating. But she would not give him away. Rachel and Jenkins were friends and allies, and they never gave each other away.

'Have it again,' said Rachel.

Rachel the peacemaker. Rachel the wise one, eighteen years old. Jenkins found his eyes straying once again to his watch. It was a fake Rolex, the kind you could come by for a hundred dollars in Tsimshatsui. Until three months ago he had had a real one. Luckily, no one had noticed the difference.

Diana bounced a ball twice on the ground and sniffed. 'For God's sake wake up,' she said.

'Ready now?' said Jeremy, sarcastically.

'Ready,' said Jenkins, his mind on the doom to come.

Diana whacked the ball over the net, in-swing, off-break. Jenkins let fly at it backhand, the whole width of his shoulders behind the stroke. He caught the ball bang on the sweet spot. Jeremy poked feebly at it as it whizzed back over the net, far too high. It was still rising as it shot over the base

6

line, crossed the mesh screens and vanished between two palm trees behind a white stucco wall.

'I think that was out,' said Jeremy, with his gleaming film-star smile.

'Game,' said Diana, looking smug.

Rachel said, 'Honestly, Dad,' and smiled tolerantly. There were many things Jenkins could be trusted to do. Dressing properly and playing tennis were not two of them.

Jenkins looked at his watch again. He knew he was looking at it too often, but he could not help it. It did not matter what time it was. What mattered was that minutes were passing, bringing closer a sequence of events so terrible he could not bring himself to contemplate it in detail.

'Damn,' he said. 'I've got to run.'

'What's the hurry?' said Jeremy.

'Office.'

'You guys work over the New Year?'

Jenkins grinned at him vaguely, unable to meet his ex-policeman's eye. It was indeed Chinese New Year, when families assemble and debts are paid.

'See you later,' said Jeremy.

'I'll try,' said Jenkins. 'I'll call. You in, Rachel?'

'Got a shoot,' she said. 'Down in Statue Square. On a horse.'

Jenkins nodded, puzzled as always by the fact that this small girl could earn a living as a fashion model, and then remembering that she was not a small girl any more. He zipped his racket back into its cover.

Diana was picking up balls at the back of the court, the curve of her buttocks showing through her white pants. Down at the Yacht Club, divorced expats told each other she had a nice arse. When she overheard, she was not displeased. She said, 'Are we playing tennis, or what?' Men's work was men's work, as far as Diana was concerned. It was the price they paid for the companionship of tanned women with blonde hair.

As Jenkins let himself out of the court, the other three were already starting a game of American doubles, bouncing around with confidence and economy. They would be getting on much better without him. He turned and walked towards the clubhouse, initiating the manoeuvres that had become second nature.

If he went past the verandah, he was liable to be hailed by somebody in the bar, which meant he would have to buy a round, which was not possible. So he turned right, along the side of the building, stooping so it looked as if he was interested in the label of a Hawaiian *ti* palm in the bed under the drainpipe. He made it to the showers without meeting anyone, took off his clothes and stepped into a cubicle.

As the water drummed on his skull, he tried not to think about how much the club was costing him. Five thousand pounds, near enough. A drop in the ocean of things poor old Diana needed to keep her in the style to which she had become accustomed.

Poor old Diana.

There had been a time when Jenkins had been Captain Jenkins, master of the Orient Line's *Komodo President*. Then, life had been divided into neat slabs: four months at sea, two ashore. The pay had been good enough to allow Diana to organize herself the kind of life unimaginable in her Poole childhood. She had her amahs, Irina and Consuelo from Manila. She had an apartment in Repulse Bay, overlooking the blue-and-grey South China Sea. She spent her leisure in the Yacht Club, and the Stanley Club, and in Raoul's Hair and Beauty. And once a year for a fortnight she went back to England, which she now called 'Home' with a sentimental but distant look in her shallow brown eyes. Home be blowed, thought Jenkins. As far as Diana was concerned nowadays, home was where the charge account was.

Not fair, he told himself, soaping a ribcage that had become perceptibly more corrugated during the last three months. Diana is the way she is, and you married her. What you are doing now is blaming her for things that are at least half your fault.

He rinsed off the soap and looked at his watch. The thought of what was going to happen crept back, restoring the flutter in his stomach. He dried himself and pulled on a beige linen suit that still looked all right by artificial light, and a pair of poncy Church's loafers Diana had bought him, with tassels on the insteps and holes in the soles. He checked himself in the mirror above the marble sinks and adjusted his dark blue knitted silk tie. He looked respectable enough, except for the face, and there was nothing he could do about that. The face was brown, with black hair in need of cutting, and going grey at the temples; distinguished, but lacking the sheen of health and aggression that burst out of successful European faces in Hong Kong.

Jenkins gave himself a polite smile and said, 'Bollocks.' It did not matter if he looked as confident as the Taipan of Swires. He was going to meet Tommy Wong, and Tommy Wong knew exactly what he had to be confident about.

Jenkins fingered the pitifully slim roll of notes in his trouser pocket. He walked out and round the back of the building. His bike was chained to the spiked iron railings. Good old Jenkins, they said. Bikes for fun. Mad as a hatter. An anti-colonialist had spat on the seat. He wiped it clean with a bit of banana leaf, climbed aboard, and aimed it back at the city.

The wind parted warm and dusty on the bridge of his nose. The road began to sink between big villas with *fengshui* lions on the gateposts. Diana would have liked to live up here in the breezes that fanned the millionaires. Between the skyscrapers Victoria Harbour lay blue and glittering, full of ships. A couple of container ships had ramshackle harbour cranes alongside, swinging rusty steel boxes through the air with reckless speed. Strewth, thought Jenkins, applying some front brake. Working cargo at New Year. They'd be paying the stevedores triple time. He was glad it wasn't him, having to explain it to an owner –

He turned his face away from the harbour. He tasted the dust and sweat of the unseasonably hot February, and felt the miserable judder of the road in his bones. He was not glad it was not him. He would have given just about anything to be out there in the harbour, doing his job, triple time or no triple time.

But there was no chance.

He turned left, diving into the apartment blocks. The harbour vanished. The streets were empty. Nobody was in the shops today, and nobody was going to the office.

9

Nor was Jenkins.

The sweat was running as hard as if he had been pedalling uphill instead of down. It was stinging his eyes and staining the spine and armpits of his linen jacket as he whizzed past the Happy Valley racecourse, across the big, empty dual carriageway at the bottom of the hill, and stood on the pedals to get up the entrance ramp of the Harbour Tower Hotel. He looked for something to chain the bike to. The doorman's eye went straight through him. Jenkins wheeled the bike back down the ramp, and glanced at the fake Rolex. He had ten minutes.

He found a railing and locked the bike. Then he flapped his jacket to dry out the sweat stains, rubbed unsuccessfully at the patch of oil the chain had left on his right trouser leg, and swallowed a few times to get some moisture back into his mouth.

Seven minutes.

In his mind, the tennis players on the hill stretched and lunged in their tidy little cage. Their lives were going to change, too. Barring miracles, he was going to have to go back to Diana, poor Diana, and say: Sorry, darling, but all this must go.

He could see the look on her face, petulant and amused and a little bit patronizing. The long brown legs, waxed to golden perfection, would cross at the ankles. The blue-dyed lashes would flutter distractedly over the shallow brown eyes, and she would frown, but only faintly, in case it left wrinkles. Darling, she would say, because that was what she had called him for years. What do you *mean*?

And he would have to explain away the Tennis Club, and the Yacht Club, and the hairdresser, and the trips Home, and the lease on the BMW. She would issue a measured dose of the fake laugh with which she paid tribute to the fact that he made jokes she did not understand. Then would come the emptiness that would sweep in from what she saw in his face, that would join the emptiness inside her head, and make her life a big zero.

He knew he would be bad at the next bit, the consolation. He would probably tell her it was not the end of the world.

When of course it would be.

The pattern would take shape the way it had when Bill got killed. First the blankness. Then the grief. Then the grief finding a focus and becoming anger.

It was his fault. He had been at sea when Bill had been killed. He had always been at sea.

Diana had been pleased when three months ago he had told her that from now on he would be working in an office. Having him around all the time would take some getting used to, of course. But offices were status, and clean shirts, and stock options of the kind she heard so much about at her cocktail parties. There had been something, well, *manual* about being at sea.

Two minutes. He shoved his hands into his pockets, re-checking the anorexic cylinder of notes. Very soon now, he was going to have to tell her the truth.

Squaring his shoulders in his sweaty linen jacket, David Jenkins walked up the ramp and into the icy air conditioning of the lobby.

Tommy Wong was a slender man in a blazer and Hermès tie. He was sitting on a red velvet sofa with his back to the window. Behind him was a splendid view of shifting water and boats beetling against the concrete frieze of Kowloon. But Tommy Wong was interested in people, not views of the harbour. Lending money was a matter of sizing up prospects, particularly when you were a moneylender to whom clients came only after they had been turned down by banks and finance companies. At Tommy Wong's end of the market, character was the only security.

Character, or a particular skill.

Wong sipped delicately at the tea on the low table in front of him. He would have preferred cognac, but he did not want the gweilo to be in the position of buying drinks. Either the gweilo would not be in a position to pay the bill or – much less likely, in Wong's view – the gweilo would have Wong's money for him, and Wong would buy him a drink to restore face after pocketing the principal plus interest.

The gweilo came in at the door of the bar. Wong observed that the beige linen trousers were too short over the highly polished but misshapen shoes. There was a stain of some kind on the right turnup, and the hemline of the jacket sagged unevenly where wear had bagged the pockets. The brown skin of the face had a greasy sheen, and the eyes were wild as a horse's.

It struck Wong that this was not the carriage of a man who had returned to repay a debt of thirty thousand dollars US, plus ten thousand dollars interest.

He raised a hand a small, suitable distance from his lap. The gweilo – Jenkins; think of him by name, thought Wong. This will be a difficult interview, and it will be wise to curb one's contempt and remember that he too is human – waved an arm of his own in the loose, uncontrolled fashion of one not used to confined spaces. Wong's trained eye detected a slight greying of the facial skin. Certainly there would be no repayment.

The gweilo – Jenkins – made his way clumsily between the armchairs. The bar was three-quarters empty; the Chinese New Year is a time for family reunions, not public roistering. Wong had been warned that this was a man of strong mind, given on occasion to violence. He saw the redness come back into the face, the hard blue-grey eyes screwed up against the light from the harbour. Certainly he had the look of a determined man.

Jenkins was not good in hotel bars. The drinks were too expensive, and the furniture too close together. Faced with this little Tommy Wong, silhouetted on the sofa against the bright water behind him, Jenkins began to feel defiant. If he was going to lose everything, he was going to lose it to someone whose face he could see.

'Budge up,' he said.

Wong looked up at him blankly.

'Move over,' said Jenkins.

Wong found himself moving over. Jenkins sat down next to him, hard enough to bounce him on the springs. The smell of him, the Stanley Club soap mixed with sweat and bicycle oil, floated across to Wong. Wong approved of the soap, but not the rest.

A waiter was standing by. The roll in Jenkins' pocket would not run to the Harbour Tower's whisky, much as he needed it. 'Tea,' he said. Now that the hour was upon him, he felt almost light-headed.

They sat in silence for a moment, looking across the maroon carpet at the spurious gilt bar. Then Wong said, 'It is hot.'

'I was playing tennis.'

'An expensive game.'

Jenkins remembered the figures in the tennis cage. The cage would be locked against him now. His defiance was leaving him. He said, 'Look. I need an extension.' It sounded as if someone else was talking.

Wong's black eyebrows rose on his café-au-lait forehead. 'Extension?' he said, as if he had never heard the word before.

Jenkins' light-headedness had become a loose, unconnected feeling, as if he was falling. There were only two weeks' money left for Diana. 'Two weeks,' he said, before he could stop himself.

Wong nodded, craftsmanlike. 'Debts are repaid at the New Year,' he said. 'This was our agreement.'

Jenkins said, 'I can't pay.'

'So,' said Wong, opening a small notebook. 'You have already sold your boat, I think. There is still the lease of your apartment. Your furniture. Your wife's jewellery.'

Jenkins said, 'That won't cover it,' and waited for the axe to fall.

Wong smiled. Jenkins felt his heart lumping about in his chest. What's so funny? he thought. He likes to watch a gweilo suffer. He's seen a friend the other side of the room. I don't matter. He'll just sell me up. Diana up. That's why –

'One moment, please,' said Wong. He was still smiling.

Jenkins stared at him, amazed. The smile was at him. It looked as if it was meant to be *encouraging*, for God's sake.

Wong pulled a little telephone from his pocket, and spoke into it in Cantonese, a language his records showed Jenkins did not understand. When he had finished he turned back to Jenkins and nodded. 'We can extend this one week,' he said, pulling a small diary from the breast pocket of his blazer and making an entry.

'Excellent,' said Jenkins. The blood was surging in his

veins. A week could see him seriously organized. Another trawl round the shipping companies and manning agencies. In a week, anything could happen.

'Thank you,' said Wong, rising, smiling. 'So nice to meet with you.' He went. Jenkins lay back on the sofa and let the sweat roll. The first surge of blood abated, and the sweat cooled.

Borrowed time. Borrowed money.

A waiter materialized with the bill. Two cups of tea amounted to Jenkins' total wealth, less five Hong Kong dollars. He left that for the waiter. Penniless and shaking, he cycled laboriously back to Repulse Bay.

Chapter Two

The apartment was a big one. Once, Diana had decorated it according to an elaborate set of principles she had prised out of a decorator called Laney Bodais. Diana had been very excited, because Bodais had won awards. Jenkins had been vaguely aware of a stout, pop-eyed man with a bald patch and a ponytail. The apartment had changed in various ways that seemed to impress people who noticed such matters. It was only the bill that had made an impression on Jenkins. Diana had soon reverted to pink and beige, with frills and dried flowers here and there. That was how she operated: a bright, expensive idea, then a falling back on the certainties. Both she and Jenkins had always been big on certainties: Jenkins' job, working his way up from cadet to third officer, second officer, chief mate, captain; four months at sea, two months at home; the tidy grid of a well-ordered life. Anything that did not fit was tidied away, out of sight, out of mind.

Nowadays, Diana's chief certainty was the Circuit. She was on the Circuit tonight; it was after all the cocktail hour, and in the gweilo world New Year is a time for parties. Jenkins found himself chilled by the pastel immensities of the drawing room. The amahs were out, twittering with thousands of cousins in Statue Square. So the kitchen was a little oasis of squalor, a half-gnawed carcass of barbecued duck, a couple of bread crusts and a margarine-smeared plate. Jenkins ate the crusts, washed up the plates and wandered back into the drawing room.

There was a photograph in a frame on top of the TV set: him and Diana in a church doorway, the cool blonde beauty and the grinning, sunburned youth. Diana's long, clean-cut face wore what now appeared to be a triumphant look. For the first time he thought he saw something dazed in his own grin. A week before the photograph had been taken, he had been at sea. His father had organized the wedding in Blandford, because Diana had not liked to get married in Poole. Her veil was thrown back. She was tanned and fit-looking even in an English April. Jenkins' Aunt Helen had tried to explain it at the wedding. 'She's got you,' said Aunt Helen. 'Now she thinks she's got us.'

For a man recently returned from the sea and due to rejoin his ship after the honeymoon, it had been hard to work out what Aunt Helen was talking about. It had become plainer, over the years. Jenkins even found it endearing. He was married to Diana, so it stood to reason that they loved each other, with all their faults and peculiarities. That was how the grid was built.

Jenkins wandered across the Casa Pupo rug, past the bookshelf full of Folio Society editions, and rummaged in the compact discs. Under a pile of James Last and Earth, Wind and Fire he found the Beethoven Piano Concerto No. 4. He posted it into the slot.

The room filled with music. For a moment he felt a huge freedom. Then, like a door slamming, it all went.

A week.

The vacancy in his stomach became a sort of Turk's head, yanked tight. Nothing that could happen in the next week could fix anything. Oh, Christ, thought Jenkins, closing his eyes. Where are the manuals for this?

There are no manuals for free fall.

He leaned his forehead against the cool glass of a William Russell Flint reproduction. Tommy Wong knew damn well that nothing could happen in the next week that had not happened in the last three months. So why the extension?

Kindness of his heart.

Jenkins laughed out loud. It sounded mad and dangerous in the empty flat. Yours not to reason why, old boy, he thought. Yours to wait for the offices to open, and get on the hooter, and call your many contacts.

Who had been so helpful already.

He found he was walking round the walls. He poked his head into the dining room, and was repelled by the heartless order of its chairs. Rachel's room was down the hall. He felt better in there. It smelled of her perfume. She had refused to be decorated, and painted it white, herself. On the walls was a collection of New Guinea masks, and opposite the bed a sort of rack on which she had laid out the idols of her childhood, partly as a joke and partly because the bit of her that had not caught up with being eighteen still loved them. Jenkins leaned against the doorpost. There was Och Scott in her kilt and her blue saucer eyes. There was Ahab the Arab and Canada Bear. Once she had hugged them every night before bed. Now they were perched precariously on their shelves, en route for the garbage.

Jenkins felt that he and they had much in common.

A voice said, 'Daddy?'

His heart jumped. Rachel was sitting at the table behind the door, her computer's screen casting green lights in her scraped-back blonde hair.

'Sorry,' said Jenkins. 'Didn't know you were here.' Why are you explaining? he thought. Sign of guilt.

She was frowning in a way that would have made Diana worry about wrinkles. 'Are you all right?'

'Fine,' said Jenkins.

'You don't look fine.'

'Things are . . . a bit up in the air,' said Jenkins, and checked to make sure he had not said too much. Qualify that, he thought. 'At the office. I thought you had a shoot.'

'Cancelled,' she said. 'Something wrong with the horse. So I thought I'd do some work.'

Rachel had left school last year, and was waiting to go to university. In what he thought of as a Rachelish way, she had got results that would have won her a scholarship to any university in Britain, Hong Kong, or the USA. But she had decided that university was for grown-ups, and that she was not ready to be grown-up yet, and would wait until she was. Meanwhile, she had run into Mavis Yee at one of her mother's cocktail parties. Mavis Yee ran Yee Ma Publicity, an advertising agency. Mavis Yee said that Rachel had the face of the year, and that a great career in modelling lay ahead.

Rachel had smiled sweetly. She did not believe there was any such thing as a great career in modelling, but she had had her book done and taken it to Fruity Models. The photographs showed her as slim and tallish, a graceful mover. Her eyelashes were long and dark, her eyes big but narrow. She was an excellent actress, who could do mysterious east, Parisian urchin, or rustic *ingénue* without make-up. People who knew no better said she looked Oriental, as if Hong Kong had rubbed off on her. To Jenkins, she had looked the same for as long as he could remember. The Oriental business was nonsense, because she had been born in Dorset, and had only moved to Hong Kong at the age of eight. Still, the modelling fees came in handy, because they bought time for her to indulge her interest in Chinese ceramics.

She said, 'What are you up to tomorrow?'

'Not much,' said Jenkins, without thinking. He sat down on the chair she used to hang her clothes on. Suddenly he caught a glimpse of her not as Rachel, but as a beautiful woman he barely knew, sitting behind an official desk. Soon, he thought, she will be moving out.

In a week they would all be moving out.

She was saying something. 'Hollywood Road,' she said. 'We could go down and have a sneer.'

It was one of their pleasures to roll down Hollywood Road, the principal antique-shop street, and expose fakes. 'No can do,' said Jenkins. 'Actually. Got a meeting.'

She ran her eyes over his bagged-out suit, the limp shirt. He had the unpleasant feeling that she could see through him. She sighed. 'It is your duty to support us in the manner to which we are accustomed,' she said. If it had been Diana, she would have meant it.

Jenkins said, 'Nothing too good for the memsahibs, bless them.'

It was not funny, but they both laughed, and Jenkins felt he had slithered away from the doubtful area and back into the grid. The illusion of closeness returned. Rachel cooked her legendary scrambled eggs on toast and told him with enthusiasm about a course she fancied at Berkeley. For a moment he managed to persuade himself it was even possible that he might one day be able to afford to send her there. At nine, Diana came back, flushed with someone else's gin, and drank a pink Slimfast. Jenkins went to bed early. Diana came in later and covered her face with sickly-smelling cream. They lay one on each outer edge of the big bed under the Casa Pupo blanket. Jenkins stared into the faint, chill breeze from the air conditioner, and tried to tune out the gnaw in his stomach.

He told himself, like a mantra, Tomorrow will be different.

He woke up early, with a jolt, and crept out of bed to get the post. There was a final demand from the car-leasing company, which he paid with just about the last of Tommy Wong's money. There was an envelope bearing the logo of a credit card company. He thought, They've billed us early. It will be a nightmare, a disaster. Diana's credit card bills were always a disaster.

He shut his eyes and tore open the envelope.

He had heard of bankrupts who pushed the whole idea away from them, letting the bills pile up unopened, locking their studies on the deep litter, so that the first thing their families knew about it was when the bailiffs kicked the door in and made off with the furniture.

He opened his eyes.

It was a piece of card, printed in four colours with a picture of a bottle of champagne, two glasses, and a flat black box that was probably some sort of electrical gadget. Tucked into the gadget's wrist-strap was a red rosebud. Fake copperplate writing said *With the compliments of your Friendship Card, on your Birthday.*

He turned it over, looking for the amount he had to pay. There were no numbers. It sank in slowly. It was a birthday card. Today was his birthday. On this date twenty-odd years ago, he had been sixteen, and his parents had stood on Barry docks, waving tearfully, watching the boy Jenkins make his start in life and hoping against hope he got it right this time, and that he had a happy birthday down there in the cadets' berths of the *Merchant Willis*. Now his parents were dead, and the only person who remembered his birthday was the credit card company, softening him up for a bill he had no means of paying.

He began to laugh, silently, so as not to wake Diana. It turned into coughing. The spout of the teapot rattled against the cups as he poured. He took the tea into the dark bedroom. Diana murmured, 'If you've got a cold, I don't want it,' and went back to sleep. Back in the kitchen he wrote a note to Rachel, pulled on a pair of jeans, yesterday's Dan Dare T-shirt and his canvas shoes, and ran downstairs to the garage where he kept his bicycle.

The librarian at the Kowloon public library was a wide-hipped, horse-faced woman whose parents had migrated from a mainland village that she remembered only as having been disgustingly muddy. She brought to her job a deep loathing for dirt and untidiness. At nine-eleven, she looked up from the screen of her electronic catalogue. Sure enough, the tall gweilo loped through the door, looking hot, wearing his child's T-shirt, the cuff of his right trouser leg tucked into his sock. Three months ago, when he had started coming in, he had worn three suits in rotation, with a clean shirt each day. The suits had become scruffier, the shirts longer-lived. The face, which had been red and full of blood in the usual way of gweilo faces, had become hollower and greyer. He was a good timekeeper, which was in his favour. But in the librarian's view he was on the way down. According to the remorseless criteria of Hong Kong, this was a matter for scorn, not sympathy.

This morning, matters followed their usual routine. The gweilo strode across the floor to the magazine rack. He pulled a handful of maritime magazines and newspapers off the rack and carted them back to his usual table in one of the carrels, from which could be seen through a forest of skyscrapers a blue slice of Victoria Harbour. Then he took a notebook from his briefcase and began copying telephone numbers from the magazines with a cheap fibre-point pen.

That took him until a quarter to ten, when he stacked the magazines neatly on the table, to keep his place, and headed for the bank of telephones outside.

The telephoning was the part of the day Jenkins hated most.

It was a fortnight since he had talked to Guy Warwick.

Warwick had sailed with him once, as first mate on the *Komodo President*. He was a moderate deck officer, but a skilled politician who had fallen easily into office life. Jenkins admired him for it. He was no bloody good at it, himself. He got the job done, but sooner or later he always rubbed someone up the wrong way.

'Southern Cross Manning,' said the receptionist's voice.

Southern Cross Manning found crews for ships. Warwick was second-in-command there nowadays. It was a good job, with stock options. Most of the people Jenkins had been at sea with were ashore by now. Jenkins did not envy them, except the way someone without a job envies someone who has a job, any job.

Jenkins was on hold for a long time before the receptionist put him through.

'David,' said Warwick, finally, in his hearty New Zealand International voice. 'What can we do?'

'Just wondering if anything had come up,' he said, trying to sound confident and hearty himself.

'Bit thin, I'm afraid,' said Warwick. 'Lot of masters and not enough vessels.'

'How about mate?'

'Couldn't do that to you,' said Warwick. Warwick knew about Jenkins, and his trouble. 'Bloody murder out there. Unless you're Filipino, course. Fifteen thousand US a year. Ha ha.'

Gloom swamped Jenkins, washing away his carefully nurtured self-confidence. 'Fine,' he said, and put the telephone down.

The horse-faced librarian watched him from behind her counter. He was leaning his head against the glass of the telephone booth, where it would leave a disgusting greasy mark.

Jenkins fed more money into the machine. He felt strange and dizzy. It's my birthday, he was thinking. But nothing is going to be different. Childish to expect it could be. His hand was shaking badly enough for him to miss the slot, and it took him two tries to dial China Shipping. When he got through, he said, 'Mr Dacre, please.'

This time there was no wait. 'Dick Dacre,' said an impatient Australian voice.

Jenkins scraped up the last traces of his confidence. 'Dick,' he said. 'David.'

'David who?' snapped Dacre.

'Jenkins.'

'Oh, yeah,' said Dacre. His voice had started cold. Now it became colder. 'What do you want?'

'I'm looking for a ship.'

'What ship?'

'Work on a ship.'

There was a short, incredulous silence. 'You want a job?'

'That's right. I rang two weeks ago. You said –'

'You've rung every bloody two weeks for bloody months.'

Jenkins' clothes were clammy with cold sweat. So far, everyone had at least been polite. He said, 'I've been looking for work.'

'Is that right?' said Dacre. 'Is that bloody right that looking for work is what you've been doing? After what you bloody did? Listen, mate. You go and sign on at the fucking labour exchange and put your wife out to whore if you want. But don't come bloody asking me –'

Jenkins found that the sweat on his body had turned hot. IN THE EVENT OF FIRE, said the notice in front of him in the box. He said, 'What did you say?'

Dacre said, 'If you want me to spell it out. You are a crazy irresponsible bastard, known for it all over the sodding Pacific.'

'Wait a minute,' said Jenkins. 'A year ago in that Yacht Club bar you told me that if anyone came aboard your ship without you asking them, you would blow a bloody big hole in them and sink their boat. So what's happened to you now?'

Silence.

'Dacre!' said Jenkins. 'Tell me, you hypocrite!' Hypocrite. Lousy word. Weak.

Still silence. At the back of the silence, a hum. The blood in his ears. And behind the blood, the dialling tone. There was a hand on his arm. He shook it off. His throat hurt. He must have been shouting. He turned round.

There were two blank, sallow faces above blue uniform collars. 'Too much noise,' said one of the faces. 'Please leave.'

'Case,' said the other security man, holding out his brief-case gingerly, as if it might explode.

Jenkins took the case. He walked out of the library and rode his bicycle aimlessly. Do something. That's what you're good at. Doing something.

But there is nothing you can do. Like they had said with Bill. Nothing to be done.

Some time later, he found himself in Hollywood Road. His hands were still shaking as he chained the bicycle to the bamboo upright of a scaffolding and sat down. He had no memory of getting there. Hollywood Road meant Rachel. Perhaps that was it.

There was some sun. There was a whiff of smoke from the incense coils hanging like giant red bedsprings in the ceiling of the Man Mo temple, dedicated to scholarship and martial valour.

It had been martial valour that had smashed the grid.

23

Chapter Three

The bridge of the *James Beeson* had been much like all the other bridges on which Jenkins had spent the last twenty-odd years of his life: a long, dark room stretching the width of the ship, with a wheel, and a radar, and a chart table, and all the other bits and pieces, predictable as a monthly pay cheque. Beyond the windows along its forward side was a hundred-and-twenty-yard deck, piled with containers, three high, seven across, a dark, rectilinear bulk against the night sky over the Zamboanga Strait. The containers were full of unlabelled cans of pineapple, produced by cheap labour at the Western Foods cannery near Davao, at the southern end of the Philippines. The task of the *James Beeson* was to transport these cans to the Western Foods cannery in Hawaii, where labour was five times as expensive. Here they would be labelled PRODUCE OF THE USA, and shipped on to the West Coast. It was an ordinary voyage, with nothing to distinguish it from hundreds of others Jenkins had made.

Jenkins was on the bridge with Juan, the Filipino first mate, and Carlos, the quartermaster. Geoff Wallace, the chief engineer, had just come up from the engine room. None of them cared how Western Foods made its money. They were truck drivers, and they earned their money pushing the *Beeson*'s ten thousand tons from crane to crane. That night they were truck drivers with hangovers, down to all the San Mig they had drunk at Edward's night club in Davao.

'Pretty, innit?' said Geoff the chief.

The *James Beeson* was moving under a sky full of heavy black clouds, lit violet at the margins by a flicker of lightning.

Over to starboard, the floodlit dome of the Zamboanga mosque was a golden tennis ball above the crust of lights from the shanties. Between the *Beeson* and the mosque, spread across the sea like a swarm of fireflies, were the kerosene lamps of the fishermen.

'Pretty,' said Geoff, insisting.

Jenkins grunted. It was too damn cluttered out there. But the captain and chief of the *James Beeson* were thrown on each other's company too much for disagreements to be pursued. That was something you learned, over twenty years of ships and marriage. Get on with the job. Get on with the people.

A bead of sweat ran down Jenkins' nose and plopped on the ledge that ran along the bridge windows. 'Hot,' he said.

'Not as hot as the bloody engine room,' said Geoff. Geoff was a small, unshaven Lancastrian, who cultivated a distressing cheeriness as an antidote to the hideous clatter of the machinery it was his duty to keep running. He was Rachel's godfather, which accounted for the collection of New Guinea masks that affronted Diana on the walls of her daughter's room.

Jenkins finished the tea in the mug. The *Beeson*'s decklights were blazing, and long practice had made the squid fishermen adept at not being run down. But the strait made him nervous.

The black screen of the ARPA, the Automatic Radar Plotting Aid, was crowded with tiny green minnows. Bigger fish glowed among them. There was no way of telling who they were or what they were doing. Full steam ahead was the way through.

He said, 'What about the deck-lights?'

Geoff said, 'I told Manuel to check the bulbs. He probably didn't. I'll take a look.'

Jenkins leaned against the aft bulkhead, looking over the quartermaster's shoulder at the pale glow of the gyro-compass. He was sleepy. The lights of the fishermen were a carpet of fire. Soon they would pick up the red blink of the Little San Pedro light, and they would be through this nasty, overcrowded little gut, and the mate on watch could take over, and the rest of them could get some kip.

He heard Geoff grunt as he pulled at the starboard door of the bridge. Sticky thing, that door. Must get someone to ease it, thought Jenkins. The size of crew owners allowed you now, there wasn't the manpower to change a lightbulb, let alone oil doors. He heard Geoff's voice say, 'Fuck bloody Manuel. Two bulbs out.'

Somewhere outside there was a curious burping, the sound of someone pulling a chair across a sticky ballroom floor. Except there were no chairs out there, and the nearest ballroom was a thousand miles away.

Jenkins' insides lurched. The mate said in a high, frightened voice, 'What that?' The chair moved again, the sound buried this time under a jackhammer clang of metal. Glass jangled. The windows were suddenly gone. Hot night air poured in, mixed with bits of metal that whipped like big, hard insects. Machine-gun bullets.

Jenkins ran out on to the wing of the bridge and hit the switch on the searchlight. It was corroded, of course. It took two tries before the beam lanced through the soupy air and slapped its white disc on the sea. The disc slid on to a big pump boat, a red hull with two outriggers, crabbing up alongside the *James Beeson*.

'Megaphone!' said Jenkins.

Someone put a megaphone in his hand. He yelled, 'Sheer off or I fire!'

A face, sharp-boned under a faded orange turban, stared up from the pump boat. They hosed us down, thought Jenkins furiously. The little bastards hosed us down. He moved the searchlight, keeping the crimson hull in the centre of the beam. It was wavering now, as if uncertain. The man by the twin machine-guns on the foredeck had his hand up, squinting into the searchlight.

He said, 'Blow the hooter.'

A voice said, 'Careful, captain. They shoot again.' It came from near Jenkins' feet. When he looked down he saw Juan, on his hands and knees. Christ, thought Jenkins. He's right.

Above his head, the ship's siren boomed, huge in the night. The wake of the crimson boat jinked. Then it sheered away. The disc of the searchlight followed it through the tiny one-man canoes of the squid fishermen. The big hull gleamed for a second blood-red in the searchlight, spewing foam from under its transom, and disappeared into the night.

Behind Jenkins someone coughed.

It was a peculiar cough, weak and bubbly, as if the cougher were trying to get rid of something in his lungs, but was not succeeding. Jenkins glanced over his shoulder.

Someone was lying against the bulkhead under the light. He was wearing a boiler suit like Geoff's, except it was the wrong colour. It was black and shiny in the mercury bulb. Black and shiny meant red and wet. The face was white.

Geoff's face.

Geoff raised his eyebrows at Jenkins. He said, 'This is bloody silly.' His mouth stayed open. Grey blood ran out.

He died.

Jenkins crouched by his side, holding the thick, hairy wrist in which the beat of life had stopped. Everything was the same: the hum of the ship, the mutter of thunder in the clouds. But the deck underfoot was sticky with Geoff's blood.

Jenkins started to shake.

This was Geoff. Any minute now, he would get up and laugh and say it was beer o'clock, and what about a swift one?

Jenkins went through the motions of getting him back. Pulse, breathing. None of that. Heart massage, mouth-to-mouth. But the air wheezed and bubbled in the shattered chest, and the pulse did not come back.

Finally, Jenkins stood up. He felt that something priceless had run between his fingers and into the sea. He wanted to turn the *James Beeson* hard-a-starboard and get it back, or anyway plough through those squid boats and find that pump boat with the red hull and mash it into the deep with the *James Beeson*'s ten-foot propeller blades.

Juan said, 'Military coming, sah.'

The screen of the radar showed its shoal of green flecks, shifting gently, like neon fish in a tank. There was no way of telling which was the red boat. There never would be.

Back in the office in Hong Kong, the beached captains behind their desks would nod wisely, and look political.

Tragedy, they would say, and, to be fair, they would mean it. Lot of pirates around, of course. American weapons, lawlessness. But if you arm merchant ships, you are inviting armed assault, went their reasoning. Retaliation is the job of the military. In this case, the Philippine military. Fine body of men, the Philippine military, thought Jenkins, spitting a trace of Geoff's blood over the rail. Bigger thieves than the pirates. But the owners did not like direct action. Hard to square with the insurers. So what you were left with was no action at all. A highly acceptable policy, for fat-arsed fleet managers.

For a moment, Jenkins did not recognize the man who was doing this thinking. He had been twenty years with the Line. He was a ship's master, a responsible servant of the company.

But Geoff was dead, and things that had seemed to be simple were suddenly not.

Four deckhands brought a stretcher. They eyed the bullet holes in Geoff with proper enthusiasm. Then they wrapped his body in polythene and took it down to the number two freezer, from which had come the steak Geoff had eaten for his dinner six hours previously.

An hour and a half later the military came alongside in a rusty grey gunboat. They proposed to arrest the ship's crew as material witnesses. Jenkins handed the lieutenant commanding the usual envelope of dollars, and the lieutenant commanding lost interest in material witnesses. The *James Beeson* passed the strait and ploughed on into the darkness.

Ross Clements had been shipping manager then. When Jenkins broke the news on the satellite phone, Ross had sounded depressed. He commiserated with Jenkins on the loss of his chief, and complimented him on his handling of the situation.

'Nice work,' said Clements, meaning, precisely in line with company policy: passive resistance, sit there and let them hose you down, then carry on as if nothing has happened.

But suddenly Jenkins found that company policy was interfering with his sleep. And it got worse after he had rung Geoff's wife in Australia.

The company had already talked to Charlene. Jenkins found himself apologizing. It was not in his nature to apologize.

Charlene said, 'There was nothing you could do.' Her voice was raw with crying, but there was something else wrong with it. Jenkins knew she did not believe what she was saying. The truth came rumbling in from a chaotic darkness he had carefully excluded from his life. There was such a thing as despair, and you could not make it go away with platitudes.

Jenkins had always managed to persuade himself that the world was a place in which order and system prevailed. But now he saw the world as a conspiracy of inaction. When Ross Clements talked about preserving the sanctity of international trade, what he meant was preserving the profits of a shipping line and a pineapple cannery.

Nice work, Geoff, Jenkins found himself thinking. Maitais for tourists in Waikiki. A Bentley for the chairman. You did not die in vain.

Charlene said, 'The company are being pretty decent.'

Jenkins said, 'Sure,' not trusting himself to say more.

Charlene said, 'Moneywise, I mean.' There was a pause. 'Shit,' said Charlene. 'I'm meant to feel all forgiving and all that. But I bloody don't. There's two kids here who want their daddy and a little brown bastard who killed him for no reason. I'm bloody angry, Dave.'

Jenkins said, 'Sure,' again, and rang off.

And there was old Geoff, stiff as a plank in the freezer.

It did not add up.

But Jenkins found that in his mind was developing an idea that did.

They had taken the body off in Hong Kong. Ross Clements had come on board.

'How do you feel about continuing with the voyage?' he said.

'Well,' said Jenkins. 'I'd like to go to Geoff's –'

Clements said, 'We've got a new chief coming aboard any minute. Dan Smith. Kiwi. Nice chap. If we've got two new chaps, well, it's not ideal.'

Jenkins said, 'So no time to go to the funeral.'

29

Clements put his freckled hands on the Formica table top. He knew his Jenkins. Good company man. Reliable, straightforward. If it needed doing, Jenkins would do it. That was probably how he put up with that wife of his. Sense of duty, or something. 'The company'll be there at the ceremony,' he said. 'Problem is, we're up against the schedule . . . I know Geoff was a friend of yours.'

'My daughter's godfather.'

'We'll fly your wife down.'

Jenkins thought of Diana, going all the way to Australia for a funeral. Diana found funerals depressing. He said, 'Don't worry about that. I'll send some flowers.'

Clements looked relieved. 'Good of you to see it that way.'

Jenkins did not see it that way. But he was not about to confide in Ross Clements about how he did see it. What he planned to do was strictly personal.

The *James Beeson* left Hong Kong and sailed via Honolulu to Oakland, California. In Oakland the agent called Jenkins a cab. The cab stopped in a street of low buildings. Jenkins walked under a cat's cradle of power and telephone lines to a shopfront whose windows were not windows, but panels of reinforced concrete. A large security man stood on the right-hand side of the door, which was made of steel. The door opened, and Jenkins went in. The sign over the shopfront said Meyer Guns.

Half an hour later he came out with a brown paper parcel, long and narrow, which he carried as if it were full of eggs. The taxi took him to a supermarket, and thence back to the dock gates, where he waved cheerily at the guards, who waved back and let him through without glancing at the contents of the cab, which now included fifty pounds of fillet steak, five cases of Corona beer and an automatic breadmaker, all piled on top of the brown paper parcel from the gun shop.

The steak went in the freezer, from which Geoff's body had been removed three weeks previously. The breadmaker went in the officers' mess. The parcel went inside a bit of redundant piping in the accommodation air-conditioning unit.

Three months later, coincidentally four months to the day since the murder of Geoff, the *James Beeson* was approaching the Zamboanga Strait. Jenkins was on the bridge with Juan the first mate and Carlos the quartermaster. It was dark. A heavy rain was swishing into the black sea. Jenkins went below with a large wrench. Half an hour later, he returned to the bridge.

The rain had stopped. Jenkins was sweating nervously. There was a feeling in his stomach he recognized as the one he used to have as a child, when he went fishing on a good day in the River Stour. He went to the curtains masking the chart room from the bridge proper. On the chart the ship's track was a pencil line drawn up the right-hand or mainland side of the strait.

'Many fishing men,' said Juan, his teeth gleaming green-white in the glow from the radar plotter.

They were there again in the black dish of the ARPA: the green neons with the bigger fish sliding between.

'Keep to the right,' said Jenkins.

'Bery good,' said Juan. Juan was a reliable man, as long as he had orders and he did not get over-excited. 'Some ships anchored.'

The plotter showed big, stationary blobs of light, coasters probably, anchored off the town. Beyond the bridge windows Zamboanga was a yellow galaxy separated from the *Beeson* by the individual constellations of the fishing fleet.

Jenkins waited, giving the orders that manoeuvred the *James Beeson* to the extreme right-hand edge of the ribbon of black water leading through the narrows. 'Steady,' he said to Juan.

'Steady.' The ship's long deck stretched ahead, a square-edged cutout against the dark horizon.

'Half ahead.'

Juan's eyes flashed nervous white. The company's standing orders for pirate waters specified full ahead. But he moved the telegraph handle back, and the sound of the buzzer filled the wheelhouse. Then he wrote the movement in the telegraph log. None of this was Juan's responsibility.

Jenkins found himself grinning in the dark. In his mind he was tying on a mayfly, and starting the walk under the willows towards the hatch where the big trout lived; size of a log, that trout. He knew he was going to get hell from his father, because it was coming up dinnertime, and the hatch was outside the water he had permission to fish, which was why he was going there at dinnertime in the first place.

He moved gently over to the lighting console, and shut off two of the starboard-side lighting switches. Carlos's head was a faintly gleaming silhouette in the lights of the fishing fleet. Jenkins said, 'Keep her steady at that.' Then he went out into the thick air on the wing of the bridge. All right, he thought. Here we go, Geoff, and everyone else who has sat still and taken it.

If you wanted to avoid attack by pirates, the IMO said, you kept steaming full chat, and you lit your ship up like a Christmas tree. The *James Beeson* was poodling along at four knots, hardly enough to raise a breeze on Jenkins' face. In the middle of her starboard side, where Jenkins had switched the lights out, was a patch of inky darkness.

Jenkins walked quickly down the iron stairs to the boat deck, where he had left the Oakland parcel, the night sight, and the hand-held VHF.

He unwrapped the parcel and took out the bazooka. He moved the bomb into the business end, the way the man in the shop had showed him. Then he sat down on the white plastic patio chair he had put there earlier, and waited. He had already sat like this once before. There was no reason the red boat should come after the *Beeson* twice. Last time, the night had been too clear for little brown peasants to go hunting ships. Tonight was better. Lousy visibility. Black as your hat. Of course, the odds against them pulling another attack were huge. Jenkins cradled the warm metal of the bazooka. Still . . .

There had been a gap in the willows through which the cunning caster could just flick a mayfly. He had sat there and waited for the big fish to come up and suck an insect from the surface. The sound of his breathing had been loud in his ears. It was loud now. Perhaps the big fish had already been caught. More than likely nothing would happen. All you could do was wait . . .

He had kept his mouth shut all these years. But now he had to do what was right.

Squid boats began to flow past, bobbing on the ship's bow-wave. Jenkins pulled the night sight from the pocket of his shorts and scanned the quadrant of sea aft. In the red world of the viewer the kerosene lamps showed up as big, smoky flares, the boats as matchstick-slim hulls heaving on the faint northerly swell. An anchored ship went by, unlit, a black hulk against the dazzle of the shore. If driving a ship nowadays was like being a truck driver, driving a ship in the Philippines was like driving a truck on an unmarked road system in which most of the other traffic did not have head-lights. After all these years, Diana still clung to the shreds of a notion that there was something respectable about the Merchant Navy. In the days when you got a clean uniform every day, starched, pressed and laid out by a Chinese steward, perhaps she might have had a point. Nowadays there were no uniforms, just as there was nobody with time to paint the ship, or send a frigate to let daylight into some nasty little bandit covered in guns swiped from Subic Bay. All that was left were decaying ships, undermanned, run according to a set of laws designed by accountants, that forced you to sit on your hands while the bandits hosed down your upperworks and killed your children's godparents –

Out in the red dark, something big was moving: some-thing too big for a squid boat, too sleek for a merchant ship.

Gently, Jenkins bowed his head. He felt the metal of the bazooka tube against his cheek. He closed his left eye, peer-ing through the ring of the sight into the patch of darkness down there where the lights were out. He could feel the hot pulse of his blood. His mouth was parched, the way it had been parched when the pyramid of the trout's nose had come out and sucked down a mayfly at the edge of the tree-shadow on the water by the hatch, and his own wrist had moved, and his own fly had landed two yards upstream of the fish, cocked, and begun its drift down . . .

Out there in the dark was a streak of white. A wake.

He had forgotten about fishing, now. He was thinking about Geoff with the blood spilling out of his mouth. With his free hand, he put the VHF to his ear.

He heard Juan's voice say, 'Breedge.'

He said, 'Stand by.'

'Iss.' Juan's voice was a small, tense hiss.

The white streak became the bow of a long, slim boat. It crept out of the black, matched speeds with the *James Beeson*, and began crabbing inwards. When it was thirty yards off, Jenkins said, 'Lights.'

The dark patch on the *James Beeson*'s side became suddenly as bright as noon. In the light was a crimson hull with bamboo outriggers that gave it the look of a surface-running water beetle. There were six small men on its deck. The one closest to him was wearing a faded orange turban. Jenkins saw the man blink in the sudden glare, and bend over the twin machine-guns on the foredeck mounting. Lit from above, his cheekbones looked sharp as knifeblades.

Above the hum of the *Beeson*'s engines, Jenkins heard a shout; perhaps several shouts. The two discs of the bazooka sight lined up on the pump boat's bow. A big outboard howled, and the pump boat's nose went up as the helmsman accelerated, swinging to starboard. The machine-guns started to hammer, spouting wild fans of tracer as the gunner fought for balance. The two discs in front of Jenkins' eye lined up on the blood-red side.

Jenkins pulled the trigger.

Chapter Four

There was a giant firework *whoosh* next to his ear, then a flash and concussion and a blast of hot air. For a split second the night turned white. Then Jenkins found himself in what seemed to be darkness, with his ears ringing and a huge red blob floating in front of his eyes. The blob resolved itself into a clot of flames drifting astern on the oily water. The pump boat seemed to have disappeared.

Jenkins stood up. There was a sharp, smoky smell, like used cartridges. He retrieved the night sight from where he had dropped it and took the bazooka into his cabin. Then he ran up the steel staircase to the bridge. It was beginning to rain again.

He could hear the excited voices even before he got to the top. There was Juan, and Carlos the quartermaster. They were both standing on the wing of the bridge, pointing back at the orange flare of the burning pump boat reflected in the black water. Jenkins said, 'Hey.' The rain swished down in a curtain. Everything vanished. He ducked into the bridge door, streaming water. He said, 'Who's got the wheel?'

Carlos said, 'Autopilot, sah.'

Jenkins said, shakily, 'Get back on the wheel, please.'

'Issah,' said Carlos.

Jenkins felt light-headed. Down in the sea, fuel was burning and six men might have been blown to bits. Up here, all was silence and order.

He moved over to the chart. The course said 350°. The bridge door opened. Dan Smith the new chief came in, trailing a smell of hot oil. 'What was that bang?' he said.

'What bang?' said Jenkins, in a voice that might have belonged to someone else.

Juan giggled. 'Capting shoot pirate with bazooka.'

Jenkins said, 'Shut up, Juan.'

'Ha, ha,' said Smith, who believed only in his engine room.

'No, really,' said Juan. Juan liked a bit of drama, and this was more than a bit. But Smith had gone below again.

Now that it was done, Jenkins could see just how far he had stepped out of line, and it made him feel sick. He said, 'I told you. If you talk about this, everybody gets fired.' He told himself that an explosion in the Zamboanga Strait was nothing too far out of the ordinary, provided nobody asked stupid questions, and nobody got over-excited. He walked round behind Carlos, glancing at the compass card on the wheel. Calm down, he told himself. Concentrate on the simple stuff. Never mind Geoff. Never mind burning pirates.

He stopped. He stared at the compass card. It read 18°. He said, 'What course are you steering?'

'Eighteen, sah.'

Jenkins said, 'I said steer three-fifty. Juan, what the hell are you playing at?'

Juan giggled. 'Sorry, sah.'

Carlos said, 'Steer three-fifty degrees.'

The rain was an opaque curtain outside the windows. Juan went and peered at the ARPA, the screen casting a green glow on his face.

Jenkins took two steps across and looked over his shoulder. The rain was heavy enough to blot out the screen. He found the sensitivity control without looking at it, and turned it up full. The collision alarm was turned off, because of the squid fleet. He said, 'Get to the GPS and put us a fix on the chart.' His stomach felt loose and bottomless. They were in confined waters at night, with traffic, blind, out of position. He should never have left Juan on the bridge. He knew Juan went to pieces when he was excited.

The arm of the radar swept round the screen, clear of rain now.

But not clear of everything.

Dead ahead of the blob that was the *James Beeson* was

another blob: a huge blob, a ship, maybe. The little green letters popped up on the ARPA screen: CPA, closest point of approach, zero metres. TCPA, time to closest point of approach, thirty seconds.

Jenkins said, in a quiet voice, 'Hard-a-port.' He found that he was running to the telegraph, had his hand on the smooth brass handle, wrenched it back to full astern. All the time he was looking forward, down the long runway of the container tops.

But the rain was coming down like a waterfall, and the wipers could not keep up, and he could not see the bow of his own ship, let alone whatever else was out there.

He felt it instead.

There was a sudden check in the deck, an almost negligible buckling of the knees. The sweat flowed off him in greasy sheets. It should have been dead straightforward. Step out of line. Knock off your pirate. Step back in. On to Hong Kong, and nobody the wiser.

But Jenkins had blown it.

He thought, You silly, silly bastard.

He put out his hand and punched the alarm. The ship became suddenly a huge steel box of bells. There was shouting. Someone was on the bridge wing with the searchlight, shining it across the water at something a couple of hundred feet away: a ship, anchored, with rusty stains running from scuppers to waterline. And on its port bow, clear now, a long black scar, the colour of the *James Beeson*'s paint.

Jenkins knew with complete certainty that he had stepped out of line so far that there could be no stepping back.

The bridge telephone rang. 'Water coming in in numbers one and two,' said Dan Smith's voice. 'Lot of water.'

'Pump it out,' said Jenkins, between numb lips.

The other ship stayed where it was for perhaps thirty seconds. It's fine, thought Jenkins, not believing it.

The other ship's stem seemed to be getting shorter. She was definitely down by the nose, like a submarine about to dive.

Oh, no, thought Jenkins.

The other ship's nose went under water. She sank in fifty seconds.

37

Well, thought Jenkins, with a peculiar detachment he only later worked out must have been shock, there goes the ol' career.

Then he started to concentrate on finding ways of getting his ship and cargo to Hong Kong.

There had been no fuss, no reporters. The *James Beeson* was in dry dock, her cargo transshipped at horrible expense. Her officers and crew had been taken off as soon as she had come into Hong Kong, and were now scattered from Norway to Tasmania. Jenkins had been told to wait at home pending the outcome of enquiries. So he had told Diana he was on leave, and waited.

The call had finally come from Ross Clements, sounding easy and pleasant, as always. 'We're having a think,' he said. 'We'd like you to sort of keep things to yourself.'

Jenkins was staring out of the window at the vapours winding among the apartment towers. The flat seemed overheated and over-scented. He was jumpy, and he could not think of a tactful way of asking the question that was on his mind. 'Are you sacking me?' he said.

'Frankly,' said Clements, 'this is a bit of a can of worms. We're looking at all the angles. Lunch tomorrow?'

Jenkins noticed that he had not answered the question.

Orient Line was a good employer; like a family, the saying went. Jenkins had worked for the Line since he had been sixteen. The Line had educated him and employed him. It had first suggested and then arranged Diana and the children's move from Lee-on-the-Solent to Hong Kong. It had advanced him the money for the apartment, and sponsored his application to join the Hong Kong Yacht Club, and given him compassionate leave when Bill had been killed.

It was a big, powerful, all-embracing, cradle-to-grave organization. Like a family.

But if you kicked over the traces, you could be sure Orient Line would kick back.

Not that there was anything like a Court Martial. There had just been Ross Clements, over a bowl of Thai green curry in the Mighty Elephant, with his eyebrows up and the beads of chili sweat bursting on his forehead, and Jenkins opposite him, sipping beer, not eating. Jenkins had been surprised to find himself feeling not shame and trepidation, but resentment.

He watched Ross pile more rice on his plate and ladle on curry. He said, 'So?'

Ross's sun-reddened nose twitched as he chewed. His blue New Zealand eyes were unforgiving over the smile. 'Things are a bit difficult,' he said. Jenkins knew that he was not going to be left to drift. He was going to be torpedoed. 'Trouble is, there's company policy, and there's international law, and you have sort of messed things up with regard to both.'

Jenkins said, 'Would you have done any different?'

Ross ignored that. He said, 'I've had meetings with directors. With the Taipan.' He laid down his fork. 'Tough meetings.'

'How many pirate attacks have you had in the Zamboanga Strait since this happened?' said Jenkins.

Ross shrugged. 'None. I grant you, Dave. But the office in Manila has had to . . . well, I don't like to tell you what the payoffs have added up to. And you bent the fucking ship, and sank a Filipino, because you were off course.'

'The mate on watch was off course.'

The thick chestnut eyebrows came down. 'Do me a favour,' he said.

Jenkins shoved his sweating hands into his pockets. That had been a stupid thing to say. The captain carried the can.

'So,' said Ross. 'What am I supposed to do?'

Jenkins knew he was not meant to answer. Ross was working his way towards pronouncing sentence by a route just as formal as a court.

'The directors wanted to hand you over to the Flips,' said Ross.

Jenkins said, 'These people killed Geoff.'

Ross frowned. He said, 'I thought you of all people might understand. Your loyalty's to the company, not the individual.' To his mind, Jenkins looked angry. On the edge of a bit of a freakout. No room for freakouts, nowadays. He paused, and said soothingly, 'Geoff was killed by gunfire, person or persons unknown. You can't go hauling off left and right with bazookas because of an accident.'

'You know bloody well that wasn't an accident.'

Ross said, 'We should probably keep our voices down.' Jenkins realized that other lunchers were looking at him. He must have been shouting.

'I will spell it out for the last and final time,' said Ross. 'Company policy is nil resistance. Plus you were off the bridge and off course and you sank a ship at anchor.' He leaned forward. 'If this went to a Court of Inquiry, it'd be your ticket.' Jenkins could smell the garlic on his breath. 'We're doing you a favour keeping it quiet. You do understand?'

Jenkins knew that he was meant to say yes, of course. But Jenkins found he could no longer say the right thing at the right time.

Jenkins said, 'No.'

Ross had known it was not going to be easy, with Jenkins. He said, 'Dave, I'm afraid we're going to have to let you go.'

Across the quarry that had opened where his stomach had been, Jenkins said, 'Redundant?'

'Fired. Two months' pay. We won't tell anyone if you don't. You get to keep your ticket.'

Jenkins could feel the blood draining away from his mind. Orient had been his life.

Ross said, 'Anything we can do to help. We can get you counselling . . .'

Jenkins got up. His chair fell over. He walked out into the buzzing crowds of Central.

In the Anglican cathedral it was cool and dark, and the good ladies of the diocese had decorated the pillars with vases of lilies. He sat in a pew behind a couple of Filipinas. The thoughts stopped crashing around like skittles. They became quiet and logical and sombre. They had nothing to do with his being orphaned by Orient Lines. They were more practical than that.

He had overspent, because he had been expecting a voyage bonus that he would not now be getting. The Orient severance cheque would leave him with enough for a month. After that, God knew.

He drew a deep, lily-scented breath. You are institutionalized, he told himself. One employer since the age of sixteen; your whole adult life, twenty-odd years of it. One employer, one wife, one daughter. Consistent and loyal, Jenkins.

He saw Geoff's face, and heard the bang of the bazooka shell. If only bloody Juan had held his course . . . Experimentally, like a man prodding a sore tooth, he tried to regret what he had done. He did not succeed. He had done right by Geoff.

But not by Diana.

Diana was accustomed to the life she led. She deserved the life she led, Jenkins told himself. She had not had it easy. She would not understand.

She definitely would not understand.

Rachel would be all right. Rachel would sympathize. Jenkins felt a great and desperate need for sympathy. But it would not be right for a father and a daughter to keep a secret of this magnitude from a mother.

Get organized, Jenkins told himself. Keep your lip buttoned.

He got up and bowed to the altar and walked out into the afternoon.

During the next fortnight he had opened his campaign, basing himself in the public library, where there were magazines and telephones. He rang every shipping company in Hong Kong. The story was always the same. He was a seaman of over twenty years' experience, with a master's ticket in good standing. But as soon as the fleet managers heard his name, their enthusiasm dived sharply.

'Ah,' they said. 'David Jenkins. Left Orient, you say?'

'Needed a change.'

'Nothing at the moment,' said the voices on the other end. Jenkins knew what it meant. He was on the blacklist.

In the weeks that followed, Jenkins told Diana he was fed up with sailing, and sold his yacht *Powderfinger* for the best price he could get, which was about half what she was worth. But he kept up the Yacht Club subscription. All his life he had moved in groups, not taking much part, but thinking his own thoughts while fitting in. Now, he found groups less attractive, quite apart from the fact that a round in the Yacht Club bar could wreck his week's budget. Diana hardly noticed, of course; she had her own friends.

He missed the yacht, though. Naturally, Rachel noticed. 'How could you bear to sell her?' she said.

'Spent enough time at sea as it is,' he said.

'But *Powderfinger*.'

'Oh, for Christ's sake,' he said. 'I sold her. All right?'

'All right,' she said. But Rachel knew him nearly as well as he knew her. She knew damn well it was not all right. But he could not tell her why.

So he had told Jeremy Selmes instead.

They had made a rendezvous a week before the severance money was due to run out, in the British Bulldog, a self-conscious London-style pub a couple of blocks from Jeremy's office. Jenkins had got there early, because he had nothing else to do. Jeremy came in five minutes late, small, dark and busy. He winked at the waitress. 'Nice,' he said, watching the black miniskirt sway back to the bar. Then he leaned back on the banquette. 'Well, our Dave,' he said. 'How's life?'

Jenkins looked at the neat blue suit, the black brogues buffed to a military shine. At that moment, he knew he could not tell him the truth. He said, 'I've decided to come ashore.'

The dark eyebrows went up. 'Swallowing the ol' anchor?'

Jenkins forced himself to grin. 'Moving sideways,' he said. 'Fleet management.'

Jeremy noticed that Jenkins' hair needed cutting, and he looked tired. Not that he would do much sleeping himself, if he was married to Diana. Bit short in the top storey, but that one would roger like a rattlesnake. 'Who for?'

'New lot,' said Jenkins, vaguely. Once you got the habit of vagueness, it seemed to come more easily than direct lies. 'Greeks.'

'Oh, yeah.' Jeremy knew nothing about shipping.

'Actually, that's sort of what I wanted to talk about. There's a bloke, one of our captains. Bloody idiot. He's got himself in a mess.' He was finding his stride now. He was telling the truth, after all. 'He needs some money. Quite a lot of money. He can't raise it through, er, conventional channels.' Jeremy had been a policeman. Jeremy was an operator, an expert on the unofficial world. 'I was wondering . . .'

'Ah,' said Jeremy. He raised his arm for the waitress and ordered more beer, simultaneously extracting her telephone number with surgical neatness. It was part of what Jenkins admired about Jeremy: his ability to move through the world like an earthworm through a pile of manure.

'So,' said Jeremy. 'This chap needs a loan.' He looked up. His eyes were hard and dark, not twinkling any more. 'Would you call him desperate?'

Jenkins paused for a moment, though no reflection was necessary. 'I suppose I would,' he said. 'Why?'

'Chap I'm thinking of,' said Jeremy. 'Not a lot of fun. Knows some dangerous people. But as moneylenders go, he's straight, I suppose. Twenty-five per cent interest, maybe fifty, depending on collateral. No violence till the principal falls due. Sound about right?'

Jenkins' stomach was a large, nauseous void. 'Better keep him away from the office,' he said. 'Get him to ring me at home.'

'Fine,' said Jeremy. 'His name's Tommy Wong.'

Chapter Five

Three months later, Jeremy was having a busy morning. By dint of one threat of maiming and two large bribes, he had just negotiated his men a job guarding the Wang container park. He was sitting at his desk under a confidence-inspiring photograph of himself in the uniform of the Hong Kong Police, shaking hands with a governor complete with cocked hat and ostrich plumes.

His direct line rang. 'Maximum Security,' said Jeremy.

'Morning,' said David Jenkins, on the far end.

'Dave,' said Jeremy, leaning back in his chair, his voice losing its businesslike smoothness. 'What gives?'

'You remember in November,' said Jenkins. 'I told you about that chap who needed to borrow some money.'

Jeremy frowned. Jenkins' voice was unreadable. 'Yep.'

'Silly bugger's made a mess of it,' said Jenkins.

Jeremy pulled a Rothmans out of his packet and lit it, blank-faced. 'Can't pay?' he said.

'That's about it.'

'Oh, dear,' said Jeremy. 'What can he sell?'

'He'd rather not.'

'Listen, mate,' said Jeremy. 'If your friend borrowed money from Tommy Wong, he'd better pay it back.'

'I see.' Jenkins' voice was still neutral.

'I told you at the time,' said Jeremy. 'No violence till due date. But plenty then. Tennis tonight?'

'Probably not.'

Jenkins hung up. He had been calling from the payphone at the Yacht Club. It was Wednesday, ten o'clock, the day after he had sat on the steps of the Man Mo temple. At this early hour the bar was almost empty, except for an elderly blonde propped on a stool. She was drunk, chatting up the barman. Jenkins recognized her as a friend of Diana's. Clambering on to a bus he felt, not for the first time, that he hardly knew Diana any more. Just as she hardly knew him.

Thank God.

In the library, a crop-headed Chinese was sitting in Jenkins' usual place. He felt a twinge of irritation. That chair at that table was the last piece of territory he had. The horse-faced librarian was behind the counter. Jenkins felt half inclined to make a fuss. Approached in the right way, she would make it clear to this interloper –

Steady.

He went to the newspaper rack, pulled down the *South China Morning Post*, and took it to the table. He sat down opposite the man who was in his seat and put the paper in front of his face. It made a little black-and-white room in which he could try to get his nerves steady again. The stories on the front page were written in the stilted Beijing press-release language that was taking the papers over nowadays. The Chinese opposite him started talking in Cantonese at normal volume into a mobile phone. For Christ's *sake*, thought Jenkins. But he could not even summon the concentration to be irritated. A single thought was running in his mind like a hamster in a wheel.

What do I do now?

He took some deep breaths. What he needed was a ship to drive. He didn't know how to do anything else. But nobody would give him a ship. So rob a bank, thought Jenkins. You may be bad at politics, but you are fine at organization. For Rachel's sake, steal something. And Diana's sake, of course. Poor Diana.

So you rob a bank. So you get caught. Rachel and Diana are in even worse trouble. Jenkins was astonished at himself. Seriously contemplating a bank robbery? Insane. What he needed was a ship.

On and on ran the hamster, round and round.

Someone came and sat next to the crop-headed man on the far side of the table.

'Excuse me,' said a voice. 'Captain Jenkins?'

He lowered the newspaper and looked up. He found

himself looking into the impenetrable black eyes of Tommy Wong.

'There is someone you should meet,' said Wong.

Jenkins found his heart thumping uncomfortably. It had happened. He said, 'How did you know I was here?'

Wong gave him a small, efficient nod. 'You are an important person to me,' he said. 'The duck that lays the golden egg.'

'Goose,' said Jenkins. The horse-faced librarian was scowling behind her counter. 'You're a day early.'

Wong laughed. 'This is not about money.' He got up. 'Come.' He spoke in a normal, unhushed voice that sounded very loud in the library. 'It is quite safe. It will be to your advantage.'

He could be lying, thought Jenkins. He could be hauling me out of here to beat it out of my hide. But Jeremy had said no violence till after the money was due. Jeremy knew about things like that.

He stood up and followed Wong out. The muscular man who had been sitting in his seat came after him, walking on the outsides of his feet, a fighter's walk.

A gunmetal-grey Lexus was parked on the kerb outside the library. The muscular man opened the door. Wong got in first, then Jenkins, then the muscular man, so Jenkins was the filling in a sandwich. The muscular man smiled, a wide, entirely unfriendly smile. The driver began to drive.

Wong was surprised at the lack of fear in the gweilo's face. Of course, you could never tell what they were thinking; but amazingly, what he saw in the horse-wild eyes looked very like relief. No sane person would feel relief at being taken to an unknown destination by a man to whom he had failed to repay forty thousand dollars. But then gweilos were different. He said, in a harsh voice, 'We are going to see my principal, Mr Chang. A most influential man.'

Jenkins nodded. A peace had spread through him. Something was happening. For the moment, that was enough.

The Lexus made a Red Sea path through the packed traffic and stopped outside the Hong Kong and Shanghai Bank building. The three of them walked across the atrium and into an elevator. The minder punched a button. Jenkins looked down upon the gleaming black crowns of his companions' heads, and felt hopeful. It was an odd place for them to bring him if they were going to beat him up.

The floor numbers flicked up to the high thirties, and the doors opened. They walked through a roomful of desks, past two impassive secretaries, and into a corner office.

It was a big room, with floor-to-ceiling windows overlooking the harbour. On the wall behind the black lacquer desk was a neatly framed sheet of handmade paper bearing a Chinese ideogram painted in ink. Under the ideogram sat a stout Chinese man wearing spectacles, what looked like a Savile Row suit, and an Old Harrovian tie. Tommy Wong said something in Cantonese, exuding deference like a slug secreting slime. The man behind the desk nodded and turned upon Jenkins a surprising smile, chubby-cheeked as a Disney chipmunk. 'My dear Captain,' he said. 'It is indeed a pleasure to meet you. I am Hugh Chang. Please sit down.'

Jenkins sat. Wong and the bodyguard withdrew. Jenkins felt his calm fraying at the edges. The character was all over Hong Kong, on canned lychees, and theatre posters, and containers in the port. It was the trademark of the Chang organization.

This was *that* Hugh Chang. You saw his picture on TV, smiling with delegations from Beijing, or on page one of the business sections. You did not get marched into Hugh Chang's office by a small-time moneylender.

Chang said through the smile, 'It is kind of you to spare a moment for this meeting. We both have many things to attend to, so if you will forgive me, I will come to the point. I am aware of your business relationship with Mr Wong. I am sure that you have this matter in hand.' The chubby-cheeks smile did not falter. Jenkins' sense of disorientation increased. 'But in the unlikely event that you are experiencing difficulty, how far would you go to discharge your obligation?'

Half an hour ago, I was thinking seriously about robbing banks, Jenkins thought. He said, 'I will do what is necessary.'

Chang nodded, still smiling his calm, chubby smile. 'And . . . forgive me . . . in the Zamboanga Strait? Were you doing what was necessary?'

'How did you know about that?'

'Mr Jenkins, many people know about that.'

Jenkins thought about Warwick and Dacre and the black-list. He said, 'Why are you interested?'

Chang said, 'Mr Wong and I are old friends. It occurred to me that we could all help each other out. Before I can help, I need to know a little more about you.'

That's not an answer, thought Jenkins. What is this?

'So,' said Chang. 'I need to know about Zamboanga.' He put his wrist on the table, glanced at his watch, and glanced up again at Jenkins.

The watch ploy galvanized Jenkins. Suddenly his heart was pumping and his forehead was wet with sweat. This could be his chance to get back into an orderly world, with structure. Grab it. What have you got to lose?

He said, 'A colleague of mine was murdered by pirates. The Zamboanga Strait is infested with them. I decided that the company rule forbidding retaliation did not meet the case. The pirate needed disposing of. I disposed of him.'

'Direct action to solve a difficulty,' said Chang. 'Even though it involved you in proceedings of dubious legality.'

Jenkins said, 'The law was a problem, not a solution.'

Chang nodded. He said, 'I am grateful for your confidence.' He looked significantly less chubby. His eyes had a bloom like a plum's. He said, suddenly, 'Did you know that my son Raymond is friendly with your daughter Rachel?' The chubby smile returned. 'When young people are friends, wise parents make each other's acquaintance, perhaps form a relationship.' He nodded, a sage's nod. 'And cooperate in matters of business. For example, to arrive at a rescheduling programme for your debt. I am also as it happens in need of an officer for one of my ships.'

Jenkins felt the blood in his face again. Chang said, 'So this is truly a fortunate coincidence. I will notify Mr Wong. A Captain Soares will call you to explain. Now if you will excuse me?'

Jenkins did not believe in fortunate coincidences. But the right words were all there: order, cooperation, programme, relationship. Words that meant he was back in the grid. Don't look gift horses in the mouth, he told himself. This is

48

the way back. The sudden lightness of his heart lifted him to his feet and out of the office.

After he had gone, Chang looked for a moment at the reflection of his face in the mirror-smooth lacquer of his desk. This Jenkins was an excellent seaman, by all accounts. That was good. He had worked twenty years for the same company. That was good, too. Yet he was not afraid to do violence in pursuit of what he saw as his loyalties, which would now be to his family and himself. That was very good.

But there were two important things that were even better. One was that the man was desperate. The other was the daughter. By all accounts, Jenkins loved his daughter.

The daughter was a definite bonus.

Chapter Six

Rachel was in her room, peering through a lens at a T'ang horseman, the deeply satisfactory meeting-place of the green glaze and the naked buff clay; a line yet not a line, an opposition of hard and soft, the ying and the yang. You see it everywhere, she thought idly, all the way through this four-thousand-year civilization.

The telephone rang.

It was a man's voice, smooth and young. 'Rachel?'

Her heart bumped heavily in her chest. Oh, good, she thought. 'Raymond.'

'Listen,' he said. 'I'll take you to Gallery Ong tonight.'

'Tonight?'

'I'll be round in an hour. Be ready.'

The bump of her heart became less pronounced. Raymond Chang was definitely pretty wonderful. He was sweet and funky and sharp and he looked lovely, and he had the cars and all that. But Rachel had a large, nagging worry about him, and it went like this: How can you have a relationship with someone who expects you to be poised on the starting-blocks at all times?

She said, 'Actually I don't think I can.'

Raymond's voice cooled several degrees. 'What do you mean, you don't think you can?'

Rachel found the nagging worry turning into something that closely resembled irritation. She said, 'Because I've got other plans.' She could have told Raymond that she was going out with her father. He would have understood that, because his own father was a traditionalist, strong on family bonds and duties. But she liked Raymond. She did not want to deal with him according to a set of rules to which she did not subscribe. She wanted a relationship, human to human. Or nothing.

Raymond said, 'What other the hell plans?'

Rachel could hear the blankness in his voice. She was faintly pleased that he was jealous, but worried that she might have given in to the irritability, overdone the curtness . . . hell, blown it. *Don't give in*, she told herself. 'Just plans.'

'Oh,' said Raymond.

'But tomorrow night would be fine,' said Rachel. After the curtness, we now do Ms Obliging.

'Maybe,' said Raymond, still using the blank voice. 'See you alound.' His 'r' sounds tended to slip when he was under stress.

'See you –' But before she could finish, he had put the telephone down.

Brilliant, she thought. Just brilliant. First man you really like, and you have with your great big foot kicked him down the stairs.

So ring back.

Certainly not. The 'r' of 'around' had slipped.

She grinned at herself. Stubborn cow. Stubborn devious cow.

Outside, the apartment door slammed, and the shower hissed on. Ten minutes later her father came in, improbably dressed in a black kimono decorated with birds of paradise. His face was still tired, but there seemed to be a new gleam in his eye. Rachel shoved Raymond into the pending file and gently but firmly closed the drawer.

As always, Jenkins' heart melted in the warmth of her smile.

He said, 'Are you going out?'

'Yes,' she said. 'With my old man, I thought.' She looked at him with her amber eyes. 'Happy birthday. I thought I'd take you to the Loon Fung.'

'Wah,' he said. 'My favourite.'

She looked at him narrowly. For weeks, keeping him cheerful had been like lifting a chair by one leg. Tonight there was a lightness to him, a – well, if it hadn't been her father, she would have called it a confidence. She said, 'What are you so cheerful about?'

'Good day,' he said. 'Makes a change. Where's your mother?'

'Out. She said she had an important tennis match. And then she's having dinner with Myra Jennings.'

'The crocodile?'

'The turtle. Though personal remarks are neither appropriate nor helpful,' she said in a schoolmarm's voice, and pursed her lips severely. 'Anyway, they'll have a lovely time and so will we. She said to say happy birthday.' She was inventing the last bit.

'I hope she won't mind missing the Loon Fung.'

Rachel looked down, avoiding his eye. 'Shouldn't think so,' she said. Her mother seemed to have been made no happier by her father's coming ashore. Not that it was the kind of thing her father was likely to notice. As long as the family were fed and watered, her father seemed to feel no need to probe deeper. Rachel was old enough to wonder how much longer they could live together on that basis.

But it was not something she wanted to think about; not on her father's birthday. She looked for a way of changing the subject and found it. The bangles on her wrist clinked as she reached for a Post-it on the side of her filing cabinet. 'Man rang. Slimy voice. Called Suarez, or something.'

'Did he, by God?' said Jenkins. He was feeling almost euphoric. Tommy Wong was under control. It looked as if he might get to sea again. And he was going out to dinner with Rachel, without Diana.

Not, he thought quickly, that Diana's absence was anything to be euphoric about. But with Diana there, they would have had to talk about her tennis ladder and life on the boring bloody Circuit. It was one thing making her feel wanted, but it was another having to sit there while it trickled over you like oil from a leaky sump.

But she was happy. That was the main thing.

He put on a seersucker jacket and a pair of dark blue linen trousers. In honour of the occasion he shoved new cardboard inside the holes-in-the-soles loafers. His hair needed a cut, he thought. Too damn grey at the temples. Otherwise ready for sea.

He went to the telephone and dialled the number on the Post-it Rachel had given him. A cold voice said, 'Yeah?'

'Captain Soares?'

''Oo wants 'im?'

'My name is Jenkins.'

'Ah, yes,' said the voice, becoming slippery. 'Captain Jenkins. What pleasure. Listen, I have 'ear so much about you, I want to buy you a beer, make you a proposition. I got things I got to do this evening. Later, maybe eleven, I'll be somewhere. The Kitten Club in Wan Chai. I guess you know the Kitten? Full of young pussy. Ha, ha.'

''Fraid not,' said Jenkins. 'How about tomorrow?'

'Tomorrow too late,' said Soares. 'We get feex up, we get feex up tonight. Eleven, OK?'

Jenkins said, 'OK,' and put the telephone down, feeling vaguely compromised. Never mind, he thought. Until eleven, it was his birthday.

They took a taxi down to Aberdeen. The Loon Fung was roaring like a waterfall. Rachel said something to a waiter in fluent Cantonese and the waiter rushed them through the crowd to a table overlooking the water.

'Would you like me to order?' she said.

Jenkins grinned at her. She would order whatever he said. She knew what he liked, and more important, she could read the menu.

He watched with considerable smugness as she barked her way through the courses. It was, he reflected, the best possible luck that she had her mother's looks and her father's brains, and not the other way round.

The food came quickly. Rachel said, 'I'm starving,' and began to eat, bowl to mouth, shovelling it in with the chopsticks. When the first frenzy was over she paused, and rested the amber eyes on him. She said, 'You'd forgotten it was your birthday, hadn't you?'

'The credit card company sent me a card.'

She laughed. 'Why don't you go back to sea?'

He looked down at the won tons floating like money-bags in his soup. He said, 'I just bloody well might be doing just that.' He saw once again Mr Chang's chubby face. 'By the way,' he said. 'One's been hearing things on the, er, cocktail circuit. What's this about you and Raymond Chang?'

She was looking at him full face – long, mysterious eyes, straight, elegant eyebrows. You could see why people wanted to take photographs of her. She brushed the heavy blonde hair over her left ear, the way she did when she was embarrassed. Jenkins felt suddenly constrained by the fact that he was her father, and that she was only eighteen. 'Raymond?' she said, with careful casualness. 'Part of the old *guanxi*.'

'Ah.' *Guanxi* was what you needed to get on in the Chinese world. It meant connections, people you knew or had done favours for, favours you could call in when you needed them. But it must be more serious that that, because Rachel had overlooked the fact that he would rather roast in hell than go to a cocktail party.

'And he took me out to dinner a couple of times. He's quite sweet. Very good-looking. I think he fancies me.'

'I'm working for his father.'

'Doing what?'

'Driving a ship, I think.' He was covered by a sudden urge to confess. 'Sounds fairly dodgy.' He was appalled at the admission.

But Rachel did not seem to notice. It looked as if this Raymond was occupying a large amount of her mind. 'Raymond says his father's a bastard. Well, not in so many words. It's all that Confucius business, fathers and sons. Dutifulness. Raymond says his father's the old-fashioned type.' She concentrated fiercely on raking crab and black bean sauce out of the dish and into her bowl. 'He doesn't approve of me.'

Rachel had never previously attached much importance to the approval of her boyfriends' fathers. Definitely serious, thought Jenkins. To cheer her up, he said, 'That's not what he told me.'

She said, 'You talked about me and Raymond?'

'His father said something about it being good for the parents of young people to meet.'

Rachel spat a fragment of crab shell on to the floor, a sample of Chinese table manners that would have mortified Diana. 'I don't know about that. The way Raymond talks, the old bastard probably believes in arranged marriages. Unmixed ones.'

He said, 'Very sound thinking.'

She put her hand on his. It was vaguely sticky with black bean sauce. She said, 'I defy you.' For a second he saw her aged ten, covered in jam and sand, on the beach with her brother, Bill. Bill had been eight; two sticky little brutes, yelling. Now one of them was dead, and this one . . . well, this one was grown-up.

The grimness had returned. It was thinking about Bill that had done it. Bill dying had knocked Diana off the rails good and proper. Since then, things that should have been natural had been a matter of duty. He had looked after her, in a dogged sort of way. A grim sort of way –

'Dad?' said Rachel.

He realized she had been talking. He said, 'Sorry,' and took a swig of tea. 'Miles off.'

'Happy birthday,' she said, and pushed across a small parcel, red with gold good-luck messages.

Inside the wrapping was a little Perspex dome. Inside the dome was a tropical island with palm trees. When he inverted it, snowflakes swirled around the palm trees. He said, 'Just what I always wanted.'

She said, 'You had all those Swiss-chalet pictures in your cabin on the *James Beeson*? You used to say they were better than air conditioning. I thought this would remind you.'

Jenkins kissed her jade-smooth cheek.

'I'm glad you're going back to sea,' she said.

He nodded. For a moment it was just her and him, in a little dome of their own. Daughters were a wonderful thing.

At half past ten he dropped her home and took the taxi on to Wan Chai.

The Kitten Club was buried in the slot of darkness below the glass migraine of Wan Chai's neon. Jenkins paid off the taxi, and paused outside the door. There was a sandwich placard with topless photographs of Gina and Dolores and Lily and Pam. He was not confident that he was going to like Soares, if the Kitten Club was Soares' idea of fun.

He pushed open the heavy wooden door and went in.

Gina and Dolores, who were not called anything like Gina

55

and Dolores in their native Thailand, quickly levered their breasts over the bodices of their leotards and assumed enticing grins. Gina said, 'You buy me drink?'

Jenkins' eyes took in her heavily made-up face and puckered brown nipples. She got the impression he was not concentrating. 'No drink,' he said. 'San Miguel for me. Have you seen Captain Soares?'

There was red flock wallpaper, a couple of booths, and a red curtain at the back. The feeble-looking Chinese youth by the curtain ventured a conniving grin and said, 'Not rong now.'

Jenkins sat down in one of the booths, wrinkling his nose at the smell of joss-sticks. The CD player ground through 'Midnight Hour' and 'The Birdie Song'. The red velvet curtain shifted, and a head appeared. The hair was black, gleaming with wet-look styling gel. The heavy moustache was black too, and so were the stubble on the receding chin and the eyes set above bags of blackish-grey skin. The eyes looked left and right, checking. The head emerged from the curtains, followed by an egg-shaped body in a white short-sleeved shirt and khaki chinos. There were gold medallions in the black mat of hair on the lard-coloured chest. The hands were buttoning the trousers.

'Captain Soares?' said Jenkins.

The eyes landed on him like something cold and wet. Under the black moustache, the red mouth stretched into an ingratiating smile. '*Mis*ter Jenkins,' said Soares. 'How kind of you to come.' A Thai woman brushed past behind him, her slanted eyes sulky behind their thick mascara, and went to whisper with the other girls behind the bar.

Soares scratched his chest hair, jangling his medallions. He sat down at the table, called for a beer, drank, and belched. 'So,' he said. 'They say you need a job.'

Jenkins nodded, watching Soares' grey tongue lick foam off his moustache.

'Yeah,' said Soares. 'We got this ship. Piece a shit, I 'ave to tell you. We got to take her to a breaker's yard. In Oakland, California.'

'Breaker's yard,' said Jenkins. Most breakers were in India or China, where labour costs were low.

The moustache gave Soares' face a glum, clownish look. He said, 'I want a first mate.'

Jenkins nodded. Beggars could not be choosers.

'The money is good,' said Soares. 'Sixty thousand dollars.'

'Hong Kong.'

'US,' said Soares.

Jenkins' beer stopped halfway to his mouth. He said, '*What?*'

'Half now. Half on delivery.'

Jenkins put the glass down quickly, in case he dropped it.

Sixty thousand dollars was the kind of money you could pay off your debts with, and start a new life. But nobody Jenkins had ever met was going to pay sixty thousand dollars to have a ship delivered across the Pacific to a scrapyard.

He said, carefully, 'So what's the ship?'

'Boxboat,' said Soares. 'Seven thousand tons. We're carrying a few containers. Empties, mostly, little sand ballast. I need a guy used to working with Filipinos, supervise cargo, supervise deck crew, keep his mouth shut. We got a Brit second mate, Flip third and fourth. Australian chief. He's bringing his wife. Filipino crew, Chinese cooks.'

Jenkins nodded. It sounded extremely dodgy. But the chief engineer's wife was an encouraging sign. Officers did not bring their wives on dodgy voyages. Besides, only this morning he had seriously considered robbing a bank. He said, 'One question.'

Soares cocked an eyebrow.

'Is this legal?'

Soares put his pudgy hand on his medallions, which his scratching had pushed to the left-hand side of his chest. 'On my mother's grave,' he said. 'You want the job?'

Sixty grand. Mentally, Jenkins took a deep breath. 'Of course,' he said.

'Welcome aboard,' said Soares. 'Maybe you need a sub.' He plunged his hand into his khakis and came out with a fat roll of dirty greenbacks. 'Thousand dollar do?'

Jenkins did not like the way Soares took it for granted, but he found he could not keep his eyes off the money. 'Nice, eh?' said Soares. Jenkins looked up. Soares was smiling, a proper smile of complicity. This time his eyes showed no tendency to shift.

The door opened and a man came in. The girls behind the bar drifted towards him. He was dark and thickset, in his late twenties. 'Leave 'im alone,' Soares said to the girls. ''E's mine.' He handed Jenkins the wad of money. The dark man came over. 'Dave,' said Soares. 'This is your second mate. Peter Pelly.'

Pelly had slicked-back black hair and a pudgy, strong-featured face. His narrow black eyes slid over the money in Jenkins' hand. At least one of his grandparents had been Chinese. 'How do?' he said, in a London accent. Jenkins put the money in his pocket. Peter's hand felt hard and dry. He was looking at the girls, not Jenkins. He bought Dolores a drink from one of the Rémy Martin bottles behind the bar, flashing a big roll of dollars with a sort of innocent enthusiasm. Jenkins liked him more than he liked Soares.

Pete said, 'C'mere, darling.' Dolores came to sit on his knee. Jolly Jack ashore, thought Jenkins. Evidence that you are part of a ship again. You should be delighted.

Soares said, 'What you need here is a little celebration.' He poked Jenkins' thigh, and pointed to the girl with whom he had come from behind the curtain. 'Suck the chrome off a trailer hitch.' He stuck his grey tongue out from under his moustache and waggled it. Behind the bar the girls laughed like sparrows twittering.

Jenkins stood up. He could feel the money in his pocket. He said, 'My wife's expecting me.'

'You quee-ah?' said the girl.

'Buoy C-11. Day after tomorrow, eight a.m.,' said Soares. 'You don't know what you're missing.' He laughed, a crunchy wheeze that rattled his medallions.

'Ta-ra,' said Pete, winking.

As he left, Jenkins felt distinctly grubby. Never mind, he told himself. The great thing about corruption is that you get paid for it.

When he got home Diana was in bed, her face shiny with cream. She was wearing a blue lace nightdress and reading *Hello!* 'Darling,' she said. 'Rachel said you had a lovely dinner.'

'That's right,' said Jenkins. The grubby feeling had faded.

His heart was light. He wanted to confide in her; to say, Diana, you can carry on living here, and it's OK about the clubs and the BMW. But of course she had not known that it had ever been anything but all right. Instead, he said: 'I've got something to tell you.'

She turned a page of the magazine.

'I'm going back to sea.' He braced himself.

She did not look up from the magazine, but Jenkins saw her lips tighten. She said, 'Really?'

'I hope you don't mind.'

She swivelled her eyes at him. They were amber like Rachel's, but cool and shallow where Rachel's were warm and deep. 'Mind?' she said.

'The money's excellent,' said Jenkins, wrong-footed into justifying himself.

Diana said, 'I know you'll do what you think is right for us all.' She smiled, the dazzling cocktail-party smile that came and went and left her face unmoved. 'I'm sure you'll enjoy it.' She went back to her magazine.

Jenkins undressed and climbed into bed. It had been much easier than he had expected.

Diana smoothed the magazine shut, and put it neatly on the pile on her cream bedside table. It appeared that they were going to talk. She said, 'Do you know who rang Rachel tonight?'

'No.'

'Raymond Chang.'

Jenkins gazed at the pink-and-beige curtains. The windows were closed. The amahs cleaned the room every day, but sleeping here still felt like being buried in dust. He said, 'She mentioned something. Nice bloke?'

Diana made an exasperated tutting noise. 'His father's one of the ten richest men in Hong Kong.'

'Oh,' he said. 'Him.'

Diana said, 'You're from outer space, did you know that?' It was only just a joke. He put his hand on her shoulder. The skin was still smooth and young; Diana would be thirty-six next birthday. He felt a dim stirring of desire; anything to get closer. He ran his hand down her smooth upper arm to the lacy swell of her hip.

She shrugged it away. 'It's late. I've got to get up, even if you haven't.'

For commitments including an early morning workout at the Strong Body Studio and a visit to the hairdresser, thought Jenkins. He slid down in the bed. Sometimes, being married to Diana was like not being married at all.

He had been twenty when he had met her: four years at sea, with a brand-new mate's ticket in the briefcase in his room at his parents' house outside Dorchester, home in the second week of a month's leave. There had been a dance at Canford School, a feverishly Gothic building where he went to play real tennis with a few of his mates. And there she had been.

It had been something or other at first sight, definitely. Jenkins had had short hair and a brown face, and the bastard of a captain on his ship at the time had made sure that he was a spruce dresser, blazers and flannels in the midst of the sideburns and loon pants of his contemporaries. And Diana – well. Diana had had long golden legs, and long golden hair done up at the back, and long white teeth, and among the platforms and the cheesecloth and the false eyelashes, she was the only natural phenomenon.

He got himself introduced. When they talked, she was not awkward like the other girls. She did not consider it weird or straight to be in the Merchant Navy. She knew how to get on with people, the way the blokes on the ship got on with each other.

It was much, much later that Jenkins began to suspect that there might be more to married life than getting on.

That night, he found he was dancing with her, awkwardly, true, but not noticing, to the strains of Noddy Holder, with the disco lights winking on the Assyrian bas-reliefs in the hall. And later, out in the car park, in his MGB, he had found the smooth skin of her upper thigh, and the lithe swell of her tennis-playing hips, and the excitable pucker of her small pink nipples. And she had gasped in his ear no, not on the first date, *please*. That had been something a bloke could respect, never mind the problems he was having with his trousers. So he had asked her to see *Superfly* the next night, and taken her to a Ralph McTell concert in Bournemouth the night after that. And the night after that they had gone for a walk on the beach out towards Studland, and on a rug in the dunes she had demonstrated that the things she did not do on the first date she did enthusiastically on the fourth.

Then Jenkins had gone back to sea.

He had written to her three times a week, long, technical letters about life on the ship. The letters that came back were shorter, written in a big, square hand, the i's dotted with circles. They spoke of tennis and people Jenkins did not know. They gave him the idea that she was in demand. In fact, they made him anxious, because here he was out here in that damn ship, and she was the toast of Poole, and God knew who she was seeing.

So when she wrote to say that she was pregnant, it came almost as a relief. He asked her to marry him by return. And they had been married, from his parents' house, because she had said that her own parents' house was too small, and she had a point, seeing it was a terrace in Hamworthy, and his father, RN (ret'd), lived in a fair-sized farmhouse with stables and twenty acres.

Oddly, as Jenkins thought, his parents did not seem too thrilled with Diana. A couple of days before the wedding, his mother said, 'You are sure about this, are you?'

'Of course,' said Jenkins.

His father had had four pink gins before dinner instead of the usual two. 'One thing you can be bloody sure of,' he said. 'David'll lead with his bloody chin.'

Jenkins remembered the feeling he had had then. It was him and Diana against the world. He liked being at sea, but sometimes he thought it might have been a bit unfair of his parents to send him off at sixteen, before he knew his mind. He had told Diana, and she had agreed.

When Rachel had been born, Diana got a nanny, because Jenkins had made second mate. There was plenty of work about. Sometimes he did not come home for six months at a time. On one of his leaves, she conceived Bill. It was an ideal marriage. Two lovely kids. Beautiful wife. The only trouble was, they saw each other on average one month in four. Still, they were grown up.

Him and Diana against the world.

Next morning, he got up early. The wind was moaning in the balcony. Diana was a lump in the bedclothes, snoring faintly. He took his suitcase from the top of the wardrobe, brought it into the living room and started throwing in clothes. Rachel stuck her head out of her door. 'Tea?' she said.

They sat at the kitchen table. 'When are you off?' she said.

'Today.' He wanted to tell her about the Kitten Club. But there was nothing tellable.

'Are you all right?' she said. She knew him unnervingly well.

'Absolutely fine,' he said. 'I met the people last night.' He hoped she was not going to cross-examine him.

But her mind was on different things. 'Raymond rang,' she said. 'Raymond Chang. When I got back from the Loon Fung.'

'Your mother said. Bit late, wasn't it?'

She dropped her eyes. 'I think he's rather keen.'

'And so are you.'

Her face pinkened slightly. 'I told him it was a bit late for ringing.'

'Great minds.'

She took his fingers in hers. She said, 'You wouldn't recognize subtlety if someone hit you over the head with it.' She kissed him on the cheek. 'Have a good trip.'

He nodded. He finished packing and took tea to Diana. She said, 'Haven't you gone yet?' and went back to sleep.

He kissed Rachel goodbye, told her awkwardly to be good, and heaved his case down to the lobby. He was used to Diana. Still, he found himself thinking an unworthy thought. Sometimes nowadays he did not feel it was him and Diana against the rest. Sometimes nowadays, he felt it was him and Rachel against Diana.

Chapter Seven

By eleven o'clock that morning, the northeast monsoon was up and wailing in the city's concrete gorges, knocking the khaki water of the harbour into short, sharp waves iced with grubby foam. There were a good hundred ships in the anchorage, most of them on eight-hour turnaround, working cargo with ramshackle barges alongside. Outside the harbour proper, in the roads to the south of Lamma Island, a dozen more were waiting their turn. There was shouting, and bustle, and the manic activity in which Hong Kong specializes.

But not on buoy C-11.

Buoy C-11 was a round float with a shackle at its centre, attached to the seabed northwest of the Macao ferry pier. There was a ship chained to it. On the ship's transom were traces of white-painted lettering that had once spelt *Glory of Saipan*.

The *Glory* looked like a rusty steel shoebox a hundred and twenty yards long and thirty yards wide. At the front end, where the sides began to converge to make the point of the bow, was a five-storey accommodation block, painted white, topped with the plate-glass windows of the bridge. Below the windows, red tears of rust streaked the pocked and blistering paint. On the aerials above the monkey island fluttered the star-and-stripes ensign of Liberia.

Aft of the accommodation, the *Glory*'s hatch-covers ran clear to her stern. On top of the hatch-covers, twenty- and forty-foot containers were stacked two high and six across. At the extreme back end of the ship a square-section funnel leaked black smoke into the stinking wind.

Jenkins approached buoy C-11 in a splintery wooden water taxi. The driver had several gold teeth, all of which were showing. 'Hah!' said the driver. 'Dirty old thing!'

Jenkins could not bring himself to answer. The *Glory of Saipan* was indeed not an encouraging sight. She had all the bad signs. The portholes in the accommodation were open. That meant that the air conditioning was not working. On her afterdeck, by the funnel, was one of the worst signs of all: a 500-kilowatt generator, with arm-thick wires snaking down a hatchway into what was presumably the engine room. That would mean that not only the air conditioning but the ship's generators had broken down, and that the owners were too parsimonious to replace them.

The taxi bucketed over the short, steep waves to the *Glory*'s stern and motored full ahead, jamming the rubber tyre on its nose against the plates of the ship's transom. Jenkins heaved his bag on to the deck and stepped aboard. The taxi spewed white water from its stern and clattered off for the shore, leaving Jenkins in the roar of the generator.

An Australian voice behind him said, 'Who the hell are you?'

He turned, feeling the crunch of rust-flakes underfoot. The man was about five feet six inches tall, with a fleshless face. The skin was ruddy pink, not with health but with a tracery of capillaries brought up to the surface and dynamited by drink. The whites of the eyes looked runny, like the whites of under-poached eggs.

Jenkins put out his hand. 'Jenkins,' he said. 'First mate.'

The Australian ignored the hand, and looked him up and down with the dreadful eyes. 'Nairn,' he said, without moving his lips. 'Chief engineer. Got the fucking water-maker in bits.' He stumped into a door at the base of the funnel.

Jenkins tried not to be surprised. New kind of ship, new kind of rules, he told himself. But he did not like the ship or the rules. He hefted his bag and crunched forward along the narrow steel deck beside the containers, dragged open the door of the accommodation and let himself in. He went up five flights of stairs through a stink of stale cooking and men's sweat. It was nasty. But there were consolations. That morning, twenty thousand dollars had gone over to Tommy Wong, and ten to Diana's bank. Wong would get the balance on arrival in Oakland.

Beggars and choosers, Jenkins told himself. You can get used to anything.

Meanwhile he had arrived on the bridge, and a bridge was a bridge. He had a poke round. The charts seemed to be in date. Most of the equipment was as filthy and neglected as the rest of the ship. But Jenkins was surprised to see a new Raytheon ARPA, and in the chart room a satellite communications setup and SSB radio. The ship might be a rust-bucket, but if she started to sink, she would know where she was sinking. Better still, it was going to be possible to call for assistance.

'Meester Jenkin,' said a voice.

He looked up. It was Soares, still wearing the short-sleeved white shirt and khaki chinos of two days ago, medallions clanking on his pasty chest, apparently unconscious of the cold. Jenkins shook the slimy hand and said, 'When do we sail?'

Soares shrugged. 'Wait for orders. Lunch half-twelve.' He picked up a telephone and dialled. 'Mess boy to bridge.'

The mess boy showed Jenkins to his cabin, a Formica box with a desk, a bunk, and a reeking shower-and-lavatory unit. A procession of ants was walking along the leeboard of the bunk. Jenkins sent the mess boy for mops and disinfectant, laid fresh newspaper on the shelves of the steel wardrobe and unpacked his bag. He put Rachel's tropical snowstorm on the shelf inside his porthole and gave it a shake for luck. The artificial snowflakes swirled round the palm trees. Bloody awful ship, he thought. But it was a ship. Things were back on course. At twelve thirty, he went down for lunch.

The messroom had a blue-and-white-check oilcloth over a steel table. Peter Pelly, the second mate, was there. He winked and nodded. The skin under his narrow plum-coloured eyes was greyish-white with hangover. Nairn and Soares were eating sardines and greasy potatoes fried with garlic. Sitting at the end was a woman of about fifty, with a long jaw and steel-wool hair in a bun. She glanced at Jenkins with suspicious grey eyes. Her mouth was a letterbox slot, as

65

if years of resignation had done away with her lips. Nairn said, 'Irma, this is the chief mate, er . . .'

'David Jenkins,' said Jenkins.

Mrs Nairn stretched the letterbox and said, 'Pleastameecha.' There was no further conversation. Jenkins pulled over a packet of Kraft cheese slices and some pale pink tomatoes, and made himself a sandwich. Nairn poured himself three short glasses of apple juice out of a cardboard carton and tipped them down his throat with a jerkiness that made Jenkins think he was more used to drinking whisky.

Soares wiped his mouth with the back of his hand. He said, 'Everybody doing OK?'

Nairn belched. His wife frowned at him, as if to say not quite nice. He said, 'Apart from the bloody machinery. And two Chinkie motormen never seen an engine room before. I want to tell you that this is not what I am bloody well used to. I was on the *Asia Ruby*. I had a second, a third, two cadets, five apprentices. The hardest job I had all day was deciding what wine to order with dinner –'

Mrs Nairn said, 'That's all over.' Her voice was sharp as a whip.

Nairn looked as if he had woken from sleep. 'Wha'?' he said.

She did not take her eyes off him. 'Over,' she said. 'Now we've got a ship to run.'

'Oh,' said Nairn, like a sleepwalker. 'Yeah.'

She rose. Nairn got up too. They left.

Peter raised his eyebrows. 'Lovely couple,' he said.

Soares had been picking his nose. He inspected the result and said, absently, 'Yeah. Dave, check stores with Rodriguez, third mate. Pete, you're navigating, I see you on the bridge. Pilot on board at eighteen 'undred.'

Jenkins said, 'Where do I find Rodriguez?'

Soares said, 'The Flips got their own mess one deck down. You like to eat fried blood and fish head, you can join them.' He rummaged in his pocket and threw Jenkins a set of keys. They were unpleasantly warm.

Down in the crew messroom Rodriguez and Johnny, third and fourth mates respectively, were watching *Die Hard* on the video machine. Rodriguez was a small man with loose lips and an oily pompadour. Johnny was stout and lugubrious, with protruding eyeballs marbled brown. Rodriguez said, 'Howdy.' They both gave Jenkins limp handshakes.

Rodriguez said, 'You like Elvis Presley?'

'"Jailhouse Rock",' said Jenkins.

Rodriguez nodded. 'My hero. In US I go to visit Graceland.'

'Ah,' said Jenkins. At least Rodriguez was interested in something and had the power of speech.

Rodriguez ran a comb through his quiff and pushed himself to his feet. Jenkins said, 'Johnny. What are you doing this afternoon?'

'Sleep,' said Johnny. 'Bad stomach. Bad heart. Watch video.'

'How about the safety gear?'

'Later,' said Johnny.

'Now,' said Jenkins. There would be order. There would be system. This would be a ship.

Johnny stuck out his lower lip and waddled, wheezing, out of the messroom.

The stores were a series of cabin-sized lockers in the root of the accommodation. The doors were of steel. Cracks radiated from the corners of the frames. Holes had been drilled to stop their spread, but they had spread anyway. The locks were good Chubb deadlocks, brand new. Jenkins pushed the key into the first one and opened it.

The locker was filled with sacks. Jenkins tried to count them. There were too many to count.

'Locker one,' said Rodriguez, reading from the list and yawning. 'Rice. Two hundred forty by fifty kilo bags.'

There was silence. Then Jenkins said, 'How much rice do eighteen Filipinos eat in a day?'

Rodriguez said, 'Twenty kilo, maybe.'

'So that's six hundred days' rice.'

'Bery slow ship,' said Rodriguez, giggling.

'Count them.'

They counted them. There were two hundred and forty bags. In the freezer were the dismembered carcasses of fifty pigs, as well as several hundredweight of fish. There were gallons of oil, and crates of onions, and carboys of soy sauce. Rodriguez ticked the items off on his list, humming 'A Fool Such as I'. When they had finished the inventory, Jenkins took the list up to the ship's office. His knees felt faintly shaky. He had the sense that an infinitesimally short honeymoon was over, and things were going wrong.

Soares was leafing through *Playboy*, absent-mindedly massaging the crotch of his trousers. 'All OK?' he said.

Jenkins said, 'How fast does this ship go?'

'Eleven knots,' said Soares.

'How long till Oakland?'

Soares' clammy eyes had turned small and sharp. 'Month,' he said. 'Depends. Why you ask?'

'We're carrying enough stores for three hundred and fifty people.'

Soares turned a page of *Playboy*. He said, 'Mr Zamboanga Boy Scout Jenkins, if you don' like this ship you can give back the money and go on the beach.' He looked at his watch. 'We sailing at seventeen hunnerd.'

Jenkins told himself, You are the first mate. You are being paid to take the captain's orders. There will be a perfectly sensible explanation. 'Yessir,' he said. He found he was sweating.

Soares went back to his *Playboy*.

Jenkins made himself stop thinking about stores. He drew a set of overalls, a pair of steel-capped boots and a hard-hat. He pulled them on, shoved a two-way radio into his breast pocket and drove half a dozen deckhands on to the foredeck. The radio in his pocket squawked. 'Pilot on board,' said Soares' voice. 'Off we jolly well going.'

This was mate's work. It was as comforting as sitting down in an old, well-used armchair. Jenkins nagged the hands into rigging a slip on the mooring buoy. He craned over the flare of the bow to watch the foreshortened figure of a Chinese step from the pilot boat to the buoy and unscrew the shackle of the slack anchor chain. Through his feet he felt the faint throb of dead slow ahead. In his ear, the pilot's voice said, 'Let go slip.'

'Let go slip,' he said. The steel hawser splashed in the khaki water and came in on the port windlass. The *Glory* was free.

And back to Jenkins came the thought of all those stores, and the sixty-thousand-dollar salary. What is this? he thought.

Too late for wondering now.

The *Glory of Saipan*'s nose swung across the harbour, round Green Island and into the channel that led to the open South China Sea and the thousands of peaceful miles beyond. Jenkins turned to the foredeck crew to organize the retrieval and reshackling of the anchor.

His two-way radio crackled in his ear.

'Mate,' squawked the voice of Soares. 'There's a problem in the engine room. Sort it out, could you?'

Chapter Eight

The engine room was hot as hell and twice as noisy. But Jorge the oiler was used to heat and noise, having worked in engine rooms ever since his rich uncle had bribed a pass out of the examiner at the MacArthur Sea School in Cebu City six years previously. Jorge felt his true vocation lay in the breeding of fighting cocks, and borrowing money from his mother to bet on them while they tore each other to bits in the cockpits of the *barrio*, and not paying his mother back, win or lose. Life at sea was usually unpleasant, particularly on a dirty old ship like this.

It was extra unpleasant tonight.

It had begun with the two new motormen, Ho and Lee. They were both Chinese. Even Jorge could tell that they did not know their jobs. But he would not have dreamed of telling them, because they were square men who put their feet to the ground with precision. Jorge's training with the cocks had taught him to recognize fighting animals when he saw them.

The motormen were in a cubbyhole by the steering gear. Between them was a steel table to which had been taped two cardboard mailing tubes. They were standing over the tubes, yelling into each other's faces. There was a pile of money at one end of the table. It looked like gambling.

While Jorge watched, he saw a small head with round ears and whiskers emerge from the right-hand tube. The Chinese called Ho picked up the pile of money.

Light dawned on Jorge. What he had here was a case of rat racing. Jorge was a man of strong sporting instincts. He went up to the table. The rat of the one called Ho stuck its head out again. The one called Lee paid up. Ho's rat impressed Jorge as having a bold eye and the look of a solid rat over distance. Jorge pulled his roll out of his pocket and slapped a hundred dollars American on Ho's side of the table.

Neither man even looked at him or his money. Jorge began to feel neglected, a sensation he had never enjoyed. So he pulled up a chair and watched, breathing hard.

Ho's rat won again. Lee paid up. Still they ignored Jorge.

In the end, Jorge could stand it no longer. He had won. He wanted paying. He tapped Lee on the shoulder; more a slap, really, or a gentle punch.

This time, he was not ignored.

Lee turned to him a face blank as a sheet of buff paper. Then Jorge felt a stunning pain on his right ear. He went over sideways on to the greasy steel deck. *He hit me*, he thought, through a blood-coloured fog. His fingers closed round the handle of his sheath knife, and he bounced upright like a Mr Wobbly toy.

Lee picked up Jorge's money from the table and stuffed it into his pocket. Jorge felt indignant and humiliated. Knife outstretched, he started forward.

Lee smiled. It was a smile that made Jorge realize all of a sudden that this was not the sort of person you waved knives at. But now the knife was out, Jorge could see no way he could decently put it away.

Lee moved his arms as if he was climbing into a tight pullover. His foot came up and whacked into Jorge's knife elbow. As the blade skittered across the floor his knuckles popped forward, aiming at Jorge's nose, to drive the bones up and into the brain. But Jorge had ducked, so the fist caught him on the forehead. Lightning flashed in his head. He shot backwards into the main engine room, coming to rest against the windows of the control booth. Inside the control booth, he saw through a curtain of blood the vision of the chief shouting into a telephone. His hand found the door handle. He opened the door, stumbled in and locked it behind him. Someone was bellowing, but he could not hear the words because of the way his ears were ringing. Anyway, he was not listening. He was looking out of the window at the engine-room floor, across which the Chinese Lee was padding with his horrible sucker-footed walk. And in the hands of the Chinese Lee was a big red fire axe.

Jenkins stood at the top of the greasy stairs, chest heaving after the hundred-yard sprint from the bridge. Below him the engine bellowed, surrounded by the three steel galleries on the topmost of which he was standing. Down at the bottom, next to the whizzing tappet rods, a man in a white boiler suit was brandishing a red axe at the shop-window of the control room. Nairn was inside, his face a bloodshot death's head behind the glass. There was a big red mushroom of a button next to Jenkins' hand. The general alarm.

He knew what you did when there was mutiny and insurrection. You pushed the button.

He pushed the button.

Next to the control room, the orange alarm light started to flash urgently. Jenkins waited for running feet. There were no running feet. There would be bells.

But nobody would be answering the bells, because this was not a ship like any of the other ships he had spent his life on. As he watched, the orange light stopped revolving. Someone had turned the bells off.

It burst into Jenkins' mind with a light bright as magnesium. For sixty thousand dollars, you made up the rules as you went along.

He looked about him. There was a sheaf of rusty iron piping jammed into a bin welded to the bulkhead. He pulled out a four-foot length and ran down into the steel pit of noise.

The Chinese Lee had taken one swipe at the glass of the control room. Instead of shattering, the glass had starred. Not an engine-room hand, thought Jenkins, or he would have known it was toughened. The man was winding up for the second clout when Jenkins came up behind him. Inside, Nairn was making faces, pointing. The Chinese looked round. He had short-cropped hair that stood in bristles on his bullet head. His eyes were narrow and black under heavy brows. The muscles at the hinges of the jaw looked big and hard as walnuts.

Jenkins pointed at the steps. The Chinese frowned.

Jenkins saw the beginnings of uncertainty on his face. Putting his length of piping to the deck like a walking stick, Jenkins pointed at the ladders leading up and away and beckoned again, more urgently, pantomiming danger. Then he started to walk up, towards the deck. Over the vibration of the engine in the steel treads, he could feel the clump of boots behind him. Two pairs of boots.

There was a little oblong of daylight at the top of the steps. He walked through it and into cool sea air.

Can't have the engine room terrorized, thought Jenkins. These were not seamen, or motormen, or any known form of seafaring life. Jenkins knew that there would only be one way of teaching them the rules, and it had nothing to do with training manuals.

He was standing in a sort of crevasse between a line of containers and the front face of the engine-room superstructure. An iron ladder led up the face. It suited Jenkins fine. Shoving his bit of pipe into his belt, he began to climb, teacher mounting the dais.

When he was at the top he looked down.

The two men in white overalls were in the crevasse, looking up. He shouted, 'Come up! Quick!'

The man with the fire axe looked at the ladder, then at the axe. He dropped the axe and began to climb. His mate came after him. Jenkins said, 'Quick!'

The fingers of the first man's left hand appeared on the top rung of the ladder. Jenkins smashed the iron pipe down on them. The man yelled. Jenkins hit him on the ear, alongside the yowling red mouth. Then he whacked his other hand.

The man let go of the ladder and fell into the crevasse between the containers with a metallic crash.

To port the dish aerials on Stanley Island were sliding by, and the pilot launch was bustling away towards the distant planet called home.

Jenkins leaned over the ladder. The second man was still there, rubbing his neck, which the first man must have hit on the way down. He said, 'Speak English?'

The man turned a hard, expressionless face up at him. 'Small bit.' Below in the crevasse, the other man was beginning to crawl.

'Stay where you are,' said Jenkins. 'I'm going to give you Lesson One.'

'Yes, Mr Jenkins,' said the man.

'You do not fight in the engine room. You do not fight on this ship. You obey orders on this ship.'

'Yes, Mr Jenkins,' said the man.

'Tell your friend.'

'Yes, Mr Jenkins,' said the man, and smiled, a wide, entirely unfriendly smile. Suddenly, Jenkins recognized him. This was the man who had been with Tommy Wong when Wong had taken him to the office of Hugh Chang. That day, he had not been a motorman. He had been a loan-shark's minder.

So what the hell was he doing on the *Glory of Saipan*?

Not important. The land was the land, and a ship was a ship. 'Right,' said Jenkins. 'We'll see the captain now.'

Soares was on the bridge, sitting in a rattan chair propped on a packing case so he could see out of the window. Soares said, 'So what's the problem?'

'Crew fighting,' said Jenkins. 'Two Chinese. Supposed to be motormen.' He was feeling ragged and jumpy. 'I shut them in the portside paint locker. I suggest you put the bastards ashore.'

'Ashore?'

'They smashed up the engine room. They went after the chief with an axe. They don't know the work they're being paid for. Someone will get killed.'

Soares scratched his chest. He smelt of deodorant plastered over old sweat. 'Hmm,' he said. 'Yeah. Thing is, we jus' might need them.'

Jenkins stared at him. 'Need them?'

'First offence, anyway,' said Soares. 'Tellyawhat. I'll go 'ave a word with 'em in my office.' He slid out of his chair with a grunt, and took Jenkins' hand confidentially in his clammy fingers. 'Seems strange, huh?' he said. 'Specially to a guy like you, regular Orient Line guy, huh? You done nice. No problem. But . . . well, you'll see.'

Jenkins pulled his hand away, and wiped it on his overalls. Soares left.

74

He began to pace the bridge, making himself a routine patrol. Portside, the rattan chair and the console with the warning lights and the engine-room telegraph, now on full ahead. Amidships, the wheel with the gyrocompass and the autopilot controls, tended this close to land by a quarter-master apparently called Bong. Starboard side, the ARPA. Aft of the ARPA, the chart room, with curtains to protect the lookout's night vision.

Suddenly, he doubted that he had done a good job, building a team, all that nonsense. He had smacked a Chinese thug with an iron bar, that was all. Twenty-odd years at sea, steady. And it had come to this.

He thought of Diana, half-asleep, her voice: 'Haven't you gone yet?'

Eighteen years of marriage, said a tinny little echo in his mind. And this is where it gets you.

Keep your lookout. Don't think.

He went to look out of the windows aft portside, walked the width of the ship, looked aft starboard side, then at the ARPA. He found the routine soothing. It almost persuaded him that this was a real job on a real ship. He plotted the rest of the traffic, which was thinning as they moved southeast, away from the islands of Hong Kong. Pete came in and went to the chart table and started fiddling with a pencil on one of the big flat sheets. Jenkins looked over his shoulder.

As plotted, the *Glory of Saipan*'s track would take her just to the north of Luzon, the northernmost island of the Philippines. It was well to the south of the Great Circle route to San Francisco. He said, 'What we doing all the way down there?'

'Old Man's orders,' said Pete. Pete carried with him a correct Merchant Navy atmosphere, dissolute yet stolid. Jenkins found him reassuring. 'Where you from?'

'On the beach,' said Jenkins.

'Me too,' said Pete. 'Bloody Seamen's Mission.' Jenkins got the idea that he was a talkative man, suffering from an overlong silence. 'Paid off in October. Sitting there thinking there's no bloody ships left on the ocean. Then up pops Soares.' Pete's narrow black eyes strayed over the peeling green paint of the bridge, the rust streaks under the windows. 'Not my idea of a ship, really. Watch out for that fucking chief, he's got a fucking chip shop on his shoulder. And you know about those motormen. I'm going to stay out of their bloody way, me personally. But you can't argue with the money.'

This was close enough to Jenkins' analysis to give him the urge to confide. He said, 'Funny sort of delivery, this?'

'Don't care how funny it is,' said Pete. 'It's better than the Mission.' He pulled out a calculator and started to stab buttons, sucking air through his bottom teeth.

Jenkins watched the islands of Hong Kong sink into the sea, and felt lonelier than he had ever felt. Goodbye, Rachel, he thought. Think of your old man.

He made himself and Pete coffee with the bridge kettle; at least there was something as normal as a bridge kettle. Heartened, he called the mess boy and told him to start spring cleaning the accommodation.

Somewhere aft, machine tools began to whine and howl. When Jenkins looked out of the bridge window he saw orange showers of sparks, and the blue lightning of arc welders, and he knew that, kettle or no kettle, things were far from normal. For no legitimate reason he could conceive of, someone was making alterations to the containers.

Chapter Nine

Jenkins had been asleep for four hours when Soares called on the internal telephone. He showered in his bathroom, in which the mess boy had replaced the smell of old urine with the smell of new bleach. He made himself a cup of coffee in the galley and walked along to the office against the long corkscrew roll of the ship in the low swell from the northeast.

Soares was in a swivel chair, feet on the desk, wet eyes in the crotch of the *Penthouse* centrefold on the bulkhead. He was wearing a singlet and shorts, exposing areas of white thigh and black fuzz. 'Mate,' he said. 'We got some cargo work for you.'

Beyond the office portholes, the South China Sea stretched to an unbroken horizon. Jenkins said, 'We don't have a cargo.'

'Yeah,' said Soares. 'Yeah, yeah. But I want some boxes shifted.' He pushed four pages of squared paper across to Jenkins. He chewed his fat lower lip, watching Jenkins sit down, glance at the papers and frown.

'What is this?' said Jenkins.

'Stowage plan.' Soares lit a cigarette and blew smoke at the genitalia on the wall.

As a stowage plan, it was frankly weird. It showed a schematic diagram of the *Glory of Saipan*'s deck. The central containers were shown as voids, extending two deep, down to the level of the hatch-covers. Fourteen twenty-foot containers would have to be moved. Jenkins said, 'Where are you going to put the boxes you take out?'

Soares pointed a thumb out of the porthole at the blue and empty sea.

Jenkins drove the gantry crane himself. It was easy work: sit in the cab, with the cables snaking down under your feet; line up on the container; lower the grab, timing it right with the long, low swell running from the port bow; lift, the ancient bearings rumbling and groaning. Run the cab towards the side until you were looking down at blue water instead of the rusty iron tops of the containers, and the stops clanked against the outboard edges of the jibs. Thumb the button, release the modified spinlocks. Splash.

The containers smacked the water in white flowers of spray. The air rushed out in a stream of fat bubbles. The rusty brown boxes turned green with depth, and vanished into the blue nothing. From that nothing a question rose with the bubbles, a question Jenkins did not want to hear, because he knew that the answer was not an answer he was going to be able to live with.

Why?

He finished at five fifteen, went to his cabin and took a shower. Mrs Nairn knocked on his door. 'Beer?' she said. He followed her bolster thighs along the alleyway.

The Nairns' cabin was intensely tidy. On the bulkhead was a picture of the chief, in shorts and a bush hat, standing in front of a combine harvester. Mrs Nairn put two frosty bottles of San Miguel and a can of Seven-Up on the lace tablecloth. She whipped the caps off the beers with a practised jerk of her thick wrist. 'Settling in?' she said.

Jenkins said, 'Yes.' She had hung antimacassars on the vinyl banquettes. There was a pink-and-blue painting of kittens on the wall. He realized that he was not the only one who wanted life to seem ordinary. He wondered if his own attempts looked as weird as Mrs Nairn's. He ran his finger round the neck of the San Mig and took a sharp, cold swallow.

'Cheers,' said Mrs Nairn, and took a sip, little finger out.

Nairn came in. He did not look at Jenkins, drank half the Seven-Up in one swallow, and made a disgusted face. He said, staring at the combine photo, 'Bone to pick with you.'

Jenkins said, 'Sorry?'

Nairn said, 'You were with Orient, right? I know you bastards at Orient walk hand in hand with God. But is it usual for Orient deck blokes to stick their noses into the engine room?' His voice was elaborately sarcastic; the voice of a man who wanted a fight, any fight. Chip shop on his shoulder, Pete had said.

Jenkins said, 'I left Orient.'

'You got fired,' said Nairn. 'And the sun stopped shining out of your rectum on that precise day. Just you remember that. Last ship I had I left of my own free will. So keep your nose out of my engine room.'

Jenkins could feel the anger like a balloon in his chest. It was too early in the voyage for a row. He stood up. He said, 'I'd better be getting on.'

Mrs Nairn said, 'Oh, no. Really . . . '

Nairn walked into the sleeping cabin and slammed the door.

Mrs Nairn smiled a bright, papering-over-the-cracks smile. 'Don't pay any attention to Edwin,' she said. 'His memory's not so good nowadays.' She bent forward. There was something not right about her smile. 'He used to drink, you know.'

'Is that right?' said Jenkins.

'So now you know,' said Nairn's voice from behind the door. 'But I'm off it now. Doctor's orders. She's the fucking doctor.'

' 'Fraid so,' said Mrs Nairn brightly.

'Remember that,' said Nairn's voice. 'In case you get a sudden Orient Line fucking urge to start handing out pills.'

'A doctor?' said Jenkins. Ships the size of the *Glory of Saipan* did not carry doctors.

Mrs Nairn gave Jenkins a little wink. 'Nice to be useful,' she said. 'Don't pay any attention to Edwin. He retired, once, but then we had to come back to sea. Circumstances. He's a disappointed man.' She emitted a trill of laughter like breaking china. 'I think everybody on this ship is, don't you? We're all victims, really.'

Jenkins forced a grin and left the cabin. He had been on ships with crazies before, including Fingers Nagwich, who, after a week on the gin in 1979, had refused to go into Singapore without air cover. But a ship had been a ship, a clearly defined society on a clearly defined voyage, with conventions. Conventions were what made ships tolerable.

And marriages, said the scratchy voice in his head.

There were no conventions on the *Glory*. The *Glory* was a big rusty box, empty except for chaos.

And more chaos to come.

He went to the bridge to begin his watch and take some deep breaths of air unpolluted by Nairn. After a while, he began to feel calmer. The sun was lighting bonfires of cloud in the western sky. Aft, the hollow squares of containers looked like three miniature courtyards. Down in the courtyards, there were straight-edged openings that could almost have been doors and windows.

Jenkins went to look at the chart. The straight line of their track bore the crossings of the day's fixes, one each hour. He bent to look more closely.

A hundred and ten miles down the track someone had marked a cross. It had not been there this morning.

The crew of the *Glory* were being paid big money for delivering a rusty ship carrying too much food and a doctor. The answers to the big question had been adding up for some time, now. Soon, Jenkins knew he was going to have to admit to himself exactly what they added up to.

At 0410 the bridge was dark, except for the green glow of the ARPA. Jenkins had just come on watch and his eyes were heavy. He was leaning on the wooden grab-handles, watching the disc of the screen.

At the point where the ship's track met the circumference of the screen, a little green blip had come into being. Jenkins knew without checking that it was in the position of the pencilled cross on the chart.

He brought up the vectors that would tell him their relative positions in two hours. As the *Glory* lumbered across the swell, he gazed into the black soup-plate, reading the future and hating what he saw.

Beyond the long line of windows a meathook moon hung in the sky. The *Glory of Saipan* climbed towards it on a silver ladder.

On the circular screen, the blip drew closer.

At five, as the first watery signals of dawn were greying the sky, the bridge telephone shrilled. 'Captain here,' said the voice. 'Who's that?'

'First mate.'

Soares vouchsafed him a wet cough. 'What you got?'

'Radar target,' said Jenkins. 'Dead ahead. Stationary. Range eleven point three miles.' A hope grew. Now Soares would say: It's a fishing boat. Give him a mile. And they would pass this fishing boat, and sail on to Oakland.

Soares said, 'Hold your course.'

Jenkins said, 'We'll hit him.'

Soares said, impatiently, 'We're going alongside.'

'Alongside?'

'*Mister* Jenkins,' said Soares. 'You got paid your money. Now you start to earn it.'

The hope vanished like a bubble.

The sky in the east paled fingernail-pink. The sea turned from Indian ink to battleship paint.

Out on the horizon, something small and square stood black against the pale light.

Jenkins picked up his binoculars, a pair of 7 × 50 Steiners dating from the days of his affluence. They were one of the few things he had not sold. He had known that in the orderly progression of events, he would find another ship.

On the wing of the bridge the air smelled warm and clean. The seas rolled regular as lynchets in the circle of the glasses' objective, ruffled with a tiny pre-dawn breeze.

The thing was a ship. It was painted black and white, and it had square, boxy upperworks, and three rows of windows, and a squat funnel on top. It looked like the kind of ship a child would draw, with squiggles of pencil smoke coming out of the funnel. It had a top-heavy look that meant sheltered waters only; the look of the ships that scuttle from island to island in Hong Kong, or slither between the mudbanks of the Pearl River. A ferryboat.

The sun stuck a blot of fire above the horizon and began to haul itself up the sky. Through the glasses, its red light cast a cosy glow over the ferry's peeling white paintwork. They were closing now. Soares was on the bridge. From inside the wheelhouse came the sound of a VHF radio. The ferry had a name, written in black Chinese characters under its bow. 'Mate!' bellowed Soares. 'Get in here!'

Jenkins took a last lungful of clean air and went in. Soares was standing with a cigarette in his mouth and his thumbs hooked in his belt. 'Call all hands,' he said. 'Get the gangway down.'

The blocky shape of the ferryboat had sprouted a dark, furry growth. It was not fur, but people: hundreds of people, on the upperworks and the foredeck and the afterdeck, guarding bags and bundles, holding children by the hand. They did not wave, like victims of shipwreck or breakdown. They just stood and watched, impassive as cormorants on a rock.

Soares said to Jenkins, 'So there you are. They don't like living in China. They want to go to America. So we're taking them there. And when we get off the US coast, our frien' Mr Chang has arranged us a rendezvous with some tuna boats. And on the tuna boats they get given their visas, their green cards, whatever, it's not our problem. And they go ashore, and live happily ever after.'

Jenkins said, 'You said it was legal.'

'These are three hundred and sixty-seven people in distress at sea. We save them from this filthy ferry, right? And we take them towards where we are going. All the time outside territorial waters. And before we get into US territorial waters, we run into those tuna boats I tell you about. And they will take them off our hands.' Soares delved in a nostril with a thick finger. 'Anyways,' he said. 'You're not stupid. It's work, you get paid. You got a problem?'

Being ready to rob a bank was not enough. You had to jam the sawn-off shotgun into the cashier's mouth, and feel your finger take the first pressure on the trigger. You had to swallow the humiliation, and think of Diana. 'No problem,' said Jenkins, using organs of speech that seemed to belong to a stranger.

The *Glory of Saipan* came alongside the ferry. Under Jenkins' direction the deck crew attached warps and springs and lashed the two ships together tight. The gangway went down. A stocky Chinese trotted on to the ferry's deck: Lee, the motorman who had smacked the control-room window with the fire axe. The people started to come aboard.

Diana and Rachel and Hong Kong were falling away, part of the neat and organized world that was disintegrating into chaos. Soares was leaning on the rail, watching a Chinese, foreshortened at the head of the gangway, checking off arrivals on a clipboard. The Chinese was Ho, the comrade of Lee, ex-minder of Tommy Wong.

Jenkins took a deep breath. He went down the metal stairs to the root of the gangway. He levelled his eyes at Ho, who gave him his wide, humourless grin. Jenkins nodded. It was part of the order and system, as per the manual. The first mate is responsible for the handling of cargo.

Down on the deck of the ferry, Fung waited his turn, jostled by the throng heading for the gangway. He was a small man, with a monkeyish face, holding his daughter Lin by the hand, dragging his three boxes and a suitcase after him a couple of inches at a time as the queue moved forward on the ferry's splintered deck. His mouth was dry, but his heart was filled with holy joy.

This little ship had been dirty, and smelly, and the food had been bad. When the crew had left, Fung and his friends had expected the worst. They had worshipped the Lord in their own way. The Army had smashed their church when they refused to pay protection. They were persecuted and kept in captivity. They had paid their money, and been delivered from captivity. But now they were being abandoned on the sea. So they had prayed to the Lord for deliverance.

And now deliverance had arrived in the shape of this tall steel ship – rusty, it was true, but reassuringly solid after the rot and splinters of the ferry. It was no more than had been promised. But Fung had had the kind of life in which a promise kept amounted to a miracle. The *Glory of Saipan* was a miracle on a level with the parting of the Red Sea under Moses' staff.

He looked to left and right at his friends. They had space allotted to them in the first courtyard. Fung had seen it on the plan; Lucy had arranged it, dogged, tireless.

He could not see Lucy, but the crowd was thick, and she was small. Around him the people started to move again, and he found himself on the gangway. Fung sang under his breath as he walked under the eyes of the two men at the top of the gangplank, the hard Chinese with the clipboard who looked like a Triad, and the tall, angry-looking gweilo with the big nose. The gweilo winked at Lin. Lin giggled. Fung jerked her hand. He pulled her up on to the metal deck on top of the containers and looked into the first courtyard with the sensation of a wandering Israelite looking upon the land of Canaan. His house was a battered container with a door hacked from the metal, inscribed with the words Hapag Lloyd.

'Alleluia,' said Fung.

He still could not see Lucy.

To Jenkins, it looked as if someone had told the people that they could only bring one suitcase each, and that they had agreed, being in the frame of mind to agree to anything, only to repent later. So in addition to the suitcases there were indispensable bundles and boxes, and even a purple-and-orange armchair. One man stumped up the gangway with a plank on which flapped five chickens, their toes stapled to the timber. Another man, older, with a bent back and an anguished grin that showed the length of his horse-sized yellow teeth, struggled up the slope carrying a sack that wriggled and screamed.

When the old man arrived at the gangway's root, Ho put a hand on his chest and started shouting. The old man looked at him with widened eyes. Ho grabbed the sack. The old man started shouting back. Ho pushed him. The people behind him on the gangway started to complain in high, stressed-out voices. Ho's hand brushed the leg of his overalls. When it came up again, it held a square-ended knife with a twelve-inch blade. The yelling stopped. The blade's edge kissed the bindings of the sack. The sack gaped open. Three black piglets wriggled out and rushed squealing against the flow of people back to the ferry.

'Pigs dirty,' said Ho to Jenkins, shooing the old man aboard with the flat of his knife. The crowd began to trickle by again.

After fifty more, the trickle stopped. Lee the axeman trotted up the gangway. 'Finish check,' said Ho. 'Now we got all them.' Since yesterday morning, Ho seemed to see Jenkins as a fellow-professional.

Jenkins climbed on to the top of the containers and walked to the edge of the first well.

It was definitely a courtyard now, swarming with people. Each container seemed to hold about five. The welders had stuck on ladders leading past the doors from the hatch-covers to the roofs of the top containers. Someone had already lit some sort of stove on the open hatch-cover, and the faint smell of starting charcoal came to Jenkins' nostrils.

All perfectly legal.

The small girl caught his eye. She was running up and down the ladders in the courtyard. At first he thought she was excited. Then he saw that her face was white and panicky. Above the hubbub he could hear her voice, shrill, calling something that might have been a name. She seemed to be looking for someone.

Jenkins walked round to the lip of the containers. He found that Ho was at his shoulder. He intercepted the girl as she came to the top of the ladder, and said, 'What is it?'

'Nothing,' said Ho, grinning. 'Very stupid girl.'

The girl said, 'Rusi.' She was crying. The monkey-faced man who was presumably her father had come up the ladder. He grabbed Jenkins' sleeve and took him to the side of the ship overlooking the ferry. The radio in Jenkins' pocket squawked. 'Get that gangway in,' said Soares' voice. 'Let go fore and aft.'

Lee was back on the *Glory*'s deck, standing by the gangway in his white overalls, cleaning his nails with a sheath knife. Jenkins gave the orders. The monkey-faced man tugged at his sleeve. 'Rusi!' he said, pointing straight down, into the steel-walled, water-floored trench between the ships.

There was a row of portholes down there. There was something odd about one of them, a flicker, as if something was moving inside. It was hard to tell, looking from above. A reflection, he thought.

Then something else happened. Something glittered briefly – broken glass. And where there had been the fore-shortened disc of the porthole, there was something else, something pale and spidery, fluttering in the air.

A human hand, waving.

Chapter Ten

The radio in Jenkins' pocket rasped. Soares' voice squawked, 'What you doing down there?'

Jenkins said, 'There's someone left on board the ferry.' The hand had gone from the porthole. The three black pigs were squealing on the empty decks.

'Fuck sake,' said Soares' voice. 'We got a Chinese gunboat on radar.'

Jenkins said, 'We're way outside territorial waters.'

'You think that matters?' yelled the radio. 'They want us, they'll have us.'

Beside the monkey-faced man the little girl was shouting in Chinese, nearly hysterical. A crowd was forming. Jenkins switched off the radio and shoved his way towards the ship's side.

Lee the axeman was standing at the top of the gangway. His eyes looked like guns in narrow casemates of bone. He was shaking his head, pointing at the Rolex on his thick wrist.

Jenkins tried to push past him. Lee grasped the rail, barring his path with a steely forearm. In the crowd of Chinese, the monkey-faced man started yelling. Then they were all yelling. The racket was like gulls fighting. Lee's smile vanished. The arm stayed in place.

Jenkins said to Ho, 'What the hell does this man think he is doing?'

Ho said something in Chinese. Lee shook his head, looking at Ho. 'Hole in bottom,' said Ho. 'Boat sink.'

In Jenkins' experience, motormen did not muck about first mates. He shoved brusquely at Lee's arm. Lee's arm did not move.

Jenkins kicked him in the balls, clambered over his retching body and ran down the steel gangway. A loudhailer seemed to be bellowing from the bridge. He jumped on to the ferry's splintered upper deck and found a door. He yanked it open. The stink made him gag: vomit, bilge, overflowing lavatories. The porthole with the hand had been three decks down. He found some stairs and began to run down them four at a time. On the third deck down, he found himself in a long, evil-smelling corridor, lined on either side with cabin doors. The deck had a soggy feel, as if somewhere under his feet volumes of water were sloshing. The only light was a dull gleam, a porthole perhaps, at the far end of the alleyway. He stopped, hearing the creak and grind of the two ships, the thump of the blood in his ears. The deck heaved sluggishly as the ferry rolled. He suspected that Soares was quite capable of letting this thing sink, whether or not his first mate was aboard.

He shouted, 'Who's there?'

From down the alleyway came a reedy sound, muffled by walls. A woman's voice, shouting, 'Here!'

Jenkins went down the alleyway until he found the door.

'Thank God,' said the voice from inside. 'I locked us in. The bolt's jammed.'

Jenkins became aware that his feet were wet. The alleyway was awash. He said, 'Stand away from the door.' He kicked it. It hurt his foot. Whoever had built this ferry had had plenty of solid tropical hardwoods to work with. The door did not budge.

Jenkins splashed back down the alleyway. The water was up to his knees, bubbling out of the stairwell. He pulled a fire extinguisher from its mount, waded back and swung it at the cabin door.

At the third wallop the wood began to split. Jenkins' breath was rasping in his chest. The water was at his thighs. The door handle twitched.

'Again,' said the voice. 'On the lock.'

He hit the lock again. The door swung open. Water poured in.

At first, Jenkins thought there was only one person in the

cabin – a woman, small and slight, dressed in a boiler suit too big for her. The water was nearly up to her waist. She had a tired, youngish face that was not, he thought, entirely Chinese.

He said, 'Quick. Get on deck.'

She was carrying a suitcase. She said, 'You'll have to help Jer.' Her English was excellent, tinged with American. She sounded remarkably calm. Over her shoulder, Jenkins saw a man lying on a top bunk. His eyes were half-closed, his cheekbones prominent, the sunken cheeks the colour of the fat on cold roast beef.

The woman said, 'He's sick.'

Jenkins said, 'This thing's going to capsize.'

'Of course.' She could have been wandering on to a bus.

Jenkins grabbed the man's arm. It was thick and muscular under the white nylon shirt. Muscular enough to unjam a bolt, if he had not been ill. 'Hup,' he said.

The man sat up slowly and slid his feet into the water. The whites of his eyes were custard-yellow. Jenkins dragged him out of the cabin and pushed him down the alleyway. The ferry rolled, and for a moment the water level sank, flapping the door. There was something wrong with the door, but Jenkins could not work out what, because his mind was full of what would happen next time the ferry rolled with all that water in her. He shouldered his bag and followed the sick man up the companionway and into the dazzling light on deck.

The double line of faces at the top of the *Glory of Saipan*'s rusty wall of containers moaned, with relief or disappointment, it was hard to tell which. The woman was moving up the gangway. Jenkins pointed the sick man after her, and followed him.

As they came to the top, the loudhailer screamed from the bridge. The mooring lines came off. The ferry made a huge, weary gurgle and lay on its side. Then, slowly, it rolled all the way over, and wallowed like a great black turtle in the turquoise sea.

The axeman Lee was leaning on the rail, eyes narrowed, staring at the woman. The woman smiled at him and gave him the finger. She said to Jenkins, 'He will tell you that he overlooked us. Or that we are stowaways,' she said. 'And that Jer has infectious hepatitis and is a danger to the cargo. He will be lying.'

Jenkins did not answer. It was not his job. He took the sick man's arm and steered him into the accommodation. The Filipino stationed by the steel door grinned at him with gold teeth, and waggled a baseball bat studded with four-inch nails. There was a cadets' cabin, unused because there were no cadets. The sick man sat on the bunk and lowered himself wearily sideways. But he must have got up again, because as Jenkins left, he heard the click of the bolt going home.

He leaned against the side of the alleyway. His legs felt shaky. He was doing the job of the conscientious first mate, responsible for cargo. Carrying out the spirit of the job, not the letter of the job. But the further he got into this, the more complicated it looked. Because he had remembered what had been odd about the cabin door.

The woman had said that the bolt had stuck. But as the ship had rolled and the door had swung to the outrush of water, he had seen the latch. There had been not one tongue of brass sticking out of the lock, but two.

The bolt might have been stuck. But it looked as if someone had locked them in as well. So as first mate of the *Glory*, he had not just taken responsibility for cargo. It looked very much as if he had also stopped part of it getting murdered.

Four minutes later, the bulbous bow of the *Glory of Saipan* hit the ferry beam-on.

The bow went into the ferry's rotten planking like an axe into a chocolate egg. Trapped air whooshed at the blue, blue sky.

'Full astern,' said Soares, scratching.

The *Glory of Saipan* lay stopped, holding the fat little hull under the water. Bubbles poured from the rent, releasing the stink of the ferry's innards. In the glassy sea the hull turned from green to blue and vanished. All that remained were some worm-eaten splinters, two lifebelts, and the three pigs.

The pigs swam confidently through the oil slick towards the steel sides of the *Glory of Saipan*, sure of their welcome.

But there was no welcome. There was only the rusty steel

wall, at which they scrabbled with their cloven hooves; and high above, a face, talking to them encouragingly, making promises: the face of Lee the motorman.

Soares yawned, and hoicked the engine-room telegraph to full ahead. White water churned under the *Glory of Saipan*'s transom.

Lee watched the three little black heads drop astern. He was yelling with laughter.

The pigs swam round in the oil slick, panicking. At first, they squealed. Then they stopped squealing. They were lower in the water now. It lapped their snouts, stinging their nostrils. Their movements became sluggish.

That was when the black fins came, trailing their vees of ripple through the sea; two tiger sharks, each fifteen feet long. The sharks rolled, gaping. They tore off the back half of one pig and the front half of another. The third paddled in the bloody sea, squealing, until it drowned.

Of course the pigs should not have been there; wrong place at the wrong time. The sharks had only been doing their job.

Lee trotted back to the engine room, all systems go, tireless. Lot of work coming up. Lot of order to keep. Couple of . . . targets. He went to his small steel cabin and did a hundred pressups, a hundred situps. His balls still ached; but soon he would fix the gweilo. America would be good. They were soft in America, or so he had heard.

Someone knocked on his door.

He got up and sat on the bunk, heavy-lidded, a light sheen of sweat on his face. 'Who?' he said.

'Captain,' said a Chinese voice.

He opened up. The captain was small and greasy, and he stank. With him was Ho. The captain said, 'That woman.' Ho translated. 'She . . . got away from you.'

Lee did not answer.

Ho said, 'The captain would like to meet her again.'

Lee nodded, once. The captain's horrible tongue went round his wet and horrible mouth. He said, 'Fifty dollars.'

'After,' said Ho.

Lee considered, and decided it was reasonable. 'It must be soon,' he said. 'Unless the captain likes cold meat.'

'That would not be surprising,' said Ho, in Cantonese. In English, he said to Soares, 'For one hundred dollars, this can be arranged. She has seen you and she likes what she has seen.'

'Sure, sure,' said Soares, and left.

As Jenkins went down to the messroom, he could hear how the ship had changed. Behind the tinny blare of the TV in the crew's messroom was the starling-roost clatter of many voices. There were the smells of three hundred and sixty-seven extra human beings; cigarettes and disinfectant, joss-sticks and charcoal braziers with things cooking on them.

In the officers' messroom, Soares was at the table, reading a newspaper. Jenkins opened the fridge door and pulled out the materials for a cheese-and-tomato sandwich. 'Two extra passengers,' he said.

Soares' eyes flicked at him with the contempt of a cold-blooded creature for a hot-blooded creature. 'You ever hear of obeying orders?'

Jenkins squashed his sandwich on to a plate with unnecessary precision. It would not be profitable to lose his temper. He said, 'What happened to your Chinese gunboat?'

Soares said, 'Why for we should carry stowaways?' He looked suddenly sharp-faced and vicious. 'This is the East,' he said. 'You want a woman, you buy one. You take a passenger, you charge a fare.'

'And if they can't pay, you kill them?'

Soares sniffed and lit a Rothmans, his eyes shifting.

'They stay aboard,' said Jenkins. 'Or I get on the radio.'

Soares let a cloud of smoke trickle out of his nostrils. Finally, he said, 'Fockin' Boy Scouts.' The messroom door opened, and the Nairns came in. 'Mrs Nairn,' he said. 'Boy Scout here brought a guy on board looks 'orrible yellow. Liver cancer, he say. Infectious hepatitis, someone else say.'

Mrs Nairn said, 'I already had a quick look. He's jaundiced, all right. Can't feel his liver. Could be either.'

Nairn had sat down, and was staring with dislike at a carton of apple juice. 'How he get aboard?' he said.

Soares said, 'First mate let him on.'

Nairn said, 'Whadde do that for?'

Mrs Nairn said, looking sideways at Jenkins, 'You can't leave people to drown.' She smiled, a sugary smile, the sort of smile she would have given Mother Teresa.

'But what if he infects the whole fucking ship?'

'Relax,' said Mrs Nairn. 'Doesn't show up for three months. They'll be long gone.'

Jenkins found himself unable to eat his sandwich.

Soares said, 'One thing, Dave. That makes two times you hit Lee. He's not a man I'd hit once, even.' His tongue went round his lips, and he grinned. 'You watch out for him.'

Jenkins took his sandwich up to the bridge, where Pete was on watch, and someone with a powerful imagination could pretend the *Glory* was a normal ship.

A very powerful imagination.

Before, the container tops had been a flat, rust-coloured platform, like the deck of an aircraft carrier. Now they were spattered with little knots of people, talking and lying in the sun. In a couple of places, enterprising launderers had stretched lines between stanchions and washing was fluttering in the warm Trade. From the courtyards and the hold ventilators there issued wisps of grey smoke.

'I went down the hold,' said Pete. 'Told them no open fires. Didn't make a blind bit of difference. Nobody speaks English.' He looked across at Jenkins. 'Bit surprising, this, innit?'

Jenkins threw the remains of his sandwich in the gash. 'It is and it isn't,' he said.

'Good business for someone,' said Pete. 'The fare's twenty grand a head. US.'

'Passage plus visa plus green card.'

'Visas,' said Pete. 'Yeah. S'pose it's worth it, if you're them. Straightforward, really. Like all of life. All comes down to money.'

Not completely straightforward. What had happened on that ferry had been attempted murder.

Of stowaways. Soares had said it, and now Pete. It all came down to money.

Be reasonable, thought Jenkins. Ask no questions. Pick up your money.

'What I say is this,' said Pete. 'What the eye don't see, the heart won't grieve over. Right?'

'Right,' said Jenkins. He had always worked for money. You worked to provide for your family. Diana would go along with that.

Rachel wouldn't.

If Rachel knew what he was thinking, she would never speak to him again. Not that he had done anything he was ashamed of. He had saved two people from drowning. It was a bent job, but he could do it straight. Diana could have her money. And Rachel need never know. Must never know. It was the kind of knowledge that could get you killed. There was a queasy feeling in the pit of his stomach. It was called shame.

Keep quiet, and it will go away. Nobody knows. Nobody will know.

Jesus.

His mind went back to his birthday dinner with Rachel at the Loon Fung. He had mentioned Chang. Said he was driving one of his ships, and that the job sounded dodgy. He had not said anything else. She had not looked as if she had been listening. But he had to make sure. This was a private battle that Jenkins had to fight himself, like all the other private battles. Not Rachel's problem. Not in any way.

He got up, walked to the chart room and pulled a chair up to the Inmarsat. He whacked out the access code and the number of the apartment, and lifted the receiver.

'Kissy kissy,' said the photographer.

Rachel draped her eyes over the camera, and stuck out her lips, and moved her body so the little silk shift dress she was wearing did the elegant-but-provocative things the designer had meant it to do. Modelling was *soo* boring. If it wasn't for the money . . .

Off the end of the jetty on which she was posing, a sampan piled with vegetables was chugging across Aberdeen Harbour.

'Just one more,' said the photographer. 'The fringe . . . *thank* you, Antoine.'

While Antoine Chen fussed with her hair, Rachel became aware of a small racket at the landward end of the jetty. A man had arrived, a Chinese, tall and high-cheek-boned, wearing a beautiful Armani suit. The other two girls on the shoot drifted towards him, twittering like linnets.

'OK,' said the photographer.

Rachel's heartbeat had quickened. She moved again, aiming herself at the lens, trying to fog it with love.

'*Perfect*,' said the photographer. It's the thing about this one, he thought. She just suddenly begins to *glow*. Just like that. Of course, it takes a genius to bring it out.

But he saw that she was looking away again, at the Chinese man in the Armani suit. He sighed. Can't compete. Not with Raymond Chang. 'Thank you, darling,' he said. 'All done.'

Rachel relaxed, and began to walk with her racehorse stride towards the fisherman's hut they were using as a changing room. Raymond Chang watched her. He had a bottle of Krug in his hand, and a couple of glasses. The other girls were giggling and making grabs for the bottle. He ignored them. He said, 'Hey, Rachel. Want a drink?'

Arrogant jerk, she thought, over the rapid thump of her heart. The sort of arrogant jerk who hung up on people, and thought he could fix it by ringing the next night, too late . . . She ignored him, she was not quite sure how. She went into the evil-smelling hut, pulled the dress over her head and climbed into her Levi 501s, Cure T-shirt and bomber jacket, camouflage for the long bus ride home.

When she went out again, Raymond was still there. He nodded at the other girls and came over to her. He did not smell of drink. From behind his back he produced a bunch of frangipani. Rachel thought that was really sweet, much better than a phone call. Actually, arrogant or not, it was impossible not to own up to the fact that Raymond was really, *really* sweet.

'Rachel,' he said. 'How's things?' He smiled.

He was bright, spoilt, lazy, stinking rich. But his smile was lovely. It made Rachel think that he had just woken from a beautiful dream, and found her more beautiful than the dream. She found herself smiling back.

'Lunch?' he said.

'Got to run,' she said.

'So I give you a lift,' he said.

'The traffic's terrible. I live in Repulse Bay.'

'I know where you live,' said Raymond. 'So I brought my *dai fei*.' He pointed at the next jetty down, where a red cigarette boat bobbed alongside.

'No,' she said. But it would be nice to miss the traffic. And nicer to be with Raymond.

'Pretty please?'

Rachel giggled. She thought, Well, what the hell? Pursued by the scowls of the other girls, she and Raymond climbed into the cigarette boat. He accelerated out of the harbour. Her hair whipped off her face, and her body pressed into the white leather seat. Like a bloody shampoo commercial, she thought. But she found she was laughing anyway.

It took half an hour to get to Repulse Bay. He throttled back. The boat rolled gently, fifteen feet off the beach. She said, 'How am I meant to get ashore?'

'Hadn't thought of that,' he said. 'Wade?'

She looked into his eyes. She said, 'Somebody's got to get wet.'

Raymond Chang was famous for his immaculate clothes. He did not say anything for a moment. Then he said, 'Sir Walter Larry.'

She had noticed before that emotion affected his l's and his r's. Good, good, good. 'Of course.'

He ducked his head. He drove the boat's nose on to the beach, jumped into the water and carried her ashore. She looked at him, sand on his feet, his trousers hanging off his legs in sodden folds. He said, 'Is my tie crooked?'

She laughed. 'Straight,' she said. She had had her revenge for being hung up on. They both knew it. And something more than that.

'See you some more?' he said.

She said, 'You could call.'

He took her hand. 'Maybe I get organized,' he said. 'This time.' Definitely an apology. Not that there was any need for

95

an apology. He shoved the boat off the beach and climbed aboard. Waving, he reversed into the green bay. She watched as he tore round the headland. There were several boats out there. But once he was gone, it felt empty. Oh, dear, thought Rachel. I seem to be in love.

The apartment was three hundred yards back, with a view of the sea if you craned your neck from the balcony. The glow of Raymond was cooling into loneliness, and she felt tired and empty. She was an hour early, so with any luck Mummy wouldn't be in, and she could do some work. Mummy would want a blow-by-blow of the shoot. Mummy took the whole thing far too seriously. She was spending a lot of time trying to persuade her daughter not to go to university. Look at your stupid father, said Mummy. Got all those master's tickets and things, and he's been stuck in that boring dead-end work for *years*. You don't want to end up like him. Modelling's money, it's glamour. *Go* for it.

Rachel stepped out of the elevator and walked along to the front door. Mummy was not the brightest. Poor Mummy.

She opened the door. Really, she thought, padding bare-foot across the living-room carpet to her door, it was about time she got a place of her own. Though she would miss her father.

The telephone began to ring. She started towards it, buoyed up by the idea that it could be Raymond. It stopped. Someone had answered.

The other receiver was in her mother's bedroom.

On the bridge of the *Glory of Saipan*, Jenkins was sweating with impatience. Come *on* –

A man's voice said, 'Hello?'

Jenkins said, 'Who's that?'

'Jeremy. That you, Dave?' Jenkins said it was him. 'Popped in to fix the TV,' said Jeremy. 'Diana said it was on the blink.'

'Ah,' said Jenkins, not interested. 'Is Rachel home?'

'Out,' said Jeremy. 'Modelling job, I think.'

Jenkins was more disappointed than he had bargained for. It was not just that he had wanted to warn Rachel. He had been looking forward to hearing her voice. 'Diana there?' he said. He could at least leave a message.

' 'Fraid not,' said Jeremy. 'She's walking the Maclehose Trail. Any message?'

Jenkins was surprised. The Maclehose Trail was a long walk over the mountains of the New Territories. Normally Diana balked at staircases, never mind mountains. 'No,' he said. 'Well . . . actually, yes.' Jeremy was discreet, and he understood how things worked. 'Could you tell Rachel something for me?'

'Of course.'

'We had a conversation. Out at dinner. On my birthday. I mentioned some work I'm doing. Can you tell her that she shouldn't mention it, to anyone at all? At all. It's important.'

'Sure,' said Jeremy, in a tone of voice that conveyed even via satellite that his eyebrows were somewhere near his hairline.

'Sounds weird,' said Jenkins. 'But please do it.' He hesitated. If anyone could give him good advice, it would be Jeremy. No, he thought. Not even Jeremy. 'It's just so nobody gets the wrong end of the stick.'

'Sure,' said Jeremy. He sounded graver, this time. He said, 'Listen, mate. Do you want to talk about this?'

'Nothing to talk about,' said Jenkins. 'Just tell Rachel, eh?' He hung up.

Jeremy put the receiver down slowly. He was frowning, his heavy dark eyebrows drawn together over his nose. He laid his head back on the pillows of the big bed.

Next to him, Diana said, 'Who was that?' Like Jeremy, she was naked. She began to kiss his neck. Her fingers crawled down his carefully tanned stomach.

Jeremy stopped frowning, and pulled her face up to his. 'Dave,' he said. 'Walk on.'

She giggled, and put one of her thighs across his body until she was kneeling astride him. 'Again?' she said.

'Long way to go afore nightfall.'

'What did he want?'

'Nothing.'

She shifted her hips. He looked up at her. The breasts were still high, the stomach still flat. Pity about the mind.

'Really nothing?'

'Come on,' he said.

She moved her hips again, tantalizing him. 'Ve haf vays of making you talk.'

'He's in the shit,' said Jeremy. 'Up to his neck.'

'As per usual,' said Diana.

The bed began to creak like a monster panting.

Neither of them gave Jenkins another thought.

Back in her room, Rachel shut the door very quietly. She had not heard what had been said. But she had recognized Jeremy's voice, and what had come after. How *could* she? With Jeremy?

She thought; You stupid, stupid woman. And Jeremy was supposed to be Daddy's friend. Jeremy was a *bastard*.

Bastards, the pair of you.

BOOK II

Chapter One

At ten o'clock that night, Soares ran a comb through his wet-look hair, squirted breath freshener on his tongue, slapped some aftershave on the black stubble and trotted down the stairs to the hold. You need a purpose in life, thought Soares. He had two: money and sex.

The guard on the hold door said, 'Evening, sah.' Soares nodded, licking his lips. He liked the smell of the Burma Road, the corridor running down the outside of the hold. It was a dirty smell, weird food and a lot of people, like some kind of foreign village. Dozens of women, all panting for it. And one in particular.

A man in a white boiler suit was sitting in the Burma Road, smoking a cigarette. When he saw Soares he crushed out the cigarette and stood up. It was Lee the motorman. Soares winked at him. Useful bloke, Lee. He said, 'Girl?'

Lee grinned. He led the way down a corridor between two sacking partitions, and pointed. Soares pushed aside the flap. ''Ello, bitch,' he said.

The partition was a tent with no roof, lit by the fluorescent tubes bolted to the hatch-covers. The woman inside was the one Jenkins had brought off the ferry. She stood up with a nervous quickness. She said, 'What do you want?'

Soares laughed, coughing. ''Ow much?' he said.

Her eyes were stretching. Green eyes. Nice. 'What are you talking about?'

Playing hard to get, thought Soares. He grinned. 'Come 'ere and I show you,' he said. This one had real tits, not Chinese fried eggs. The mouth was full and promising. *Very* nice. Soares unzipped his fly.

The woman's eyes got bigger. Soares liked that, the way he liked running a ship, hiring guys like Jenkins. Sense of power. He put out his pudgy hand and fingered the swell of her breast through her T-shirt.

The woman backed away. She said, 'Stop that.'

Soares had not known she could speak English. Good, he thought, he would be able to explain his special requirements. He said, 'Come up to my cabin. You can use the shower. I'll bring food.'

The woman was not looking frightened any more. In fact, Soares realized, she was looking angry. She said, in a sort of lawyer-type voice, 'If you're looking for a prostitute, you should try at the end of the alleyway.'

Soares found himself a little taken aback. But lawyer or not, she was part of the cargo now, and Lee had cleared the way. He took her hand, and pulled it to his fly. He said, 'I'm looking for you, baby.'

She smiled with that nice big mouth. All *right*, thought Soares. She said, 'Captain Soares, I don't screw for money. In addition, I regret to inform you that I find you physically repulsive. So unless you wish me to communicate forthwith with the owners of this vessel, I suggest you take your business where it will be welcome.'

Soares stared at her with his mouth open.

'Out of the door,' she said. 'Turn left. I'm told she's very good.'

Soares found himself walking out into the alleyway. A head appeared round a sacking curtain at the end. It was smiling a wide red smile, looking at Soares under heavy black lashes. It belonged to a Chinese woman in a little black dress that showed a flash of bright red underwear. She pulled him inside the screen. 'Captain,' she said. 'How you find me?'

Soares said, 'Woman told me.' He jerked his thumb down the corridor.

'Ah,' said the woman. 'Lucy Moses.' She folded her arms round his neck and bit the bristles under his chin. 'Stupid woman,' she said.

'Yeah,' said Soares. He was planning to have a little talk with Lee. Except that Lee was not someone you would want to mess with.

On second thoughts, no little talk with Lee.

Back in her enclosure, Lucy heard the moans and grunts from the end of the alleyway. She sat on her suitcase with her knees pressed together, and tried to make the shaking stop. How to shorten your life. Get stuck on a ship with Lee the killer. Then sexually humiliate the captain.

She was going to have to find help. Soon.

Jenkins had spent most of the night in the ship's office, drawing out charts and schedules. When you reduced it to numbers, it was possible to imagine you were doing a legitimate job.

There were a hundred and fifty-seven people in the hollow squares of containers on the hatch-covers, and two hundred and ten in the hold. They divided up into ninety-three family groups, and a good handful of singles. There were requests that various groups of families be accommodated together. And there were instructions that some passengers, mostly young and male, were to be placed at the aft end of the hold, where the engine noise was big and the heat intense.

Jenkins had arranged the distribution of a hundred and twenty empty five-gallon bleach drums, for use as water breakers. The welding gang had attached six-hole latrines with canvas screens to the ship's sides, ladies on the starboard side of the transom, gents to port. Jenkins had called in the surly Chinese cooks, and given them their briefing. At ten in the morning and four in the evening they were to ladle boiled rice and some form of meat or fish into the hundred and twenty white plastic buckets provided, five hundred grammes per person.

For the ten o'clock distribution, he went out on to the wing of the bridge and looked aft over the containers. It was a new world down there. The people were like ants, spilling forward on to the narrow deck between the containers and the accommodation on which the cooks had set out their cauldrons. At the foot of the steps leading up to the deck, Rodriguez the third mate checked the passengers off on a list. From the queue rose the sound of quarrelling.

It is a system, thought Jenkins. Quarrelling apart, it

seemed to be working well. There was a lot to be said for organization. It helped people. And it kept your mind off things that for the sake of your sanity were best not thought about. Like running a cattle ship for human beings, for the benefit of a woman you were married to but no longer knew.

Jenkins was shocked. Where had that come from? Wherever, it was wrong.

Suddenly, the noise of shouting increased, and the crowd eddied round a man in a T-shirt and shorts and a woman in a straw hat. The man in shorts was screaming, grabbing at her bucket of rice.

The woman clutched her bucket to her with both arms. The man grabbed the handle. From above, Jenkins could see it laid out as if on a map. On the deck by the cooks, a white-overalled figure was moving purposefully through the crowd: Lee. Relieved at the diversion, Jenkins yelled, 'Hey!' A couple of faces looked up, looked away again. Then, suddenly, between the man and the woman there was a third figure: a woman, small, wearing a black T-shirt and jeans. Even from the bridge, Jenkins recognized her as the woman who had been locked in the cabin on the ferry. Lucy, she had been called. Lucy took a bowl from the hand of one of the crowd and scooped a tablespoonful of the rice from the woman's bucket into the man's. The sound of laughter floated up to Jenkins' ears.

Lucy looked up at Jenkins, and said, 'OK now,' smiling. Jenkins felt a sudden sense of warmth and complicity.

On his way back to the wheelhouse, he ran into Soares. Soares said, irritably, 'Word with you. I saw you watching that girl. You get in Ho and Lee's way, you get discipline breakdown, and that finishes with a knife in the guts.' He sniffed, a wet, disdainful sniff. 'The one you brought off the ferry. She's a shit disturber. You can end up with big trouble. Leave it to Ho and Lee, it's what they're paid for. Someone's out of line, *whap*, they're experts. Only language these people understand.'

'Is that right?' said Jenkins.

Soares did not like his eyes. They were too blue and too wild. Like some kinda goddamn Nazi, thought Soares, or one of them monk statues Mama used to take him to see in the cathedral in Lisboa. 'I had a word with Lee,' said Soares. 'I told him, don' kill Jenkins. Meanwhile, you got a shipload a pussy. You get out there and grab some, get a fucking life.'

Jenkins said, 'I'll think about it.' He was still appalled at the way he had thought about Diana; resented her, even. He had no grounds for resenting her. It was the other way round, if anything. The shame crawled on him like a skin disease.

All those years, Diana had held the fort at home. Still in Lee-on-the-Solent, at first. That December he finished a voyage on the *Penang Bridge*, carrying tinned mackerel and Australian beer round Indonesia and New Guinea: sun, sand, palms, and a sea that slopped like gin under hot and bloody sunsets.

He had arrived in Lee-on-the-Solent on Christmas Eve. A cold rain had been falling. What light there was had been blackish and dirty, and the front path of the house had squinched wet and gritty under his shoes. The house itself had been hot, full of the stench of drying nappies. Rachel had been three, Bill one. Neither of them had recognized him. But Diana had bought a Christmas tree, got decorations sorted, put a smile on her face, the still beautiful but now tired face. And they had drunk sweet sherry which her parents had given her, and later they had gone to visit his parents at the farm, and there had been no sweet sherry, only gin and whisky and red wine, which in those days Diana had not liked.

Later, Diana had cried. And Jenkins, who had spent twenty months of the last twenty-four on the far side of the world, had not known what to do. He knew how to handle a New Guinea ship's company who had beaten a Norwegian ship's company 28–0 at football, and wanted to eat the referee. But that was nothing to do with bringing up a family with a wife his parents did not like, and whom he saw so seldom.

Him and Diana against the rest. But he hardly ever saw Diana. And when she cried, he knew it was his fault.

Things got better, of course. His shipmates got divorces. He and Diana learned to live together; well, live apart, really. And then the terrible thing had happened.

Diana had told him about it. She and the children. Rachel had been ten. Bill had been eight. They had been in England – Home, Diana called it – at the end of a visit, spending three days in London. Bill was a dinosaur enthusiast, so they had done the Natural History Museums. Rachel was a Christopher Robin freak, so they had watched the changing of the Guard. Then Diana had a small orgy at Harvey Nichols and they all had lunch at McDonald's, Marble Arch. Bill had been wearing new jeans and new trainers and a Victoria Harbour T-shirt, of which he was very proud. They had walked across Hyde Park, heading for Harrods. There are no really big parks in Hong Kong.

Bill saw the squirrel in open ground, far from a tree. He started after it; there are very few squirrels in Hong Kong. He wanted to catch it and feed it the stub end of the packet of peanuts he had in his pocket. The squirrel did not want to be caught. It ran away, due south. Bill ran too.

He could imagine Diana permitting herself a faint, well-bred smile, and tossing her hair for the benefit of a passing jogger. The squirrel paused by the edge of South Carriage Drive, looking over its shoulder. That had been one of the bits she had stressed, later. *It actually looked over its shoulder*.

Then it ran straight across the road and Bill went after it.

The taxi hit him with the geometric centre of its radiator grille. It threw him fifty feet, end over end. When they got there his eyes were open, blue, reflecting the sky. He said, 'Where's Dad?' Then he had died.

That had been the other bit she stressed later. She had stressed it a lot; almost every day.

The worst day of Jenkins' life. And he had not even been there. It was not the sort of thing you could put behind you.

He had tried to make it easier for Diana. He was her husband, after all. He put up with the things he had to put up with, did his duty, supported her at all costs, because that was the way things were organized. Jenkins supports Diana, Diana supports the children. She had had a terrible time. One terrible time deserved another. He loved her. Stood to reason; they were married.

But as he looked at the glare of the sea and the sky through the bridge windows of this rusty bargeload of gangsters and fugitives, that shameful idea came back to nag at his mind.

Once you were outside the lattice of how-things-were-done, you saw things differently. And what he was seeing was that for a long time now, love had had nothing to do with it.

Chapter Two

Mrs Nairn took sundowners seriously, because she knew that it was at the end of a long day and a couple of beers that you got to know people. A lot depended on your people, on a trip like this. So at five thirty she filled up the fridge with San Migs, put out a bowl of peanuts, and arranged some dried pampas grass and an ostrich feather in a vase. Homely, she thought. Nice change of surroundings to put the boys at their ease.

At half past five, Jenkins and the second mate turned up, left their shoes in the alleyway, and sat down.

Mrs Nairn decided she had no worries about Pelly. He might look a bit on the Chinky side, but he was a decent professional bloke. He did not appear to have too many outside interests. The Old Man was a bastard, but he was a greedy bastard, out to earn his money, so Mrs Nairn had no worries about him, either. Jenkins was a bit more complicated, and Mrs Nairn liked things simple. Best get to the bottom of Jenkins, thought Mrs Nairn.

'Well,' said Pelly, after a beer. 'Better go and do some navigating.' He left.

'So,' said Mrs Nairn. 'They settling down, in the hold?'

'Early days yet,' said Jenkins. 'Poor bastards.'

'Too true,' said Mrs Nairn, insincerely. Poor bastards or not, the cargo was there because it wanted to be. And a job was a job, and the world was tough as hell, and there was no room for sentimental galahs. She had a suspicion that Jenkins might be a bit on the sentimental side. Someone was going to have to win his confidence. Extend the hand of friendship, and the bastard would probably eat out of it.

'Must have been nasty, leaving Orient,' she said.'

'Yes.'

In general practice in Western Australia, Mrs Nairn had been famous for her bedside manner. Now, she injected the results into a sympathetic shake of the head. 'What happened?' she said.

'Collision,' said Jenkins, disinclined to talk.

'And you carried the can.'

'It was my fault,' said Jenkins, extremely uncomfortable. 'None of us are here because we want to be.'

Not getting anywhere, thought Mrs Nairn. 'You mean Edwin,' she said, looking at her hands. 'He had a breakdown. Landed up in, er, hospital.' She levelled at him a gaze of glutinous frankness. 'Edwin has an addictive personality. So he retired. Came ashore, where I could keep an eye on him. This is retirement work for us,' she said, as if speaking of macramé or model-making. 'Edwin used to be at sea. We went farming with the payoff.' She pointed at the photograph of the bush-hatted Nairn and the combine. 'Next-to-desert. Ten thousand acres of wheat. You use the provident fund and a bank loan to buy your machinery, and you pray for rain. You need one year's rain in ten, to make your money back.'

Jenkins looked at the picture. Nairn was leaning against the combine's wheel. He looked drunk. 'And it didn't rain?'

'Oh, it rained,' said Mrs Nairn. 'But Edwin got shickered and bet the farm on a horse two weeks before. So Edwin went back to the clinic and some other bastard did the harvest, and we landed up looking for a ship again.' She sipped at her beer, little finger extended. 'And found one.'

'Must have been hard,' said Jenkins.

Mrs Nairn shook her head, her neck creasing and uncreasing like a concertina. 'You will never know,' she said. Soft as butter, this one. You could see it in his face. 'And it's left Edwin a bit edgy. Conscious of his position, as it were. He's an older man, nowadays. He feels threatened.'

Jenkins nodded. In his view, Nairn was suffering from paranoia, much of it justified.

'We must try to understand each other,' said Mrs Nairn. 'If you have a problem, I'm here for you.'

Jenkins had lived with Diana long enough to deal with this kind of trickery. He said, 'I'll bear that in mind.' There was a cargo matter. 'Have you got any further with that jaundice case?'

'Pursuing it,' said Mrs Nairn. She had indeed been giving it a lot of thought. 'So anyway, this trip's for our new provident fund,' said Mrs Nairn. 'I go back to work. Edwin stays sober. Everybody keeps their eye on the ball.' Her eye was suddenly steely. You too, it said to Jenkins.

Jenkins looked non-committal. As soon as he decently could, he finished his beer and left.

Once, Edwin Nairn had worn a white uniform, trodden wooden decks instead of rusty steel, and directed the operation of a shiningly clean engine room staffed by thirty men. In those days he had spent his time in his cabin, or with the second and third at drinks before lunch and dinner, during which discussions of technical matters were lubricated by gin and tonics with the gin poured up to the church windows and the tonic a half-inch splash for the sake of form.

Ashore, Nairn had always felt at a loss. The world was not hot enough and not noisy enough, even when you were next to desert. What Nairn liked was big heat, a hell of a racket, and plenty of order and system.

What it boiled down to was this. Human beings were a bunch of bastards, but with an engine, you knew where you were. And these last few months, human beings were getting worse. It had been bad enough on his last ship, a glorified barge called the *Nome*. He was not clear about how he had landed up on the beach. He dimly remembered that there had been a plot to kill him by spiking his food with ground glass, a plot in which the whole crew had been involved. So he had jumped overboard in the Malacca Strait and tried to swim to Java. After that there was a blank period. Then he had suddenly been on a tractor, and the bastards had been plotting again, and next thing he knew the farm had gone and he was in hospital again, and Irma had been screaming at him. Since then it had been Irma in the driver's seat, and the bastards plotting away in the background. The thing about Irma was that she did not see things as clearly as he did. Clever she might be, tough as old boots; but she did not have his insight.

Not that you would ever tell her that. You had to watch what you said, with Irma, or life got really nasty.

At eight thirty the next morning, he felt jumpy and queasy. Must have been something he ate, he told himself. Or nervous indigestion. Couldn't stand them all swilling San Migs while he drank pop. And coffee for breakfast was not enough. Right fuel for the right purpose. Same as an engine. You had your light oil, for manoeuvring. You had your bunker crude, for sea. You had your steam boilers to blast steam into the pipes that snaked through the tanks, heat your bunker crude until it turned runny enough to pass through your filters and cleaners to spin the crap out of it until you had your nice clean black oil at about $130\,°C$ that could squirt through your injectors into the cylinders of your seven-cylinder MAN diesel, where it exploded, and drove the pistons, which drove the crankshaft, which drove the propeller, which screwed this rustbucket through the hoggin . . .

Nairn found he had lost his thread. He ran his eye over the dials, three times, because nowadays he found it hard to hold the readings in his mind long enough for them to make sense.

The watermaker did not look good. It was a low-temperature distillation unit, with pumps that made a partial vacuum so the salt water would boil at room temperature. The pumps were knackered and the seals were dodgy. If he lost the watermaker, there would be no fresh water for the boilers to boil, and the bloody fuel would turn back into road tar. And of course there would be nothing for the passengers to drink, which would make the passengers even more dangerous than they already were. And that Pom mate was so busy trying to steal Nairn's job that he'd have no time for keeping the cargo under control. Nairn knew the type.

He frowned.

In the soundproofed control room, the noise of the engine had been loud, but steady. But for a moment, it was mixed with a new vibration, like running feet. Out there in the engine room, something new had happened.

His eyes swept the dials. Nothing had changed.

It came again – a pounding he did not hear, but which arrived through the soles of his feet and the surface of his skin. He stepped out of the control room and into the noise.

A Chinese man barged into him, knocking him into the face of the fuel oil tank. He caught a glimpse of a blur in a white boiler suit running up the steel ladder towards the next gallery. By the time he realized that the man who had collided with him was the blur on the stairs and opened his mouth to shout, the blur on the stairs had gone.

Shakily, he dusted himself down. He had had one lot of trouble, and he did not intend to have another. There had been a time when rather than collide with his chief, a motorman would have thrown himself overboard. Not any more. They were all after him, now . . . He looked nervously around him, his head moving on his scrawny neck like a camel's.

As usual nowadays, everything felt wrong. But there was something especially wrong in the filter room.

The oil cleaners stood in a row, three of them, their covers like inverted woks, streaked with oily prismatics. On the deck between them a man was lying face down. He had longish black hair. He was dressed in jeans and flipflops and a T-shirt that had been white until he had hit the floor. Safety, thought Nairn. Nobody wears flipflops in my engine room.

The man writhed on the diamond-patterned steel, hands over his face. Nairn peered down at him. One of the cargo, he thought. What does the bastard think he's doing down here? Between the fingers, the skin looked odd, white and puckered. Burned himself. Lot of hot things down here. His own bloody fault for wandering round the ship as if he owned it. None of my bloody business. Cargo matter. Bit of work for that mate.

He shuffled back into the control room and picked up the telephone.

Mrs Nairn stumped down the alleyway, beginning her rounds. Surgery was not till ten, but there was business she wanted to do first.

She stopped outside the door of the cadets' cabin and knocked. A man's voice, sleepy and full of phlegm, said, 'Who?'

'Doctor.'

The door opened a crack. In the crack was the face of the sick man Jer, narrow-eyed and suspicious. He opened the door.

'Lie down,' said Mrs Nairn, pushing him towards the bunk.

He lay down on the bunk, closing his eyes. 'Pull up your shirt,' said Mrs Nairn.

Hesitantly, he exposed his yellowish belly.

Mrs Nairn began to palpate the skin under the ribcage on the right-hand side. Jer groaned.

'Hurt?' said Mrs Nairn.

Jer groaned again.

'Yeah,' said Mrs Nairn. 'Nice to have your own cabin.'

Jer made noises expressing incomprehension.

'Very nice,' said Mrs Nairn, gripping his hand and pulling him up. His eyes were open now. They reminded her of prunes and custard. 'Money?' She made finger-and-thumb gestures.

Jer rummaged under his pillow, came out with an envelope, from which he extracted an American twenty-dollar bill.

Mrs Nairn made expansive fisherman's gestures with her arms. 'More than that.'

Jer went back into the envelope and pulled out a hundred-dollar bill.

'And again,' said Mrs Nairn. 'You wouldn't be happy in the hold.' Her face was blank and leathery, her eye penetrating. 'Someone wants to kill you, by the look of it.'

Slowly, Jer pulled out another hundred and passed it over.

'That will do nicely,' said Mrs Nairn. She tucked the bills into her brassière. Outside the door she met Jenkins. There were bags under his eyes, as if he hadn't slept well.

'Poor bloke,' she said.

Jenkins seemed distracted. 'Who?'

She jerked a thumb at the cabin door. 'Not too good,' she said. 'We'd better keep him isolated.' She sighed. 'We do what we can.' She brightened. 'Isn't it a lovely, lovely morning?'

'Hate to spoil it,' he said. 'Could you come with me?'

He led her along the Burma Road. Chickens were clucking in the tent city, and there was a smell of stove smoke and excrement.

The engine room was hot and noisy. Inside the control room Nairn was sitting in a one-armed vinyl chair, staring at a sheaf of papers. When Jenkins stuck his head in, he jerked a thumb at the oil cleaners without looking up.

The man in the filter room was lying with his knees drawn up to his stomach. He still had his face in his hands. His mouth was visible. It was open. He looked as if he might be screaming.

Mrs Nairn squatted on her thick haunches beside him. She patted him on the shoulder. The man's eyes rolled at her. She caught his little fingers and gently moved his hands away from his face.

'Christ,' said Jenkins.

On each cheek, an area of skin the size of a cigarette packet had a dead, cooked look. Mrs Nairn slid a syringe into his arm and pressed the plunger. The man's face relaxed, and his eyes rolled up. Jenkins and a couple of oilers dragged him out and into the Burma Road.

'Fried hisself,' said Mrs Nairn. 'Poor chap.'

'Not himself,' said Jenkins.

'Sorry?'

Jenkins said, 'He'd have had to put his face on the oil cleaner, take it off, put the other cheek on.'

'Point,' said Mrs Nairn, not interested.

'This was the man who told me there were people left on the ferry.'

'That right?' said Mrs Nairn. 'Listen, we should get him to the hospital.'

As the doctor, Mrs Nairn would only be interested in the medical problem. As first mate, Jenkins was interested in the cargo problem; not your usual cargo problem, but still a cargo problem. Lee had tried to prevent Jenkins rescuing Lucy and the jaundiced man, Jer. The little man with the burns had told Jenkins they were still on the ferry. It seemed entirely possible that Lee was taking revenge.

They laid the man on the sick-bay bunk. Mrs Nairn had given him morphine. 'Who did this?' said Jenkins.

The man mumbled something in Chinese.

'You don't want to worry,' said Mrs Nairn. 'They fight. There's nothing you can do about it. They don't speak the language. They don't bloody think like us.'

She was right about the language. But Jenkins had sailed with Chinese crews for most of his life. The language was the only thing that Mrs Nairn was right about.

He needed an interpreter. He found he was thinking of the Chinese woman with green eyes. She spoke English. Better than that, she had sorted out the quarrel in the food queue. She had a sort of authority. And Lee had wanted to kill her. They were all outside the law, but it occurred to Jenkins that Lee would have to behave differently towards a high-profile figure like a ship's interpreter than towards a mere passenger.

He found himself enthusiastic. And something else. The feeling of warmth he had felt last night had returned.

'I'll take care of it,' he said, and went to look for Lucy.

In the forward courtyard, a group of small girls were playing a skipping game. One of them was the child who had come aboard with the monkey-faced man with the burned cheeks. He waved to her. She waved back hesitantly, her long black eyes narrow and wary. He said, 'Lucy?'

She said, 'Rusi Moses.' She handed her end of the skipping rope to a friend, and flapped her hand at him to follow.

They went out of the containers and down to the hold. The heels of the girl's trainers had red lights that blinked as she wove through the maze of tents and screens.

They were outside a screen made of two bedsheets. A couple of thin, nervous-looking men were sitting in folding chairs. The *Glory of Saipan* was sensitizing Jenkins in new areas. He knew that these men were bodyguards, and he guessed that they were not professionals. The little girl pointed at the screen. Jenkins nodded and grinned, feeling like a giant.

One of the bedsheets twitched back two inches, like a suburban lace curtain.

The face was small and hard and suspicious. It did not change when she saw him.

He said, 'I need your help.'

'What for?'

Jenkins reminded himself that this was a woman whose life was in danger. He said, 'There's been an accident.'

'What sort of accident?'

'Someone you know. Come now, please.'

The hospital smell of the sick bay was mixed with Marlboro smoke from the crew's messroom down the alleyway. The injured man was lying on the bunk, the burned skin of his face gleaming with tannic-acid jelly. Lucy watched him for a moment, blank and quiet. Then she said something in a language that was not Cantonese. The man replied in a slow, thick voice.

She said in a high, blank voice, 'His name is Fung. He was looking in the engine room. Out of curiosity. He's an engineer. He fell.'

Jenkins said, 'This is the guy who told me you were on that ferry. I think Lee was not pleased about him telling me, so he dragged him down to the engine room and fried him.'

'Why should he tell lies?'

'You were on that ferry. You tell me.'

She shrugged, her face unreadable.

'I need to know,' he said. 'Someone could get killed.'

She said, 'Why should you care?' Her face was still hard.

Jenkins found himself weary and frustrated. He said, 'I get paid for it. It's my job. The fact that I work on a rustbucket illegal-immigrant ship doesn't mean I'm not going to do what I'm paid for. I'm first mate and I'm responsible for the cargo, and what that means at the moment is that I want to know what the hell is going on. Understand?'

'Yes.'

'So I need an interpreter.'

Her eyebrows made dark, delicate arches on her forehead. 'Meaning me?'

'You speak English.'

'And the pay?'

'Pay?'

'You don't expect to get an interpreter free.'

China, thought Jenkins, where everything has its value. 'What do you suggest?' he said.

'I want a cabin. Near Jer. With a key.'

Jenkins looked at her small, closed face. There were spare cabins. An interpreter would be useful. And perhaps there was something else: the residual glow of the warmth and complicity he had felt. Oddly enough, he found himself definitely looking forward to working with Lucy Moses. He said, 'Wait here.'

Soares was in his chair in the ship's office, smoking a cigarette and leafing through *Penthouse*. He rolled his dead-spaniel eyes up at Jenkins. There were tendrils of smoke hooked into his moustache. 'What do you want?' he said. Jenkins explained.

Soares said, 'That bitch.'

'An interpreter means we can stop trouble before it happens. You on a delivery bonus?'

Soares farted and fanned the air with the magazine. 'Yeah,' he said. He trod his cigarette out on the deck. He got up and squinted out of the office porthole, which had a view of the boat deck. The girl was framed in the port-hole, elbows on the rail, still staring out to sea. Her shoulders were small-boned but square, pushed up by her elbows on the rail. The breeze lifted her short pageboy of black hair. Nice neck, thought Soares. Nice butt. He licked his lips and winked. 'Lucy Moses,' he said. 'So you human after all. If it's in a cabin, it's a handier fuck. Right?'

Jenkins stood quiet. It did not matter why Soares thought he was doing what he was doing. What mattered was getting it done.

'Why not?' said Soares. A cabin would certainly be more private. It would be nice to get her alone in a cabin. 'She get lucky, I might give her one myself.' He pulled a key from the drawer of his filing cabinet and slung it to Jenkins, laughing. 'And if you want the pass key, I got 'im. Dave, you may turn out a hokay guy after all.'

Jenkins reviewed that warmth he had felt. I hope not, he thought. I really do hope not.

Chapter Three

Lucy's cabin was eight feet long and eight feet wide. It had a lavatory that just about worked and a sink that did not work at all. It had a chipped steel wardrobe and a sticky carpet and a stink of ancient cigarettes. It was not much bigger than the cell where she had spent three months after Tiananmen Square. As then and before, there were people outside who wanted to do her damage. Then, the key had been on the outside of the door. This cell stank; it was hot and filthy. But in this cell the key was on the inside of the door. It was just about perfect.

Lucy sat there and put her hands on her shoulders and literally hugged herself. She could hardly believe she had dared ask for it. It was even harder to believe the mate had given it to her. Without asking for money, too. He must be crazy. Though of course she was going to have to work for it . . .

She sat on the safe bunk, and drummed her nails ratatat on her safe wall, and shouted, 'OK, Jer?' Next door, Jer thumped twice with his jaundiced hand.

Everyone on this ship had friends around them. There were the passengers, in their groups, of course, the crew and the officers, and Lee and Ho, a group on their own, small but horribly potent . . . She stopped herself thinking about Lee. The important thing was that everyone fitted into a group, except her and Jer. Not fitting meant you were not noticed. Not missed. She thought of the ferry, and shivered. Fung had missed her. Dear Fung, a true friend. But an ally among the officers – that was priceless.

Cheered, she began with almost sensual delight to unpack

her case into her wardrobe. Her own wardrobe. She shook out each object and refolded it, placed it with mathematical precision on the green-and-rust shelf. There was the cotton underwear, the three good dresses she had brought to wear in America, the spare pair of jeans. And the straw hat, miraculously undented. She hung the straw hat on a rusty nail in the wall. Designer living, she thought, and giggled. It was a long time since she had found anything funny enough to laugh at.

The best thing was that now it seemed likely that she and Jer would be safe from Lee. And she was in a position to start doing things that would change probability into near-certainty. Then she would be free to turn this voyage in the direction she wanted.

There was a knock on the door. She jumped, her belly rigid again, on the defensive. She said, 'Who's there?'

Jenkins' voice said, 'First mate.'

She opened the door a crack, and put her foot behind it.

He said, 'There are things I need to know.' He was a big man. He had a gentle face, but there was an odd aura to him; as if once he had decided to do something it would not be possible to stop him. Now, he walked straight into her cabin, and she found she had opened the door for him as if there had been no problem and no danger, and he had been a friend.

But of course he was not a friend. When he was inside she hooked the door open, and went to stand by the desk, as far away from him as she could get. He had agreed to work on this cattle ship, and that meant they were on opposite sides.

She said, 'Thank you for fixing this up.' She smiled at him. She knew it was a powerful smile.

He said, bluntly, 'It was your idea. Look, if we're going to have a nice quiet trip, I want to know what's going on.'

She knew he was asking about Lee. She chose to misunderstand him; there was no reason to know about Lee.

'We came out of the Pearl River a week ago.'

Jenkins tried to imagine a week on that ferry. He could still taste the stink of it. 'What happened to the crew?'

'They left,' she said. 'In the night, on a motor boat. Then you came, three days later.'

Jenkins said, 'What if you'd been found by someone who wasn't us?'

She shrugged. 'They said that when we were outside territorial waters with the engines stopped, we were a ship in distress. And nobody would want to pick us up, because people on a ship in distress are the responsibility of the rescuers. They said that the only person who would want to pick us up was you, because you were being paid for it.'

Jenkins tried to get back to Lee, tactfully. Tact was not his strong point. He said, 'Why did you and your friend get left on the ferry?'

She said, 'The bolt on the cabin door jammed. We were overlooked.'

That was the official version, and certainly not true. But there was no point in carrying on with this flannel. He said, 'You're not Chinese.'

'Half by blood,' she said. 'Whole by nationality. My father was American.'

'Mr Moses.'

She frowned. 'Who told you that?'

'Another passenger.'

She laughed, for no reason he could detect. He said, 'So why not get an American passport?'

She said, 'My parents weren't married.'

It had been the question of a conventional man; a man who had spent twenty-odd years in a steady job, eighteen of them married, not questioning the rhythms of life, four months on, two months off. Not really questioning anything, getting on with it, marching to the same old drum.

And for the first time, he found himself realizing that, even though that drum was not beating any more, he had still been marching in the old rhythm.

For absolutely no reason.

'Now if you don't mind,' she said, 'it's a week since I saw a shower.'

Dinner that night was oxtail, flash-fried in a form of sweet-and-sour sauce. It was like eating rope. 'Bloody 'ell,' said Pete, shoving his plate away. 'Nobody could eat that stuff.' He got up and pulled the telephone off the wall and dialled.

'Cooky?' he said. 'You ever heard of chips?' There was a silence. 'Chips,' he said. 'Fried potatoes. Jesus Christ.' He looked round the room. 'What's Chinese for chips?' Jenkins got the idea that he knew damn well, but he was making a statement: *I am one of you, not one of them.* 'Nobody knows,' said Pete. 'Chips, you bastard.'

'Shut up,' said Soares. He seemed edgy about something. He sat at the head of the table, tearing at the brown tailbones and spilling sauce on the grubby napkin tucked into his medallions. 'Water,' he said. Pete passed him the jug.

'Steady,' said Nairn. 'Water not unlimited.'

'What the fuck you talk about?' said Soares.

'Watermaker's on the blink,' said Nairn.

'So order some fucking spares.' Soares spat gristle on to his plate. He got to his feet fast enough to knock his chair backwards, and left, slamming the door.

'Temper, temper,' said Mrs Nairn, with a merry laugh.

At six, Johnny the fourth mate rang Jenkins. 'Heart bad,' he said, wheezing. 'Bad shit in toilet. Too much ill to go on bridge.'

'You sure?' said Jenkins.

'Come down, see,' said Johnny.

'I'll stand your watch,' said Jenkins. At eight he made his way up to the bridge.

Beyond the windows, the night was black as velvet. The pencil line on the chart led east, shaving the little targets of contour lines marking the shoals and islets on the southern margin of the Balintang Channel, at the northern tip of the Philippines. They were a long way south of the track Jenkins would have sailed if it had been him heading for California.

He gripped the handles of the ARPA and watched the screen. Ahead and to port was the green hatching of an island, and the dots of fishing boats. When he walked to the window he could see them, little yellow kerosene stars in the black void. Beyond the islands and the lights lay the empty Pacific: six thousand miles of it, nearly a month's plugging for the *Glory of Saipan*. The bridge was homely. Jenkins indulged in a little professional fretting, partly because he was worried, and partly because it made him feel like a craftsman, not a bandit. He hoped that Nairn had been exaggerating about the watermaker. Three hundred and sixty-seven passengers drank a lot, never mind washing and cooking and laundry. For an ocean, the Pacific was a very dry place.

A blast of stale deodorant enveloped him. Soares was standing at his elbow, squat head and shoulders limned by the glow of the screen. 'I'll take the rest of Johnny's watch,' he said. 'You get some sleep.'

Jenkins said, 'I'm fine.'

Soares said, 'Fuck off below and shag your bloody interpreter.' The flame of his lighter shone in the sweat on his face.

Jenkins felt the anger grow. Steady, Jenkins told himself; you're the mate and he's the captain. He can do what he wants. So he went to the log, and wrote that the captain had taken over the watch at 20.03 local time. Then he went to his cabin.

He lay sweltering on his bunk, gazing at the dirty Formica of the deckhead. The ants were still marching, and the smell in the lavatory had made advances against the disinfectant.

He lay there for ten minutes, sweating. His heart was beating like a drum, and the stink of the lavatory was choking him. He did not like being sworn at by Soares. You could not pretend that it was the normal dealing of captain with mate. Any more than you could pretend that this was a normal voyage.

A normal voyage to support a normal marriage, said the scratchy voice in his head. He thought about Diana. Her face grew large and cartoon-like in his mind, taut yellow-brown skin, the sticky red lips –

The telephone by his head rang like a bomb. He jerked upright, picked up the receiver. A voice whispered, 'Jenkins. Get on deck. Starboard side.'

'Who's that?'

The receiver went down.

Jenkins rolled his feet out of bed. He pulled a T-shirt and a pair of shorts on to his sticky body and padded out of the accommodation block and on to the boat deck.

Down in the containers, the passengers were quiet. The

Trade was blowing soft out of the eastern stars. He leaned on the rail, breathing deep. A VHF was chattering on the bridge. Lightning flickered overhead. It reminded him of Zamboanga. Except that there had been no telephone calls off Zamboanga.

He became aware that he had ceased to breathe.

The flicker was not lightning. It was too yellow, and not bright enough. As he watched, a pencil of light lanced from the next deck above him. Someone was using a flashlight on the wing of the bridge. Not at random, either. Three dots. Pause. Three dots.

The *Glory of Saipan* hummed on, all seven thousand tons of her, lit up like a railway marshalling yard. The bow made its consoling *whoosh* as it plunged into a swell. Jenkins strained his eyes into the blackness to starboard. Red blotches floated; the blood behind his eyes.

But out there to starboard, something gleamed white. Something that could have been a boat's wake.

The sweat on Jenkins' body turned suddenly cold. He ran up the ladder to the bridge wing.

Up here the deck-lights were masked, and the only illumination came from the green radar and the silver stars. Against the stars was a black cutout he recognized as Soares. Jenkins said, 'Someone was signalling with a flashlight.'

Soares' silhouette said, sharply, 'I drop my lighter. Looking for it. You dreaming.'

He's right, thought Jenkins. I'm overheating, listening to whispers in the night. The only person who could have been signalling was Soares. Why should Soares be signalling? He said, lamely, 'I thought I saw a wake.'

'You wrong,' said Soares. 'Get back to bed.' There was a jingle as he fumbled in his pocket for his lighter. He was moving back towards the wheelhouse door, away from the bridge wing, into the shelter of the screen by the wheelhouse door, flicking his lighter at his cigarette. The flint stung Jenkins' dark-accustomed eyes. In its flash, Jenkins saw Soares' sweat-sheened face.

Soares' eyes were closed.

At that moment, he heard the snarl of a big outboard behind him.

The red patches in front of his eyes were clearing. He ran to the rail.

A big pump boat was crabbing up alongside. Five small brown men were balanced on the bamboo outrigger. As it touched the *Glory*'s side, they jumped for the rail and clambered over.

This time, he had no bazooka.

Soares said, 'Wait.'

Jenkins understood.

Emigrants travel light but valuable. Pirates loot the valuables. Soares gets the kickback.

'What did you expect?' said Soares. 'Missionary work? Come 'ere, Jenkins. We make a deal.'

But Jenkins saw that his right hand was moving stealthily across his body at waist level. It fumbled in his jeans. When it came out again, it held something long and pale that threw back wicked green glints from the ARPA. Soares held the knife out in front of him. He came towards Jenkins at an odd, shuffling waddle.

Down in the containers, people began screaming.

Jenkins stepped behind the binnacle. His mouth was dry, his eyes fixed on the sliver of pale light in Soares' hand. He could hear the wheeze of Soares' breath over the hiss of the wake. Soares made a fencer's lunge forward. Jenkins could smell old sweat on his body, drink on his breath. Ten minutes ago, he had been thinking about the normal relations between captain and mate.

Normal relations did not include knives.

This time, he was allowed to get angry.

He got angry.

He stepped out from behind the binnacle, knowing now what he had to do. Soares lunged again. Jenkins jumped back, felt the blade swipe across the front of the T-shirt. He took a step back, and found himself pressed against the steel shelf that ran under the rail. Soares' bulk was squat and threatening. He saw himself lying on the deck leaking blood, heard the receding howl of the pump boat's engine. *'Silly bastard. Boy Scout. He fight those pirate. They kill 'im, course.'*

The *Glory* rolled. On the shelf at his back, something

124

rolled with her. Something cylindrical. His hand found it. The flashlight Soares had been using.

Soares said, 'Now I kill you, Mr Boy Scout.'

Jenkins found the switch of the flashlight with his left thumb. He had a glimpse of Soares' black moustache and the orange-peel skin of his nose, the eyes screwed up against the sudden dazzle. Then Jenkins hit him as hard as he could in the middle of his face. He felt cartilage give way in the nose. Soares said, '*Oof*,' and fell down. Jenkins heard the clatter of the knife on the deck. He bent and picked it up and threw it over the side. He was breathing fast, and his knees were weak in the aftermath of fear. The bridge was quiet, except for Soares' snuffling. There was more noise in the containers. He hit the alarm, ran on to the bridge wing and went down the steel stairs to the boat deck.

Fung had been lying on his back on the bunk in his container in the forward courtyard, praying. To tell the truth, he would rather have been sleeping. But Fung was finding it hard to sleep, since the burns. He could not rest either cheek on a pillow, for one thing. For another, he was worried. What had been a march from captivity, a march like the one the Israelites had made from Egypt, had taken a worrying turn. There were wolves in the cargo. They had turned on Fung. And they would do worse. Fung was desperately worried that they would prove too strong. Lord, he said, we are few, and they are many –

It was at this point that bells started ringing and the rectangular cutout of the door had suddenly turned from grey to floodlit white. A woman screamed. Somewhere nearby, a hoarse voice spoke in an unknown language. Fung swung his feet out of bed and into the flipflops on the container floor. 'Stay there!' he yelled, for the benefit of his daughter in the bunk above, and the three cousins on the floor.

Feet rang on the container top and the ladder outside the door. A bright light shone in Fung's eyes and flashed on something that was unquestionably the barrel of a gun. The man with the gun was broad and squat, wide-mouthed and bulging-eyed. He reminded Fung of a toad. He made a gesture Fung understood.

'Everybody out,' said Fung to the other people in the container, between teeth that wanted to chatter.

'And leave our stuff?' said Yu the first cousin. 'You're crazy.'

'Quick,' said Fung.

Cousin Yu started to argue. Lin, Fung's daughter, told him not to contradict her father. Fung pushed her out of the door and down the ladder. The courtyard was already full of people. The noise was enormous. Someone said, 'What is it?'

'Pirates,' said someone else. 'Thousands of pirates.'

'So where is Lee? Ho?'

'Hiding.'

The wolves flee the fire, thought Fung.

Up in Fung's container, the brown man had already ripped open the cardboard boxes, shaken out the books, and found five hundred-dollar bills in the lining of a suitcase. Fung's cousin Yu was still on the ladder. 'Hey!' he said. 'You –'

The pirate's light came at him. A foot hit him on the side of the jaw. He plunged back into the courtyard, which fell silent. The pirate's name was Bing. He looked at the mass of yellow faces and ground his teeth, a merry amphetamine grind. Money, money, money, said the tune in his head.

Bing's friends Jojo and Inky were on the bridge, at the ship's safe. Only Jojo and Inky were here on serious business, by invitation. Binky and Julio and Lupo had come along because they were whacked out of their skulls on ice, and they wanted a little excitement and amusement, plus anything they could pick up. These slit-eyes were like chickens with no heads: gabble, gabble, gabble, thought Bing. It's rob, rob, rob for me, he thought, stuffing the money, money, money into his Y-fronts.

Yeah.

Up on the wing of the bridge, Jenkins was thinking, Ship's safe. The safe was in the office. Soares would have told the pirates how to get at it. They would be expecting him to meet them there, with the keys. Can't let that happen, said twenty-odd years of conditioned reflexes. He ran down the outside steps, pausing on the boat deck to snatch the short steel tiller from the lifeboat. Then he kicked open the accommodation door and ran into the alleyway.

And stopped.

The light was yellow. The bells were ringing. There was a small brown man standing outside the office door. The man was naked except for a pair of lime-green satin shorts. He was holding an assault rifle. Jenkins thought: in the planning phase, Soares would have told this man not to hurt officers. At least, that was what he had to hope.

The little hole in the assault rifle matched the little black pupils of the brown man's eyes. All three of them were looking at Jenkins' belly. Jenkins said, slowly and carefully, 'Put that bloody thing down.' He started walking towards the man.

The eyes shifted first one way, then the other, meeting Jenkins' one at a time. They were crazy eyes with blood-red whites. They shifted away. The gun muzzle dropped. Sweat ran out of Jenkins' hair and into the collar of his T-shirt.

Behind him, at the end of the alleyway, the door crashed open again. Suddenly Soares was behind him, screaming in what sounded like Tagalog. The little brown man frowned, the words not penetrating the chainsaw buzz of the amphetamines in his head. Soares shouted again. The man's face cleared. The rifle came up.

Jenkins understood that he had been sentenced to death.

His mouth became full of dry cement. He jumped forward and to one side of the gun, swinging the lifeboat tiller. It hit something metallic. Shots thundered next to his ear. There was a crash and a wheezing moan behind him in the alleyway. His hand landed on a narrow brown neck, and slammed it away from him as hard as he could. The neck went limp. Jenkins found himself on all fours. His right knee was on the pirate's carbine. The pirate was lying face up, showing a mouthful of teeth red with blood or betel nut, Jenkins neither knew nor cared which. He picked up the carbine. The office door was open, the lock smashed. The safe was shut. Another brown man was standing in front of it.

Jenkins pointed the carbine at him. He had no idea how it worked. The man dropped his knife.

'Out.'

The man had a squat, violent face. He said, 'Huh?'

Jenkins gripped the carbine hard. Suddenly it was thundering, bucking in his hands, and the porthole glass was splintering. The man scuttled into the alleyway.

The alleyway seemed full of people now. There was Rodriguez the third mate, patting nervously at his pompadour, and Ramos the second engineer, shouting in Tagalog. The pirate Jenkins had hit was snoring on the deck. Jenkins pointed to the squat man. He said, 'Take this man up to the deck aft of the bridge and hold him.' The only person who seemed to be missing was Soares.

He looked at the end of the alleyway, where Soares had been standing. Mrs Nairn was squatting there, her solid thighs bulging a dressing gown with pink parrots on it. There was a body on the deck. Red and grey stuff lay under her feet and splashed up the cream plastic walls of the alleyway.

Jenkins remembered the wheezing sigh he had heard.

The body was Soares. The red and grey stuff was what had been inside Soares' head before the burst from the assault rifle had taken the top off.

Into Jenkins' mind swam an infantile memory: breakfast on Sundays in Dorset, when his father had been home from sea. In the unvarying rhythm of the weeks, Sunday meant best behaviour and boiled eggs, with the top lopped off by Dad. His stomach rolled. This was no time for being sick.

Rodriguez's Elvis nonchalance had slipped. He showed his prominent teeth in a nervous grin. He said, 'What we do?'

'Send a Mayday.'

Mrs Nairn looked up. Jenkins saw her polite little smile in the foreground. In the background were Soares' waxy skin and dead-fish eyes, and what was left of his brains in what was left of his hair. She said, 'That might not be such a great idea. What happens when the Flip military sees this lot?'

The words did not seem to mean anything. She said, gently, 'You're the captain now.'

Jenkins swallowed, thinking of Geoff, dead in the

Zamboanga Strait, and the Filipino military taking delivery of their fat envelope of dollars. Nobody had yet invented an envelope fat enough to take care of the *Glory of Saipan*. The job was to keep the *Glory of Saipan* on the water. No military. He said to Rodriguez, 'Get these little bastards up to the bridge.'

Bing finished robbing the first courtyard, went up the ladder, and headed for the next one aft. His Y-fronts were full of money, the ice was cool in his head, and he was feeling mellow, mellow, mellow. A large iron voice started to talk high overhead. Bing realized with a shock that it was talking Tagalog.

Bing's mellow feelings evaporated. He unslung his M-15 and pointed it at the sound. 'COME ON TO THE TOP OF THE CONTAINERS,' said the voice. 'BING AND JULIO AND LUPO.'

Bing was suddenly furious. What iron dog barks our names in the night?

A light came on up there by the bridge, a searchlight, shining on a skull. Not a skull. The face of Inky, hollow with terror. Inky's mouth was open. There was something in the mouth, shoved in hard so the head twisted sideways on the neck. Bing looked at the M-15 in his hands. Yup. That was it. What was in Inky's mouth was the barrel of an M-15.

Bing's guts turned to water. Inky closed his eyes. The gun came out of his mouth. His iron voice screamed, 'GET ON DECK! HOLD YOUR GUNS BY THE BARRELS!'

Bing looked back down the flat iron field of the container tops. Julio and Lupo had appeared under the harsh lights of the gantry, holding their guns by the barrels.

'LAY THEM ON THE DECK!'

Bing was impressed by the agony on Inky's face. Also, there was no way of telling how many guns were in the dark behind the lights. Shit, thought Bing. This was meant to be a groove. He laid his gun on the deck.

Inky's iron voice said, 'DROP THE MONEY.' Bing groped in his crotch, pulled out a handful of money, let it flutter into the courtyard. 'NOW CALL THE BOAT!'

Bing trotted to the edge of the containers. With a hand

that shook, he groped in his shorts for his flashlight, and blinked three long dashes into the dark.

Up on the rail of the bridge, the sweat was running off Jenkins like water from a tap. Down there alongside the darkness thickened and the pump boat crept back. The three small brown men from the containers were scrambling over the rail.

'Overboard,' said Jenkins.

Rodriguez said, 'Wha'?'

Jenkins pointed over the side. The pirate who had done the talking began to struggle.

'Ta-ra, sunshine,' said Pete. He lifted the pirate, and threw him into the sea.

'And the other one,' said Jenkins.

The man he had knocked unconscious stirred and muttered as they lifted him. He fell limply, and made an untidy splash. The pump boat dropped astern, circling, flashing lights.

'See if anyone's hurt,' said Jenkins. 'Pete. You'd better take Lucy. Get those people calmed down. Find out what was stolen. Get it back to its owners, if you can.'

Pete said, 'Where were Ho and Lee?'

Jenkins thought of the telephone call. *Get on deck. Starboard side.* He saw the red-and-grey fragments of Soares' head, the white flower of spray as the unconscious man hit the sea. He said, 'Don't know.' He leaned over the rail and was sick into the sea.

Pete said, 'Looks like you're running the show now.'

Jenkins felt terrible. The world was far away, spinning greasily. It was one thing being first mate, obeying orders. It was another thing being Old Man, taking responsibility. Inch by inch, he had waded into the swamp. Into the arms of Tommy Wong; first mate of a rustbucket; then first mate of an illegal-immigrant ship; and now acting captain, privy to murder.

He could feel the swamp lapping at his nostrils.

This is how they made ordinary soldiers into concentration-camp commandants, thought Jenkins. So how will you resist?

As well as possible. The way you did your job. The way you run your marriage.

Very encouraging.

He walked stiffly to the chart room and sent a sparse, factual datacom report to the owners in Hong Kong. Locked in the groove of the autopilot, the *Glory of Saipan* hummed on towards the stars.

Chapter Four

Pete reported back an hour and a half later. 'Done,' he said. 'That Lucy bird made 'em give it all back to each other.' He made coffee, sat for a while in silence. 'Can't get over it,' he said. 'He must have been being paid a shitload of money. But he still has to get his little mates in after the bleeding ship's safe.' He fell silent again, his chunky head still against the lightening sky. There was a curious atmosphere on the bridge, as if the death had suspended the barriers that normally stood in the way of communication.

''Scuse my asking,' said Pete. 'But you're not the type for this kind of ship, are you? I mean I heard you had a bit of bother at Orient, but what brought you here?'

Jenkins meant to say something anodyne, about a job being a job. But it did not come out like that. With Pete he was on familiar blokes-in-the-messroom ground, and in the messroom you did not tell the truth where a bad joke would do. So he said, 'I wanted to get away from the wife.'

But as he said it, he realized that he was not saying what he ought to say. He was telling the truth.

Pete did not seem to find this even slightly amazing. He said, 'Mine naffed off with an airline pilot. Better hours, she said. Two kids.'

'So why this ship?'

'All that time keeping the lid on,' said Pete. 'Lid blew off. Went on the piss. Hit people. Word got round. You know?'

'I know,' said Jenkins.

Johnny came on watch, wheezing. Jenkins went to bed.

Almost immediately, the dream came galloping out of the dark. He was in a garden, with trees, oaks and ashes, Dorset trees. He was at a table. On the table was a chess board. On the other side of the table, her hair the colour of butter, was Diana. Diana was playing white.

'Your move,' said Diana.

When he looked at the board to make his move, the pieces were all white.

But that was part of the rules.

Diana needed rules like that.

Then the scratchy voice said, 'She doesn't need any special rules. She's a cheat, that's all.'

He was awake, and the clothes were sliding on his body with the sweat that was between them and his skin. Soares was dead, and it was five to four in the morning. Time for his watch.

He took a lukewarm shower and went up to the bridge. The place where Soares had lain smelt of bleach. Johnny was by the ARPA. The screen was blank. Beyond the windows was the great Pacific blackness, lit with the billion lanterns of the stars.

'Morning, sah,' said Johnny. The 'sah' was new.

Jenkins made his way to the coffee machine, and mixed himself a paste of Nescafé and sugar and water. His head felt dull. He said, 'All quiet?'

'All quiet,' said Johnny, rolling his sick eyes. 'Not well with heart.'

'Sorry to hear that,' said Jenkins.

'Yes,' said Johnny, taking it for granted. 'When I get money, pay for good operation in US. Now I sleep.'

Jenkins sat at the desk in the chart room. He kept hearing the telephone exploding, the odd, whispering voice in his ear, the warning. The voice itself was hazy, half-heard through veils of sleep.

He got up and paced the bridge. On a ship containing four hundred people, someone would always have his eyes open.

Thank God.

The sky paled. The stars faded, and on the container tops a scattering of men, mostly elderly, pranced cranelike through t'ai chi exercises. Beyond the bridge windows, the dawn began to paint a strip of sky a faint, optimistic pink.

At eight, Rodriguez appeared on the bridge. Behind him

were Lucy, Fung and three other Chinese men. Rodriguez said, 'These people want talk with you. I searched 'em for weapon. No –'

Lucy pushed him aside. 'The passengers of the *Glory of Saipan* wish to thank you for your prompt action in repelling last night's pirate attack,' she said, briskly. Fung and his companions nodded enthusiastically. 'They say they admire your quick thinking, your bravery, and your ruthlessness in preserving their interests. While they deplore the death of the captain, they cannot bring themselves to mourn too deeply, since it seems likely that he and the pirates were acting in concert.'

Jenkins said, 'Who told you that?' As far as he knew, only three people knew about Soares' signals: Soares, Jenkins, and the owner of the voice that had woken him.

She shrugged. 'It is generally known.'

Jenkins said, 'Someone rang me last night. A man. He warned me that the ship was under attack. Who was that?'

Lucy smiled, a polite, official smile. 'Any public-spirited person,' she said. She moved on. 'Now we look forward to a smooth voyage and a happy outcome under your captaincy.'

The first time Jenkins had been given a ship, it had been different. It had been a rite of passage: the day he arrived at the apex of the pyramid. The ship had been an oil-rig support vessel – a glorified barge, really, filthy and sweltering in the Gulf. But that was the moment when Diana had become Mrs Captain Jenkins. And that was the moment when his father had grunted more approvingly than usual, as if to say twenty-six was a goodish age for a first command; maybe David was showing a bit of bloody sense at last. He had arrived, and was fitting in.

The *Glory of Saipan* was not like that.

Jenkins bowed. He said, 'I am not the captain.' It was a testimonial, and testimonials were in short supply in his life at the moment. But he was not ready to be captain of the *Glory of Saipan*. Being captain meant taking responsibility; letting the swamp close over his head, and nothing he could imagine would induce him to do that.

★

'Tennis, darling?' said Diana.

Rachel looked up from her desk at her mother. She wanted to say, I know what you're up to, and it's not fair on Daddy or me or anyone. But she did not know if that was the way to go about it; whether the consequences for Daddy would be good or bad. Or for her. And anyway, affairs did not necessarily last for ever. This one could be temporary, an aberration. Perhaps Mummy had been under strain, like Daddy, and just not shown it.

Like hell.

Diana looked well-scrubbed, even pretty, in an ecru silk sweater with the usual too-shiny gold chain round her neck, and her hair ash blonde all the way to the roots. But Rachel could see the collagened-out wrinkles, the vertical lines in the skin around the mouth, the shine of grease on the eye-bags. Temporary nothing. Fake, fake, *fake*, thought Rachel.

'Darling,' said Diana. 'Mummy's in a hurry.'

Rachel found it was difficult to breathe properly. I must get out of here. Get a flat, or something. It was all right when Daddy was here. But this is . . . well, I can't stand it any more. She said, 'I'm busy.'

'A shoot?' said Diana, thrilled. 'Who for?'

'No.' Actually, she was going to spend the day with Raymond Chang, but she could not face the flood of coyness this information would unplug. 'Book work.'

'Oh, I see,' said Diana, in whose life books were for propping up dressing-table mirrors. 'Big *brain*.'

'Goodbye,' said Rachel.

Diana made a sticky red *moue*. 'Kiss Mummy?' she said.

Rachel pretended not to hear her. Horrible woman, she thought, and felt guilty, even though it was true.

The door closed. She sat and failed to read Arthur Waley's *Secret History of the Moguls*. She kept seeing Raymond, barefoot in his Armani suit, holding his cigarette boat by the nose in the bay. He was a notoriously snappy dresser, Raymond. She really thought he would not have got his trousers wet for anybody else; or anyway she hoped so, just as she hoped passionately that he would ring.

The telephone rang.

She picked it up, and it was him.

Suddenly birds were singing, and the sun was pouring in at the window. She was full of warmth and excitement. Raymond sounded excited, too, insofar as his rich-kid drawl could convey anything in the nature of enthusiasm. He said, 'You want to do something interesting?'

'What?' said Rachel. Stay cool.

'Listen up,' he said. 'My old man wants me to go to Xian with him. We have a house up there. He has some business to do, and I have to help him out, and he says there's some archaeology going down. New pottery armies, or something? So I wondered.'

New pottery armies, thought Rachel. She had heard rumours. But it was a closed dig. Her heart was galloping. She made herself say, 'Xian? That's miles away.'

'We're going up in the jet,' said Raymond. 'At six o'clock tomorrow morning. *Soo* early. You want to come?'

A closed dig, and Raymond. Rachel found her cheeks were hot, and it was hard to frame words. Cool it, fool. 'How long for?'

'Week,' said Raymond. 'Ten days. Hard to tell. You can come over to our house for the night, save hassles in the morning. If you can stand to be nice to my old man. He's, um, old-fashioned, if you understand me.'

In the circumstances, Rachel would not have minded if Raymond's old man had been a five-toed dragon. She said, 'That sounds very suitable.'

'Yeah,' said Raymond. 'Nice. I'll come and get you in a half-hour.'

And in twenty minutes there he was, outside the lobby, grinning his beautiful white grin in a red Mercedes with more white leather upholstery.

Rachel had completely forgotten about playing it cool. She picked up her bag and ran out to meet him. She had cancelled two weeks' work, ignoring the squeals of Mavis Yee, and left a note on her mother's bedroom door. If she had trouble with the big words, Jeremy could read it for her.

'Sorry I'm early,' said Raymond, leaning his neat black hair against the car's window. 'Couldn't wait.' He gave her that smile. Rachel felt her heart melt. She slung her bag into the back. He drove up to the Peak slowly, because he knew

Rachel would enjoy the car. She noticed that, and the fact that there was a policeman at each pillar of the drive gates into his father's house.

He led her past the bronze lions flanking the steps up to the front door and into a room where a small, chubby man was talking into a telephone. When the small man got up, she recognized him as the Mr Chang she had seen in the newspapers. He was smiling. She was surprised and delighted by the smile. A chubby little smile; sweet, she thought. But perhaps that was only because he was related to Raymond. 'So,' he said. 'Miss Jenkins.'

'Rachel,' said Raymond. She thought he seemed nervous.

'Yes,' said Chang, without a flicker. 'I am very pleased that Miss Jenkins can join us in our little house on the mainland. Jiang will show you your room. Then a small dinner, probably quite tasteless?'

At dinner they spoke Mandarin. Mr Chang managed, without saying anything directly, to convey that he was impressed by her command of the language, and she found herself telling him more than she had meant to about her university plans. Raymond seemed to become less tense. After dinner, which ended early owing to their six a.m. start the next day, Mr Chang said a charming goodnight and she went to her bedroom, which contained a collection of bronzes that would have done credit to an emperor's tomb. She had been examining them for half an hour when the telephone by her bed rang. Raymond's voice said, 'Goodnight.'

'Goodnight,' she said.

'One thing,' said Raymond. 'Be careful with my father. Like I told you. He's . . . old-fashioned. Night.'

'Night.'

She sat on her bedspread, blue silk with red *feng-huang* phoenixes, symbol of conjugal union. I should be so lucky. Victorian life with intercoms, she thought. Of course she would be careful with Mr Chang. Mr Chang was an old sweetie. She could tell.

In the morning, there were croissants and coffee. Mr Chang drank tea and ate congee. He looked puffy under the eyes, as if he had slept badly. When he had finished, he looked at his watch. 'There is time,' he said. The butler came in with a telephone. Chang pressed the buttons, and handed it to Rachel. 'Your father,' he said.

Rodriguez said, 'Satellite. Call waiting.'

Jenkins picked up the receiver.

'Daddy,' said a voice.

Rachel's voice. For an unguarded second he felt light and joyous. He said, 'Where are you?' He would be asking what the weather was like, next. 'How did you find me?'

'Raymond's dad told me. I'm calling from his house.'

Whomp, said Jenkins' heart. 'Raymond's dad?'

'Mr Chang. We're off to the mainland. That's why I'm up so early. We're going to Xian, where they dug up the pottery army. Mr Chang knows someone who's excavating a new one.'

Jenkins found his mind. He said, 'Mr Chang.'

As always, she detected the worry in his voice. But she got the wrong end of the stick, thank God. 'It's perfectly all right. He's got a house there, old style, spirit screens, three courtyards. Raymond showed me pictures. Mr Chang doesn't want Raymond mixed up with gweilos, worse luck. So it's not your orgy of fornication and drug abuse. It's sleeping on opposite sides of the courtyard, boring, and archaeology, wow!'

Jenkins said, 'Listen –'

'Must dash,' she said. 'Mr Chang's next door. He'd like a word.' And she was gone, like a whirlwind.

A new voice said, 'Hello.'

Jenkins could see the jolly eyes, the chubby smile. Be careful, he thought. Oh, be careful. He said, 'I hear you are . . . having my daughter to stay.'

The voice was full of the smile. It said, 'She has done me and my son the honour of visiting our house. She is much looking forward to our archaeological trip. Captain Jenkins, my office passed me your datacom. It was certainly lucky for these pirates you mention to stumble on such a prize.'

'They didn't.'

'Sorry?'

'Stumble. Soares was signalling to them by VHF and flashlight.'

138

Chang made tutting noises across the ether. 'Really,' he said. 'And then he died. I am greatly in your debt. Captain Jenkins, I should be greatly honoured if you would accept a promotion.'

Jenkins waited.

Chang said, 'This ship and its cargo are important.' He laughed, a dry little cough of a laugh. 'I have much respect for you as a person. I know, for instance, that you are a dutiful father and husband.'

Jenkins found himself enveloped in a horrid stillness.

'And in particular,' said Chang, 'you love your daughter. I know you will be pleased that we are looking after her so carefully.'

There was a pause that felt a million years long.

'Of course,' said Chang, 'there will be the captain's bonus, amounting to twenty thousand dollars, and a recommendation to the college of her preference that your daughter Rachel be awarded a scholarship. I endow many scholarships. I am really very grateful.'

Jenkins told himself, Whatever you do, don't get angry.

'So congratulations, captain,' said Chang. 'So glad we understand each other. Your orders will arrive by datacom.'

The connection broke.

Jenkins got up and stumped to the front of the bridge, and leaned his elbows on the Formica, and watched the flying fish skitter on the blue, blue sea.

Rodriguez trotted on to the bridge to begin his watch, and fiddled with the kettle. He said, 'Cup of mud, capting?'

Jenkins took the cup. But when he came to drink it, he found his hand was shaking too badly to get it to his mouth.

There were inducements that were beyond imagining. The swamp had closed over his head.

Mud was right.

After Bill had died, the Line had given him compassionate leave. He had flown back to Lee-on-the-Solent from Guam. They had delayed the funeral for him. Diana had been hostile and distant. He had understood; or he had thought he understood. It had all been his fault, for not being there. He had held Rachel's hand, and they had stood in the sun outside the crematorium, and people had said what he supposed were the usual sort of things. His parents in particular.

His father had had two destroyers sunk under him in the war. He had clapped him on the shoulder, and fixed him with his blue naval eyes, and said, 'Damn shame. Can't be helped. Life goes on.' His mother had said, 'Darling. We hardly *knew* him,' which of course was a dig at Diana, who had never taken the children to their grandparents because, in Diana's view, the grandparents saw her as a fortune-hunter who had snared their boy . . .

In fact the funeral had been a mess. Immediately afterwards, they had returned to Hong Kong. Diana had sold the old flat; too small, too full of memories, she had said. They had leased a bigger one, at huge expense. Diana had withdrawn. She wanted nothing to do with families. Families had caused her pain and grief, so the logical thing to do was to sever contact. Jenkins had found himself looking after Rachel, partly to take the strain off poor Diana, and partly, if he was honest with himself, because having spent too little time with Bill he didn't want to make the same mistake with Rachel. He got to know Rachel better than he had imagined possible. In fact, it was he who had brought her up; Diana seemed to feel that relationships beyond the flimsy camaraderie of the Circuit were too much trouble, too potentially wounding. One day, he told himself, she would come round. Patience.

And in the meantime, he and Rachel had grown closer. On his leaves, he spent more time with her than with Diana. They had become friends.

And now this.

At ten, the cooks dragged their cauldrons on to the little platform above the containers, and the passengers filed past for the morning rice. Pete came on watch, and Jenkins arranged Soares' funeral. At five past, the datacom printer began to whizz and a long tongue of paper rolled out of the machine.

Orders from Mr Chang, on a bridge like any other bridge; another room in the suites of identical rooms that had made up his life.

He spread the paper on the chart table.

ON ARRIVAL AT LAT 40°N 135°W, YOU WILL HEAVE TO
AND BROADCAST THE WORDS 'IRON HOTEL' ON CH72
VHF, I WATT LOW POWER, FOR FIVE MINUTES AT 1310
GMT AND 0110 GMT. RELIEF WILL BE AVAILABLE FOR
THE THREE-WEEK PERIOD COMMENCING MARCH 7.

March 7 was three weeks from now. Relief of a rescuer
outside territorial waters was not at all illegal.

At the end of the telex, an order had been appended.
WITH REGARD TO WATERMAKER SPARES AS REQUESTED
BY CHIEF ENGINEER. THESE WILL BE DELIVERED TO YAP
C/O CHEE AGENTS. NOTIFY ARRIVAL WHEN 20 (TWENTY)
MILES OFF. SPARES WILL BE DELIVERED PER LAUNCH.

Yap was in the Caroline Islands, one of the Federated
States of Micronesia. He said to Pete, 'Distance to Yap?'
Pete began to fiddle with his calculator.

'Eleven hundred miles,' he said. 'Funny way to go to Oakland.' But Jenkins had left. Pete raised his eyebrows. 'Sorry,
I'm sure,' he said. Make a bloke a captain, and he was never
the same again. He returned to his calculations.

Jenkins went to his cabin and climbed into his whites.
Then he walked to the ship's office and rummaged through
the sticky books till he found the *Ship's Captain's Medical
Adviser*. He shoved the volume into his pocket, clapped his
cap on his head and walked on to the containers. It was a
job, and jobs needed doing properly. Some sense of duty,
said the scratchy voice. There are brains up the wall, and
Rachel is under the hammer. Everything is normal. He told
the voice to shut up. It was time for captain's rounds.

The ship smelled of hot iron. Down in the courtyards,
little groups of Chinese were hunkered in the narrow strips
of shade. They looked up as his shadow fell into the brilliant
squares of sun, saw he was invisible, and looked away. But
one of them, an old man with a white sunhat and blue
boxer's shorts, raised a hand and waved. Jenkins recognized
him as one of the t'ai chi practitioners. The cargo was turning into separate, recognizable people. He found that
encouraging.

Lucy was sitting in Fung's container watching a game of
chess. There were a dozen people crammed in there under

the crucifix on the wall, all of them but her Christians from the front courtyard. It was hot. But it was sociable, too. The dozen people were there because they liked each other's company. Naturally, they took a strong interest in each other's lives. Which was why two of them, members of Fung's congregation, had homed in on Lucy.

'It's dangerous to come out here on your own,' said one of them, an old woman with deep creases in her parchment skin.

'That animal could try again,' said the old woman's husband. 'That kind doesn't try once, then give up.'

Lucy said, 'Don't worry.' It was not like on the ferry, where nobody would have known her death had not been an accident. The captain was watching her now.

The old woman patted Lucy on the knee. 'Care,' she said. 'We depend on you, Moses.'

Lucy laughed. She got up and climbed the ladder. As her head came level with the container top she saw the captain himself, wearing ceremonial clothes of mourning white, an official cap under his arm. He looked grim and harassed. He did not look like a Soares. He definitely looked like a man who would take responsibility. But perhaps she was reading too much of herself into him.

Time would tell.

Jenkins had never sailed on a passenger ship. The closest he had got was second mate in a freighter converted for the hadj. The pilgrims had been jammed into the holds like pilchards, under the care of some kind of mullah, who had acted as their spokesman. Their only requirement had been a lot of rice, and a compass welded to the deck so they would know which way to face for their prayers.

The pilgrims had been a large, homogeneous mass, all with the same object in view. This lot were different. The forward courtyard was clean and tidy, with plastic awnings shading straw mats on which a crowd of people were talking about a book. It looked to Jenkins like a Sunday school. In the second courtyard, the feeling was different. It was less crowded. A radio was playing distorted Canto-pop, and outside one of the container doorways someone had erected tin tables. It was a café, more or less. People were playing mah-jongg and drinking tea and beer. A man was paying for a Fanta from a large bundle of dollar bills. He looked up as Jenkins' shadow fell on him. He had a fleshy, self-confident look: a businessman relocating his business from one side of the Pacific to the other. Jenkins nodded to him. The man nodded back, offhand, the way a hotel guest might nod to the manager. Everything was in order in the Iron Hotel.

The aftermost courtyard marked a perceptible shift downmarket. It was noisier, and there were more people. There even seemed to be a small market in one corner, an affair of oranges and noodles, brought aboard in someone's bundle. Jenkins found himself thinking that Rachel would have liked to see this, the wonderful adaptability of these people.

Of all of them.

He went down a ladder and into a door at the base of the funnel.

Lucy followed him.

She watched from the top doorway as he stood on a railed gallery overlooking the engine. He turned away, inspecting his white duck trouser leg for oil stains. He was human. Curious; she had not expected to be dealing with humans. She followed him down two flights of ladders and found herself at the after end of the hold. If the courtyards had been like a village, the hold was a village full-fledged. There were two eighty-foot rooms and one forty-foot, connected by the watertight doors of the Burma Road, lit by fluorescent lights on the underside of the hatch-covers, floored by containers filled with sand ballast that left ten feet of headroom between the roof and the floor.

It was a very full ten feet.

The passengers had divided up the space with tents, sacking partitions, boxes and anything else they had brought or could find. The noise was terrific: the organ-pipe drone of the ship's passage through the sea, overlaid by dozens of tape machines and videos, and a multiple yell of conversation. Mixed with the stink of food and shit and joss-sticks was the reek of woodsmoke. Can't have that, thought Jenkins, and plunged into an alley in the sacking.

The alley was a street. Over the sacking he saw a pale man asleep on a pile of rags, and two muscular youths doing situps, and a woman suckling a baby. When their eyes met his, they slid away. Down here he could feel hostility, pressure-cooker hunger and ambition. The smoke from the fire was rising ahead of him, spreading out on the steel roof. He walked into a sort of square, in the middle of which was a small bonfire of packing-case fragments. Round the bonfire a dozen young men were sitting. Their eyes turned on him, bland and hostile.

'Put it out,' said Jenkins.

Blankness.

He picked up a bucket that was standing just inside the entrance of a cubicle. He threw the contents on the fire. There was a hiss and a cloud of steam. The young men began to yell. One of them fumbled in a pocket. Knife, thought Jenkins. That was not clever. A voice barked words Jenkins did not understand. Ho's voice.

Ho walked into the square, yawning.

'No fires,' said Jenkins.

Ho said something to the men. They sat down again, ignoring Jenkins. 'So sorry,' said Ho, smiling his artificial smile. 'No more fires.'

Lucy had stayed in the alleyway. She could see Jenkins' head and shoulders above some of the partitions. She heard the hiss of the fire, the roar of voices. If he knew the character of some of the people down here, she thought, he would not have gone in alone. This was where the thieves were, the scum. Already, after not even a week, there were prostitutes working, and she had heard that some of the gangsters were fighting about women and heroin.

That was where Lee saw her.

He was standing with two idiots. The idiots were hard men, but they were smoking fat three-skin cigarettes of tobacco and brown heroin. Lee did not mind junkies, because they made him feel extra powerful.

But what Lee really liked was the flap and shiver of a body dying, mingled with the sense that he was carrying out a task for which he was going to make serious money. Plus there was the sense of loyalty.

Lee set great store by loyalty.

The other holds had what felt to Jenkins a better atmosphere. He wandered through the streets like a mayor. Cocks were crowing and ducks quacking. In an open-fronted booth, a tailor was measuring a man for a suit. Mrs Nairn was examining a baby, watched anxiously by its mother. Against one of the bulkheads, a girl was playing Bach on a violin. Jenkins stopped to listen. When she saw him, she stopped, her face blank and frightened.

'Go on,' he said, trying to look encouraging.

She played on. She played really well. At the end, he clapped. She smiled and bowed.

It was not so bad.

Then the noise started.

When the captain had disappeared from view behind a tall sacking partition, Lucy had suddenly realized that it was not just him who was alone down here. She was off her territory, without protection. I must be mad, she thought, in a sudden sweat of terror. What has changed that I can take a risk like this? She turned to run back on deck.

A man in a white boiler suit was standing in her path.

Lee.

His right hand moved to the ruler-pocket in the leg of his overalls. It came out with a long, square-ended knife.

She jumped backwards. A hessian partition gave way, and she fell on to a body. Someone roared with anger. She screamed, the fluorescent lights on the hatch-covers in her eyes, waiting for the hiss of the knife, and thinking, I have failed. There was more shouting.

But instead of the knife, there was a heavy Occidental voice. Then there were bouncy footsteps pounding on steel deck, the clash of a watertight door dogged home. The sound of Lee running away.

She scrambled to her feet. The man who had been asleep behind the partition decided it was a joke. Several children were watching, saucer-eyed. The captain was standing over her.

'What's all this?' he said. He looked nervous and angry.

She was so flustered that she nearly told him. Just in time, she remembered that the fact he was not trying to kill her did not necessarily make him a friend. 'I slipped,' she said.

She wanted to cry. It had been horribly close. She wanted to thank him, tell him the truth. She had watched him. He would probably protect her. Almost certainly.

No, no, she thought. There were more reliable people on board than the captain; people who knew what was going on. They would look after Lee.

The deckhands had sewn the corpse of Soares into a sheet of dirty green tarpaulin. It looked like a mouldy spring roll, lying on a plank on the afterdeck, supported at either end by an oil drum, washed by the roar of the generator.

Mrs Nairn and Pete were by the body. Mrs Nairn sighed. She said, 'Funerals at sea.'

Pete's eyes swivelled from the horizon to her grey, craggy face. 'He was an arsehole,' he said.

'Captain likes to see a thing done properly,' said Mrs Nairn, shifting her bra. The two fifty-dollar bills she had gouged out of the baby's mother were digging into her breast.

'Good bloke, Dave,' said Pete, looking away.

'He'll need help,' said Mrs Nairn. 'Support.'

'That's right,' said Pete, flat-eyed.

'Can't be too careful,' said Mrs Nairn for no apparent reason, and pasted a welcoming smile on her face. 'Ah. There you are, Dave.'

Jenkins had arrived. There were sweat marks on his white shirt. He said, 'All ready?'

There was a straggle of Filipinos smoking Marlboros, and, surprisingly, thirty Chinese. Jenkins leafed through *Medical Adviser*, from abscesses to venereal diseases. Funerals were at the end.

He took off his cap and began to read. The words made a soothing drone, barely audible over the roar of the generator. Finally, he said, 'We commit his body to the deep.'

The Filipinos stuck their Marlboros back in their mouths, picked the plank up by its sides and aimed it over the rail. The green roll plunged into the blue sea with as little splash as an Olympic diver. A strange, high sound mingled with the throb of the engine.

Jenkins turned round.

The thirty-odd Chinese had formed up into two blocks, women on the left, men on the right. They were singing a Chinese hymn to the tune of 'Onward Christian Soldiers', faces bright with sun and exaltation. Fung was at the front, his face bandaged, conducting. Jenkins turned to look at the white lace ribbon of the wake, straight as a ruler back to the western horizon.

'Good riddance,' said Pete.

Back in the wake, something like a green pancake roll surfaced and wallowed.

The singing faltered. The generator roared on. A voice by Jenkins' ear said, in tones of scorn, 'What a balls-up.' Nairn's voice. Jenkins realized that the scorn was directed at him.

He said to the red veins of the face, 'You could have told your wife to put some weights in.'

Nairn flushed purple. 'What are you trying to say?' There was violence in his eyes. Jenkins saw it turn to terror. 'You want me out of the way,' he said. 'The way –' He stopped. The way you got Soares out of the way, he had been going to say. A revelation. Plain as the nose on your face. This Jenkins, this . . . pipsqueak, had killed Soares so he could take over. And where does that leave us? Kill one, he could kill the lot of us. Like when they told him he could retire, and when they conned him out of the farm. They all had those eyes. Looked friendly. But they'd kick you off your ship, steal you blind –

'The way what?' said Jenkins.

'Nothing,' said Nairn, not meeting his eye. *Kill you*, his mind screamed.

'Edwin,' said Mrs Nairn, sharply. 'What's the problem?'

'No problem,' said Nairn, slyly. Nose like a fucking beagle. Keep her happy. Terror when roused.

She gave him a narrow-eyed glare, and went forward.

Nairn knew what he needed to help him think all of this out. He said to Pete, who was still leaning on the rail, 'Got a drink?'

'Not on me,' said Pete. His eyes looked sharper than Nairn remembered.

'Wife doesn't hold with it,' said Nairn, man to man.

'Ah,' said Pete. 'Vodka, then? You don't get the niff, with vodka.'

'Vodka would be fine,' said Nairn, through a mouthful of saliva.

'Hundred bucks,' said Pete. 'Litre bottle.'

'Bring it to the engine room,' said Nairn. 'And don't let her see.'

Chapter Five

Nairn pulled the bottle of Smirnoff out of the plastic bag and cracked the seal with hands that needed no instruction from the brain. He tipped three inches into a glass, and added an inch of Seven-Up. Not that he needed any of this, he told himself, but funerals were upsetting. And this killer bloody pipsqueak Jenkins was worrying. Not only because he wanted to take over. There was another angle. You wouldn't have caught Soares cocking up funerals, or having anything to do with them, matter of that. Over the side, no questions asked. Hard bastard, Soares. With a cargo like this, you needed a hard bastard. Everyone out for number one. The watermaker was going to be no picnic. Thirsty meant touchy. They'd be rioting about this.

Need a drink.

Cheers.

The vodka drilled a red-hot hole to his stomach. He poured another. The second one went down even better than the first. The dim green control room had turned bright and happy, with a faint flicker. Time for number three.

Number three was odd. It made him confused and discouraged and shaky.

Those bastards stealing the farm had knocked the stuffing out of him somehow. Not his fault, of course. Anno Domini, though. Time was, he would have sailed a trip like this before breakfast. But now, he was . . . well, if he had been anyone else, he would have said he was frightened. He knew what was frightening him, besides all those people, of course. It was the future. The future without his bloody provident fund, the one those bastards had taken off him. He saw himself in old age, watching the wife crochet beermats. Him. The chief, who had worn snow-white uniforms and trodden teak decks, and been God to a dozen cadets at a time. He saw a trailer by a garbage dump, two incontinent wrecks – poverty, death . . .

At about eleven thirty, he drank number four or possibly five, he had lost count. There didn't seem to be a lot left in the bottle. Enough, though. Poverty and death had vanished, as if behind a curtain. He wavered his way into the racket of the engine room, relieved himself on to the spinning propeller shaft, and looked at his watch.

Time for the daily tour. He bent an ear to the deafening clatter of the tappets on the big diesel, scowled at the dials on the boilers and the oil cleaners and the watermaker, particularly the watermaker, and moved his lips in front of the blackboard with the day's fuel-pumping plan.

Rounds done, he walked back into the control room, sat down. Time for a refreshing lotion. He picked up the Smirnoff bottle. His fingers were oily, clumsy with drink. They slipped off the bottle's shoulders. The bottle fell on the steel deck and smashed.

Nairn looked at the clear pool with its remnants of glass. *Shit*, he thought. No more bottle. Run out, have to go back to Pete, hundred dollars, haven't got hundred dollars. Someone might notice that he had had a couple, and tell bloody Irma. Bastards. Man of his age, been in engine rooms when Jenkins sucking his mother's –

Need a drink, thought Nairn, because drink's run out. Need a drink to deal with lack of drink.

A species of whirlpool came into existence in Nairn's head, accompanied by a shrill ringing in the ears. He began to cry.

The crying was not now specifically about the vodka. He cried because his wife would not leave him alone. He cried because ships were not what they used to be. He cried because he had done bloody well at that farming, and it wasn't his fault that he had lost the bet; just his lousy luck, right? And he cried because he was all the way down here at the bottom of the hole, and this was a rustbucket full of Chinks and bandits, run by this murdering bloody Jenkins pipsqueak who couldn't run a piss-up in a brewery. When the water ran out, as it would, there were going to be great big Chinese riots, in which they were all going to be sliced into, well, slices.

Into Nairn's mind flashed an appallingly clear vision: himself with a huge, stinging wound in his throat, gasping arterial blood into his lungs. Ho and Lee, the motormen who were not motormen, were standing over him with dripping machetes, laughing out of their dirty yellow faces.

Oh, Christ, thought Nairn, clenching his fists to stop his hands shaking off the ends of his arms. Oh, God help me. We are sitting on a floating bloody bomb.

OK, then. Concentrate. Have a drink. No drink. Well, think clever. Irma had the first part of the money in a no-tax false-name deposit account in Singapore, where the Chinkies could never get it back. Fifty grand US. Half a loaf better than no bread. It was definitely time to bail out. Yeah, thought Nairn, his blood beginning once again to move in his leathery veins. Do it right, and there could even be reward money to make up the shortfall. Dangerous, thought Nairn, shivering. But when the going gets tough, the tough get, can't remember what they get. But no poverty. No death.

He lurched out of the engine room and along the Burma Road, with the tents of the steerage migrants on his left. He kept his gaze averted, but he could feel their eyes on him, black and evil, can't tell what they're thinking. His teeth were chattering with terror as he stumbled past the guard on the door of the accommodation block. He brushed past a Chinese woman as he lurched up the stairs to the bridge. He said, 'Outta my way. I'm going to fix you.' *Bastards*, he was thinking, or possibly saying. Yellow bastards. You won't cut my throat. You won't get a fucking chance.

Go a bit careful here, he thought, as he arrived on the bridge. The pipsqueak could be there. Even these Flips might spot me. They're all in it together. There is me, Nairn, chief engineer, who understands what is happening; and there is them, the rest of them, bastards of all colours, malign, inhuman. Nairn could not remember why they were bastards because of the fog in his head. The bastards were bastards. That was enough for him.

Pete straightened from the chart, saw who it was, and said, 'G'day again.'

Nairn surveyed him with a wild yellow eye. 'Fuck off,' he said.

Pete grinned. He said, 'Did you get through that whole bottle?'

Nairn said, 'Mind your own fucking business.'

Pete looked faintly nervous. Mrs Nairn was not going to like this. He said, 'Better make you some coffee.' He took Nairn's shoulders, and sat him in the rattan chair. Nairn's face was bluish-white, his breath like petrol. 'Stay here. We've run out. I'll get some from the galley.'

Played into my hands, thought Nairn. He groaned, and let his head slump, feigning sleep.

'Fucking idiot,' said Pete.

See? said Nairn in his mind. They hate me. Everyone does. And they'll kill me.

He waited for the door to close. Then he shot the bolt and stumbled into the chart room. The satcom screen watched him with its blank eye, making plans. He reached out his fingers to its keyboard. But the keys suddenly became teeth. He had a prophetic glimpse of bleeding stumps of fingers, and felt hideous pain.

He screwed up his face to stop himself whimpering with terror. Go on, he thought. Do this. You can do it. On pain of poverty and death . . .

He began to type.

The keys dodged around a bit, but he found cursing kept them still. He typed. When he had finished, he thought, that should do it. He waded through the flickering chart room, pulled down an almanac and found the coastguard number. Then he sat down again and began to run through the transmit menus, slowly, referring to the almanac. Something was creeping across the chart table. He ignored it, because he knew of old that it was probably not there. Something was breathing behind him. But all he had to do was hit the return button, and go and get a drink, and the thing would go away. If he could not find any more vodka, he could have sworn he had smelt Aqua Velva on the second mate.

His finger came down on the return key.

It did not reach it.

A hand had grabbed it, a thin brown hand that dragged his away from the keys and caught his other hand and pulled his chair backwards on to the deck. Nairn had seen the creeping things before, and felt the breathing things. But they had never grabbed him and thrown him around. It came to him that he was dying and being dragged off to hell. He began to scream and lash out.

Jenkins heard the screaming from his cabin. He went out of the door and up the stairs in what felt like two steps. The door was locked. He ran to the outside stairs.

There were two figures on the chart-room floor, and a stink of alcohol. One of the figures was Nairn. The other was Lucy.

He said, 'All *right*!' He dived at the struggling figures, grabbed Lucy by the arm and pulled her away. Nairn rolled into a ball and began to whimper. Jenkins said to Lucy, 'What the hell are you doing? You're not allowed up here.'

Lucy pulled her arm out of his grip. Her face was flushed and angry. She said, 'Look at that screen.'

OFFICER COMANDING US COASTGUARD W COAST MS GLORY OF SAIPAN APPROACHING US TERRITTORIAL WATERS WITH CARGO OF 370 CHINESE ILLEGALS STOP VESSLE REPRESENTS SEVERE POLLUTION HAZZARD STOP I CLAIM REWARD FOR THE SUPPLYIN GOF INFORMATION LEADING TO THE PREVENTION OF BREECH OF US IMMIGRATION AND COASTGUARD REGS SIGNED NAIRN CHIEF ENGINEEER GLORY OF SAIPAN.

Jenkins picked up the telephone and with a slow, inaccurate finger dialled Mrs Nairn.

She came quickly, bringing a medical bag, two deckhands and a stretcher. She bit her lips. 'I'm sorry,' she said. 'It won't happen again.' She loaded a syringe and jabbed it without finesse into the wasted muscle of Nairn's shoulder. Nairn whimpered, shuddered, and became still. Pete came on to the bridge with a jar of coffee. He looked at Mrs Nairn, put down the coffee and left hastily.

'What happened?' said Mrs Nairn.

Jenkins showed her the datacom screen, and sat down, carefully, so as not to cause vibration.

What was on the screen was one keystroke away from killing Rachel. He moved the cursor on the menu, cancelled the message and erased the screen.

When he looked up, Lucy was still there. He wanted to grab her and thank her for saving his daughter's life. But that was not how captains behaved. He said, stiffly, 'What were you doing here?'

'I saw that man coming up here. Drunk. Shouting and cursing, talking about the coastguard. Then he locked himself in. I came up the outside stairs and read . . . that.' She lowered her eyes demurely. 'I thought he'd better not be allowed to send it.'

'Yes,' said Jenkins. 'Thank you.'

She smiled. It was a highly intelligent smile, packed once again with warmth and complicity. 'We are all in this together,' she said.

He nodded, forcing himself to clear Rachel from his mind. Someone had warned him about a pirate attack. Now this woman had been on hand to stop Nairn turning them in to the coastguard. Things were happening that as captain he needed to understand. He said, 'What was that fuss in the hold today?'

She wondered if she should tell him. She liked his eyes. But that was no reason for trusting him. She had taken other steps. 'Someone knocked me down,' she said. 'An accident.' She watched those eyes. Gossip in the cargo said they were crazy, those eyes. They were sharp and blue, and sometimes, in unguarded moments, they even looked kind. But just at the moment she found them not so much kind or crazy as calculating.

He said, 'It is important that I should know what is going on.'

She widened her own eyes, to let the innocent green work. She watched it have its effect. She said, 'Are you asking me to spy on my fellow-countrymen?'

'A finger on the pulse. That's all.'

She shrugged. 'I'll give it some thought.'

'Please do.'

She left, clenching her fists with pure glee. To have the captain's ear would make things very much easier. To have him as an ally. Possibly as *more* than an ally. Very much easier indeed.

First, hook your fish.

Then reel him in.

She walked down to Jer's cabin and knocked three times. Jer let her in. She sat down.

Jer said, 'I heard shouting.'

'That's all right,' she said. 'The captain wants me to be his spy.'

Jer bowed his jaundiced head. 'I'm sure you'll be very good at it,' he said.

They laughed. Jer laughed hard, a vigorous laugh for a sick man. Lucy had to put more effort into hers. She liked the captain. When she examined herself, she was surprised to find how much she liked him.

When hooking a fish, the wise angler took care not to hook herself.

Mrs Nairn closed the door to Pete's cabin and relocked it with the skeleton key. It was neat, the cabin; wardrobe closed, blonde pinup pouting from above the bunk, bottle of Johnny Walker on the desk. Mrs Nairn went through the desk drawers, and found six hundred Rothmans and three more bottles of whisky. She smashed two of the bottles into the cigarettes. Then she went into the lavatory, put the seat down, and waited.

Twenty minutes later, a key rattled in the lock and Pete came in. He was whistling. When he smelt the spilt whisky, the whistling stopped. He shut the door and walked over to the desk.

That was when Mrs Nairn stepped out of the lavatory and belted him round the right ear with the last Johnny Walker bottle.

Pete said, 'Urrh!' and turned round, clutching his ear, eyes watering. She hit him on the other ear, hard, but not hard enough to break the bottle. He said, 'Fuck,' and fell into the chair. She unscrewed the cap of the bottle and tipped the contents into his lap. She said, 'You sold Edwin vodka.'

Pete said, 'No.'

Mrs Nairn pulled a Bic lighter from her pocket. The fumes of whisky were suffocating in the hot cabin.

Pete said, 'Yes.' His eyes were on the lighter. 'Please.'

'I am a poor defenceless woman,' said Mrs Nairn. 'But next time so help me I will fucking light you.'

Jenkins stayed on the bridge. He had to do his job properly. To do the job properly, he had to understand the cargo. The officers and crew were not going to be any help. So he needed Lucy.

He wished he trusted her, that was all.

He took the manual for the satcom from the shelf, sat down at the keyboard and programmed in a new password: BILL JENKINS, poor Bill. He removed the handsets from the bridge VHFs and the SSB, took them to his cabin, and locked them in the safe by the bed.

From now on, the four hundred people on the *Glory of Saipan* had one voice that could connect them with the outside world.

His.

Chapter Six

In a hot makeshift tent in the corner of the hold, Chiu was working, loosing off the salvo of moans and gasps, grinding her pelvis against the body of the man between her legs and driving her red fingernails into his nape. Chiu glanced covertly at her platinum moonphase Patek Philippe, and began to speed it up. There were a couple more waiting, and there had already been two today. In Shanghai, she had specialized in long sessions; her best client, a Triad called Tsing, called her Three Hour Rainbow. But on this ship the money was not so good, so quantity not quality was the name of the game. Wailing quietly, Chiu wound her groin round the client's, and totted up what she was making. Five hundred US a day was not bad, she thought, sucking air as she began her artificial orgasm. Less expenses, call it four. Added to the deposit she had paid in Shanghai, she should have cleared her fare by the time she arrived in America. And then it would be soft pink lights instead of the oil lamp in her tent, and a waterbed instead of a foam mattress on the rusty deck, and sleek millionaires instead of scrawny shopkeepers like the one on top of her –

The shopkeeper's teeth showed. He said, 'Wah,' and collapsed on her breasts. Skilfully, Chiu rolled from under him, combining speed and efficiency (excellent business practice) with an embrace that pressed her stiff-nippled breasts against his hairless chest (reinforcing customer loyalty). The client lit a cigarette and lay in afterglow. Afterglow was not cost-effective, and it pissed Chiu off. But she lay there anyway, stroking the client's hair, because it made commercial sense to be civil with your regulars.

She was looking at the wall of the tent, giving him a couple of minutes, wondering if she could start repairing her make-up yet. She thought she heard a step outside. Next client, she thought, looking at the Patek Philippe. Then her smeared mouth opened, and her eyes became almost round.

The cloth wall had bulged in faintly. A long, square-ended blade appeared through the sacking and hissed from top to bottom. Through the slit came a stocky figure in white over-alls. Misfortune, thought Chiu, scuttling to crouch in the corner. The Hung Kwan, or Red Pole. The Warlord.

The client scrambled off the mattress, hiding his naked-ness with his hands, in one of which he still held the cigar-ette. The Hung Kwan grabbed him by the hair, kicked him through the slit, and threw his clothes after him. The client did not make a sound. Chiu's cubicle was in a special place, tucked into an angle of the bulkheads in a dead end of the canvas street. If the client kept quiet, it was probable that nobody would know what he had been up to.

Chiu wrapped a sarong round her breasts, pulled a mirror from a bag and began to fix her lips and lashes. 'It is my great pleasure that you visit,' she said. 'Might I impertin-ently ask the reason?' She knew the reason perfectly well, and the knowledge frightened her so much that she stuck her mascara brush into her eye.

The Hung Kwan said, mildly, 'To give pleasure to beauty is always delightful.'

She did not like the mildness. She said, 'You could have used the door.'

He said, 'My pleasure is in different doors.' There was the noise of rustling cloth. In her make-up mirror she saw the boiler suit on the floor. His body was thickset, with a spare tyre of fat round the belly. Trembling inwardly, she hoped that this would be all. She pasted a smile on to her face, let the sarong fall, and laid herself down on the sheet of foam.

'How you like,' she said. He was so big that her arms would not go all the way round him.

'There is the matter of the money,' said the Hung Kwan.

She became stiff and unresponsive. 'Money?'

'Thirty-one visits from clients,' said the Hung Kwan. He

put his hands on her hip bones and turned her over sharply, so she was lying face down on the foam and he was kneeling behind her.

'One hundred dollars per visit,' said the Hung Kwan, touching her buttocks, first the left, then the right. 'Plenty for all. So we shall take a mere half.'

'Half!' said Chiu, outraged. She tried to roll over, but the Hung Kwan put the weight of his body on hers and brought his face next to her ear. 'Listen,' he said, in a whisper. 'Give me the money and I will look after you. Or would you rather seek protection from the God people?'

The God people were a joke, of course. But Chiu was damned if she was going to hand the Hung Kwan her money, all that labour in vain. He'll look for it, she thought. But maybe he won't find it. He entered her, violently. She groaned. Then she thought, This is only work. And she began to make the movements that brought the money.

Afterwards, she said, 'There is no money.'

The Hung Kwan was not one for afterglow. Chiu watched him apprehensively as he stepped into his boiler suit and began to search the little pile of boxes in the corner. Shall I run? she thought. But she had no clothes to run in, and nowhere to run to.

Five minutes later, the law-abiding families of the tent city stopped their talking, and turned to listen to the sound coming from the direction of the bulkhead.

The sound of Chiu screaming.

When the knock came on the door, Jenkins was in a thick, sweaty sleep. He swung his legs out of his bunk and staggered across to unlock it. Mrs Nairn was outside. She was wearing a white overall with red blotches. She said, 'We've got an unpleasantness in the hold.'

Jenkins stumbled through the lukewarm air to the washbasin, and splashed tepid water on his face. He followed the clump of Mrs Nairn's heels down the stairs and into the accommodation.

As soon as they were past the watertight door into the Burma Road, he could tell that something had happened. Yesterday, the maze of tents and partitions had been full of voices. Now the alleys were empty and quiet except for the huge drone of the hull through the sea.

He followed Mrs Nairn down a blind alley to a burlap partition erected against one of the hold bulkheads. She pushed aside what looked like a recently cut flap of the sacking and said, 'In here.'

In there was a pile of boxes draped in a shawl embroidered with dragons. There were red-and-gold-lettered posters on the wall, and a foam-rubber mattress on the floor. Lying face down on the mattress was a woman, covered by a blue cloth. Her long black hair was spread out on the pillow. Her face was smeared with the remains of lipstick. The skin was startlingly pale, the eyes crescents of white in the mascara. She was breathing heavily through her half-open mouth.

'Gave her a shot,' said Mrs Nairn. There was blood on the floor, and flies on the blood. Grunting, she bent and whipped the blue cloth from the woman's naked body. It was thin and pale, the waist narrow, the fingernails long and varnished red. There was a thin gold chain around her waist. Just below the chain, where the buttocks began to swell, was a long strip of surgical lint. Mrs Nairn pulled it off.

'Bloody hell,' said Jenkins.

Across the flesh at the base of the back ran a red slit an inch deep, as if someone had taken a butcher's knife and started to cut her in half.

Mrs Nairn was rubbing her hands with surgical spirit. 'She'll probably tell you she fell,' she said, jamming a syringe full of Novocaine into the lips of the wound. The woman moaned and stirred. 'Hold still.'

A Filipino deckhand was standing in the Burma Road. Jenkins said, 'Get me Lucy Moses.'

'Lucy Moses?'

'The interpreter.'

She arrived a few minutes later. Mrs Nairn was cobbling away two-thirds of the distance along the cut. Mrs Nairn looked up. Her face was cold and absent, empty of suburban coquetry. Jenkins said, 'Ask her who did this.'

Lucy spoke in Cantonese. The woman answered in a high, drowsy voice. Lucy said, 'She fell.'

Mrs Nairn looked at Jenkins, rolling her eyes heavenward.

The curved needle went in, out. Blunt fingers knotted the gut.

When Jeremy had been a policeman, Diana had liked him to freeze their blood with tales of gang violence. It was the trademark, the slashing of the big muscles – calves, biceps, pectorals, buttocks.

Jenkins said, 'It looks like a Triad punishment chop.'

Mrs Nairn said, 'You got it all the time on the *Tan Shan*, Chinese crew. It stands to reason. It'll be that Ho or that Lee. What does it matter?'

Jenkins looked at Lucy. 'What do you think?'

Lucy said, stiffly, 'I'm afraid I've never had occasion to find out much about prostitutes.'

Mrs Nairn looked at Lucy without interest. She said, 'This one's part of the cargo. She's the problem, not the solution.'

Lucy said, blank-faced, 'Of course the doctor is right.' She walked away.

'Wait,' said Jenkins.

She did not look round.

Mrs Nairn yanked a knot tight. The tart had beaten her down from a hundred dollars to seventy-five, so she saw no need for delicacy. 'They'll stick together. Bunch of low-life Chinks.'

Jenkins said, 'There are things going on down here that we need to know about. So how about you stick to your job and leave me to do mine?'

Mrs Nairn sniffed. 'That sounds a bit like Edwin,' she said. 'I tell you, mate, by way of advice only.' She smiled the suburban smile. 'Get mixed up with this lot and they won't thank you for it. They'll take you for a ride. You tell 'em what's what, shit on 'em for three weeks, it's the only language they understand. Few get the chop, put it down to natural wastage.' She slapped Chiu on her white buttock. 'They're not people. They're cargo.'

Jenkins said, 'I'll leave you to it,' and went on deck.

The sun blazed down from a milky sky. In the fore courtyard the Christians were holding another prayer meeting. In the second a group of old men was sitting at a round tin table in the café slurping noodles out of bowls. On a mat in the corner, four little girls were staging a dolls' tea party. When Jenkins went down the ladder he found the air under the awning cool, the perfume of tea and joss-sticks overlaying the bilge and latrine. One of the little girls threw a ball crooked. It missed the catcher, and hit Jenkins in the stomach. The girl covered her mouth with her hand, pale, eyes round with horror. Jenkins threw the ball back. She blushed and giggled. An old woman washing clothes in a bucket grinned at him, and the little girls stared and whispered.

Diana would have agreed with Mrs Nairn. Do what you have to do. You carry pineapples, you don't eat pineapple. You carry people, you don't get involved, except to get paid.

But cargo did not giggle.

Chapter Seven

Pete's philosophy in life was that you could put up with just about anything, as long as you got paid for it. But the profit on a hundred-dollar bottle of Smirnoff was no compensation for the pain in his ears. Certainly did step into the whirling knives there, thought Pete, concealing from himself the fact that he had been terrified. Mad old cow. He thought of the Bic, and shuddered. Like the teachers at school had said, before they slung him out into the Seven Sisters Road, be more careful in future.

The telephone rang. The chief's voice said, 'Where's that fuckin' Pom?'

'The Old Man?'

'Not in my book.'

Pete knew from long experience that getting between a chief and an Old Man was putting your dick between the train and the buffers. Particularly when the chief had just got big rocks from his wife about drink you had flogged him. So he said, soothingly, 'Can I give him a message, chief?'

'Water ration,' said Nairn. 'Total available for crew and passengers one ton per day. Got that?'

Pete knew his Chinks. Bloody hell, he thought. Here we go. He said, 'Hope your missus got plenty of thread for her needle.'

'You tell him,' said Nairn. 'I'm staying down here. Locked in.'

Pete was bored. The money was OK, but life was getting samey. It would be interesting to see how the Old Man handled this one. He smiled and licked his lips. Then he dialled the captain's cabin and told him the news.

Jenkins said, 'Thank you,' nice and calm. He did not feel nice and calm. The wind was hot, and salty, and it made you sweat. A ton a day was two and a half litres a head. A drop in the ocean.

He dialled Lucy.

Her voice was high and cold. He said, 'Could you come to the office?'

'I suppose.' When she came in, she was wearing black jeans and a black T-shirt, with her hair tied back into a sort of topknot, so her eyes had a stretched, hostile look. She said, 'What is it?'

Jenkins sighed. He said, awkwardly, 'It may be Mrs Nairn's . . . er . . . view that you are part of the problem. It is not mine.'

Lucy was expressionless. 'Cargo is indeed a problem,' she said. 'I understand.'

There was no time for this sort of stuff. 'For God's sake,' said Jenkins. 'Mrs Nairn thinks one way, I think another. You think one way . . . *Lee* thinks another. Sod it. I know that and you know that, and Mrs Nairn is too bloody stupid to work it out.'

Lucy met his eye. 'Not stupid,' she said. 'She doesn't care.' And this one does, she thought. That was something of a surprise.

'OK,' said Jenkins. This was not a conversation about caring. It was about doing the job, making things add up. 'What I think is this. We are all individuals and we have our individual reasons for wanting to get across the bloody Pacific. So there are two things I have to say to you. One is that until we can pick up spare parts at Yap, water will be rationed to two litres a day. I'd like you to make the announcement.'

She said, 'How long till Yap?'

'Four days. Not long. I'll put a seaman on the tap by the cooks' deck. I want everyone to take their water breakers up for numbering this evening, four o'clock, when we give out the rice.'

She said, 'Someone will make trouble.'

'If we don't do it this way the water runs out, and the ship stops working, and we put out a distress call, and we are all in trouble. All of us.' He watched her. She was looking at her hands. Try now, he thought, while she remembers we are both on the same side. He took a bottle of Soares' Wild Turkey and two glasses out of the bottom drawer of the filing cabinet. 'Drink?'

She shrugged. Being tactful was not his job. He wanted people to understand.

'And the second thing,' he said. 'There are things going on that need explaining.'

She sipped the whiskey, raised an eyebrow at him. He felt the distance between them. 'Such as?'

'You and Jer were locked on that ferry for no reason anyone will tell me. From the outside, whatever you say. Someone rang me in my cabin the night the pirates came. Warned me.'

She said, mildly, 'Both these things had a good outcome, never mind how they happened. Which I don't know. So why worry?'

'That's Mrs Nairn philosophy.'

She smiled and ducked her head.

He said, doggedly, 'I need to know what's going on.'

She said, 'You're a liberal. We don't have too many of you in China. You're too interested in other people's business.'

'I'm captain of a ship, with four hundred people I need to deliver in good order.'

She said, 'Why should I trust you?'

Jenkins' never-deep reserves of finesse were dry. He said, 'I bloody saved you and your mate Jer from drowning.'

She laughed. She was really pretty when she laughed. 'That's Chinese,' she said. 'Calling in the *guanxi*.'

'Is that it?' he said. 'So will you tell me what's going on?'

'OK,' said Lucy. 'The reason Jer and I got left is that Lee thought Jer would infect the cargo. I was Jer's friend. I would have made trouble. So he tried to leave me too. As for your voice in the night, I've no idea.'

'Why do you trust Ho but not Lee?'

'Lee had made a deal with Soares,' she said. 'He took Soares' orders, and Soares paid him extra. That's why there was no sign of him when the pirates were on board.'

'No sign of Ho either.'

She said, 'Ho is what you'd call a pragmatist. I guess he thought there was not much one man could do.' She looked at Jenkins under her lashes. 'Wrongly, as it turned out.'

Jenkins realized that this was a compliment. He hung on doggedly. 'So why trust Ho?'

She said, 'Ho's efficient. Scrupulous in his way. Lee's crazy. Pathological.'

'So?'

'That's all there is.'

'He tried to kill you. Now he's stopped. Just like that.'

'Jer's not a threat. Mrs Nairn says he's not infectious. Lee doesn't have to kill anyone. The word is pragmatic.'

Pragmatic was it. Pragmatic enough to take your breath away. 'So Ho and Lee are . . . monitors.'

'As you had already guessed.'

Jenkins grunted, and sipped his drink. 'Can you talk to Ho about the water problem?'

'Of course.' In different circumstances, she would have liked to confide in this man. Things being as they were, he got an edited version of the truth. Now it was time to change the subject.

'So here I am sitting on a ship, drinking with a liberal.' She sighed. 'You can't imagine how *luxurious* that feels.'

Jenkins felt vaguely uncomfortable. He liked her. She had a quickness, a practical streak mixed with a simplicity that reminded him of . . . hell, it reminded him of Rachel. But he could not help thinking she was trying to get round him. He said, 'They don't think I'm a liberal in England.'

'Believe me,' she said. 'I've lived with slaves long enough to know a free man when I see one. My father was a free man.'

'The American.'

'Not just any old American,' she said, nose haughtily in the air, mocking herself. 'Professor of English Literature at the University of Buffalo.'

Jenkins said, 'How did he meet your mother?'

'He was on a lecture trip,' she said. 'In Shanghai, just before the Cultural Revolution. He fell in love with her and smuggled her out. Very daring. He was your radical academic. Free man. Didn't approve of marriage. She loved him too much to argue. They came to the US and lived together, common law, you'd call it. I was born in Buffalo. My father moved to California. We all did. Of course.' She was not playing the fool any more. 'Can I have some more whiskey?'

Jenkins gave her some. Water shortage or no water shortage, trust or no trust, he liked this. Two people, talking person to person, on this giant tin can. He never talked person to person with anyone. Not even Rachel. Certainly not Diana.

'But my mother didn't like California. She was ashamed. She wouldn't let herself mix with Chinese people in case they found out she was shacked up with a gweilo. And Americans worried her, specially the ones she met where we lived, right out in the suburbs in a little white house with a green yard, and space everywhere, and a flush toilet. I had a bedroom painted pink, with a record player and the complete works of Nathaniel Hawthorne bound in olive-green cloth. Library surplus. I went to school on my bike. Blue bike. I loved it. But my mother hated it. She thought the suburbs were a desert, because the houses were far apart and there were no uncles and aunts and goddamn cousins. So she was unhappy, and being unhappy made her mean, and her being mean kept my father away from home. So she got lonely and he met another woman. He married the other woman, and died of a heart attack. So nobody really knew we existed. Then my mother heard that they had jailed the Gang of Four and things were better in China. So she went home, and took me right back with her.' She fell silent, remembering the crowds, the stink, the roar of strange languages. Then she caught herself. You are not here to confide in anyone. You are here to lay a trail.

So she laughed. 'Everyone on the ship's got a story,' she said. 'Fung's a Christian, but the wrong kind for the Party. Ho's a gangster who wants dollars. Chiu's a whore who wants a better class of customer. There are crooks, political radicals, shopkeepers, you name it.' She got up. 'I talk too much.'

'Not for me,' said Jenkins.

She gave him a quick smile. He felt it again, the warmth,

the complicity. Stronger, this time. She stood up. She said, 'I'll tell them about the water.' She left.

Jenkins was sorry to see her go. There were not many people you could talk to on the *Glory of Saipan*.

Or anywhere else.

Lucy gave her usual triple knock on Jer's door. When he let her in, she told him about the water rationing. His muddy orange face didn't move, but she could tell he was worried. He said, 'Lee's not happy about Soares. He'll be looking for an excuse to make trouble.'

'Probably.'

'Is there anything you can do?'

'I think the captain will be watching what happens this afternoon,' said Lucy.

'How did you do that?'

Surprisingly, Lucy found herself wanting to defend the captain to Jer. 'He'll be there,' she said. 'He's an honourable man.'

Jer looked at her strangely. 'That may not be enough,' he said.

'You've got a suspicious mind.'

He grinned at her. It was an unexpectedly charming grin. 'You should be a missionary,' he said. 'Then you could do all the social work you want, at no personal risk.'

She punched him lightly in the shoulder. 'No risk involved with you around,' she said. 'Thug.'

He laughed. It was not the laugh of a thug, or indeed of a sick man. It was merely the laugh of a man with a sense of humour that had been tested more severely than most.

The two of them went on deck together. When Jer stood up you could see just how big he had been, exceptionally tall for a Chinese, almost bearlike, with a deep chest and a neck still thick and muscular. Curiously, his size made him appear more benevolent than threatening, perhaps because his back was stooped with illness, and the blue work-shirt and loose trousers hung from his bones as if they were a couple of sizes too big. He held Lucy's arm as they went out on deck, and sat on a small stool next to her while she stood on the cooks' stairs and shouted out her explanations about the water rationing through a loudhailer.

The crowd stood quietly and listened, apparently docile. But Lee, sitting in a hot, reeking cubbyhole halfway up the funnel, knew different. Lee was a man closely attuned to violence, and violence was what he could smell blowing back from the huddle in front of the steel stage on which the doll-like figure with the loudhailer yelled and gestured.

About time too, thought Lee. It was time that woman died. So far, through luck or cunning, she had always had someone with her. Luck, probably. Lee had a high opinion of his own cunning. Take Ho, for instance. Ho was a simple man, loyal to a single employer. Ho had assistants down in the hold, foot-soldiers upon whom he could call when it was time to keep order. But Lee had found it profitable to serve two masters, minimum. What he needed now was a good riot to give him cover for a killing.

Lucy had finished her announcement. Someone shouted a question about the blue plastic drums the water was issued in. Lee thought, Wait for the distribution. Jealousy and greed would do the job. And in the middle of that battle, me and her.

He licked his lips. He loved the way the world changed when it saw his knife, the knife moving at normal speed, but everything else like a Jackie Chan movie slowed down, ready to fly apart, disassemble in beautiful red flowers of blood.

Lee permitted himself a quiet moment, in which he saw himself and that woman alone in the crowd, like lovers. The woman's neck was a column of bow-taut ivory. And the heavy blade was sweeping at it, through the slowed-down time that turned the air to syrup, and Lee could feel the hot joy of it in his groin.

Up at the front of the containers, by the white steel wall of the accommodation, the water queue was forming. Lee got up, stretched, and swept the sweat from his forehead. There could be a chance here.

The queue was restless, but not violent. Jer had hobbled off for a constitutional.

To begin with, matters arranged themselves in the usual way. Ramos, the second engineer, appeared at the base of the steps, holding a clipboard. Another man had a pot of paint and a brush. Each person in the queue held a blue water breaker. Ramos nodded. The queue began to move.

Lucy patted her knees with her palms, and waited.

As the queue passed Ramos, Ramos ticked the list and put out his hand. Into the hand each person in the queue pressed two US dollar bills, and passed on for the painting of the number on their water breaker. Ramos received a total, Lucy had calculated, of two hundred and four dollars per food queue, and the water ration would come in the light of a bonus. Her enquiries had revealed that a quarter of his fees went to the cooks, and the rest to the engine-room hands. It was good business. But these people had bought their passage inclusive of food. To make them pay for it twice was no better than piracy. Her theatricals in Jenkins' cabin had given her a chance to put this right. And also to test Jenkins for other things she had in mind for him. She glanced covertly up at the deck abaft the bridge.

Ah.

He was up there, a tall, awkward figure, with a big, sun-burned nose and baggy blue shorts. Arms folded on the rail, he was looking down at the distribution taking place on the deck above the containers. His eyes had settled on Ramos, who was concentrating on taking the money. Lucy could not see the eyes, but she felt a gleeful delight as she imagined their expression.

After a couple of minutes, the captain left the rail. Two minutes later, the mate Peter materialized with a burly deck-hand. They took station one either side of Ramos. Peter said something to Ramos. Ramos took a fistful of money out of his pocket, handed it to Peter, and walked aft with a heavy face. Grinning, Peter gave the money back, two dollars by two dollars, to the people who had already paid. A hum of satisfaction rose from the crowd on deck. The gangling figure in blue shorts was back at the rail. She felt the warmth of having been right. Then she examined herself further, and was amazed.

The warmth was not just self-satisfaction. Part of it was definitely connected with the captain.

Trust nobody, Lucy reminded herself. Or die.

*

Lee watched her sit on the steps under the captain's feet, looking smug. The passengers were disappointingly calm, drifting aft with their water containers. He would have loved to kill her right there, cut her into pieces under the eyes of that captain. But Ho would object. Swallow your pride, Ho was always telling him. Your time will come . . .

Lee was beginning to hate Ho.

The hate was jumping in his blood so he could no longer sit still. He walked out on to the afterdeck, next to the generator, away from the people, and lit a Mild Seven.

The wake was like a great wound the ship tore in the sea, white, the colour of mourning. Lee liked the wake.

A man stepped from behind the generator.

Lee's mouth fell open. He dropped his cigarette. Then he smiled, feeling the tightness in his groin as the man moved towards him. The sun blazed, and the generator howled, and the wake hissed in his mind like a jet aeroplane. His hand fell to the ruler pocket in the leg of his overalls, and closed round the haft of his knife.

From his vantage point abaft the bridge, Jenkins saw an eddy of people at the aft end of the containers. A strange noise had begun to rise.

It started off as a single shout. Then people started screaming. And above the screaming there were words.

Man overboard.

Chapter Eight

Jenkins followed the pointing fingers with his binoculars. He caught a flash of white in a wave that was not breaking, and held it.

The white object in the water was no more than a glimmer in the blue swell, rotating as Rodriguez took the ship through the tennis-racket-shaped Williamson turn. It became a figure lying in the water, drifting down the starboard side. 'Stop engines,' said Jenkins, and heard the buzz of the telegraph. The *Glory of Saipan* coasted on, propeller stopped. There was an orange lifebuoy fifteen yards from the figure. The figure seemed to be making no effort to swim to it. Silly bugger, thought Jenkins. He said, 'Where's that lifeboat?'

Johnny's liverish eyes rolled up at him from the boat deck. 'Stuck,' he shouted. 'Can't launch.'

Bloody hell, thought Jenkins. This was bad. This was very bad. His heart was going like a triphammer, and he was sweating. The figure in the water didn't move.

Swim, you idiot, thought Jenkins, chewing his lips. He said, 'Dead slow astern.'

The telegraph buzzed. White water churned under the transom. He was five yards away, not swimming. It had been a good bit of ship handling, but if the stupid idiot would not swim . . .

'Stop engines.'

The rusty hulk of the *Glory* lay wallowing in the blue swells. Jenkins ran down the iron ladders to the deck.

The figure in the water was lying face down. What was stopping it from sinking was a pocket of air trapped in the back of its white boiler suit. As Jenkins watched, a long, dark shadow glided out of the blue nowhere of the sea.

The shark rolled, its belly flashing white in the sun. Oh, *no*, thought Jenkins. The figure in the water jerked and twitched. Jenkins found he was looking into a face.

It had dead-white skin, an open mouth, and eyes that looked at nothing at all. Last time he had seen them they had been shiny with violence and the feet, now limp in the blue sea, had gripped the deck as if with suckers. The face was the face of Lee.

Jenkins stared, not understanding.

Below the mouth was another mouth, wide and pink.

Sharks do not attack people in the water unless they are bleeding. Lee had been doing a lot of bleeding. Because before Lee had gone overboard, someone had cut his throat.

There were three sharks now, coming in from three sides. Lee's body danced in the water, and the cloud of what was left of his blood hid the shreds of the boiler suit. When the turbulence had stopped, there was nothing left.

Jenkins squeegeed the sweat from his forehead with the edge of his hand. Then he radioed the bridge and called for half ahead. He tried to feel regret, shame, horror. But the horror had been used up when he had seen the face. As for shame and regret, it had been Lee. Try as he would, he could not feel anything, except that the man had probably deserved it.

You are going native, he told himself.

Not so. Lee gone was a problem gone. What he felt now was curiosity.

The propeller churned. The crowd returned to its cooling rice. Jenkins called Johnny and gave him a bollocking about the state of the lifeboat, and told him to get it fixed. Johnny wheezed excuses. The *Glory of Saipan* resumed her slow, rusty corkscrew towards Yap.

Last time Nairn had felt like this he had been twelve years old, and his ma had just caught him smoking a Winfield behind the bike sheds at Woop Woop High. Ma had got shickered on Beefeater and told his dad, who had already been shickered on Ned Kelly. His dad had whaled the tar out of him, then and every time he had caught his eye for the next fortnight, to show him what he thought of little nicotine addicts. Nairn's principal memory, besides the mental and physical agony, was his father's smell, whiskey and tobacco mixed. It had been a confusing moment, one of the first of many.

So just now Nairn was keeping a profile lower than a scorpion's abdomen with regard to Irma. He was sitting in the messroom, picking at his burned milkfish, and trying not to catch the eye of Pete, on his left, or Irma on his right. And of course he was absolutely dying for a drink.

Irma pushed her plate away. 'So,' she said, grimly. 'It's started.'

'What's started?'

'First the tart. Now this Lee. They're cutting each other up.'

'Oh, I don't know,' said Pete diplomatically. 'Tarts get cut up in the like natural way of things. And that Lee bloke wasn't typical. He was a hard bastard, right?'

Nairn opened his mouth to say that he knew his engine-room hands, and that a bastard was what Lee had definitely been. Then he realized that that would look as if he was siding with Pete against Irma, which since the vodka incident was by no means politic. So he shrugged, and carried on eating.

Jenkins came in. 'Milkfish,' said Mrs Nairn, with what Nairn thought of as her shit-eating smile. '*Burned* milkfish.'

Jenkins said to Nairn, 'Who do you think killed Lee?'

Nairn picked a bone out of his milkfish. 'No idea.'

'He worked for you.'

Nairn put down his knife and fork. His heart was suddenly thumping. 'Are you trying to tell me I don't know what is going on in my own engine room?'

Jenkins said, 'I'm trying to find out who killed this man before he kills anyone else.'

Mrs Nairn said, 'I recall Edwin saying he used to argue with his mate, Ho.'

'Among others,' said Nairn, glancing at her resentfully.

'Good riddance,' said Pete.

It was quite obvious that none of them was interested. As long as they got paid, a murder here or there did not matter. It bore a disturbing resemblance to the way Jenkins had found himself thinking at the ship's rail. He manufactured a sandwich, went to the office and rang Lucy.

She answered, high and clear.

Jenkins said, 'Lee's dead.'

'I know.'

'Useful for you.'

'Sorry?' Her voice was blank and metallic.

'Who do you think killed him?'

'I told you. He was a psychopath. These people have enemies.'

This is getting me nowhere, thought Jenkins. 'Think,' he said.

'No idea.'

'Who burned Fung's face?'

'Lee, I guess.'

Jenkins said, 'You didn't tell me this.'

'It wasn't your business,' she said.

'From now on, it's my business,' said Jenkins.

'Maybe.' Still the blank voice. She was not going to help. Jenkins did not want to press her, in case the voice stayed blank, and all that warmth and complicity faded away, and he was alone again.

Not that being alone mattered, he told himself. What mattered was doing the job. In the back of his mind, the scratchy voices were tuning up to ask him why he felt so alone, and for whose benefit he was doing the job. Luckily, the telephone rang.

A voice said, 'Satellite on bridge.'

Jenkins got up. 'Thank you,' he said.

Down below, Lucy stretched out on her bed and gazed at the cream Formica deckhead. It had been a good day. Lee was no longer waiting in the dark, ready to kill her. The captain thought she was refusing to help him find a murderer. For the moment, he did not trust her. But that was just a phase. She could feel him starting to turn. He would come round.

Beyond the bridge windows, night had fallen, black as tar.

175

Jenkins picked up the receiver of the satellite telephone and said, 'Yes?'

'Captain,' said the smooth voice of Mr Chang. 'I am informed that Lee has been killed.'

Jenkins found he felt nervous. He said, 'Mr Chang, I have to tell you that this man is no loss.'

'So I am informed,' said Chang. 'I am grateful to you.' He laughed, a dry laugh. 'Direct action to cure disruption. It is just what I hoped of you.'

For a moment Jenkins floundered, with absolutely no idea what he was talking about. Then the truth burst like a magnesium flare. *He thinks it was me that killed Lee.*

'It is nice to think that you are acting on your initiative,' said Chang. 'But as you discovered after your incident at Zamboanga, initiative should be combined with control. I would not like to think you are making a habit of this type of drastic action.'

'A habit?'

'Twice, now.'

Chang's voice came into his mind, talking of Soares' signals to the pirates: *And then he died.*

He thinks I killed Soares, too.

'I appreciate that piracy is reprehensible, and that you are protecting my investment,' said Chang. 'But when I heard about Lee, I thought we should talk.'

When I heard about Lee.

Jenkins had total control of the *Glory*'s communications. Nobody had told Chang about Lee from the *Glory*'s bridge. So someone had a radio or a satellite phone of his own.

And that was why Chang had called, to jerk Jenkins' chain.

Jenkins' very short chain.

Chang said, 'Now you would like to talk to Rachel. We are growing most fond of Rachel.'

Smile, thought Jenkins. You're being watched.

Then Rachel said, 'Evening, Dad.'

He croaked, 'Are you all right?'

'Should I not be?' Her voice was homely, slightly husky, unfazed by captivity.

'No,' said Jenkins, thinking of telephones through bullet-proof glass screens, visiting time: talk, but don't touch. The voice had infused him with strength. 'What are you doing?'

'We're staying in Mr Chang's villa,' said Rachel. 'Me and Raymond. It's beautiful.'

'You and Raymond,' said Jenkins. The *Glory of Saipan* heaved a long, slow roll, and a coffee cup fell off the window ledge.

Rachel laughed. 'I told you,' she said. 'The staff have been instructed to keep us apart, in the name of Confucius. It's going really well. They've asked me to stay on. A month, maybe.'

A month would see the voyage out. Jenkins had a great urge to start shouting *Chang is a murdering bastard, get out of there!* But there was nothing to worry about, as long as he did his job. Instead he said, 'Watch your step.'

'I'm watching. How's the ship?'

'Lot of containers,' said Jenkins. 'Same old stuff.'

'Hurry up,' said Rachel. It was an old joke; Jenkins often talked to her from his ships, when Diana had been out, or in more recent years when Diana had been in, but not to be disturbed.

'I'll hurry,' said Jenkins. 'Won't your mother miss you?'

'No,' said Rachel, with surprising sharpness.

'A month is a long time.'

'Not long enough.'

So now all I have to do is toe the line, thought Jenkins. Still, I'm being well paid. The passengers are here because they want to be. Why should I do anything else?

Jenkins heard confused sounds at the other end. 'Lunchtime,' said Rachel. 'Must dash.' She switched off the phone.

Her father had sounded tired. But she did not think about him for long, because she was sitting at a lacquer table by the french windows of an enclosed terrace flanked by walls roofed with green tiles. Beyond the terrace the winter-brown valley stretched away to a distant blue fence of mountains. On the red lacquer table was a blue-and-white bowl containing tea. There was a pool, in which two carp dozed by a single white water-lily. Beside the pool, Raymond was talking on another telephone to the professor of archaeology at the Xian Institute, arranging a visit to the dig.

Perfection.

Raymond looked across at her and smiled his lovely smile. When they had arrived in Xian in his father's private jet, he had at first proposed drinking heavily and watching videos. But she had been firm with him and he had given in, the way she had found she could persuade him to give in. His better nature coming out, was how she saw it.

So he exercised his *guanxi* with the professor, and they ate lunch, and after lunch she pulled on a pair of old Levis and made him drive her to the dig.

It was a closed dig, so there were no tourists. But Mr Chang's *guanxi* unlocked all doors. There were mounds of sandy soil, a few trucks, many bicycles, an ant-like swarm of labourers in padded coats, and the professor.

The professor greeted them with a fawning humility that Raymond took for granted, but Rachel found ludicrous. She drank tea in the overheated site office, and accepted the tour the professor offered. During the tour he used a Mandarin suitable for children and foreigners, and explained the dig in terms that would have been patronizing to a party from a cruise ship. When the formalities were concluded, she said to Raymond, 'Let's go.'

'Sure,' said Raymond, with his easy, languid smile. He pulled out his telephone. 'Where to?'

'Look at the dig,' she said.

Raymond's eyes travelled out over the grids of tape and mounds of dun-coloured dust. 'We already saw it,' he said.

'Properly.'

Raymond sighed and slid his telephone back into his pocket. His father sometimes told him he was easily led. You did not have to be easily led to be led by Rachel. He followed her along the alley between the mounds and down a ramp to a face at which women were working with soft brushes. His shoes were getting dirty. He could hardly believe he was doing this.

It was just a wall of mud, thought Raymond. *Bor*ing. But Rachel did not look bored. She was talking to a woman, one of the diggers, technical stuff about the T'ang dynasty that he was only beginning to understand. The woman smiled, and passed Rachel her brush. Rachel smiled back, with that tiny lift of the eyebrow that weakened Raymond's knees every time he saw it, and began to work at the mud face. The woman she had taken the brush from giggled into her hand, half-shy, half-amazed.

And stopped.

Raymond found he was holding his breath.

Something marvellous was happening.

The dried mud under Rachel's brush had developed a ridge and a dome of buff clay: a nose and a mouth, with a forehead above, helmeted. The head of a warrior.

The warrior came out of the earth slowly, scowling as if furious at being woken from sleep. Raymond was no longer bored. He found another brush and worked alongside Rachel, not noticing the gouges the Xian grit made in his beautiful shoes, the black crescents forming under his correct fingernails. He could smell his own sweat, mixed with Rachel's, but he was not offended by it. Raymond owned two Maseratis, a string of racehorses, and more houses than he could remember the addresses of. Scrabbling with Rachel in that gritty trench near Xian, he was having the best day of his life.

The professor came and shook his head. 'So quickly?' he said. 'Very lucky.' He beamed at Rachel. Raymond found himself feeling prouder than he could remember feeling, ever.

It was only when it was too dark to see that they went back to the Lexus and he turned the bonnet for the villa. As he threaded the way through the trucks and bullock-carts and laden bicycles, she said, 'That was terrific. Can we go again?'

Raymond found himself surprised. It was almost as if she was asking permission. He was the one who felt he should be asking.

Be reasonable, he told himself. There were strata here. On top was his father, who had issued instructions that Rachel be kept here at all costs. Next there was him, Raymond, and below him, more or less nowhere in the order, came Rachel, the gweilo with whom Raymond was amusing himself at the moment.

Raymond ran it by in his mind. It did not seem to ring true.

He turned the long black car down the cobbled avenue and between the *feng-shui* lions flanking the villa's gates. Rachel put her hand on his knee and leaned over and kissed him on the cheek. Raymond found himself excited by the pressure of her hand and the softness of her lips, but also by the mere fact that she was there. His previous relationships had been unambiguous. The girls had been out for what they could get, and so had he, and usually they had both got what they wanted.

The weird thing about this gweilo was that she seemed to be *giving* him things all the time. He wanted to give her things in return, but there seemed to be so little she needed. It was confusing; the strata were becoming mixed up. Raymond felt himself to be at the bottom, down among the buried warriors, and the odd thing was that, bottom or top, it just did not bother him.

He got out of the car. A servant took it away for cleaning and polishing. Another servant said, 'A meeting with your honoured father, sir?'

He said to Rachel, 'Excuse me?'

'Of course,' she said. 'I've got work to do.'

Raymond's shoes were scuffed, so he threw them away. He showered, changed into a black Armani suit, and went into his father's office for a telephone conference with a PLA colonel on Hainan Island, where his father was opening a casino-and-girls venture. It would be an excellent earner. But as Raymond sat down in front of the spreadsheet and started to calculate the house percentages in the casino, he thought, If Rachel knew what I was doing, she would disapprove. Violently.

His father said, 'Raymond?'

'Father?'

'Are you having an interesting time with the girl?'

'Rachel?'

'The girl.'

Raymond knew better than to seem too interested. Family duty was important. Girls were a diversion, even Rachel. Girls could be got rid of, if they became a threat to duty.

'Sure,' he said. 'She's OK.'

'Good,' said Chang. There was dirt under two of Raymond's left-hand fingernails, he observed. What did this mean? 'I think she will be with us for a while. Her father is a very ruthless man.'

'Huh?' said Raymond.

'You will not mind looking after her?'

'I guess,' said Raymond, coolly, to hide the quickening of his heart. Rachel was some kind of bargaining chip, then. She faded a little in his mind as he leaned back in the big, soft chair. The soldier in the mud sank into perspective. It was only buried money. There was no reason to have gotten so excited about it. Someone else could dig it up.

He had the fleeting thought that Rachel would have disapproved of that thought, too. He tried not to give a damn. He was in control, and control was what mattered, whatever she said.

Somehow, he could not make it work.

BOOK III

Chapter One

Two thirsty days later, Jenkins left his cabin just after dawn and climbed the outside ladder for the sake of the breeze. It was a fine morning, still cool. The bridge wing rail was still wet with the night's dew. He ran his finger along and licked it. The liquid soothed the parched surface of his tongue, and left him wanting more. When he went into the bridge and made a half-cup of coffee, Johnny's bulging eyes followed him like the eyes of a child watching another child eat sweets.

'Datacom message for chief,' said Johnny.

Jenkins tore the paper from the datacom printer and slumped into the rattan chair. The only bonus about dehydration was the apathy it had brought to the cargo. Since Lee, everything had been quiet.

Beyond the windows, the rusty V of the *Glory*'s bow nosed towards the pyramid of clouds over the volcanic stubs of Yap. God knew why Chang's people had arranged for the parts to be delivered down here, a thousand miles south of the track to San Francisco.

He glanced at the GPS. They were coming up to the rendezvous position. He picked up the glasses and scanned the sea ahead for the launch. There was only the shifting blue glitter of the waves. He wondered how the launch's crew had been squared. Presumably Chang had contacts on Yap who would not think it remarkable to make a delivery to a ship festooned with Chinese emigrants. He unrolled the datacom message.

PARTS UNAVAILABLE YAP DIVERT TO SAIPAN AVAILABLE AT THREE DAYS FROM THIS DATE.

He read it twice, climbed out of the rattan chair, waded over to the console and dialled the chief's cabin.

Nairn said, 'Whaddya mean, not available?'

'Not available till Saipan. Three days. Unless we can get any more speed?'

'Not if you want to get across the rest of the Pacific.'

Jenkins said carefully, so as not to offend him, 'I don't suppose it's possible to make any more water?'

'Listen,' said Nairn. 'We've been using the bloody seed corn. That watermaker's completely knackered. As of today I've got enough to heat my fuel, and that's it.'

'So what are the options?'

'Quarter-litre a person a day.' Nairn said it as if defying Jenkins to find fault.

'No good.'

'I'm not asking, I'm telling. You want more, make it yourself.'

Jenkins put the telephone down. A quarter-litre. A coffee cupful. For three days, minimum, till they got to Saipan.

He dialled Lucy. He was falling into the habit of accepting her advice on passenger matters.

'It doesn't sound good,' she said. 'There are city people down here. They won't understand. They'll go crazy.'

'How crazy?'

'Listen,' said Lucy. 'There was a guy in the hold selling water for ten dollars a pint. Another guy tried to kill him. I had to tell Ho, so Ho could stop it. But there's only one of Ho.'

Beyond the bridge windows, the sky was blue as a baby's eyes, decorated with white puffs of fairweather clouds.

Lucy said, 'I thought we were near Yap. They must have water there.'

'Sure they do,' said Jenkins, with irony, and hung up.

That had been the attraction of working for Orient Line. Your life ran in grooves, cadetship to retirement. That was why his father had slotted him into the Merchant Navy. At the age of fourteen, he had been given to riding motorbikes on the Dorset lanes; why not? There was never any traffic, and even fourteen-year-olds needed to get around.

Until one day he had wrapped himself round a flock of

sheep, and landed up in hospital, and missed the Dartmouth exams, and arrived in the magistrate's court instead. Fined fifty quid. Disqualified for four years. It had not been worth going for the Navy again, in his father's view; you needed a sense of responsibility for the Navy.

So he had joined the Merchant Navy, done the responsible thing. And then he had married Diana, and his father had had his doubts. But Jenkins was not listening to his father any more. Jenkins had worked out that all that Navy stuff had been a load of codswallop, and so had the discreet fuss they had made about Diana. Jenkins had started thinking for himself. That was why he had blown up the pump boat in the Zamboanga Strait.

Just at the moment, his job was to bring his cargo safe across the Pacific. Probably Chang would not mind some rioting, a few deaths, even.

Jenkins thought about the passengers: the old man with his t'ai chi, Lin, daughter of Fung, the mah-jongg players. It would be the innocent who got hurt.

He looked out of the window at the waterless sky. Then he picked up the telephone and rang Nairn. He said, 'What state are the double bottoms in?'

'What state do you expect them to be in?'

'Cleanable?'

'Within reason,' said Nairn, grudgingly. 'Why?'

The double bottoms were tanks between the ship's bottom and the floor of the hold. Normally, they were used for sea-water ballast. 'I want to put twenty tons of fresh water down there,' said Jenkins.

'Where are you going to get twenty tons of fresh water?'

'Yap,' said Jenkins, and hung up.

You could lose the lot, he thought. Entering Yap with this cargo was illegal. Hiding the cargo was even more illegal. So far, everything had been legal.

Chang's sort of legality; the sort that could take a couple of murders for granted.

Chang would rather some of them died than that all of them be arrested.

Jenkins steeled his mind. He would not consult Chang. He would be risking arrest; risking Rachel's life. But he knew what Rachel would have said if he had asked her to choose between people dying of thirst and her own safety. Chang would find out, of course. But by then it would be done.

There was nothing like a *fait accompli*.

He rang Lucy. He said, 'We'll do it.'

'We will?' There was a sort of purr in her voice. 'Go alongside real *land*?'

'We'll be alongside three or four hours. We'll be fine. Unless someone does something stupid. I'd like you to arrange that.'

She said, 'Sure. And while we're alongside, I'll buy you a drink.'

'Sure you will,' said Jenkins. There was no time for amusing jokes. The Yap channel was a slot in the reef with the tide sluicing past it, and it needed thinking about. 'Come up and get the loudhailer.'

The water queue began to form six hours early, and the passengers drew the last of what was in the tanks. Below decks, Coke and Seven-Up had been selling at fifteen dollars a can. The extra ration knocked the bottom out of the market. It bred a mood almost of gaiety in the passengers. Fung watched with equanimity as one of the deckhands climbed into the cab of the gantry crane and the containers blotted out the sky and descended into his courtyard. Chiu, rinsing out her underwear for the first time in four days, watched with a professional eye as the deck passengers filtered into the hold. They were below the waterline there, so the heat was not disastrous. It had been announced that any problems would mean immediate return to China. To reinforce the announcement, the watertight doors between the holds were closed and guarded by two-man teams consisting of one crew member with a baseball bat, and one of the muscular little Chinese from the aft end of the hold. Chiu found this all satisfactory. Most satisfactory of all, she had managed to attract the attention of stout Mr Wong, a household-furnishings store proprietor from the second courtyard, who had contrived to get his wife and two children shut in a different hold. She had beckoned Mr Wong into her cubicle, and had unbuckled his trousers. Mr Wong moaned. 'Silence!' hissed Chiu, dropping to her knees and sliding down the zipper with her teeth. 'Obey orders, or we perish!'

It was good to be back at work.

On the bridge, Jenkins picked up the VHF mike, tuned to the port channel, and said, 'Yap harbourmaster, this is *Glory of Saipan*. Request alongside berth to take on water.'

'*Glory of Saipan*,' said a large voice. 'Come right in.'

The *Glory of Saipan* moved round the western point of the island, her funnel spewing a black plume into the clear Trade. The reef slid by, blue shading to turquoise into brown. Jenkins stood dry-mouthed at the bridge windows, squinting down the azimuth, muttering directions to the quartermaster. Yap was your hot, wet tropical island, with inhabitants who slept a lot, and a couple of hotels catering for divers seeking visions of paradise on the reef. Nobody paid much attention to anything except the reef fish and the inside of their eyelids. If you had to go alongside anywhere with a cargo like this, Yap was the spot.

The shallows were dotted with crisp white dive boats, the scalloped edges of their awnings fluttering in the breeze. A brown child was playing in a catamaran built of sheets of corrugated iron.

Sweating with heat and fear, Jenkins lined up the leading lights and steamed through the slot in the reef. By noon, the *Glory of Saipan* was tied up alongside a white concrete quay.

The Customs and Immigration authorities of the Federated States of Micronesia were led by a chocolate-coloured Melanesian bulging out of a pair of pink shorts, carrying his official papers in a fringed coconut-leaf handbag. He accepted a San Miguel in the ship's office, blotted the sweat from his fat cheeks with a copy of the *Herald Tribune*, and thumbed listlessly through the crew's passports. 'How long you staying?'

'Four hours,' said Jenkins.

'Too bad,' said Customs and Immigration. 'Barbecue tonight at the Shark Bay Hotel. Where you bound?'

'Oakland. Breaker's yard.'

Customs and Immigration squinted at the rust. In harbour, without the breeze, the air in the *Glory*'s accommodation was all but unbreathable. Jenkins wondered how he could fail to smell the people in the hold. 'Rather you than me,' he said. He drank his beer in one gigantic swallow, heaved himself up and led his team out of the office.

Jenkins watched him on to the dock. A couple of men were unrolling a fire-brigade-sized hose from a stopcock on the quay. Nairn came out on deck, blinked his watery eyes against the white glare off the concrete and started shouting peevishly at a couple of oilers. The hose swelled. The water started coming aboard.

Down in her cabin, Lucy checked her lipstick in the mirror and adjusted her hat. Then she walked out into the alleyway and put her head round Jer's door.

She said, 'Wish me luck.'

Jer's yellow eyes blinked at her from the bed. He said, 'What are you going to do?'

'Something stupid. Give him a push.'

Jer's teeth were white in the ochre of his face. He took her hand. 'Cool it, little sister,' he said. 'Rock the boat too far, and you'll fall out.'

Lucy said, 'I'll look after my department. You look after yours.'

He sighed. 'It is only because we get on so well.'

'Yellowbelly.'

They both laughed. He said, 'When pushing, be sure not to lose your own balance.'

She said, 'Save it for the karate students,' and closed the door.

Jenkins was in his cabin, turning Rachel's tropical snow-storm in his hands, and trying not to think about the danger he was putting her in. The heat was appalling. There was a knock on the door, and Lucy came in.

Jenkins got up quickly. This was not Lucy in black T-shirt and jeans and dirty feet. This Lucy was wearing a white linen dress that stopped well above the knee, and a wide straw hat, and low-heeled shoes that even Jenkins could see had been expensive. She said, 'Are you coming?'

'Coming where?'

'Ashore. I'll buy you a drink. I said I would.'

Jenkins said, 'You're crazy.' But at the same time, he was thinking, Nice legs, too.

She frowned. 'I am?'

'You haven't got a passport. If anyone sees you –'

'Ah,' said Lucy. 'I see. You don't want to come. Fine.' She smiled.

Jenkins found himself wrong-footed. He could not make himself ignore the fact that she was beautiful. 'Can't be done,' he said, with genuine regret. 'Do you want a beer here?'

She lifted an eyebrow, her eyes flashing like go lights. 'Not really,' she said, and left.

Jenkins shook up the tropical snowstorm again. There was nothing he would have liked better than to step out of the squalor of the *Glory* and walk down with Lucy and have a drink at the Shark Bay.

In an ideal world.

His telephone rang.

'Bridge,' said Pete's voice. 'I, er, I think you should get up here. Quick.'

Jenkins went out of his cabin and up the stairs. Pete was on the inshore wing of the bridge. He turned as he heard Jenkins' footsteps. The fleshy face had fallen into creases of puzzled displeasure. He pointed over the side.

The quay was an empty white pan of coral dust, sizzling under the sun. Except for one figure: a slim woman in a wide straw hat and a white linen skirt that stopped well above the knee, handbag held over the shoulder by a finger, stepping delicately over the water hose and walking towards the gate.

Jenkins was already on the stairs, grabbing his passport from the office safe, running down the echoing steel gangway and on to the quay.

He caught her as she was going through a rusty chainlink gate with a much-battered plywood sign that read NO OUTER ISLANDS ALLOWED IN – AUTHORIZED PEOPLE ONLY – KEEP OUT!! When she saw him she said, 'Captain,' mildly surprised, as if they had met by chance at the Hong Kong Yacht Club.

'For Christ's sake,' he said. The sweat was running through the dust on his face. 'Where do you think you're going?'

'I hear there's quite a nice hotel here,' she said. 'I'm going to get a drink.'

Jenkins thought, Three hundred and seventy people alongside. Rachel in Xian, hostage for their safe arrival. Quite a nice hotel.

She was walking on, through the gates, past a stained cement building that bore the faded legend FEDERATED STATES OF MICRONESIA – DEPARTMENT OF THE INTERIOR.

'Come back,' he said. 'Now. Or I'll take you.'

She smiled. She said, 'That wouldn't be wise.' She was looking past him.

'Hi,' said a big voice. Jenkins turned. It was Customs and Immigration, standing with the parts of him that would fit in a wedge of shade. 'Help you folks?'

Jenkins was loose-bowelled with horror. Oh, Rachel.

'We were looking for a drink,' said Lucy, giving him a smile that lit up the shadow under her hat. 'A decent drink.'

'We should get back to the ship,' said Jenkins.

Customs and Immigration looked at him, then at Lucy. 'Nah,' he said. 'It's hot. You relax, take the lady, get a beer.' He pointed down the road. 'Shark Bay's right down there. I'd come with you, only I have work to do.'

Lucy put her hand in Jenkins' arm. 'Why, thank you, suh,' she said, Shanghai Southern belle. 'Have a nice day.'

'You're welcome,' said Customs and Immigration.

Jenkins could feel his benevolent eyes on their backs as Lucy led him stony-faced down the road and into the trees. It would have looked odd if he had not let himself be led. Oddness would mean questions.

In the shade, he said, 'Do you realize how stupid that was?'

She did not look at him. She walked on, neat and under control, her fingers light in the crook of his arm. 'Come ashore for a drink, by special permission of the Customs and Immigration,' she said. 'Absolutely no problem.'

'No.'

She smiled up at him from under the hat, her eyes lit with

mischief. 'Customs is watching,' she said. 'And they'll be watching from the hotel. Act normal.'

Sweat rolled down his face. They were walking under green coconut palms on concrete that was not rusty and did not roll. The passengers were below hatches. The tanks were filling.

Jenkins was out of his depth.

The hotel was a white wooden box with a green corrugated-iron roof and a palm-shaded verandah suspended over a creek. When he opened the door for her, the air conditioning lapped over him like cool water. Three or four couples were sitting at tables, and somewhere Jimmy Buffett was singing 'Margaritaville'. The Australian behind the bar smiled welcomingly. Beyond the window, down the brown alley of water between the mangroves, was a view of the coral-white quay with the rust-coloured bulk of the *Glory of Saipan* alongside. It might as well have been on a different planet.

Lucy gave a small sigh, sat down in a bamboo chair and crossed her legs. Jenkins sat opposite her, rigid with apprehension. She raised a hand to the barman, who was watching her with admiration. She said, 'Do you have a bottle of champagne?'

'French or Californian?'

'French.'

'Moët,' said the barman.

'Fine.'

The champagne arrived quickly. She paid the barman. When he had poured, she took a sip and closed her eyes. 'I am really sick of that ship.' She took note of Jenkins' face, wooden and shining. She smiled at him, a smile not tough, like the one she used on the ship, but almost affectionate. 'Thank you for joining me. It really is all right, you know.'

Jenkins gulped champagne and blinked away the icy little needles. It really was not all right.

She rolled the cool glass on her cheek. 'I tell you what I really hate about that ship,' she said. 'You can't talk about ordinary things. Like what's the weather like, or what shall we have for lunch, or you've got nice eyes.' She let her eyes rest on his.

Jenkins looked at his hands. He said, 'Or bring a bottle of Moët.' He clung to his churlishness like an anchor, because the wine was warming him, and he could feel himself drifting towards her.

She shrugged. 'We drink quite a lot of this in Shanghai.'

The Australian barman had come over. He was large and blond and fresh-faced, with weak spaniel eyes and a deep small-boat tan. 'You folks off that ship?' he said.

Jenkins grunted.

'Sure,' said Lucy.

'Out of Hong Kong, right?'

'That's it,' said Lucy. 'This is the captain. I'm his wife.' She levelled her green eyes at Jenkins.

Jenkins wished more than he had ever wished anything that she would shut up. But he also felt a ludicrous urge to smirk, like a child playing truant from school.

The barman was staring at him, frowning. Suddenly his face cleared. '*Powderfinger*,' he said, snapping his fingers. 'I'm Harry McFee. Remember?'

The blood seemed suddenly to have drained away from Jenkins' head. 'No,' he said, more curtly than he intended.

'Start of Macao race last year,' said the barman. 'You blew us away, right?'

'I don't remember,' said Jenkins stiffly, averting his face.

'Yeah,' said the barman. 'I was crewing for a bloke, mate of yours, Jeremy Selmes. We were coming up on you, you luffed the hell out of us, put us right over the line. Christ, Jeremy was pissed off. Been sailing this year?'

'No.' Any minute now, he was going to sit down. Jenkins remembered him, all right. He had met Diana in the Yacht Club bar. In fact, he had got on really well with Diana, according to her.

The barman was finding Jenkins standoffish. 'How's old Jeremy?' he said. You didn't get a lot of company on Yap.

'Fine.'

'Small Pacific,' said the barman. 'It's what I always say. Where are you headed for?'

Voices sounded outside. The door opened, and three men

came in. They were wearing white polo shirts, long blue shorts, deck shoes and deep suntans. They were all talking at once.

Jenkins said, too quickly, 'You'd better go and look after your customers.'

He saw the barman's face stiffen. He knows he's being got rid of, he thought. I've offended him. He wanted to leave, now, immediately. But there was still three-quarters of a bottle of champagne left. They had drawn enough attention to themselves already, without leaving behind pints of the most expensive wine in the Pacific.

The barman grinned, an insincere, professional grin. 'Captain,' he said. 'Mrs Jenkins.'

When he had gone, Lucy said, 'You knew him?'

'Friend of a friend.'

'Relax,' she said. 'Having drinks is normal.'

Jenkins nodded. They were Captain Jenkins and his wife, talking quietly in a private corner. Customs and Immigration believed it. Maybe the barman had forgotten Diana. Calm. Think about something else. He finished his glass. He said, 'Why did you want to leave China?'

She took the stem of her glass between her pointed fingers. She said, 'Couldn't stand it any more.'

And she could afford champagne. Jenkins said, 'I thought the ruling classes had a great life.'

'There are prices you pay.'

'What do you mean?'

She would not meet his eye. She took a sip from her glass, as if gathering strength. She said, 'I told you. I came to Shanghai when I was seven. I went to stay with my Aunt Daisy, in her apartment.' She frowned. It was difficult to get used to the way her face expressed emotion: Chinese features, Western body language. 'Aunt Daisy wasn't pleased to see me. Hard to blame her, really. She'd been beaten up by the Red Guards because my mother, her sister, had emigrated. Her husband was a professor at Shanghai University but they sent him off to a farm in the north and he caught TB and died. All my mother's fault, she thought. Now we were back, she took it out on me. I told you about that pink bedroom? No pink bedrooms in Shanghai. I shared a little one, maybe the size of my cabin on the ship, with my cousins Chee and Yin. Not nice girls. Not to me, anyway. They decided that if their mother didn't like her sister, there was no need for them to like their cousin. So they told me my face was too pink and my eyes were too green and my feet were too big. And they stole all my clothes. And to piss me off they spoke Cantonese, which I didn't understand properly, because I had been brought up to speak Mandarin. And of course in America the kids had called me a slant, and a Chink. So I began to feel I didn't fit in anywhere at all. It was a lonely feeling. Sorry,' she said, 'this is boring.'

Jenkins shook his head. The champagne was working. He had forgotten to be worried. It seemed like weeks since anyone had told him the truth about anything. This sounded true.

She said, 'So when something like that happens to you, you have to decide to sink or swim. It could be the East, I don't know. But you have to work out what's inside you. And if you're hollow, you fall to pieces.' She looked at Jenkins. 'Does that make sense?'

It made sense.

She was looking at the bubbles rising in the glass, as if each one were a crystal ball in which she was seeing her past. 'My mother died. The cousins were using me as, well, as a maid. I decided that if I didn't learn anything, I'd be a maid for ever. So I went to school and I went to university. That is, I made my cousin send me.'

'Made her?'

'I told her I'd denounce her if she didn't do as I asked. She had stuff to hide; one of the girls used to steal oil from the garage where she worked. You get good at manipulating people.' She looked at Jenkins. 'As you have noticed. So anyway, I was a physicist, and I had good *guanxi* everywhere. Not just in the university. In business, and with political cadres. Climbing the ladder.' She made a face. 'Then I blew it.'

'How?'

'Fell in love.' She emptied the glass. Jenkins filled it again. 'Piao was his name. We met at the university. At a lecture given by Isaiah Berlin. He was a nice guy. Thin. Pianist.

Nice hands. Funny. Loved politics. Hated politicians. We had a daughter in 1988, Little Lucy, he called her. Then in 1989 there was all that business, we were faxing news, poems all over the world, and he was in Tiananmen Square, and those assholes picked him up. They picked me up too. They sent him to a camp in Manchuria, making automobile jacks for the Western market. And they kept me in jail for a while. I left Little Lucy with the neighbours. When I got out of jail, they told me she had died. Cot death. I think she was hungry.' Again the grimace. 'And Piao fell into the rolling mill.' She let her hands fall on the table. 'People dying is the only thing *guanxi* won't fix. Sad, huh? So I decided to get out. I was doing, well, sensitive work, so I couldn't get a visa. But I took it real slow – five years, it took. So I used *guanxi*, and got on that ship. And here I am. I guess it's the kind of thing that happens to everyone.'

'No,' said Jenkins. Losing a child was not the kind of thing that happened to everyone.

'What do you mean?'

He could not talk about Bill. 'I went to sea when I was sixteen. Nice safe life.'

'You're working for Hugh Chang. That's not safe.'

'You can get desperate.' *You have to work out what's inside you. If you're hollow, you fall to pieces.* So what was inside him?

Diana. Twenty-odd years at sea.

There must be something else.

'Sounds like the same thing,' she said. 'You get a chance, you take it.' Their hands were an inch apart on the table.

It might have been the champagne. But it seemed only logical that their fingers should touch, and lock.

Jenkins thought, How did that happen?

Oh, *shit*.

Chapter Two

He pulled his hand away. He was the captain, and she was the cargo. He poured more champagne. It was time to leave.

The Australians at the bar had called for another round. It was not their first, or even their fourth. Now, one of them was taking Polaroid snaps of the others. There was heavy laughter. A voice that travelled said, 'What do we do for a woman on this island?'

'Bring the wife, Len,' said the barman, with a conciliatory grin.

Len ignored him. He had long flat cheeks and a bullock's eye. He allowed the eye to stray out of the window, where a woman dressed in an indigo lap-lap was walking down the concrete road under the coconut trees, her brown breasts rolling. 'That one's too fuckan huge,' he said.

Marv was the smallest of the four men at the bar. Marv had freaked this morning when he had come nose-to-nose with a manta ray off the reef, and he was anxious to worm his way back into Len's good graces. He looked round at Dozzie and Lurch, to gather them in. He said, 'What about that little Chinky number, eh?'

They had all noticed them, talking quietly in the corner, the big bloke in jeans and a tie-dye T-shirt, with black hair going on grey and a tired, beat-up-looking face; and the Chinese or anyway half-Chinese woman with him. She was tasty, all right. She had a nice pair, and decent legs. But she looked too crisp for Yap. Too . . . well, *grown up*, Chrissakes. It would be like shagging a lady lawyer.

But Len and his mates were five beers up, and this was the wild Pacific, where anything went.

Len took a draw of his San Mig, leaned back with his elbows on the bar, fixed his eyes on the straw hat, and said, 'My favourite fabric.'

Nobody listened. He said it louder: 'My *favourite* fabric.'

The hum of conversation in the bar faltered and stilled. 'And a *lovely* colour,' said Len. 'My *favourite* colour. Yellow.'

His friends were smirking now.

'Yeah,' said Len, walking stiff-legged across the room and sitting down at the table beside Lucy. 'Lovely little piece of yellow velvet.'

Jenkins looked at the big, stupid face with the hostile eyes and the long jaw. The warmth and intimacy had gone. He found he was suddenly covered in freezing sweat. He made himself raise a gentle eyebrow at Lucy. He said, 'Perhaps we should go.'

Lucy nodded. She stood up. Jenkins stood up. Len frowned. 'Woz zis?' he said. He brought up a big brown hand and reached for Lucy's right breast.

A lot of things happened.

McFee saw the Chinese woman's fingers jab at Len's eyes. Len bellowed, and hit Jenkins. Jenkins hit Len. Len's head hit the wall with a sound like a coconut falling on a rock. McFee thought, Nice one, Len, spoilt that snotbasket Jenkins' run ashore. Then, more rationally, What about my bloody furniture? But by that time he was halfway over the bar, and a lot more had happened.

Len was on his back on the floor with blood running out of his left eye. Marv and the other two were baying like hounds, weaving towards the tall man and the Chinese woman. Jenkins was pulling out the table for the Chinese woman, so she did not have to step over Len. He looked as if he had a bad smell under his nose. Snotty bastard, thought McFee.

Marv grabbed a San Mig bottle from a table, and shouted in his shrill, stupid voice, 'Die, you bastard.'

'Don't do that,' said McFee mildly, and took it out of his hand. Bottles were overdoing it.

Marv looked surprised, but gave the bottle up, and loped over to the table to stand beside Dozzie. Jenkins grabbed the edge of the marble slab and heaved. 'Nooo!' shouted McFee.

Too late.

The table went over: a big slab of Carrara, hauled at fantastic expense halfway round the world.

It took Marv and Dozzie on their bare brown shins and slid down to their feet, rending skin. Then it broke into five pieces.

Lurch had managed to jump back in time. He felt suddenly nervous. His mates were on the ground, so it looked like two against one, which was not fair. This bloke had a nasty play-for-keeps look to him. He was . . . well, *violent*. He did not want to get hurt. Luckily, he landed in McFee's arms. McFee put his arms round him, trapping his fists. Feeling himself safe, Lurch began assuming pugnacious attitudes.

'Thank you,' said Jenkins. 'We'll be off.'

'What about my fucking table?' yelled McFee over Lurch's shoulder.

Jenkins pointed at Len. 'Ask him,' he said.

'Goodbye,' said Mrs Jenkins.

'Hey!' said McFee. 'Who do you think –'

The door opened and closed, admitting a blast of wet heat. They were gone. Just like that. Ponce bloody Jenkins. Trash the joint and piss off. This wasn't a bloody yacht race. Who was going to pay for the table, McFee would have liked to know.

He let go of Lurch.

Then he said, 'Fuck me.'

Because he had just remembered something.

There had been a party after the Macao race. He did not remember whether or not Jenkins had been there. But there had been a woman, a woman whom Jeremy had introduced as Mrs Jenkins.

And that Mrs Jenkins had been a brassy blonde, not a tasty Chinese with green eyes. Only a year ago. The barman knew damn well that you didn't get rid of a wife and find another in twelve months. Plus there was another thing. When the Chinese babe had paid for the drinks, there had been no rings on her fingers.

Which all added up to a new marble table, thought McFee.

He said to Lurch, 'Gimme that Polaroid.'

Lurch handed him a Nikon with a Polaroid back. OK, snotbasket, thought McFee. Here is where we rain on your fucking parade.

The tall man and the woman in the hat were walking down the pale road under the trees. Backs to him. Shit, thought McFee. Back views are no fucking good. He raised the camera to his eye, opening his mouth to shout, make them look round.

Then he had a bit of luck.

The woman stopped. The man stopped. They turned to face each other. They were an easy hundred yards away, so McFee could not hear what they were saying. But he could see, all right, through the long lens of the Nikon from where he was standing in the shadows of the hotel porch.

The woman reached up and put her hands one on either side of the tall man's head and pulled it down to hers. Her lips touched his, light as a feather. The two heads were silhouetted against the fresh tropical gleam of the mangroves behind them.

The camera whined, ejecting the prints. And there they were, Jenkins and not-Mrs-Jenkins. Fix you later, thought McFee. No point in chasing you on to your ship. Hit you where it hurts. And he went back to start clearing up the mess.

Lucy and Jenkins walked back to the ship quickly and in silence. At the bottom of the gangway, they stepped on to the rusty steel plating and walked back to the real world.

Jenkins had forgotten the stink, the bitter reek of bilge and old oil and human sweat and stale cigarettes, overlaid with sewage and cooking smoke from the containers. He went to the bridge and with shaking fingers dialled around the ship until he found Nairn.

Nairn said, 'Any minute.'

'Speed it up,' said Jenkins, and slammed the phone down on Nairn's shrill protests.

The soles of his shoes stuck to the deck as he walked to

the bridge window. He had blown it. The authorities would arrive in the shape of the police and Immigration, and Rachel would be dead.

But the sun glared down on the empty quay, and nobody came to arrest a Caucasian man and a Chinese woman who had been in a fight. Ten minutes later the telephone rang. Nairn's voice said, 'What are you waiting for?'

Jenkins gave the order to cast off. Slowly, the *Glory of Saipan* unstuck herself from the quay, nosed into the channel and crawled through the gap in the reef. Outside, Jenkins turned the ship's nose to port. Then, limp as a rag, he sat down at the satcom and banged off a new order for watermaker parts to arrive in Saipan.

McFee was also sending a message. *This is your mate Jenkins*, it said. *Tell him he owes me $1,500 for the table.* He put it in an envelope with the Polaroid, and addressed it to Jeremy Selmes in Hong Kong. It went out on the evening plane.

The sun fell into the sea, and Yap and McFee inched below the horizon. The deck-lights came on and the gantry engines started to moan as they shifted the containers back into their courtyard formation. Leaning on the rail of the deck aft of the bridge, Jenkins watched the figures spread over the decks again, the flutter of washing on lines as the passengers took advantage of the new water ration. It was three days to Saipan. There would be no excuse for the parts not to be there. And from Saipan, it would be a clear run across the Pacific.

Barring accidents.

He waited until the messroom was empty and made himself a tuna sandwich. Then he went up to the bridge. Pete was there, leaning against the rail of the wing.

'Bit of breeze,' he said, when he saw Jenkins. 'Bloody 'ot.'

'Cargo OK?' said Jenkins.

'Two heat exhaustion,' said Pete. 'Mrs Nairn's got 'em fixed up.' He coughed, and lit one of his infrequent cigarettes, screwing his face up against the glare. 'Er,' he said. 'Not my place and all that. But she's a bit pissed off with you.'

'Really?' said Jenkins.

'Reckons you're fraternizing,' said Pete. 'Going ashore with that Lucy. Nice bird.'

Jenkins nodded. He had done a bloody stupid thing, and got away with it by the skin of his teeth. But there was more to it than that. All these years he had been part of something. Now he felt detached; on his own. *If you are hollow, you smash.*

He went to his sweltering cabin and took a shower. The new water had a a rusty tinge, and smelled of chlorine. When he came out of the shower, he was immediately sweating again. He sat on his bunk and took Rachel's tropical-island snowstorm from the ledge of his porthole. He turned it upside down. The little flakes floated down among the palm fronds. He thought of Rachel, her confident, controlled voice calling from the lion's den. Rachel was inside him.

But that was all. The rest of it was guilt, regret for things that had already happened and could not be changed. All those years in the groove that led nowhere; Bill, and what had come after he had died. Was it enough?

The tropical snowstorm was sweaty in his palm. He put it back on the shelf. It would bloody well have to be enough. He lay down on the bunk and fell into a hot, uneasy sleep.

Chapter Three

When Mrs Leung had married Mr Leung, she had known that he was a man of independent mind, given to fits of rage. Indeed, this had been one of the points that had decided her in his favour.

Leung was a tailor, working in competition with a thousand-odd other tailors in his twenty blocks of Shanghai. The competition was by no means fair, and racketeering was common. On one occasion, when a freelance enforcer had demanded two free suits as insurance against the shop mysteriously burning down that night, Leung had sent the enforcer away with his lips sewed together with button thread by way of a hint that in future he should keep his insurance policies to himself. It was this independence of mind that had made him think it would be wise to seek out Mr Chang's emigration agent, and led to the establishment of Mr and Mrs Leung and their six-year-old daughter Ma in the forward port-hand corner of number two hold.

Ma was a great one for her dolls. On the afternoon of the day following their departure from Yap, she was giving them supper. Big Doll was complaining to No Nose about the quality of the rice. No Nose was keeping quiet, because if Ma did both voices, her throat ached. Actually, her throat was aching anyway, and there were other sensations in her, not aches but unpleasant none the less. Big Doll went on complaining that the rice had not been white, but brownish, with a nasty metallic taste, and a hint of something that might have been lavatory cleaner, or even (said Big Doll, who had been known to exaggerate) actual lavatories.

Leung sat there watching his daughter, his energies

directed by his morning t'ai chi, his fingers moving over a length of canvas he was stitching into a tent for Mrs Wa, next door but one in the shadowy, airless hold; undignified work, but work. He was very proud of Ma. In America she would get a good job in a bank, or possibly as a lady ranch owner of the kind he had seen played in Westerns by Barbara Stanwyck. And she was right about the rice. The rice had been evil to look at and vile to taste. Now that the cooks were no longer getting paid for the rations, it was only natural that they would be taking their revenge.

He looked down at the small, regular stitches of the seam he was sewing. Three more, then the corner –

There was a most unpleasant sound. When he looked up, Ma was sitting still, her eyes bulging. Big Doll and No Nose were little islands in the lake of vomit in front of her. She said, 'Bad rice,' and began to cry.

The ship's bell rang twice. It was four o'clock, time for the afternoon rice. The fact scarcely registered with Leung, because he was clambering to his feet shouting for his wife, and his wife was coming round the canvas partition from the neighbours', and seeing poor Ma and the pool of vomit, and he was explaining to her what had happened and that it was the fault of the rice, and she was telling him that as a man he knew nothing of cooking rice, for as any fool could see the problem was not the rice but the water it had been cooked in, and the neighbours were giving their opinions. And pretty soon there was a dense crowd round Ma, and each of its members was yelling, and the blood was jumping in Leung's veins.

So while his wife cleared up the mess and made Ma lie down and brewed her some soothing tea with a drop of decent water left over from yesterday's ration, Leung rose on wings of fury to the deck.

The light at the top of the companion ladder hit him like a fist in his face. The containers stretched away in front of him, ending in the rust-and-white wall of the accommodation. At the base of the accommodation, the poisoners had erected their cauldrons of filth. A disorderly queue was forming. One of the poisoners was actually smiling.

The smile was the final straw. With a howl of fury, Leung

waded through the queue and clambered up the steps. The chief cook smiled at him insultingly. Ma's poor little face rose in Leung's mind. Seizing the cauldron, he wrested it from its stand and rolled it across the deck, spilling the odd, brownish rice on to the rusty plating. There was a moan of disappointment from the queue. One of the cooks pushed him. Leung took a swing with his fist. Two men tried to restrain him. Assisted by three friends from the mah-jongg school he frequented, he fought them off. Within twenty seconds, the area of the container tops just aft of the accommodation was a mass of fighting bodies.

Jenkins had stood the midnight-to-four watch, and worked all morning. Now he was in a thick afternoon sleep.

In the beginning of his sleep was a surf of voices. Suddenly Jenkins found himself awake. He rolled out of bed and stumbled through the fetid air to the bridge.

Rodriguez was up there, crooning 'Love Me Tender' through a yawn, directing the *Glory*'s rusty nose at a metallic blue horizon. He looked at Jenkins, jerked his thumb aft, at the source of the noise, and grinned. 'Bery big fuss,' he said.

Jenkins said, 'Get Miss Moses on the bridge,' grabbed the loudhailer and ran on to the bridge wing. There seemed to be a crowd on the containers, yelling abuse, with here and there the little vortex of a fight. There was cheering. A small, stick-like figure had thrown one of the rice cauldrons over the side. Several people were stamping in unison on one of the containers, producing a sound like war drums.

Lucy came on to the bridge. She was wearing her black T-shirt and jeans, and her eyes when she looked at Jenkins held no trace of yesterday's intimacy.

Jenkins said, 'What the hell's all this about?'

'There's a girl poisoned by bad water in the hold.'

'There's nothing wrong with the water.'

'You'll have to prove it.'

Jenkins looked down at the groups on the containers. The deck for the cauldrons was like a stage, 'Public tasting,' he said.

She nodded. 'We'll need Ho.'

'Ho?'

'Some of those people only trust Ho,' she said.

'Then fetch him.'

Jenkins called Mrs Nairn, and sent her to the sick girl. As he put the phone down, Lucy came back with Ho. Ho's dark eyes moved round the bridge without curiosity, checking its possibilities for violence. He was only a man in a white boiler suit, but he looked as out of place as a chainsaw on a coffee table.

Jenkins said, 'Watch this.' He went to the bridge lavatory, drew a glass off the cold tap and brought it on deck. 'Bloody awful colour,' he said, eyeing the brown murk. He sniffed it, feeling Ho's eyes. 'Chlorine. Old iron. Both medicinal inorganic chemicals.' He drank the glass at a gulp. Ho's face cleared. He nodded. 'OK,' said Jenkins. 'So now we do a public demonstration. Us three.'

Outside the crowd roared again. 'Quick,' said Lucy.

They went down, Jenkins, Ho and Lucy, and stood above the containers on the little deck from which the mob had recently ejected the cooks. One of the rice cauldrons was still upright. Lucy had the loudhailer. Ho went in front. People got out of his way fast.

Lucy yelled something. The crowd became quiet.

'Tell them what we're going to do,' said Jenkins.

Lucy spoke again. The mess boy appeared, carrying a tray on which were a glass jug and three glasses that jingled to the tremor of his hands. He put the tray down on the table vacated by the cooks.

Jenkins picked up the jug. The crowd became quiet and intent. He carried it to the stopcock where the water rations were issued. He filled it with water. Then he took it back to the little deck and handed it to the mess boy.

The mess boy glanced apprehensively at the silent crowd on the container tops. He poured the glasses full.

'Hand them round,' said Jenkins.

Ho took a glass. So did Jenkins and Lucy. The mess boy doled each of them a bowl of rice from the cauldron. The low sun cast their shadows on the paint of the accommodation block, nearly pristine white down here where it had been masked through the *Glory*'s working life by the top layer of containers.

'Raise your glasses,' said Jenkins. 'Tell them we drink to their excellent health.'

They raised their glasses. The sun turned the shadows of the glasses into blotches of amber on the white paint.

'Down in one,' said Jenkins, and drank. The others drank too. Then they ate the rice.

The crowd watched them intently. Jenkins smiled benignly, feeling a fool. Lucy wore a bright, public-relations grin. Ho belched and fanned the air in front of his mouth, and resumed his impassive, tough-guy glare.

Then his mouth fell open. He clutched his stomach and doubled up, moaning.

Jenkins noticed that an element in the crowd, particularly the young men from the aft end of the hold, became suddenly rigid and watchful, emitting a low, ugly roar. At the front of the crowd, another element, older and of mixed sex, watched with expressions of polite curiosity. Fung's monkey face looked actively enthusiastic.

But suddenly Ho was upright again, and his moans had turned to high, idiotic laughter. And the hard lads at the back had relaxed, and were laughing too, loudly.

Jenkins said, 'Thank you, Ho.'

Ho walked away without looking back.

'If they die, he doesn't get paid,' said Lucy.

Jenkins was no longer thinking about Ho. He was thinking about the people on the containers watching Ho's pantomime, the hissing roar of the people at the back, and the cheer of the people from the forward containers. It had been a football-crowd sound – Ho's supporters, and the other team's supporters.

They had been at sea seven days. There were twenty to go. By the sound of it, they were not going to be peaceful.

In the corner of number two hold inhabited by the Leungs, Mrs Nairn diagnosed appendicitis, and removed the affected organ later that evening in the ship's hospital. Afterwards, she went up to the bridge.

Jenkins was on watch. He turned from the dark windows, saw her standing block-like inside the door. She cooed, 'Successful op. Come and have a beer.'

Jenkins followed her down to her cabin. The chief was not there. She snapped the tops off two San Miguels, popped the rim with her thumb, getting rid of any glass crumbs, and poured the beers into glasses that said A PRESENT FROM WOOP WOOP. 'Cheers,' she said.

Jenkins waited.

She dabbed white foam from her grey lips with a pink Kleenex. She said, 'How's the schedule?'

'Two days to Saipan for watermaker parts. Then two and a half weeks to rendezvous.'

'If we can keep the lid on the cargo.'

Jenkins said, 'Quite.'

She was manoeuvring towards something she wanted to say, in spirals, like a vulture. He sipped his beer and waited.

'They found a ship last year, west of Baja California,' she said. 'All officers killed, passengers dead of thirst. It happens.'

It was not a story Jenkins had heard. He suspected her of making it up. He said, 'Dear me.'

'That's right.' She pushed her handkerchief into her sleeve. 'Clever girl, that Lucy.'

So that was it. Jenkins sat very still.

'Don't get me wrong,' said Mrs Nairn, smiling her sugary smile. 'I just wanted to say something to you straight out. I'm sure you understand. Best way of doing it, eh?'

Jenkins gave her no encouragement.

'We've all got our problems,' said Mrs Nairn. 'Or we wouldn't be here. But no matter how we feel individually, we have to remember that everyone on this ship is on this ship because he or she wants to be.'

So Lucy was trying to corrupt him, and Mrs Nairn was the voice of common sense. Lucy, who knew what it was like to lose a child. Mrs Nairn, who did not care what she did as long as she got her provident fund.

He said, 'Why would Lucy Moses want to get round me? We're all after the same thing, aren't we?'

Mrs Nairn smiled. 'I've seen a lot of the world, Dave. And you've been at sea most of your life.' She smiled, a smile that contained as much compassion as the girls in the Kitten

Club contained true love for their clients. 'You don't have to understand,' she said. 'We're us and they're them, that's all.'

Diana would have said she was dead right. Not Rachel, though. She was talking about Lucy. Lucy was not 'them'.

It was Mrs Nairn and Diana who were 'them'.

He got up, before he could get angry. He said, 'Thank you for the beer,' and left.

He walked down to Lucy's cabin and knocked on the door. The sound of Chinese argument was coming from inside. Her voice said, 'Who's there?' It was the high, suspicious voice she used on the public.

'Captain,' said Jenkins.

The door opened. Her face appeared, narrow-eyed and suspicious. There was cigarette smoke in the air. Over the shiny black top of her head he saw Ho, frowning, stubbing a cigarette in an ashtray. Lucy said something to him over her shoulder. He pushed past Jenkins and left.

Lucy liked it when Jenkins frowned. It was a good hard, steady frown, which spoke of earnestness and decision.

Jenkins said, 'What was Ho doing here?'

She said, 'We were having a meeting about public order.'

'I thought that was my job.'

'Of course. But Ho has . . . insights into the way their minds work. And so do I. You've got enough on your mind. Between us, we can sort this out.'

'I don't need to know?' Jenkins' voice sounded almost petulant in his ears. That was what Mrs Nairn had told him, in so many words.

'Why should you be interested?'

He said, brutally, 'I get a delivery bonus.'

She watched him carefully. His eyes were seldom as hard as his face. He was not like the other white officers. She had the distinct impression that he cared.

In which case, what was he doing on this ship?

It was not logical. But it came to Lucy that this was a moment for instinct, not logic. It was the moment, she thought. Seize it. She said, 'Ho knows one section of the passengers well. I know another. We both want our people to arrive fit and well. And heat and bad water make people quarrel. We were . . . resolving some quarrels.'

'What quarrels?'

Now, she thought. Do it now.

'Stupid things. Irrelevant. But dangerous because they're beginning to realize what's happening to them. It's one thing getting your stuff packed and paying your deposit and climbing aboard a ferry, and taking a trip on a ship. That part's easy compared to the next part.'

Jenkins said, 'You climb on to a tuna boat. Someone hands you a green card and a visa. What's the problem?'

Lucy felt the happiness drive warm blood through her body and into her cheeks. She had guessed right. Suddenly, the world was a bright and hopeful place.

She said, 'Who said anything about green cards and visas?'

Then she sat there with her eyes on his face.

Chapter Four

Jenkins could hear the blood humming in his ears. He said, 'Soares told me that when we put you aboard the tuna boats, you would be issued with visas and green cards.'

She laughed at the absurdity of the idea. Or at Jenkins, naïve enough to believe something that Soares had told him to keep him quiet. She said, 'He knew you are an honest man, and that worries thieves. They laugh at honest guys, sure. But they're scared of them. Soares was scared of you. Did you know that?'

If she was right, it meant that Chang was frightened of him, too. That was why Chang had taken Rachel. Big money was not enough. Like Soares had said, Mr Zamboanga Boy Scout Jenkins. Being honest made you unpredictable.

He said, 'So if you don't get a visa and a green card, how do you think you're going to find a place to live, work to do, that kind of thing?'

Lucy looked at her hands. 'We get looked after,' she said. 'It suits everyone, really. Most people couldn't afford the full fare. So we paid a deposit. Ten thousand dollars, some people much less. When we get to this rendezvous, we transship to tuna boats. The tuna boats belong to friends of whoever owns this ship. They ship us to San Francisco. And we work until we have paid the fare. We have jobs ready, in places where you don't need papers to work. When we've worked our time, earned our fares out, they'll get us green cards.' She rummaged in a blue cardboard folder, pulled out a card with a scrawl of Chinese writing. 'Look,' she said brightly.

'I can't read it.'

'It says Venus Mountain Massage Parlour.'

Jenkins sat and stared at her.

'Only for a year,' she said. 'Then I'm free.'

Jenkins found his voice. He said, 'Do you know what that place is going to be?'

Lucy said, 'Of course. But what would be the alternative without visa, green card, all that stuff?' Her eyes dropped. 'This will be a picnic, compared to China. Anyway. What are you doing if it's not whoring?'

Jenkins opened his mouth. Then he shut it again. He said, 'And you really think they'll give you a green card at the end of it?'

'Nothing in life is certain.' She smiled, a tight, bitter smile. 'Anyway. A fate worse than death is probably better than being dead.'

'Dead?'

She seemed to blush. She said, 'I didn't tell you quite the whole story yesterday. The reason I left China in the end was because someone wanted to murder us. Me and Jer, I mean. They found out Lee was coming on this ship. They paid him to kill us.'

'Who paid him?'

'A gang. A Triad.' She shrugged. 'So it was lucky for me when you chose me as an interpreter, because that made me useful to whoever's running this operation, and so to Ho. So he agreed to protect me against Lee. And finally killed him. Great, huh?'

They were all in the swamp together, holding hands in the filth. Jenkins said, 'Just like that.'

She said, hard-faced, 'They say you blow up pirate ships. Just like that.'

Jenkins would have liked to argue. But when he opened his mouth, the swamp silenced him.

She said, 'There's nothing to be ashamed of. That's the way it works.'

There was another question in Jenkins' mind, nothing to do with murder, or pirate ships, or the *Glory of Saipan*. It had to do with Lucy and Jenkins and nobody else. Jenkins said, 'So that stuff about your daughter dying. That wasn't true?'

Lucy looked him bang in the eye. 'Oh, yes,' she said.

'That was true.' Two tears appeared and ran down. She wiped them away angrily with the heel of her hand.

Thank God, Jenkins caught himself thinking. Then he brought himself up short. She could still be lying. He pushed his . . . sympathy, if that was all it was . . . into the background. He said: 'Why would a Triad want to kill you and Jer?'

'I told you I was an academic? That wasn't quite all. I was working in the Shanghai Institute. Holograms. They use them on credit cards. Jer was my boss. He found a way to duplicate the moulds you make them with. There was a colonel in the People's Liberation Army who was supervising our work. Jer was the brains. I was, well, his public face. We thought it was interesting, that's all. But the colonel was . . . aware of the commercial possibilities. So he used Jer's process to turn out four million fake Visa cards.'

Jenkins tried to imagine one of Diana's statements multiplied by four million. He did not have an imagination that powerful.

Lucy said, 'Stupid idea, of course. Four thousand, yes. But with four million, you can unbalance an economy, and maybe if Jer and I did not have good enough *guanxi* we would go to jail for ever, and this colonel would be driving around in his Rolls-Royce. So I went to someone I knew who was a political cadre, and I said, watch out for this colonel, close him down. Mistake. This colonel was a cousin of somebody too important, untouchable. So instead of closing the colonel down, they came to close us down, Jer and me. They caught a couple of Jer's associates, and put bullets in their necks. Jer and I decided to get out of China. I knew someone who had a place on this ship – Fung, the man whose face was burned. So we came on board. But Lee had been tipped off by a Triad contact of the colonel, Ho told me. His job was to kill us, and make it look like an accident. After you found us on the ferry, I told Ho that if anything happened to Jer or me, you would kill him and Lee. He believed me.'

'Why?'

She looked him straight in the eye. 'He could see you were a man of integrity.' Her lashes came down. 'And that you and I understood each other.'

Jenkins found himself embarrassed, as if he had just been paid an undeserved compliment. He felt like a slave trader, not a man of integrity.

Their fingers touched. He squeezed her hand. Venus Mountain Massage. Oh, Christ. Something needed doing about this. But what could he do, as long as Diana was counting on him, and Chang had Rachel?

Someone knocked on the door. 'Captain,' said the voice of Rodriguez. 'Satcom. On bridge. Urgent, they say.'

Jenkins climbed to his feet as if surfacing from deep water. 'On my way,' he said.

Lucy watched the door close, and locked it behind him. He was a sweet guy, she thought. A really sweet guy. But sometimes you had to use sweet guys for the greater good.

Diana wondered if Jenkins would ever realize the courage she had needed to make this call. It was not likely. David had no feelings to speak of and did not understand what it was like when someone who did have them had them walked all over.

Actually, it had been Jeremy who had turned it all round, without knowing it, of course. Jeremy was so sensitive. He really understood how women's minds worked. It was funny, Diana sometimes thought, the way wonderful, well, *happenings* clustered round Jeremy. While David was just a nothing. Since Bill had passed on she had put up with him out of basic kindness. But this was the final straw.

It had been an amazing coincidence. Madam Lao, the Vietnamese lady who did her stars, had peered at her charts and said, 'Watch for amazing coincidences that will change your life. I see a dark man.'

Well of course that was it, cut and dried. Jeremy was very dark, and Madam Lao had always been right before, like about when David had been mean about that sweet Laney with the lovely brown eyes and the ponytail who had made the apartment over, the chance of a lifetime.

But it was too late now. And this was why.

Jeremy had this boat, a sailing boat, bigger than the one David had had and much more comfortable. Diana had only put up with David's boat because she quite liked the people you met in the Yacht Club bar, like Maxine Davison, fat and drunk but quite a chum of the Pattens, apparently, not that Patten had been any good, but after all a governor was a governor, and he was faster. David, in his boat, not Patten.

Anyway. With David on some ship and Rachel away in China with the son of that *really very nice* Mr Chang, she had been seeing a lot of Jeremy. And quite reasonably, Jeremy liked to take her to nice places. Which meant the old grind, of course: the gym, the beauty parlour, manicure, long, sweaty bath with the aromatherapist's prescription globbing up around her nipples. Then into a little Versace something and down to the old Y. C. to have a chin-wag while Jeremy did his sailing, and a bite of dinner after he got back, quite often with some important business contacts. It made Diana feel *useful* at last – something she had never felt in the dreary old days with David.

Awful how she was thinking of David as a thing of the past. But it was his own silly fault. He had made his bed, thought Diana, and now he had to take his medicine.

It had been a fantastic coincidence. Almost a miracle, really.

She had been sitting in the Yacht Club bar, and Jeremy was just back from sailing when the steward said there was mail for him.

There seemed to be a photograph in one of the letters. But Jeremy did not like people looking at his mail, had got quite sharp about it the first time she had peeped; of course he was in security. So she paid no attention and thought that when he had finished looking at it, she would drop a hint about another gin.

Jeremy laughed. She loved the way the corners of his eyes crinkled. He said, 'Look at that, then,' and tossed her the photograph.

It was a Polaroid. She looked at it with a nice smile, ready to find it funny.

Then the smile went.

Christ, thought Jeremy. Wouldn't like to meet that on a dark night.

Diana's mouth, which had been soft and obliging, had gone hard as nails and turned down at the corners. Her forehead was suddenly a music-stave of wrinkles, and her chin was tucked in so her neck in its bright gold chain reminded Jeremy of one of those little pumps you use to blow up inflatable boats.

He craned over to have another look at the man and the woman, silhouetted against a background of fresh green leaves. The woman's head was tilted back. The man was leaning over her. Their lips were touching.

'Romantic, eh?' said Jeremy.

Diana said, in an odd, tight voice, 'Where did you get this?'

'Yap,' said Jeremy. 'Friend sent it. Harry McFee. Recognized Dave. Dave wasn't at all pleased to see him. Apparently Dave introduced his bird as Mrs Jenkins. Then he got pissed and smashed up the bar. There's a bill to pay, too.' He moved closer to her so their knees were touching. 'I'm sorry. I really am.'

'Sorry?' Diana's smile looked as if it might crack the top half of her face clear off the bottom half. 'What should you be sorry for?' She picked up the photograph. 'I think that's really lovely,' she said. 'Could I keep it?'

'One for the album,' said Jeremy, and laughed.

Diana laughed too, snuggling up to his nice blue blazer, smelling his nice aftershave-and-Rothmans smell. Because she had just spotted the bright side.

Lovely Jeremy had just presented her out of the blue with a future in which she could be *herself*: get rid of stupid old David, and make it his fault. Fancy him sailing off with some floozy, after her years of selfless devotion.

'Gin and tonic?' said Jeremy.

'Sorry,' said Diana. 'Miles away. I tell you what. I'll get you one.' She ran her tongue round her mouth. Jeremy's eyes followed it like a dog watching a rabbit. She stretched, showing him her breasts. 'No. Tell you what. *Champers*.'

They had a lovely time. Later, back at the apartment, she showered off the baby oil and dialled the satcom number of the *Glory of Saipan*.

'Yes?' said Jenkins.

'David?' said the woman's voice on the end. Diana's voice.

It was tinny with distance, and something else that he recognized with foreboding: the sound of Diana keeping the lid on. His heart lurched guiltily. 'Are you there?' she said. She was definitely angry about something. 'I hope you are. Because listen to this. I want a divorce.'

A bomb seemed to explode silently between Jenkins' ears. He said, '*What?*'

'D-I-V-O-R-C-E. You can spell.'

Jenkins' ears were ringing. He said, 'What are you talking about?'

Diana was quite a spotter of openings. She drew breath, and let him (as she told Jeremy later) *have* it. 'I am talking about you never being here,' she said. 'I am talking about you spending your life on bloody ships and not being there for your children. And not being there for poor little Billy running across a road and getting killed by a taxi, not that you cared –'

'Hey!' said Jenkins, wrung.

'Oh no you didn't.' She was properly wound up now, and she would not stop until she had run down. 'You *bastard*. You got a perfectly decent job ashore when you know I can't stand you being away and you drop the whole thing flat to get back to sea. And if you really want to know what I'm talking about, I'm talking about a picture someone took of you on an island with a girl. A *Chinese* girl. What do you call them? LYFMs? Little Yellow Fucking Machines. How do you think I feel when someone says, so that's why he went back to sea, I think you're awfully brave, let's hope he doesn't come back with a *disease*? Do you think that's *fun* for me?' She was sobbing now, convulsions of self-pity. 'So of course I want a divorce. You *bastard*.'

For a moment, Jenkins was paralysed with guilt. Poor Diana, left on her own. Then his mind started to work again. Someone had been taking *photographs*? On Yap? He said, 'Wait a minute. Whoever told you this has got it all wrong –'

'Oh, no,' said Diana. 'Oh, no no no. I've seen the photograph. A colour photograph. It's all there in black and white. Terribly romantic, under the coconut trees. You and your little bit of yellow velvet.'

An ant was walking across the keyboard of the satellite phone. Jenkins watched it stop at the space bar, turn round and walk off in the opposite direction.

Yellow velvet.

He thought of the vulnerable delicacy of Lucy, the over-done brassiness of Diana, sure of her rights and her slot in the Circuit. How dare she throw Bill in his face? And his perfectly decent job ashore that she had never been interested enough in to ask about?

Yellow velvet.

He heard a voice saying, 'There's nothing to explain. If you want a divorce, go and get one.' The voice sounded tired. It was his own.

There was a hiss of indrawn breath, poisonous even by satellite. 'Do you know something?' She didn't wait for an answer. 'When Bill was killed.' She was crying properly now. 'I told you. He said, "Where's Dad?"'

'Diana –'

'I was lying,' she said. 'He didn't say anything. He just died. I told you he said that to make you feel better. But he hardly knew who you were, did he? David, you are useless, and you always have been, and I hate your guts, and I'm going to make you *pay*.' She slammed the telephone down.

Jenkins hung up the receiver carefully, as if it were made of porcelain. He leaned back in his chair and shoved his hands into the pockets of his shorts.

He was captain of a slave ship. And Rachel had been more or less kidnapped by Mr Chang. But now by Diana's wish he was no longer responsible for Diana, who had been the reason he was here in the first place. And he did not have to believe anything she said about their children. He had known his children, too.

He felt light and cheerful, as if he were breathing new air, untainted by guilt.

The air of freedom.

The ship felt different, now that it was full of that air. It was as if the depth of field had increased. The faces of the officers and the crew were still there in the foreground. But now there were visible behind them the sharply focused faces of the passengers, with Lucy's face at the centre.

In fact, Lucy's face was occupying most of Jenkins' mind, now that Diana had set him free. He wanted to tell her about it, but of course that would have been impossible; she didn't even know who Diana was, let alone the sense of liberation that had covered Jenkins after that telephone call. Actually, Jenkins was by no means clear himself about the roots of his liberation, except that, absurdly, he remembered feeling this way after he had given up smoking – cured himself of a socially unacceptable habit, which would allow his senses to operate with a new efficiency.

But of course things were by no means straightforward. Always in the back of his mind was the idea that he was not a free agent, that Rachel was a prisoner of Chang, and that Lucy, much as he wanted to believe her, might not be telling the truth.

So that evening, instead of drinking San Miguel under the gimlet eye of Mrs Nairn, he slid a couple of San Migs into his pocket and went down to Lucy's cabin. The door was locked. He knocked. There was no reply. But Jer's voice from the next cabin called, 'Who?'

'Not important,' said Jenkins.

'Captain?'

'That's me.'

'Come in, please.' A bolt rattled. Jer's door opened. Jenkins went in.

The cabin was hot. It smelled of sweat, with a sweetish chemical edge that might have been medicine. Jer's face was bile-yellow, his chest hollow. He was smiling, the smile of an invalid who does not see many people, and craves company. There was a chess board on the desk. He grinned, and sat down on his bed, and waved Jenkins into the desk chair. 'Chesses,' he said.

'Well,' said Jenkins. 'I dunno –'

But Jer was already laying out the pieces with a dextrous ochre hand. So Jenkins pulled the beers out of his shorts pockets, snapped the top off one with his Swiss Army knife, and held it out to Jer.

Jer frowned, and put his hand against the right side of his

stomach. 'Bad here,' he said. Then he pointed to his head, and grinned. 'But good here.' Jenkins uncapped the other beer. 'Chin-chin,' said Jer. He held out two fists.

Jenkins said, 'Where's Lucy?'

'Ah,' said Jer. 'Your friend Lucy. Later, at music. Choose.'

Jenkins tapped his right fist. The skin was hot, faintly sticky. Jer said, 'You start.'

Rachel had tried to teach Jenkins chess, with no success at all. This amused her greatly. Jer was a player of Rachel's standard, but politer. After a couple of lucky breaks, Jenkins was on the run. It was all over in quarter of an hour.

'Bad luck,' said Jer.

'Bad play,' said Jenkins.

Jer laughed. He had a pleasant laugh, the laugh of a healthy man. Despite his monosyllabic English, he struck Jenkins as a human being built on the large scale, intelligent and sympathetic. 'Now,' he said. 'Before music, one more game.'

'What is this music?'

Jer pointed upwards. 'Middle yard,' he said. 'Susan.'

'Susan?'

Jer pantomimed a violinist, and pointed at his Rolex. 'Six half clock.' He set out the chess pieces again, drank beer, and belched. 'Begin.'

Fung watched with a certain smugness as the middle courtyard began to fill up. Naturally, this had been Lucy's idea. Get Susan Hong, she had said. Ask her to play. Make no charge, but get Yip who runs the café to sell tea during the performance. People will be happy. There will be peace, and harmony, and the suspicions felt by the middle courtyard for the forward courtyard will yield under the influence of Yip doing business, and people will come up from the hold to listen, and solidarity will be unconfined.

And of course there would be the music.

Susan Hong was fourteen years old, a studious girl with large spectacles, a wide forehead, and a mouth that at first sight seemed too full and sensitive to go with the rest of her. Her parents, unhappily, were not musical. Furthermore, they loathed her because she was not a boy. So they had sold

her at an early age to the friend of an uncle, who while
waiting for her to be of marriageable age had inadvertently
exposed her to a Shanghai film maker with an ear for music.
The film maker had recognized her talent the same week he
had been editing a documentary comparing 1930s Japanese
imperialism on the Pacific rim with 1990s Chinese imperialism in the same area. The film maker had wanted to make
sure that Susan received training. But his *guanxi* could not
penetrate the barbed wire of the labour camp in which he
had found himself. So Lucy Ng, now known as Moses, had
brought her on board the *Glory of Saipan*, in the hope that
things would be better in California.

And there she was, on a small dais in the white glare of a
floodlight, the steel walls of the middle courtyard all around
her, a slight girl in a black shift, with a violin that looked the
size of a viola against her small body.

Jenkins sat on the container's edge, next to Jer and Lucy.
The breeze blew soft, and the ship loped at a gentle
rocking-horse canter across the low swell. The generator
was a distant rattle, almost drowned by the susurrus of the
crowd.

Down there, the small figure in the black shift tucked the
violin under her chin and began to play.

Solo violins were not generally something he listened to,
and the tune Susan played was not one he recognized. But
it sounded fine down there, amplified by the hard steel
surfaces of the containers. And as he listened, it became
more than fine. It grew wings, and it moved out of the
hollow square of steel and up into the sky where the moon
hung among the impossibly bright incrustations of the Milky
Way.

Under its influence, the *Glory of Saipan* ceased to be an
iron boxload of misery, and became a missile packed with
hopes and fears and ambitions, aimed at a new life. Jenkins
felt the excitement of it. He also felt the sadness of parting,
of leaving friends and family and stepping into a future as
uncertain as it was hopeful.

The first tune ended, to reflective applause. She began
another. 'English,' said Lucy, next to him. ' "*Salut d'amour*".
Elgar.'

It was a long, winding tune, and it took Jenkins away again, into the black deeps in between all those stars. Captain Durant, one of his first captains, had had a sampler in his cabin, to which Jenkins had been admitted only for ritual gin before Sunday curry. The sampler had been a quotation from Conrad: *The true peace of God is found a thousand miles from the nearest land*. And sitting in the dark on a rusty container, listening to Elgar –

Behind Jenkins, someone started shouting.

Chapter Five

Fung's daughter Lin was of an age at which she could take or leave violin music, but mostly leave it. So she had gone wandering the tops of the containers, watching the flecks of phosphorescence in the water. Then she had wandered back to the Christian courtyard, which was empty –

Which was not as empty as it should have been.

In the pale glow of the lights on the accommodation block a face appeared at the door of a container. It was not a face she recognized.

Dry-mouthed, Lin tiptoed back into the crowd round the second courtyard and found her father. Her father got up and collected half a dozen other men. More followed. As the violin lassoed the stars, they walked forward and waited on the lip of the courtyard.

The courtyard should have been empty, the steel doors of the containers closed. But one of the doors was open, and as Lin had said, something was moving inside.

Fung opened his mouth to shout. But whatever he had been going to say was drowned in the roar of outrage from the men at his back. A face appeared in the doorway, a round face, glossy with sweat and pale with fear. In the dim light Fung recognized one of the small-time gangsters who lived in the back end of the hold. Fung felt almost sorry for him.

With a noise like a wave breaking, the crowd poured into the courtyard.

When the roar from the containers silenced the violin, Jenkins felt momentarily dazed. Then he ran up the ladders to the deck abaft the bridge and turned on the working lights. In their white glare he saw people milling like ants on the container tops. Feet clashed on the iron stairs. They belonged to Fung and four burly men he recognized as belonging to what he now thought of as the Christian faction. Lucy was with them. They were holding two thin youths who looked as if they belonged at the aft end of the hold near the engine room. One of the youths had a squint. The other was short and moonfaced, and his teeth were chattering like jug-band spoons.

Jenkins said, 'What's all this?'

Lucy said, 'These men waited until the Christians were at the concert. Then they went to steal from their quarters. We say they should be punished. But not killed.'

Jenkins said, 'They can go in the portside paint locker.' It was hot in there, and undesirable, but better than being torn apart by a mob.

Lucy translated. The Christians nodded, satisfied. Jenkins thanked Lucy, and they all left.

Jenkins went into the bridge, where Pete was on watch. He said, 'Give me an ETA off Saipan.'

'Bit of a fuss?' said Pete.

'That's right.' Jenkins felt as if he had woken from a dream that had been more real than the dim, humming world of this latest in an endless series of bridges.

'Never could stand the fiddle,' said Pete, stolidly.

Jenkins thought, You knew about the work permits and the visas, but you didn't care. But then why should you? Eat, sleep, get paid. Man is the animal who gets paid . . .

Who gets the job done.

Pete was fiddling with the long ruler and the square. 'Tomorrow 06.00,' he said.

Jenkins sat down at the datacom. He smacked in his password, transmitted the arrival time to the agents in Saipan, and requested that a boat or chopper be sent to intercept the *Glory*. Pete was still at the chart table, scratching dandruff on to the Pacific passage chart. 'And while you're there,' said Jenkins, 'make me a Great Circle course from Saipan to 40°N 135°W.'

'About fucking time,' said Pete. 'I just cannot bloody wait to get this over with.'

Yes, thought Jenkins: empty Lucy and Jer and Fung and the Christians, Susan and Leung and their friends and neighbours into the tuna boats. Collect a wad of money, leave them to the sweatshops and brothels.

The air of freedom tasted stale and mawkish. There was no new life after Diana. There was only a string of grubby compromises, until you turned into something like Nairn.

He waded through the soggy heat to the empty messroom and made himself a cheese-and-tomato sandwich. Then he went to his cabin and fell into vivid dreams of stars and violins.

He was woken by a hammering on his door. He was getting used to it. There was the stagger into the shorts, the easing of the slimy T-shirt, the splash of lukewarm water on his face, and the blunder into a dark world with the metallic taste and hot eyeballs of no sleep. His watch said four thirty. The watch had changed half an hour ago. He opened the cabin door.

Pete was waiting outside. The worn-out fluorescent tube in the alleyway cast a blue-white flicker in the sweaty skin of his forehead. 'What is it?' said Jenkins.

Pete's face had fallen into grim, rubbery folds. 'Rodriguez says something happened to those buggers in the paint locker.'

Pete led Jenkins down the alleyway and on to the stairs. There was the usual stink of dirt and old tobacco. But as they went down the stairs a new ingredient made itself felt, a flat, alkaline smell that flared Jenkins' nostrils and settled in his stomach like a cannonball.

The paint locker door hung open, swinging to the *Glory of Saipan*'s long, staggering roll. Inside, the floor was littered with cans of paint, rolling to the ship's roll, clashing first one side, then the other. Some of them had spilled. There was some white, and a lot of red lead, and even more crimson.

The crimson had splashed in fans out of the door and into the alleyway. It looked as if someone had gone berserk with a pump. Why the hell, thought Jenkins, would the *Glory of Saipan* be carrying crimson paint? He walked to the door and looked in. Pete said, 'Shit,' and doubled up in the alleyway, retching.

Jenkins held on to the doorpost. He understood the colour, and the smell.

The crimson was not paint.

Someone had opened the door of the paint locker. That person had been carrying what might have been a kitchen knife or a cleaver. That person had walked in and started in slicing. He had done a good job of it; it was hard to work out where one burglar began and the other left off.

Mrs Nairn shoved past him, wearing a flannel nightdress already stained with blood at the hem, brisk and business-like, doing her job. 'Tch, tch,' she said. 'Pig's breakfast.' She squatted. 'This one's alive,' she said, rummaging in the pile of slashed meat. 'So's this one. There was only two, right?' It was a joke.

'Right,' said Jenkins, nauseous.

She looked up at him with a diagnostic eye. 'Someone's been careful,' she said. 'Intelligent bit of non-lethal maim-ing.' She sucked her teeth appreciatively 'Well,' she said. 'First mate's bright green in the alleyway. You'd better get out and succour the bastard.' She swabbed blood from what might once have been a thorax. The sharp smell of disinfect-ant mingled with the blood.

Jenkins said, 'How long ago did this happen?'

Mrs Nairn licked the end of a length of what looked like sail thread and pulled it through the eye of a curved needle. 'Half-hour,' she said. 'Twenty minutes, maybe. Blood's hardly drying. Listen, do you mind?'

As Jenkins moved towards the door, he saw a white boiler suit in the litter of paint cans. It was saturated with blood. He bent and picked it up, and walked out into the alleyway.

Rodriguez was hanging around outside with three or four Filipinos. This was nearly as good as a chop-chop video. Rodriguez shook his head 'Lot of blood,' he said, appre-ciatively.

Pete looked pale and worried. Jenkins said, 'You were on watch.'

'That's right.'

'Still?'

'Johnny said he was ill.'

'Who's on the bridge now?'

'Johnny, ill or bloody not.'

'What happened?'

'I was doing the 0400 position. There was a hell of a racket. Crashing and banging and screaming. Rodriguez said it was coming from the paint locker. I came straight to your cabin. Christ.'

'Water!' yelled Mrs Nairn, from inside the locker. The mess boy scuttled out.

'Who had the key?'

'It was on the board in the ship's office.'

My fault, thought Jenkins. 'Where is it now?'

'In the locker door.'

'Fine,' said Jenkins. This was a disciplinary chopping. 'Where was Ho?'

'Haven't seen him.'

Jenkins walked to the ship's office and sat down in the sticky swivel chair. Pete was waiting in the doorway. He dialled. A Filipino voice said, 'Engine room. Ramos.'

Lucy arrived, her face blurred with sleep. He motioned her to a chair.

Jenkins said, 'Captain here. I'm looking for Ho the motorman.'

'Ho just here,' said Ramos.

'How long's he been there?'

'How long?'

'That's what I asked.'

'Half-three I came on watch. Early. Couldn't sleep, captain. Banging by anchor made me awake –'

'Ho.'

'He was here half-three.'

'Did he leave?'

'Not leave.'

'Sure?'

'We talking.'

'All the time? What about?'

Ramos giggled. 'Womans,' he said.

'Put me on to him,' said Jenkins. He said to Lucy, 'Pick up the other phone.' There was a pause. A voice said, 'Ho.'

Jenkins said, 'Two men were in the portside paint locker.'

'Wha'?' said Ho. 'No understand.' Lucy translated.

228

'Someone chopped them between half past three and four o'clock.'

There was a pause. Jenkins could have sworn that he detected surprise in it. Finally Ho said, in English, 'They dead?'

'No. Was it you that chopped them?'

Ho did not give Lucy time to translate. He said, 'This time you ask you friend Lucy.' He laughed, a yell of a laugh that made Jenkins jump. He was still laughing when Jenkins put the phone down on him.

Jenkins' mind was working slowly, the ideas plodding in careful sequence. The men in the locker had offended against the people in the forward courtyard: Fung's people, Lucy's friends. But Fung was not a chopper, and nor was Lucy.

He said to Lucy, 'Ho didn't do this.'

'Then who?'

'I thought you might have an idea.'

'No.' Her face was blank. 'I'm tired.'

Jenkins said, 'I don't want a war on this ship.'

'It's a couple of thieves, not a war.' She did not meet his eye. 'Maybe someone decided to teach someone a lesson.' She yawned. She said, 'Now I really have to go to bed,' and left.

Jenkins clambered wearily to his feet and picked up the overalls he had found in the paint locker. The right sleeve and the right-hand side of the chest were saturated with blood. There was nothing in the pockets. They were clean, except for the blood and a smudge of yellowish paint at the left wrist that might have survived a wash or two. Jenkins thought, We are looking for a man of average height, homicidal, right-handed, with reason to dislike people who steal from Christians.

Of the four hundred people on the ship, there were about a hundred who might fit that description. And Lucy was not going to help him find out which one.

Forget it. Hope for the best. Do what you're paid for. Even if you hate yourself for it.

The telephone rang. Johnny said, 'Tug approaching. Got watermaker parts.'

229

Jenkins went on deck. A red sun was billowing out of the eastern sea. Far on the western horizon, Saipan was a conical smudge twinkling with lights along its coastal strip. Japanese honeymooners and Filipino whores, thought Jenkins. Innocent as children, compared with us.

A grubby tug nuzzled its rubber-tyre fenders against the *Glory*'s port side. Two crates went up on the derrick. The tug sheered away. The *Glory of Saipan* steamed into the growing light of the new day.

Home stretch, thought Jenkins.

Wherever home was.

In the chart room, the satellite phone rang.

Jenkins picked it up. 'Got your parts?' said the voice of Hugh Chang.

'Thank you,' said Jenkins. 'Your agent is very prompt.'

'My agent,' said Chang. 'Ah, yes. There is one more thing.'

Jenkins' stomach tightened, as if to receive a blow. Rachel is all right, he thought. Please let her be all right.

'About discipline,' said Chang. 'It is not safe to permit your cargo too much latitude.'

Jenkins said, 'What do you mean?'

Chang's smile was almost audible. 'Two men were injured. These men should not have been injured. Ho has my full confidence, in this respect.'

'The injured men were thieves.'

Chang said, 'I wish no injuries,' and laughed, closing the subject. Jenkins thought, Ho has talked to him on that mobile phone he has down there. Now my chain is being jerked. He waited.

'And Rachel is well,' said Chang. 'You will be pleased to hear. I am in Hong Kong. She has remained in Xian, where she has introduced my son to the delights of archaeology, I think.'

Jerk, went the chain.

'But I fear archaeology is a dangerous business.'

Jenkins had stopped breathing.

'Particularly,' said Chang, 'when there is a failure of teamwork.' The line went dead.

Jenkins walked to the wing of the bridge. He stood and

watched the ship drag its wake eastward, and thought about Susan Hong's concert, and Jer's chess set, and teamwork. He went into the chart room, picked up the handset of the satellite phone, and with a shaking hand dialled the number of Chang's house in Xian.

Chapter Six

The voice that answered was a young man's. Jenkins said, 'Who's this?'

'Raymond Chang.'

'Good evening,' he said, keeping his voice steady. 'This is Rachel's father.'

'I know,' said Raymond.

'Could I talk to Rachel?'

'One moment, please.' The receiver was half-covered by a hand. Jenkins heard him say, 'Do you want to talk to your father?' He consoled himself with the thought that if she were in danger, she would either not be allowed to talk to him, or be assumed to be desperate for contact. He began to relax.

Rachel came on the line. 'Father, dearest,' she said, as if in a Victorian novel.

Jenkins listened intently for danger signals in her voice, but detected none. 'You all right?' he said. He wanted to tell her to watch those bastards, do what she could to get away, not trust this Raymond a centimetre.

'Fine fine *fine*,' said Rachel. 'We're digging up a T'ang army. Then we're off to Beijing. Aren't we, darling?' Jenkins told himself that, far from disliking hearing her call Raymond 'darling', he should be encouraged. 'And how's your ship?'

Jenkins had not properly thought out what he was going to say. He repressed the urge to confide in her. He wanted to tell her to get out of there, fast, if she could. But that would be alarming. Subtlety, Jenkins. Not your strong suit. 'Er, not bad,' he said. 'Look, something rather terrible's happened.'

'What?'

There was a silence while he tried to find a tactful way of saying it, and failed. 'Your mother and I . . .' That was the one. No big explanations. Just tell her enough to make her go back to Hong Kong, now, as soon as possible. 'Your mother wants us to separate. Well, divorce.'

There was a silence. Oh, Christ, thought Jenkins. Now she'll hate me for ever.

'You poor darling,' she said, finally. 'What's she done this time?'

'I'm always away,' said Jenkins, blundering on, saying the first thing that came into his head, not really listening to the question. 'Can't blame her, really.'

'You can,' said Rachel. 'Actually. Silly cow.'

He wanted her away from Chang. But if he told her the real reason, she might panic and give herself away. 'I want you to go back,' he said. 'Talk to her.'

Rachel said, 'Whatever she said, she'd be lying.'

'Sorry?'

'Nothing. But honestly, nothing I say is going to make any difference. She . . . well, she's on a different planet.'

There was a silence. Poor devil, thought Rachel. Out there in the middle of the sea, trying to earn a living. Bloody Mummy running round the Yacht Club with her tongue hanging out and shagging Daddy's best friend. How can you tell your father something like that?

Jenkins wanted to scream at her, For God's sake, can't you see, you're a prisoner, don't trust a soul, get out of there, set yourself free, and me as well. But how could you tell your daughter something like that?

Besides, Chang's people could be listening on an extension, even recording the call. So he said, feeling feeble, 'It would really be a big help if you could go and see your mother.'

'I'll ring,' said Rachel. 'I can't go back yet. There's a lot to do.'

'Please.'

'She's a silly bitch. You're well shot of her.'

'You can't talk about her like that,' he said. 'Please see her.'

233

She sighed. 'I'll call her.'

Jenkins recognized the note in her voice. Over the past eight years, she had applied it to everything from eating spinach to going on dates organized by Diana. It meant she was unpersuadable, and that was that.

'Darling Father. Don't worry.'

After she had hung up, Raymond looked at her with his black-fringed eyes. 'Your father doesn't sound too happy,' he said.

She said, 'He's fine.'

She was ashamed to tell him the truth. He might tell his father about the divorce, and Mr Chang the moralist would be shocked, and tell Raymond to have nothing more to do with her. Sod you, Mummy, she thought. For a stupid woman, you have a genius for making things complicated. I will not go back to Hong Kong to see you, for Daddy or anyone else. In fact I never want to see you again.

Raymond was throwing grains of rice to the carp in the green pond. He said, 'You want to go to the dig?'

'Of course. You want some help with that?'

'It's pretty arduous.' He grinned at her. He had been wanting to get bored with the dig, but somehow it had never happened. Raymond could not work out whether it was clay warriors or this golden woman. Not that he had tried too hard; for the first time he could remember, Raymond was actually happy.

For Rachel, the house and the dig and Raymond were a radiant foreground. Mr Chang was irritating, because of his views on shared bedrooms; and her father was out of luck, and her mother was monstrous; but they were all in the background.

She went and sat next to Raymond, and helped him throw rice.

That evening, Mr Chang called to discuss business with Raymond and asked to speak to her. He said, 'I hear you're enjoying your digging.'

'Very much.'

'I'm glad. And your father's enjoying his ship?'

'A ship's a ship,' said Rachel. 'That's what he says.'

'Wise man,' said Chang, chuckling. 'Could I have

Raymond again?' And he gave Raymond a list of tasks that kept him busy till past midnight.

Rachel did not mind. She had work to do herself. Nowadays her mind was so full of the T'ang dynasty that she barely noticed where she was. She was beginning to work out the organization of the buried army. But the libraries in Xian were bad. Most of the material she needed was in Beijing. And Professor Yu at the dig had references that needed verifying.

When she suggested the trip to Raymond, he grinned and nodded and changed the subject. So next day she took the bull by the horns.

It was lunchtime. They were sitting by the window looking on to the terrace. She was counting his fingers, of which he had ten. She said, 'Beijing tomorrow?'

'Yes,' he said. He took his hands away and clasped them. She thought he looked nervous. 'Well . . . actuarry, something's come up.' Actuarry. Definitely nervous.

'Up?'

'My father has taken the jet.'

'Then let's get a commercial flight.'

'There are problems.'

Normally Raymond had a funny, mobile mouth, and eyes that said more than his voice ever did. Now the mouth was as inexpressive as a letterbox, the eyes blank and hooded. Rachel heard her mother's voice: *You can't tell what they're thinking*. Racist crap, Mummy; your usual. This is just distance.

Whatever it was, she found it horrible.

She said, 'What problems?'

'Problems.' He pulled his telephone from the pocket of his suit, dialled, and started talking business.

Rachel's heart had become a lump of cold stone. When he stopped talking, she said, 'Raymond?'

He raised an eyebrow.

'What are these problems?'

'Business.'

'What business?'

'Just business. You wouldn't understand.'

It was all crumbling. She was being humoured. The chill

in her became a quick, unhealthy heat as the fear turned to anger. She said, 'Because I'm a woman.'

Pain flitted across Raymond's face. 'No,' he said. 'We can't go, that's all. My father doesn't wish it.'

Rachel said, 'Your relationship with your father is your business, not mine. If we can't go to Beijing, I want to go home. Now.'

'No transport,' he said.

She put out her hand. 'Give me the telephone,' she said. 'I'll get a flight. No problems.'

He made no move to give it to her. She found herself furious. She thought, How dare you drag me out here into the middle of nowhere and stop me going where I want to go? Who does your father think he is?

Raymond's face had changed, particularly around the eyes. She could tell exactly what he was thinking, now. He was thinking he wanted to beg for mercy. In a sudden rush of empathy, Rachel thought she understood.

Perhaps Chang the traditionalist was disappointed that Raymond had not taken up with a nice Chinese girl, done the rounds of charity balls and shopping orgies, made plans to produce dear little Chinese grandchildren. Perhaps Chang the crafty thought the best way to remind Raymond of what he was missing was to keep him up here with nothing to occupy his mind but business and archaeology. After all, this was Raymond Chang, the playboy. Raymond Chang could be skiing in Gstaad or diving in Barbados, or blotto in one of his father's Australian wineries. Instead, he was stuck with this British girl, digging up grubby old pottery in a cold desert in central China.

You old bastard, thought Rachel, with the clarity of complete fury. I'll fix you.

Gradually, she became calm. It would have to be done slowly, because Raymond was a well-brought-up lad, who respected his father's wishes with a deference that had cultural foundations going down 2,500 years. Careful, Rachel. One step at a time. She said, 'So are we allowed to go to the dig?'

Raymond brightened. 'Sure,' he said. 'Now?'

'Sure.' He got up. She took his hand. The bases of the

fingers were faintly calloused. That was astonishing in Raymond Chang, the playboy. He had acquired those honourable scars for her. She felt a sudden glow of tenderness, and kissed him on the lips, thinking, I will rescue you, poor baby. His arm went round her waist. They walked out to the car.

'Hey,' she said, once they were on the road. 'While we're passing, let's stop off at the airport and book some tickets.'

Raymond stared through the windscreen. 'I told you,' he said. 'Not possible.'

They went to the dig. They went every day for a week. Raymond was lovely, but he would not budge.

On the seventh day the horizon was still wide and dusty, whipped by an icy breeze. The airport was still a long chain-link fence with a couple of big iron hangars. The gate still came up on the left. Raymond still drove past it without slowing down.

By the time they arrived at the dig, the warm glow of reconciliation was nothing but a grey ember. Raymond would not look at her. It was over, thought Rachel. When you go out with Raymond, you go out with his father. You are a chattel. How did you expect to change that?

The security guard waved them through, grinning the grin she reserved for cadres and visiting firemen. Professor Yu hailed them as old friends. Raymond seemed suspiciously enthusiastic. Rachel watched the two black heads nodding over a clay warrior. She could not concentrate. The comfort was gone. She was in a stuffy hut on a cold plateau, and all around her for thousands of miles the world was a strange place in which she could not move without the goodwill of her hosts. She was a prisoner.

She needed air. She said, 'I'm going outside.'

She climbed into the end of a trench in an area mapped as unimportant, and helped a gang of eleven blue-overalled women dig and barrow soil under a cold blue sky. The work made her warm and the women chattered hearteningly, making jokes about their menfolk's uselessness in and out of bed. She had got to know one of the women well. Her name was Suyin. She was married to a truck driver and she had a ten-year-old daughter. She talked a lot about her daughter, ignoring the patronizing remarks of the rest of the gang, who by dint of pitiless abortion had borne sons.

When the digging stopped for tea, Suyin said, 'What's happened to your man?'

'In the office,' said Rachel. 'With the professor.'

'You're crazy,' said Suyin. 'Down here, digging holes. Why aren't you with him, in the warm?'

'It's warm down here.'

'It is always warmer with someone who loves you.'

The fear and gloom came down like a black fog. Rachel looked at the lidded mug of tea between her hands, so as not to show the tears. She said, 'It is very cold when you are with someone who pretends to love you.'

Wrinkles spread in fans from the corners of Suyin's eyes and bracketed her mouth. She laughed like a mynah bird. 'Pretend?' she said. 'If he's pretending, my arse is blue.'

Rachel finished her tea, picked up the spade, and drove it into the mound of yellow-brown earth. 'It's blue,' she said.

Suyin said, 'My eyes are ten years older than yours. They are reliable eyes.'

'He won't let me go anywhere,' said Rachel.

'So?' said Suyin. 'You love him. He loves you. He wants you for himself. Be grateful.'

I do love him, thought Rachel. It's that if he behaves like this, he doesn't love me. But as she dug, and the blood spread round her limbs, she found herself thinking that Suyin could be right. It could be the reason.

Half an hour later, a shadow fell across the pit. She looked up. It was Raymond, the breeze blowing his elegantly cut trousers around his thin legs. She was suddenly afraid – not, this time, of being alone in a strange place, but that she would lose this man.

Raymond said, 'We should go.' His voice was soft, almost tentative.

Suyin said, quietly, 'Think of my arse,' and gave a high, manic giggle.

Raymond put his hand out, the hand calloused from digging, and pulled Rachel from the trench. The low red sun was casting black shadows from the mounds of the excavations. Normally, Raymond walked a correct distance from her, aloof and dignified, as befitted a rich man and his gweilo woman visiting a group of treasure hunters. But this evening he held her hand, and did not speak as they walked towards the car.

They drove back to the house in silence. Rachel could still feel the warmth of his grip. She was sure Suyin was right.

But what would his daddy say?

She did not give a damn what his daddy said, Confucius or no Confucius. She was a grown woman with the man she loved. The ball, as that trite bastard Jeremy would have put it, was in her court.

Raymond turned the Lexus between the lions. A servant came into the courtyard and drove the car away. They walked into the hall, where lights made watery translucencies in jade screens, and incense burned in archaic Shang braziers. What Rachel had to say felt like a tennis ball in her throat.

She said, in English, 'Why are you keeping me here?'

He looked around. She thought, He's looking for a servant to call, to avoid the issue. There were no servants in sight, and the hall was fifty yards on a side, so there was no one in hearing. She realized that he was checking that whatever he was going to say was to be for her ears only. He was going to mean it.

He said, 'I love you.' The lamplight gleamed on his teeth.

She thought, Suyin, your arse is not blue. She heard herself say, 'I love you too.' She thought, God forgive me, everyone forgive me. I am probably being a bloody fool, but I mean it, and my knees have turned to sugar. And by then she was hanging on to Raymond for support, and his arm was round her waist, and his mouth was looking for hers. And her last coherent thought was, *At last*.

A lot later, they were lying in Raymond's ebony bed, playing chess.

She looked into his eyes and thought how wonderfully thick and black the lashes were. Then she thought, It's you and me now, and your father is nowhere. The power is back in balance. Yin and yang, the phoenix on the bedspread.

She smiled. The golden woman, he thought. She had the

power of gold, but she was softer, and more fun, and gave a lot more pleasure.

He moved towards her on all fours, licking his lips.

She reached out a hand and moved her bishop. 'Check,' she said.

Normally, he hating losing. This time, he didn't care. He shoved the chess pieces to the floor, but not the board, which was made of cool stone. He rolled her on to it, manoeuvred between her thighs and looked down at her looking up at him with her round, golden eyes. 'Mate,' he said.

Next morning, pale and somewhat nervous, he drove her to the airport and purchased tickets for Beijing.

BOOK IV

Chapter One

During the next week the *Glory of Saipan* steamed north and east, away from the scattered volcanoes of the Carolines and into the empty blue bulge to the west of Hawaii. The north-east Trades were faint and warm, and the sun blazed down on the containers from a metal sky.

On the eighth morning after the watermaker had been repaired, Jenkins had put his head down after the four-to-eight watch. As usual, sleep had descended like a ton of black feathers. Then, suddenly, he was awake.

He lay there, watching the serene tropical island inside the plastic dome. It was a cool, still world under the dome, no past, no future. The kind of world it would have been nice to crawl into and go back to sleep in. But there was another world waiting: a world paralysed by Hugh Chang, and what he might do to Rachel. A world in which for the past week Jenkins had moved between his cabin and the bridge, ignoring the passengers, doing only what was absolutely necessary to keep the ship running.

A world in which this morning something was not right.

The *Glory* gave a long, slow roll, not the corkscrew of a ship heading diagonally across a corduroy of waves, but a side-to-side wallow, as if she was sitting in the trough of a sea. It was quiet.

Horribly quiet.

Jenkins fumbled for the telephone. The receiver felt sticky in his hand as he dialled.

'Engine room,' said a Filipino voice, too loud and too clear in the absence of background noise.

Jenkins said, 'Why are we stop engines?'

The voice said, 'Engine break.'

'Give me the chief.'

There was a short, dreadfully silent pause. Then Nairn's voice said, 'Yeah?'

'Captain –'

'Bottom-end bearing gone,' said Nairn, with something like relish. 'Five minutes ago.'

Jenkins thought of that quiet, domed world. 'How long?'

'Six hours, maybe.'

Jenkins said, 'Good luck.'

'Luck's got fuck all to do with it,' said Nairn. He slammed the telephone down.

Jenkins showered and went on to the bridge. Pete was up there, sweating in the chart room. 'Position?' he said. Pete prodded the plotting sheet with his finger. It left a damp mark east-northeast of Wake Island. 'Hot,' he said.

The sweat dripped. The ship rolled. A soupy breeze eddied in the thick air. Jenkins went out on to the wing of the bridge. The passengers were spread over the container tops, half-melted. Lucy was there, in the shadow cast by the accommodation, playing cards with Lin, daughter of Fung. Jenkins shouted, 'Hey!' and beckoned her to the bridge. When she arrived, he did not meet her eye; this was business. He led her into a black slice of shade. He had hardly seen her for a week. Seeing her was one of the dangerous things that he could not do, for Rachel's sake. He said, 'The engine's broken down. They're working on it. It'll take six hours to fix.'

Lucy gave him a sharp, ironic smile.

She said, 'Ten days plus six hours to the tuna boats.' She held his eye. 'Lin will be disappointed. Fung's daughter. She can't wait. She thinks she's going to school.'

'Thinks?'

'No visa, no school. She'll probably work in a garment factory. The money'll be great. When she's paid the fare, she can earn some more and go to private school to catch up on what she's missed.'

Jenkins kept his face still. He said, 'What am I meant to do?'

Lucy's face was a grim, impenetrable mask. 'You have a conscience.'

Jenkins frowned. Then he realized what she was saying and felt a sort of guilty panic. He said, 'I have a daughter.'

'So?'

'She is . . . a guest . . . of Mr Chang.' The words tasted ugly and bitter. They made him angry, with a self-justifying rage. 'She is the only child I have left. Perhaps you will understand.'

Lucy stared at him. He thought her face might have softened, but he could not tell. Anyway, he did not care. It was none of her damn business.

'Ask her,' said Lucy.

'Ask her what?'

'Ask her what she thinks about your . . . situation.'

'Is that what you would do if you were me?'

Lucy said, 'Maybe.'

'That's not an answer.'

She bowed her head. She said, 'Only you have that answer,' and walked off the bridge.

All very well, Jenkins howled inwardly. All very well for you. It's not your child.

Her child was dead, like Bill.

Christ.

It was time for Jenkins' rounds, but he could not face all those people. So he sat in the chart room, in the heat and the stink, and listened to the ship. Now that the engines had stopped he could hear the people, a sort of ragged choir of voices and tape decks and feet on metal: the hum of life. He was not part of it. He was detached, the way he had always been detached, part of the machinery.

It was not like being alive.

Out on the wing of the bridge, someone was shouting. Jenkins looked through the window and saw Fung, with a Chinese woman he did not recognize. They had come up the outside ladders. Now they were standing quiet-faced and stolid in front of Pete, who was waving his arms and roaring, 'Piss off back where you came from. Private property. Off bleeding limits –'

Jenkins walked on to the bridge wing. He said, 'What is it?'

Fung nodded and grinned and bowed in a sort of paroxysm

245

of pleasure at seeing him. The woman with him raised her thin eyebrows. 'Prease, captain,' she said.

'Piss off!' roared Pete.

'Hang on a minute,' said Jenkins. 'What is it?'

'Plivate talk needed,' said the woman. 'From Fung.'

Jenkins shrugged. 'OK,' he said. 'Thanks, Pete.'

Pete faded away, blank and stolid, and expressed his feelings of shock and indignation by setting fire to a cigarette.

'Yes,' said the woman. Fung spoke, earnestly and at length. The woman nodded, an odd upwards jerk of the head. She said, 'Fung says Lucy Moses not happy because she make pain for you about child. Yes?'

Jenkins shrugged.

'Fung wishes to tell you of Lucy Moses' child, story Lucy will not tell. Lucy in jail, many friends. Lucy not tell policemen names of friends because friends get big trouble. So policemen get child Lucy and give her none foods. You talk, we give foods, they say. But Lucy no talk. Child die. Friends safe.'

Jenkins stared at her, then at Fung. Fung was nodding with a sort of manic earnestness.

'True,' said the woman.

Jenkins nodded. He could feel the blood in his face. So what? he was asking. So bloody what?

But there was another voice. This voice said, It is how you make a monster. Push a man into inhumanity an inch at a time, dirty little deed by dirty little deed. Then hold what he loves most hostage, and he is yours; compromised by his actions, prisoner of the last and only sympathetic act of which he is capable.

There is no escape.

Lucy had escaped. Lucy had resisted conversion into a monster.

Lucy's daughter had died.

He said, 'Thank you. I hear what you say.'

Fung and the woman left. Sweating, Jenkins went back to the chart room, picked up the satellite phone and dialled the number in Xian. A Chinese voice answered. He said, 'Rachel Jenkins?'

The voice made interrogative noises.

'Raymond Chang?'

'Ah. Laymon. No.' The telephone went down, there was no way of telling why.

No more contact, then.

Jenkins saw the *Glory*. He saw his iron hotel, crammed with people, six million dollars of Chang's money, linked to Chang by an umbilical of bridge communications and his love for his daughter, and somewhere in the ship a satellite phone.

And at that moment, the *Glory* changed aspect. Jenkins was out here, in command of a great deal of Chang's money. Did not that give him as much leverage over Chang as Chang had over him?

Look at it like this. Every little bit of power Chang hasn't got is a little bit of power you have got.

Jenkins walked into the bridge, picked up the telephone, and dialled the crew messroom.

'Rodriguez?' said Jenkins. 'I want you to search the ship for a portable satellite phone.'

'Yes?' said Rodriguez.

'Reward for finding it, one thousand dollars US.'

'Yes,' said Rodriguez.

'Go down with Pete.'

'Yes, *sah*.'

Pete said, 'What's this?'

'Searching the hold for a satellite phone. Someone's talking to the shore.'

Pete frowned. 'So?'

'From now on, all communications come through the bridge. So get down there and tell the passengers to clear the hold, would you? Tell them vermin control. I want them leaving by the portside exit. No luggage needed. We'll have them back in half an hour.'

Pete said, 'They won't like it.'

'Then they can bloody well lump it.'

Pete gazed upon him, black-eyed, sceptical. 'If you insist,' he said.

The heat had brewed the hold's usual stench into an ammoniacal fog. When the people saw the cans of disinfectant

247

Rodriguez had brought to add credibility to the vermin patrol, some of them even looked cheerful.

With Rodriguez were five Filipino deckhands carrying buckets and stirrup pumps. He said to Pete, 'It hot. You sit down. We make search,' and started rattling Tagalog orders. The hands fanned out and trotted away into the maze of tents and partitions. Pete lit a cigarette with hands that dampened the paper, and began to walk aft, fast. The smell of disinfectant began to float over the partitions. As he approached number four hold there was a shout. 'Sah!'

Pete stamped on his cigarette and dived into the partitions, following the voice. He pushed aside a sheet of sacking and found himself looking at the aft bulkhead. In the bulkhead was an inspection panel. The cover was off. A deckhand was standing by the orifice, grinning. 'In here,' he said. 'Was hided. In corner.' He was holding a Samsonite briefcase in his right hand. There was writing on the case, small and neat: *Scansat*. Inside was an aerial and a handset, black plastic, anonymous. Pete snapped it shut. They went on deck.

Jenkins was waiting by the door from the hold. Pete was carrying the briefcase. Rodriguez was combing his hair and grinning. One thousand dollars meant a stunning bathroom in the house he was building in Cebu City.

The inhabitants of the hold began to stream back, over-heated and ill-tempered. There was a lot of shouting. In this heat, thought Rodriguez, it was not surprising. He clambered up on to the deck that looked down on the containers. Some of the hard men from the aft end of the hold were standing in groups, making threatening gestures towards the bridge. The captain was up there, the briefcase in his hand, asking questions of Pete, blah, blah. Rodriguez let his eyes stray over the crowd on the containers. A thousand dollars, he thought. A flush toilet, maybe same model as the one Elvis died on. The cousins would be stunned.

In the sea of faces, one face in particular caught his eye – square and toad-like, eyes fixed with a horrible concentration on the case in the captain's hand. The face of Ho.

As Rodriguez watched, Ho turned away and disappeared. Jesus Maria, thought Rodriguez, chilled. That guy looks angry. That guy looks *killer* angry.

He became aware that the captain was saying something to him. 'Sorry?' he said.

'Get out there and hose down the containers.'

'Hose?'

'With seawater,' said the captain. 'Cool 'em down.' Rodriguez had confidence in the captain. 'Get a hand on each of the hoses. Otherwise they'll all fry while the ship's stopped.'

Rodriguez said, quietly, in case he had forgotten, 'One thousand dollar?'

'End of voyage,' said Jenkins.

Rodriguez nodded, the lavatory gleaming in his head. He rounded up five other men, trotted down on to the deck, unrolled his flat canvas fire hose, plugged it into the hydrant and spun the tap.

White fans of seawater arced over the containers, made rainbows in the sun and drummed on the steel. A cool, salty mist floated on to the courtyard awnings.

In her corner of the forward courtyard, Lin, daughter of Fung, heard the drum of spray on metal. When she looked up, the sky was laced with rainbows. It had been a boring week. This was the second thing that had happened today, and it looked like a good one. So she loosed off a yip of delight and started for the ladder.

There were six other children in the forward courtyard. They got the message fast. Within thirty seconds they were on the top of the containers, dancing in the silver rain. People in the other courtyards heard them. Heads appeared. Soon there were more children up there, from the hold as well as the courtyards. There was little Ma who had had her appendix out, healing up nicely, with the pugnacious Leung flying close support. And after the children came the young, unmarried folk, hot too, with nothing to lose in the way of dignity. On the *Glory*, that meant people like Chiu the prostitute, taking the air in a little black dress and red-varnished toenails, and half a dozen muscular men aged between eighteen and twenty, from the back end of the hold.

The water played. The ship rolled. Chiu the prostitute sat demurely on the edge of the outside container, baring her face to the sun. One of the young men nodded at her. More or less out of habit she smiled back, a promising, sharp-toothed smile. The young man tensed his corded shoulder muscles, all gleaming with water droplets. Chiu felt a small surge of holiday mischief.

'Nice bod for a kid,' she said.

The young man gave her a drop-jawed leer. He called himself Larry, because thanks to long practice he was able to pronounce it.

'Playing in the water is one thing,' said Chiu, drumming her round heels on the container wall. 'Real men swim.'

'Swim?' said Larry, eyeing the heaving blue Pacific.

Chiu stuck her tongue out and waggled it lasciviously. Larry's Adam's apple jumped in his throat. He recollected his toughness. He nodded sharply, and dived in.

Chiu clapped her hands. Perhaps the ship's engine would start, and this cocksure moron would be left for the sharks. She simpered prettily at him. Two other young men, desperate for simpers of their own, stripped to their Y-fronts and dived after Larry.

How insignificant their little black heads looked in the big sea, thought Chiu; how divinely small and impotent. The starboard side Filipinos watched, grinning, hanging on to their hoses and blowing Marlboro smoke into the soupy air.

The faces in the water looked pale and frightened. The sea was bigger than they had expected, the ship's rusty side more distant. But they had to stay in, or lose face.

A voice from the container tops said, 'Hey!'

Chiu looked round and saw the Hung Kwan. Fear tingled in the long scar above her buttocks, but she was not inclined to show it. She said, 'Good afternoon, Limp Wand.'

The Hung Kwan ignored her. He said, 'What are these people doing?'

'Cooling off. You wouldn't understand. If your blood was any colder, you'd be dead.'

He flushed. But a whore's abuse was beneath a Hung Kwan's notice. To her joy, one of the Filipinos moved his hose, and a fan of white water fell on the Hung Kwan, soaking him from head to foot. She tittered, high and scornful. The Hung Kwan's face darkened with rage. 'All right!' he screamed. 'End of stupid games!'

The heads in the water swam quickly towards the ship. The Filipino kicked the pilot ladder down the side. They climbed up fast, and stood at the top like angular birds, lifting alternate legs to let the water run out of their underpants.

'Enough stupidity!' shouted the Hung Kwan. He turned on the children, twenty or thirty of them now, who had been playing in the hose-jets. 'Piss off, you!'

Fung's daughter Lin was beside herself with joy at being cool, and wet, and in the sunshine. It was just like a lovely summer holiday. The square man was very angry, and wearing smart big-man clothes that were soaked with water and clung to him so his big belly stuck out. Her father had told her to be good, but she was too excited for that. So she screamed, 'Piss off, you!' Then she dug Ma, who was her new friend, in the ribs with her elbow, and they both began to giggle so hard that Ma's stitches hurt, and she had to bend double, so of course Fung's daughter had to bend double too. And within ten seconds, all the children were in hysterics.

The Hung Kwan stood glowering, his lower lip jutting. There was a clashing of feet on ladder rungs, and Ho was by his side; a granite-faced Ho, with eyebrows low over his eyes and his teeth bared in a snarl of rage. The Hung Kwan said, 'We should talk later,' and walked away. Ho said, 'Back to your quarters!'

Little Ma said, 'Back to your quarters!' in a cheeky falsetto imitation of the Hung Kwan's Fukienese accent. The rest of them took up the refrain. Ho took a step forward. His hand flicked out, and he clouted Ma on the ear. Larry had some time ago decided that if there was someone he wanted to turn out like, it was Ho. So he stepped forward, grabbed Lin by the shoulder and hissed, 'Evil small brute!'

She punched at his legs, trying to wriggle free. One of her punches landed by pure accident in the crotch of his Y-fronts. He doubled up. As he doubled, he loosed a wild backhander that caught her on the side of the head and knocked her over the edge of the container and into the courtyard, where she tumbled into an awning, rolled down, and came to rest with a crash on a tin table round which four middle-aged women were playing mah-jongg.

She lay there for a moment, eyes wide, mouth open but silent. Then she remembered to scream. 'Help!' she yelled. 'They are killing the children!'

The people in the forward container had always known that their day would come. This was not the day they had been told to wait for. But in the heat and the anger, nobody waited for the code word. Preparations had been made.

From under the foam mattresses of the Dexion bunks, people snatched iron bars cut from container ties, filed to needle-points at one end, bound with tape or string at the other.

Up on the container top, Chiu rested her eyes impassively on Larry, who was kneeling on the deck, clutching his groin. She said, 'Not many people would have been brave enough to hit that child.' She got up, smoothing her tiny skirt over the tops of her thighs. There were voices in the containers like angry bees. If she was any judge of people, life up here would soon be dangerous and unpleasant. 'Come and see me sometime,' she said. 'For you, special rate. Double normal.' She wiggled away, nose in the air. As she went down the ladder to the hold she heard screaming, and the deeper shouts of men.

The children were frightened when the man hit Ma. Then they saw her land on the card table, and scream, and they thought that was quite funny. Then they saw the courtyard suddenly flood with running people, their mothers and fathers, who had been resting in the cooled containers. The mothers scooped them away, but their fathers went on, carrying their iron bars, towards Ho and the swimmers, and there was a hard, ugly look in their faces, as if the long hot week and the week before that had swelled in their minds and burst. Perhaps this was not the summons. But the time for turning the other cheek was past. This was Holy War.

The first five were three Christians, and another two of whom Larry had heard it said that they had spent time in prison, not for reasonable offences like rape and theft, but for making films or writing books or some other stupid crime against the state. Larry climbed painfully to his feet. Ho was yelling at the five men, who were hesitating. They lacked the no-flinch reflexes necessary for real violence. Larry walked crabwise to his jeans, fumbled in the special pocket and came out with his cleaver. It was eighteen inches long, sharpened razor-keen on the engine-room grindstone. The taped handle felt good in his hand. Out of the corner of his eye he saw his fellow-soldiers had theirs out, too. He began to feel proud and invincible, felt the warm rage heal his traumatized scrotum, spread through his stomach and into his chest and up until he was beginning the shout of fury that accompanied the slash of the cleaver at the scabby face of the moron Fung.

But he had not heard the footsteps behind him.

Down in the courtyards, the women had not been idle. There were holes between certain containers, made for a moment like this. Through one of these holes Mrs Fung had yelled to her friend Mrs Lee in the next courtyard that the gangsters were trying to murder the children. It had taken perhaps ten seconds for Mr Leung the tailor, who chanced to be measuring Mrs Fung's friend for a pair of trousers for evening wear in San Francisco, to hear the news and grab an iron bar that was leaning up against a corner of the courtyard. He elbowed his way on to the ladder, past three other men, all clutching weapons, who were also trying to clamber on to the container tops.

Leung arrived just as Larry began his swift, flat-footed charge on Fung. Leung did not hesitate. Holding his iron bar like a baseball bat, he sprinted up behind Larry and swiped his right arm. The bone broke with a sound like a firecracker. Larry screamed, and the cleaver clattered across the deck. Leung turned his attention to the other three men who had wheeled to face him. They had cleavers of their own. Leung had been hot for days, cooped up, deprived of tranquillity. Now he felt the righteous fury surging through him, driven by the surf of shouting and the war-drum boom of feet on the containers.

It was at this point that Jenkins heard the noise.

253

The cargo was crawling over the containers like ants on a carcass. The Filipinos had turned off the hoses and retreated. The sun gleamed in water, and on the blades of knives and cleavers.

Jenkins stuck his head into the bridge and said, 'Fetch Lucy.' It was Johnny's watch. Johnny's sick eyes bulged with fear. The crew were unarmed. These people could take over the ship. And then what? Jenkins grabbed the loudhailer and ran out on to the bridge wing, yelling, 'Get back to your quarters!' Nobody down there paid any attention.

He tugged the portable radio from his pocket and said, 'All hoses full power on containers. Rest of crew to bridge.' He ran down to the boat deck and, for the second time on this voyage, yanked the steel tiller out of the lifeboat. It felt chunky in his hand. Boots rang on the iron stairs. Six Filipinos appeared. Jenkins said, 'We're going to stop this fight. No knives.' Pete was leaning against the rail with his hands in his pockets. His face was mildly intrigued, but otherwise expressionless. He said, 'They've got bloody great choppers down there.'

'They won't hurt us,' said Jenkins. 'We're the ones who know how the ship works.'

Lucy was there. She said, 'Careful with yourself. Please.' She had underestimated this man. She needed his protection. But if he got himself killed, he would be no use to her. She would have to do something.

'Try the loudhailer,' said Jenkins. 'If it gets out of hand, lock yourself in your cabin.'

She watched him clatter down to the container tops, a man going to fight a war without knowing which side he was on.

The Hung Kwan also saw Jenkins head down the outside ladders of the high white accommodation. He walked through the evil-smelling lower regions of the ship until he found Ho. Ho nodded to him. Ho's telephone had gone. Ho was deaf, dumb and angry.

The Hung Kwan said, 'Perhaps it is time for another captain.'

Ho said, 'Today?'

'There are undesirable influences at work. In the confusion, anything could happen.'

The Hung Kwan left. Ho groped for the haft of his knife, loosened it in the ruler pocket of his overalls. Then he trotted purposefully towards the deck.

Chapter Two

Down at the aft portside hose, Jorge was losing heart. It was all very well for the captain to say 'full power', but it was not possible to train the hoses directly on the container tops. All you could do was arc the jets up and over. More like a cool shower than a water cannon, thought Jorge gloomily. He dropped the hose and wandered away from his station and up to the boat deck. There was a better field of fire from up there. But the stopcocks on the boat deck were painted shut. Sighing, Jorge went into the paint locker, found a hammer and a block of four-by-two, and strolled back up the steps. Ramos was also on the boat deck. He had lit a Marlboro and was watching the fighting with enjoyment. Jorge bummed a cigarette off him, lit it, and began to tap lethargically at the stopcock.

When the hoses dried up, the fighting really got going. Hitman, one of the original bathers, found himself crouching in a ring of men, each with an iron bar. Hitman's face was a shining mask of sweat and seawater. There was blood on his cleaver. 'Bastards,' he was saying. 'Scumsucking gutter-crawling motherfucking child-defiling sons of unburied migrant labourers. What are you waiting for?'

None of the men replied. The man in front of him raised his iron bar. Hitman started forward. The man behind him reached out and whacked him on the inside of the knee. Hitman went down, slashing furiously at nothing. One of the men stamped on his wrist. Another took the cleaver and threw it into the sea. Hitman closed his eyes and waited for someone to bash his head in. But these men were by the standards of Hitman's upbringing practically non-violent. Someone shouted, 'Leave him!' The battle surged away.

Lucy watched Jenkins run on to the deck. She saw the deckhands fan out, look around, and bunch up against the accommodation, protecting their backs. She saw Jenkins run forward between the knots of struggling men. Her hand went to her mouth as she saw him hesitate, look round for his backup, then up at the boat deck for the fire hoses. But there was no backup, and the men on the boat deck were still tapping away at the stopcocks with their four-by-twos. From above she could see that the men from the court-yards were paying no attention to him, the fools. But there was a little knot of men moving towards him now; young men from the after end of the hold, and an older one. The older one was Ho.

Lucy pressed her fingers against her mouth until her teeth cut into her lips. She had done what she had to do. She only hoped she had been in time.

Jenkins was out of breath, and sweating. And he was frightened.

He was standing with his back to the edge of the second courtyard, holding the steel tiller of the lifeboat. His backup seemed to have vanished. Facing him were four young men and Ho. One of the men was holding a cleaver.

He said, 'Go back to your quarters.'

Ho eyed him with intense dislike. The captain's face was red and hard. He had made a simple voyage complicated. He had taken his eyes off the objective, which was to make money. He had stolen Ho's satellite phone. He was in the way. With the captain gone, the rest of the voyage would be easy.

Ho was a killer only when he thought it necessary, but that did not interfere with his enjoyment of watching people die. He smiled, a smile that took the bottom clear out of Jenkins' stomach. 'Kill him,' he said to the man with the cleaver, for Jenkins' benefit. Then he translated into Cantonese.

The cleaver went up. It seemed to take for ever. Jenkins felt the twenty-foot drop at his back, was dazzled by the line of sunlight on the cleaver's blade. No, no, he thought. Not like this. Too stupid. He swiped with his lifeboat-tiller at the bather. It missed, slid out of his sweaty hand and clattered on metal far away. Jenkins understood that he was looking at death.

There was a sound halfway between a thump and a roar. The deck behind the man with the cleaver bloomed white. Something salty hit Jenkins in the face and smacked him backwards into mid-air. Blood, he thought, as the ground went from under his feet. But it was too cold for blood, and the wrong colour. Water. From the boat deck fire hoses.

He hit the deck with a crash.

He lay there for a moment, stunned. He was in the middle courtyard, flat on his back. He flexed his arms and legs, fingers and toes. Nothing seemed to be broken, he could not imagine why. There was the sound of squawking in his ears. Under his back was not steel but wicker. Feathers drifted in the blue square of sky. A woman was shouting.

He was lying in a pile of baskets. There were chickens in the baskets, kicking up an indignant clucking. It seemed to be raining seawater. He got his legs under him and crawled out of the smashed wicker.

He was not the only one to have been blown into the courtyard by the fire hoses. At the far side of the quadrangle, men were picking themselves out of a wrack of bodies. And beside him, stirring in the wicker, were Ho and the man with the cleaver.

Jenkins' heart walloped the wall of his chest. The man with the cleaver found him with his eyes and bounced on to the soles of his feet.

Same nightmare. Chapter two.

Then there was a new figure in the quadrangle.

Jenkins knew most of the people on the ship, in the sense that he had got used to them, the way they looked and the way they moved. But there was something wrong with this one.

It was a tall man, wearing jeans and a T-shirt, and he moved fast and springy as any of Ho's young friends. What was wrong with him was that he was wearing a black Balaclava-type hood, closed face. The eyewhites shone ice-clear in the holes, and in his right hand he carried a long, swordlike knife.

The eyes flicked at Jenkins, then at Ho and at the man with the cleaver. The man with the cleaver had not seen him. The man with the cleaver planted his feet on the rusty steel, grinned, and swung up the cleaver in a sort of salute.

The man in the Balaclava bounced up behind him and chopped his hand off.

Jenkins could taste the dirty air. He watched the hand continue its upswing, over and over into the sky, connected by a lanyard to the cleaver. He saw the blood fountaining from the stump of the cleaverman's wrist, the grimace of hatred turning to shock and then agony. He saw the man in the Balaclava scurry up the ladder with the horrible energy of a monkey and vanish over the lip of the containers. The world began to swim and waver. Ho, he noticed vaguely, seemed to have disappeared. Two people were bending over the man without a hand. The blood was coming in pulsing squirts. He clambered up the ladder and on to the top of the containers. The flat expanse of rusty metal was dotted with puddles. There were no people. The fire hoses would have swept them away. He pulled out his radio, but the water or the fall seemed to have broken it. There was no sound of fighting any more; just a scuttling in the containers, and the moans of the man with one hand.

Pete was on the bridge, pale, staring straight ahead through the windows. Jenkins said, 'Get yourself four men and go and fetch Ho. And be careful.'

When Pete had gone, Jenkins dialled Lucy. He said, 'Come here.'

When she arrived, he said, 'Ho was going to kill me. But a man I have never seen before came out of nowhere and chopped up the man who wanted to chop me. Who is he?'

Lucy was letting her jaw hang. She said, 'What are you talking about?'

'You know bloody well what I'm talking about.'

The telephone rang.

Pete was on the end. He sounded pleased with himself. He said, 'Bastard's overboard.'

'What bastard?'

'Ho. We talked to two guys who saw him go. Or pushed him, God knows. But he's gone.'

Jenkins said, 'Who were these people?'

'They were with the Christians.'

'Hold on to them.'

'They've gone,' said Pete. 'They were bloody terrified.'

'How did you talk to them?'

'One of them had about four words of English.'

Jenkins said, 'Did you believe them?'

'No reason not to.'

Jenkins said, 'I'll send Lucy down. Take her to them. Wait in the ship's office.'

'*Sir*,' said Pete, and hung up.

Ho was dead. The nightmare was only a nightmare.

He said to Lucy, 'Ho's gone overboard. They say they saw him go, pushed him, who knows? Find out. I want to know.'

Lucy came and stood by the chart table. He could smell her shampoo, a weirdly clean smell on the *Glory of Saipan*. She put her hand on his. She said, 'I'm very happy for you.' Then she kissed him.

Her lips were unbelievably soft. It felt like coming home.

This is not a dream, thought Jenkins. This is real.

The bridge door opened. Lucy sprang back. Mrs Nairn said, 'Sorry, I'm sure.'

Lucy blushed. She said, 'Excuse me,' and walked quickly out of the door.

Mrs Nairn was wearing a cardigan with a design of Westmorland terriers, and a blue denim skirt with splashes of fresh blood. She said, 'Into the bamboo, eh?' and compressed her lips into a grey line. 'None of my business,' she said. 'But I expect you've got a wife. I know it's hard for men. But is it fair on her? Specially with that one. Ask yourself, what's she after?'

Diana's voice again. The words did not mean what they said. What they meant was: If you behave like this, our money is in danger. 'You've got responsibilities,' said Mrs Nairn. 'I've been watching. You're out of line. Miles out of line.' She sounded like a golf club secretary telling off a member for spitting on the ninth green. 'Get your head together, Dave.'

Jenkins could still feel the softness of Lucy's mouth. In comparison, the financial health of Mr and Mrs Nairn seemed a distant and trivial matter.

'Any advice I can give you,' said Mrs Nairn. 'An older head. Wiser.'

'I'll bear it in mind,' said Jenkins.

The telephone rang.

Jenkins said, 'Thank you, Mrs Nairn,' and lifted the receiver.

'Starting engine,' said Nairn's voice.

There was a faint tremor in the deck now. Through the aft windows in the chart room he could see the funnel, blowing fumes at the fiery sky. He rang down for full ahead, entered it in the log, set the autopilot, and sent the datacom report Nairn had left on the keyboard reporting the engine failure. When he had finished, Mrs Nairn was still leaning against the windows in her cardigan with the little dogs on it, watching him with a face grim as if she had been carved from grey stone.

'Beer o'clock,' she said, playing her psychological trump card. 'Want one?'

Jenkins shook his head. When Rodriguez came on watch, he went down to his cabin.

You've come a long way these last three weeks, he told himself. You started out working for Diana, supervised by Soares, and Ho, and Lee. Now there is no more Diana, no more Soares or Lee. And by the looks of it, no more Ho.

He heard a chirruping from the wall.

He went to the safe on the cabin wall, opened it with the key on the string round his neck. The chirruping was Ho's satellite phone.

He carried the briefcase on to the dark wing of the bridge. The wake hissed like a knot of vipers under the flare of the bow.

He lifted the receiver.

Chapter Three

A voice said, 'Ho?'

He did not answer.

The voice spoke rapid Cantonese. He thought he heard the word 'Jenkins'.

There was a quiet wash of atmospherics in the earpiece. Jenkins could feel the darkness out there, miles of it, full of enemies.

He dropped the case into the sea, and went down to Lucy's cabin.

There was no reply, but he heard voices from next door, one of them Lucy's. So he knocked on the door, saying, 'Captain.'

Lucy opened the door. 'I was taking Jer some water,' she said.

'How is he?'

She opened the door. Jer's face was yellow against the white pillow case. The bedclothes were pulled up to his chin. He raised a hand. 'Captain,' he said. 'Chess?'

'Not now,' said Jenkins.

The cabin smelled of sweat and disinfectant. Jer's face was shiny with moisture. 'Aren't you hot?' said Jenkins.

'Fever,' said Jer.

Lucy said, 'My room's cooler.' They went in. She locked the door. She turned to face him. She said, 'I talked to those people. They said that once that guy had his hand cut off Ho ran away, aft, down the containers. Someone hit him with an iron bar, they didn't know who; or maybe they did know, but they weren't saying. And he fell off the top of the containers and into the sea. That's what they told me.' There was silence.

Then she said, 'You found your telephone, radio, whatever?'

'We found it.'

'Why did you go to look for it? Wasn't that . . . rocking the boat, with your daughter and everything?'

'I'm not much good at the abstract stuff,' said Jenkins. 'I worked out that it wouldn't make any difference. I mean if I've got the satellite phone, how's Chang going to hear about me having it?'

She laughed. Jenkins thought about saying that he felt more in control of his life, but changed his mind. Instead, he rested his head on the back of the chair.

So there was no more Ho, and he was in here with Lucy – the only place on the ship where he was at home. The only place in the world. Inside the bubble, in the tropic of cool, with the fake flakes floating through the fronds . . .

There was a hand in his. 'Come and sit on the bunk,' said Lucy.

He allowed himself to be led. 'Take your shoes off.' It was quiet down here, with the drowsy hum of the engine. He could smell her hair, which puzzled him, until he realized that her head was on his shoulder. Mrs Nairn rose hazily in his mind. He told Mrs Nairn to go to hell. His fingers were in the nape of Lucy's neck, in the silky black hair. You should not be doing this, he told himself. But Lucy said, 'Please,' and took his hand to her breast. And anyway he no longer cared whether that was truth or self-delusion, because such distinctions had got lost somewhere between her mouth and his, which were joined together now. The ship had vanished, the copper-sulphate sea and the iron-oxide hulk with its shoals of unreadable eyes and razor-edge blades glittering in the sun. What was left was this narrow bed in the Formica box of a cabin with the straw hat on the wall; the bed with the two people on it, large man, small woman. Lucy's body, naked now, him too. Then even the cabin disappeared. Somewhere, a voice was muttering to him: Compromise, making love to the cargo, giving the bastards ammunition. The voice persisted as Lucy's mouth began to gasp in his ear, and she twisted against him as if she needed to engulf his mind and his body all at once. Shut up, voice, he said. Because this feels like home, and I just don't care.

Afterwards, they held on to each other like drowning sailors clutching straws.

He sat up and pulled on his shorts and T-shirt. Lucy rolled over. 'Captain?' she said.

He stood up, avoiding her eye. He loved her. Was that wrong? He was losing his perspective. He wasn't sure whether it was wrong or not. But it was . . . undesirable. *Inappropriate*, said a scratchy voice that might have been Guy Warwick's, or Ross Clements', or even Jeremy Selmes'.

She stood on tiptoe and kissed his lips. When he reached his cabin he let himself in and sat down, and shook the snowflakes up in the bubble. They were shreds of paper in a plastic dome. No peace, no coolness.

What have I done?

Stepped off the rails. Led with your chin. Done what comes naturally. Done what felt right. Done what felt wrong.

Visited home. After twenty-odd years adrift, eighteen years with Diana. Finally, you have visited home.

And now you are back in the real world. Except that when you have visited home, there is no real coming back.

He went to the door and out under the urine-yellow lights in the alleyway. He ran down two flights and stood in the landing at the bottom. He could hear the clatter of pans in the galley and the Tagalog holler of the video in the crew messroom.

He went into the messroom and rooted about in the fridge. He found some orange cheese and some chutney, and compiled a sandwich with stale white bread from the bin. It reminded him of sandwiches on the boat in Hong Kong harbour, him and Rachel, doing a bit of light yachtigation. It was not the sort of sandwich you ate when Diana was around; high-fat, low-fibre, penalty a week of colonic irrigation. But that was all in the past now.

The door crashed open.

The plate went on to the floor, and the sandwich followed it, face down in the ratshit and salmonella.

Nairn stood in the doorway. 'Wanted to see you,' he said.

He made a new sandwich. It tasted of felt and acid, the way a cheese-and-chutney sandwich should taste. 'What's the problem?'

Nairn said, 'That datacom you sent for me. Owners want us to pick up spares.'

'Nobody said you needed spares.'

'That bottom-end job was a lash-up,' said Nairn. 'Could go any time.' He paused. 'Unless of course you know better.'

'Your engine,' said Jenkins.

'Glad you noticed,' said Nairn. 'So anyway. They want us to meet a tug out of Kauai. They're confirming position later.' He left. Jenkins went up to the bridge.

Johnny was on watch. 'Over soon,' he said. 'Fourteen days now?'

'Maybe less.'

'Great,' said Johnny. 'I not feeling good. Heart, stomach. When I get money have operation. Ulcer, bypass.' He began to intone a long list of symptoms. Jenkins watched the stars gliding behind clouds. The world was changing. Soon they would be out of the tropics, and it would be March.

The datacom beeped in the chart room. Jenkins unrolled the paper. Someone in Chang's office had been extremely efficient. There was a position a hundred and fifty miles northwest of Kauai in the Hawaiian chain. There were part numbers, and a rendezvous time in two days. Jenkins put the position on the chart, and matched up the ETA.

'Long way south of track,' said Johnny, breathing stertorously over his shoulder.

Jenkins frowned at the pencil mark on the chart. Johnny was right. There were other problems, too.

Jenkins said to Johnny, 'Why would the owners want us to go so close to US territorial waters?'

'Crazy?' said Johnny, with a lugubrious twitch of the eyebrows. 'Too much coastguard.'

It was a big risk to take to collect parts for an engine that had not broken down. Like Johnny said, a crazy risk. It was not like Chang to take crazy risks. So he must be doing it for a reason.

Jenkins did not like things done for reasons he did not understand. They made him feel paranoid. On the *Glory of Saipan*, paranoia was usually justified.

The satellite phone warbled at him. He picked up the receiver.

Chapter Four

The Changs' house in Beijing crouched behind a high cement wall. In the ostentatiously large garden, the leaves of carefully arranged rhododendrons rattled in a wind gritty with dust from the plains to the north. Rachel liked the brand-new Mercedes that had met Raymond and her at the airport. She liked the wide grey boulevards, and the step-roofed arch over the gateway into the house. She liked the way Raymond discreetly held her hand. But she did not like the fact that he was nervous.

Well, thought Rachel, sticking her chin out at the glass partition between her and the Mercedes' chauffeur. Tough luck, Confucius. This is Rachel in the driving seat.

A wide, slab-faced man met them at the door. He was wearing a black jacket and striped trousers, smiling a blank-eyed butler's smile. 'Mr Pei,' said Raymond, using the Western title. 'Our major-domo in Beijing.' There seemed to be at least half a dozen servants. Mr Pei showed them to single rooms. Raymond made no objection. Rachel took a shower in a pristine marble-and-jade cubicle, and wandered out into the shadowy corridor leading back towards the centre of the house.

It was like all Chang's houses she had seen: courtyard after silent courtyard, somewhere between a museum and the *Marie Céleste*. It was beautiful, but the servants flitting in its vast internal spaces seemed like ghosts, and human voices rang eerily among its spirit screens and arcades.

Mr Pei smiled his butler's smile at her as she went across the hall. She could hear the faint sound of Raymond's voice on the telephone. She stopped to examine a T'ang jar.

Raymond had scarcely managed to dry his hair when Mr Pei told him the honoured father was on the line. There was no way out of talking to the honoured father.

The old man had barked, 'I told you to stay in Xian.'

'Change of plan,' said Raymond, bracing himself. 'People I needed to see in Beijing.'

The old man said, 'Night clubs. Casinos.'

'If you know a decent casino here, please give me the address. This is business.'

Chang's voice was low and dangerous. 'I make you a very large allowance. This can stop. You have acted in direct contravention of my wishes.'

'Other people work for a living.'

'Other people are not my son.'

'How did you begin your respected career?'

'That is a matter for me.'

'Forgive me,' said Raymond. He could feel it all pressing in on him, thousands of years of it. *Honour your father. Work for your family*.

Then Rachel's face came into his mind, the golden woman, who understood all this but was not a slave to it. The world had moved on.

Raymond found himself grinning. One thing was very lucky, he thought. The honoured father was so old-fashioned that his imagination could not encompass the fact that it was Rachel who had persuaded him to come to Beijing, not vice versa. 'Naturally, I revere you. Also naturally I must have interests of my own, as well as the ones I share with you.'

'Naturally,' said Mr Chang, in the snake-in-dry-leaves rustle he used to freeze his adversaries.

Raymond found himself hurt by it. Further, he detected an irreverent thought. *Silly old man*.

'Listen,' said Mr Chang. 'A job for you, while you are in the city. You will visit my friend Jing Zhimin at the following address.' He gave an address.

Raymond said, 'That is People's Liberation Army headquarters.'

'Correct. You will ask Zhimin in complete confidence to arrange for a visit to a ship, the *Glory of Saipan*, off the Hawaiian Islands. Write down this position.'

Raymond said, 'Is there nobody else who can do this?'

'Everything that concerns this ship is a matter of the utmost confidentiality. I am dealing with it personally. With your help and your help only.'

'Thank you, Father.' Raymond wrote down the position.

'You will tell Zhimin to instruct a man to attach himself to a tug of Stein Marine Services, out of Kauai. The company has already been briefed. This man is to remove the captain of the *Glory of Saipan*.'

'Remove the captain of the *Glory of Saipan*.'

'One hopes he can swim,' said Chang.

Raymond's mouth had become dry. He said, 'Swim?'

'It is hard to be sure of his loyalty now his daughter is not under my direct control.'

'Of course,' said Raymond, with correct deference.

'If you can spare time away from your other business.' He put the telephone down.

Raymond sat and stared at the telephone. He thought, My father could have asked any of his employees to do this, but he asked me. And the reason he asked me is that he wants Rachel to blame me for arranging her father's death.

He is asking me to choose, and he thinks I have no option.

Thank you, Father, he thought. Thank you for giving me the chance to test my love. He felt a sudden rush of anger. And thank you for misunderstanding so well, because you have made this easy for me.

He felt a sensation like a tooth being wrenched from its moorings. He ignored it. Father, he thought, I have been a dutiful son. But duty extends in two directions.

Rachel came into the room. Look at her, thought Raymond. The golden woman. She smiled, a smile that was the only natural thing in this tomb of a house. He wanted that naturalness to illuminate his life. For ever.

Raymond thought, In my father's eyes I am nothing. I am an unhatched egg, an unweighted lever, a house with doors and no walls. Honoured Father, in every life, in every thousand-year sequence of lives, there are moments when loyalties must change flow.

Rachel looked at the wooden face, the meaningless eyes. She said, 'Is there something wrong?'

He reached for the bottle of Johnny Walker Black Label on the green malachite bar and poured himself half a tumblerful. Rachel saw that his hand was shaking. He said, 'I talked to my father.' His eyes came up to meet Rachel's. She felt them like an arrow in her heart. 'I have been . . . accustomed . . . to obey my father. In everything.'

Rachel could not let her eyes leave his. It was as if their contact was a rope between them and they were suspended over an abyss into which if either of them let go they would both fall. 'He is a dangerous man to those who disobey him,' he said.

Rachel wanted to ask him what was wrong. But that would be too straightforward. She knew that what she said next would affect the way her life ran from that point forward. She said, 'Do you feel yourself in danger?'

He took her hand across the table. 'No,' he said. 'Not me.'

She relaxed. She said, 'You're ditching him for a blonde.'

'Gentlemen prefer blondes.' There was an awkwardness in the room. He smiled. Not, she thought, a genuine smile. His eyes slid away from hers. He said, casually, 'The danger is to your father. It would be best for your father if he did not take his ship anywhere near Hawaii.' A servant put a duck on the table, with pancakes and a tray of sauces.

'My father?' she said.

He nodded. 'Duck?' he said, his eyes on hers again.

She stood up. She looked suddenly white, the skin under her eyes shaded grey. She said, through stiff lips, 'Excuse me. I must make a telephone call.'

Message delivered and understood.

And now there were only the consequences.

Rachel's voice came clear and sharp over the satellite. She said, 'Dad?'

Jenkins said, 'Where are you?'

'Beijing. We've been here a while.' There was something wrong with her voice. 'Independently, as it were.'

'What do you mean?'

'You wanted me to be able to come and go as I please. Well, I am, and I have.'

'That's bloody marvellous.' Jenkins felt hot with relief. 'Does Mr Chang know where you are?'

'He knows. But he's not . . . in control. Not like before, anyway. Listen,' she said. The thing in her voice was nervousness. Fear, he would almost have said. 'I can't be long. They're trying to get you to rendezvous with a tug out of Hawaii.'

Jenkins said, 'How did you know that?'

She ignored him. 'Don't do it.'

'What are you talking about.'

'*Listen.*' Her voice was not merely nervous. She sounded close to tears. 'Someone will be on the tug with instructions to . . . remove you.'

Jenkins heard the last ring of the portable phone, saw the cleaver glinting in the sun. 'Who told you?'

'Doesn't matter.' Pause. 'What kind of ship is this that you're on?'

What was he supposed to tell her? Shipload of illegals for the San Francisco white slave trade; money's terrific?

But if she was free now, that changed everything.

He did not answer the question. He said, 'I want you to get back to Hong Kong. As soon as possible.'

She said, 'I'm quite safe with Raymond. You'd realize if you knew him. I've got to go.'

'Wait –'

She said in her strange, tight voice, 'Be careful.' She hung up.

Chang loses Rachel, thought Jenkins. The last point of contact. So he needs to get rid of me, too.

He went over to the chart table. He rubbed out the rendezvous point, plotted the Great Circle course for San Francisco and set the autopilot. Then he called Nairn's cabin.

He said, 'We can't pick up your parts.'

Nairn said, 'Why the fuck not?'

'Too dangerous.'

Nairn said, 'If I don't get my bloody parts it's stop engines.'

Jenkins said, doggedly, 'You can do without.'

Nairn said, 'Are you trying to tell me how to run my engine room?'

270

'No.'

'So get me my parts.'

Jenkins said, 'I want to speak to your wife.'

The telephone went down.

Ten minutes later Mrs Nairn arrived. By the chart-room light Jenkins saw she was wearing her Westmorland terrier cardigan over a pink nightie and nylon fur mules. Her face looked aggressive and puffy. She said, 'Goodness, Dave, Edwin's terribly upset.' Her voice was saccharin sweet. 'What seems to be the problem?'

Jenkins said, 'I want you to explain something to your husband.'

'Can't you explain it yourself?'

Jenkins said, 'Apparently not. Just tell him that the rendezvous with his parts takes us too close to Hawaii. If we get boarded or overflown by the US coastguard they will find outside latrines, washing on lines and three hundred and seventy no-visa passengers. And that will be it. Jail for us. Repatriation for the passengers. No money.'

Mrs Nairn chewed her bottom lip. 'So what happens if we don't make this rendezvous?'

'We head north. A long way north. Outside territorial waters. If the engine breaks down, we radio the tuna boats. They'll come and find us. Once we've transshipped the passengers we send Maydays, get towed in.'

She thought about that. The voyage was not being kind to Mrs Nairn. Her skin seemed to be turning from leather to paper, and her manner seemed separate from her, like a mask coming unglued. Behind the mask, Jenkins could almost hear the grunts as fear and greed slugged it out. Greed won, of course. She put a blunt, consoling hand on his arm. What looked like dried blood rimmed the nails. 'Leave it to me,' she said.

Two hours later, the bridge phone rang. Nairn's voice said, sulkily, 'One-forty RPM is maximum.'

'Everything OK down there?' said Jenkins.

'*Jesus*,' said Nairn, and put the phone down.

Jenkins went out into the cool breeze on the wing of the bridge. If the engine didn't hold out, he was in trouble.

For what was in his mind, you needed an engine.

*

For the next two days, the *Glory of Saipan* churned northward. The sea grew greener, and heavy grey bubbles of cloud rode the horizon. The Nairns were almost silent, but Jenkins could feel their eyes on him, intent as the eyes of a gambler who watches the ball in the roulette wheel, wanting to influence the outcome but conscious of his powerlessness. There was a brittleness to them, now. Things were developing, but not according to their plan. Jenkins had the sense that they might do something rash, explode. They needed careful handling, not shocks and bumps; like nitroglycerine.

So Jenkins stayed away from Lucy. He spent a lot of time on the bridge in the rattan chair, wearing a long-sleeved shirt now. He thought about the cold grey sea a week to the northeast. When you were down there in the flying-fish zone, you could not imagine it could do anything but last for ever. And then suddenly there was grey water bursting on the bridge windows, and you were freezing your ears off. And the unimaginable was all round you. It was like being in love, in that respect.

The unimaginable was already all round Jenkins. On the third day, he decided it was time to tell Lucy about it, and explain where she fitted in.

When Johnny came on watch at noon, Jenkins went down to Lucy's cabin and knocked on the door.

When she opened it her eyes looked big and shiny. Too shiny. He realized that she was nearly crying. He said, 'What is it?'

She blinked. Tears spilled over and ran down each cheek. She said, 'I can't talk. I'm working.'

He found himself nonplussed. He had come down to walk into a new life and slam the door on the old one. He had expected to find her alone, so he could tell her he was free, and what he intended to do about it. But there were two men in the cabin with her. One of them was Fung, the other was Jer. Fung grinned. Jer lifted a languid ochre hand.

She stood there, looking at him, defying the magnetism that was dragging them together. 'It ought to have been different,' she said. She touched his cheek with the flat of her hand.

'What are you talking about?' he said.

She slammed the door in his face. He heard the key turn.

He wanted to kick it in. He wanted to say, This is what I propose to do for you, so you do not have to be a slave, and these are the sacrifices I have made and am making, because I love you.

It would keep until he could get her on her own. Not too long, though. It was a big step, and if he waited too long he might lose courage. It was easy to be brave if you were brave on the spur of the moment. It was waiting that sorted out the brave men from the cowards.

He walked up the stairs slowly, heading for the bridge, his legs heavy with disappointment. Pete was coming out of the ship's office. He said, 'You ill or something?'

'No,' said Jenkins.

'Look bloody awful,' said Pete. 'Come and get a bite of lunch.'

Jenkins could not face the thought of the messroom. He shook his head. 'Rounds to do,' he said.

He went over the accommodation, then headed aft for the engine room. He hardly noticed where he was. *Why won't she talk?*

Jenkins, you are sulking.

He went on deck. The sun was hot, but not as hot as it had been a week ago. He began to walk forward down the narrow, rusty strip of deck between the containers and the sea. Ahead, the bow crunched into a blue-green roller. A cloud of spray lifted lazy as a dancer's arm and drifted aft, drumming on the sides of the containers. More of that coming, thought Jenkins. Three, four days now, at this rate. Maybe less. Better check the container lashings.

She will have finished her meeting by now. I'll go and see. Tell her.

He marched forward towards the bridge. A booby flicked overhead, riding the slipstream. Bit far north for you, he thought.

Another shadow moved across the corner of his vision. It seemed too big and too solid for a booby, and it was coming from the wrong place, a dark, crevasse-like alleyway in the containers. He looked round.

It was not a booby. It was a squat man with violent eyes and spiky black hair, and in his upraised hand was something silver that was coming at his head. He ducked. The thing that had been meant for his head hit his shoulder with a crash that sent pain all down his arm and up into his neck.

Ho.

But Ho was overboard, dead.

Something dreadful had happened to his shoulder. His legs went from under him. He fell to the deck, writhing. The cleaver blade flashed sun into his eyes and rang on the diamond-pattern iron of the walkway. There were little orange sparks, like meteorites. Jenkins thought with an odd deliberation, Ho can't be dead, because this is Ho.

His shoulder emitted a blast of pain that nearly made him vomit. The cleaver was going up again. Jenkins' skin crawled with horror. He writhed his body, panic-stricken.

He fell.

It was a five-foot drop from the walkway to the side-deck. He landed on the bad shoulder, and bounced. Bouncing was not a good idea. For one thing it hurt like hell. For another, the side-deck was four feet wide, with a metal wall on one side and the edge of the ship on the other. The *Glory of Saipan* was a merchant ship, not designed for passenger safety. There were no railings.

Roaring with horror, Jenkins skidded across the side-deck and under the single strand of rope that was all that separated the *Glory of Saipan* from the hissing green-white sea. The little steel coaming of her hull-deck join bruised his back.

Fifteen hundred miles from land.

He went over the side.

Chapter Five

His hands scraped across the side-deck. Roaring water kicked and buffeted his feet. He clawed his fingers, felt nails break, flakes of rust drive into his skin. The coaming came under his fingers. The fingers of the right hand caught. There was something wrong with the fingers of the left, on the end of the shoulder Ho had hit. He hung on.

The left hand lost its grip. He hung there by the right, his face pressed into the rusty plating. A little space became immediately, tediously familiar. There was a speck of black paint in the shape of Australia, a sea of orange rust, and a ragged-edged blot of white, spilled in some long-ago touch-up job. It was the thing you looked at while the wake plucked at your ankles, and the tendons in your armpit and elbow and wrist cracked, and the rust-sharpened coaming sawed into your fingers, and you waited for Ho to step down and chop those fingers right off and drop you screaming into the wake. It hurt enough to make you want to let go even without the cleaver, but you hung on anyway, because the fingers were the only chance you had. And that bastard Ho would be up there, saving the edge on his cleaver, prolonging the agony. Ho the Chinese torturer. Waiting for Jenkins to let go on his own.

Never.

But the arm tendons were red hot, and the joints were stretching, and the fingers were going numb. Jenkins rolled his head back, away from that boring little patch of plating. He saw his arm, the ship's side, the blue-white glare of the sky.

And against the sky, the shape of a man.

He thought it was Ho. He screwed up his face and yelled, an incoherent roar of defiance.

The shape of the man bent towards him. Come on, you bastard, thought Jenkins. Cut my hand off –

But the nerves and sinews would not take any more instructions from the head. His fingers had decided to straighten on their own. Jenkins could feel them sliding over the rust. *You bastard*. He felt himself going.

The shape above him extended two hands of its own. The hands closed on Jenkins' wrist and plucked him out of the sea and on to the deck. As he reached the top of his arc he saw a black cloth face, eyes gleaming behind eyeholes.

Not Ho.

He landed face first. He lay with his face pressed into the stinking iron. Soon, he was able to breathe. Having his life back renewed the fear of losing it. Carefully, he rolled away from the greedy hiss of the side.

He was alone.

The walkway was a straight, rusty road stretching fore and aft between the cliff of the containers and the blue dazzle of the sea.

He began to crawl.

It was Rodriguez who found him. He helped him to the ship's office, sat him down, and left to fetch Mrs Nairn.

'Don't leave me,' said Jenkins. 'Use phone.'

Rodriguez observed that above the blood-soaked collar of his shirt the captain's face was a silvery white. His eyes were glassy, jumping from his face to the door, as if he expected someone to come barging in.

'OK,' said Rodriguez.

When the telephone rang, Mrs Nairn reached automatically for the bag with the rubber gloves and half-moon needles. She took it up to the ship's office, dumped it on the desk, and eyed the figure in the chair.

Jenkins was a nasty colour and there was a lot of blood, fresh and dried. He did not look at all good. Mrs Nairn derived considerable comfort from this. Lately, she had the sense that this drongo was getting away from her, wind under his tail, feeling his oats. Slumped in the chair, he had lost his power to frighten. Meat on the slab, thought Mrs

276

Nairn, snapping on her rubber gloves in honour of the white man. The human race was a pain in the arse to deal with on account of it was so complicated. But when it was meat on the slab, it was easy as bloody pie. She cut the T-shirt away from his shoulders. Under the shirt there was the usual mess. Healthy torso, mind you; decent bit of muscle, no fat. Not much chance of overweight on the *Glory*. When this was over and they were paid off, Mrs Nairn was looking forward to taking Edwin on a long, expensive cruise, a temperance cruise maybe, but a cruise with a real platestacker of a buffet.

She said, 'Well, you've been in the wars.'

Jenkins' pupils were large, his skin clammy. Shock, she thought. 'Ho did it,' he said in a blurred voice. 'Threw me overboard.'

What did you expect? thought Mrs Nairn. A Chink was a Chink. Get lovey-dovey with a bunch of them and you were asking for trouble. 'Dear me,' she said, insincerely. 'I thought he was dead.'

'So did I,' mumbled Jenkins.

'Well,' said Mrs Nairn, 'I won't say I told you so.' She threw disinfectant into a bowl and began to swab, skilfully but urgently, the way a vet might have swabbed a semi-domesticated animal. 'Could have had your arm off,' she said. 'Wasn't really trying, though. Didn't break the collarbone, not much damage to the muscle.'

Jenkins thought, He wanted me to drown, not bleed.

When she had finished the shoulder, she did the right hand, no stitches required, just a bit of cleaning up on the inside of the fingers. She snapped the rubber gloves off her square white hands and gave him an envelope of pills. 'You'll feel pretty bloody awful for a bit. Shock.' She wagged her finger, happy to be on top again. 'And like I said. Steer clear of our Chinky chums.'

When she had gone, Jenkins reached for the telephone. His shoulder was emitting a heavy throb, and dialling was difficult with the thick pads of dressing on his fingers.

There seemed to be padding on his mind, too. When Pete answered, he said, 'Find Ho.'

'What do you mean, Ho?'

'He's alive. Bastard tried to chop my bloody arm off, toss me overboard. And find whoever it was told you they saw him go overboard.'

'Christ,' said Pete.

'Any problem, kill the bastard.'

'What –'

'Do it now,' said Jenkins. 'Send two men outside my cabin door. Bodyguards.' His tongue felt the size of an oarblade. He fumbled the phone back on to the hook, washed two of the white pills down with Wild Turkey from the filing cabinet and stumbled to his cabin.

There had been a man with a Balaclava. A man with a Balaclava who had got rid of Ho in five seconds and dragged Jenkins up the ship's side. Must have been following me around, thought Jenkins. Why the hell?

He fell on his bunk. In his mind a severed hand and a cleaver looped up into the blue sky, linked by a lanyard.

He held up his own right hand, the fingers mummified in their dressings. Above the wrists, where Mrs Nairn had not cleaned, the arm was smeared with blood and black grease.

And something else. A greasy substance, faintly sticky to the touch, the colour of yellow ochre. He had seen something like it before. It was the stuff that had been on the boiler suit left in the locker where the two thieves had been sliced up.

Inspiration dawned.

I know who you are.

He fumbled the telephone to him, and dialled Lucy's cabin. She answered. When she heard his voice, she said, 'I was told he was dead. I swear to you, those men told me he was dead.'

'Yes,' he said in the scratchy, laborious voice that seemed to be his. 'Very probably. Listen. I know what you're up to.' She started to say something. But Jenkins had fumbled the telephone back on to the cradle and passed out.

Some time in the darkness, the telephone rang. When he picked it up, Pete's voice said, 'Can't find him.'

'Find who?'

'Ho. Maybe the bloke who rescued you put him over the side.'

'Look again.' Outside the door, the bodyguard coughed. Jenkins fell back into his confusing dreams.

He stayed there for a long time. He had no idea exactly how long, because he could not tell whether he was awake or asleep, sweating and shivering, leaving his bunk only to unlock his door when the bodyguard said it was Mrs Nairn or the mess boy with bowls of rice that he could not eat. In his lucid moments he was conscious of fear, focused on the spiky black hair and bared teeth of Ho. At less lucid times, he became mixed up in complicated dreams in which Diana and Lucy were arguing about duty. Then the dreams went, and he fell into a long black sleep.

When he woke, he felt like a length of wet bandage. But he was in the usual dirty cabin, and he could get his legs over the edge of the bunk and on to the deck. And his shoulder, instead of throbbing, was merely achy, and the eroded patches of skin in the finger-crooks of his right hand had scabbed over.

He sat for a moment, his head faint and spinning. It was cold. Somewhere in the accommodation, a door was slamming, opening with the ship's roll, slamming again. It struck him as a lonely sound. He looked at his watch. The date panel told him he had been ill for three days. He could feel that everything had changed.

Before, the *Glory of Saipan* had proceeded at a steady corkscrew trudge across the regular blue rollers of the Trades. Now her motion was bigger, less regular, with more pitch and less roll in the corkscrew. The seas seemed to be coming from on the nose. He shivered and rubbed his bare arms below the sleeves of his T-shirt. Three days could mean the best part of a thousand miles northeast of their last position. Approaching the rendezvous with the tuna boats. He was running out of time.

He rummaged in the steel locker, found a flannel shirt and a blue jersey with padding on the shoulders and pulled them on, being careful with his bad arm. The effort was exhausting. He opened the door. The Filipino bodyguards looked surprised. Jenkins said, 'We'll go to the bridge.'

The alleyway was empty, except for a puddle of water on the linoleum and a cold draught from somewhere. Below, the door was still slamming. Clinging to the handrails, Jenkins led the bodyguards up to the bridge and collapsed into the rattan chair.

Outside the windows, the Pacific was a new ocean. The boobies were gone. So were the flying fish, and the razor-cut line of the horizon. In their place was a low grey mat of stratus fading into a blackish murk. The sea was a range of moving grey hills, over which the *Glory of Saipan* was clambering laboriously. As Jenkins watched, her stubby bow struggled up a grey slope, hung weightless for a moment, and commenced a long plunge into the next valley. At the bottom of the valley the steel bulb of her ram squashed out fountains of ice-white spray, kept on plunging as the next hill rose up and over and thundered on to her foredeck, creaming round the windlass and slamming the anchors back into the flare of the bow with a crash that made her leprous plates shudder. White spray shot up the front of the bridge windows and drifted aft in lazy clods. It would be wet in the containers. He pulled the phone towards him and dialled Pete.

'*There* you are,' said Pete, relief in his voice.

'Where's Ho?'

'Still couldn't find him.'

It was what he had expected Pete to say. He rang off and hobbled over to look at the Navtex.

The slip spoke tersely of intense depressions in the North Pacific, and issued gale warnings. The GPS gave a position two days from the US coast. Jenkins thought about what was waiting up there behind the grey clouds, the tuna boats bobbing like boxers, dirty little steel buckets with stinking holds and crews armed with tuna gaffs and cattle prods. In another twenty-four hours they would be in VHF range. There were another twenty-four after that, perhaps a bit more, to Oakland and the payoff. In his mind he saw people swarming down a cargo net hung from the *Glory*'s rail. There were women, and children, and luggage: suitcases now, no chickens, no cooking pots. The Christians were there, and Fung. And Ho, watching from his blank black eyes. Ho's job was over. The crews of the tuna boats were his fellow-soldiers and business partners.

Jenkins watched Fung and his daughter climb on to a separate raft, with the Christians and Jer, yellow and shaky. And last of all, Lucy.

The rafts dwindled towards the rolling deckhouses of the tuna fleet. The *Glory of Saipan* lay empty on the sea, except for her crew and her officers.

Jenkins thought, We are all going to America, because that is where you have paid to go, and we have been paid to take you.

But not that way.

He had known that for some time. Since before Rachel had called from Beijing, in fact.

He collected his bodyguards and headed for Lucy's cabin.

There was no answer at the door. Ramos the second engineer was letting himself into his cabin down the alleyway. 'She went to forward courtyard,' he said.

On deck, the wind slapped him in the face like a wet rag. Someone had rigged stanchions on the container tops, with double rope lifelines. The metal roofs of the containers shone with water. As he took the shaky step up on to their tops, a wave burst against the accommodation. Heavy spray sleeted aft and landed with a metallic thunder.

The stanchions made a walkway from the accommodation to the top of the steel rungs running down into the first courtyard. Jenkins found he was panting as he went down the rungs. The stitches in his shoulder pulled, and his body was slimy with sweat.

There was a little lake of water in the courtyard, sloshing backwards and forwards with the ship's roll. Jenkins tried to time it right, but he got cold water in his shoe. He heard the bodyguards curse. A thin rain had begun to fall.

The courtyard had changed. All that remained of the awnings were shreds of plastic tarpaulin fluttering in the wind. The doors of the individual containers had been closed with bits of old pallet wood, the cracks stuffed with polythene. The metal of the containers was running with condensation. There was no washing, and no people. But of course there were voices. In a Chinese courtyard there would always be voices.

Jenkins waited for the dry roll, and skipped across the

hatch-cover to the ladder that led up to the Hapag Lloyd container inhabited by Fung. He rested for a moment, hanging on the iron rungs by the red-checked oilcloth table covering that was doing duty as Fung's door curtain. From behind the curtain came voices. Fung's voice, then Lucy's.

Jenkins stopped breathing. He found his hands clamped immovable to the ladder.

Fung spoke only Chinese. That was why Lucy had set up as ship's interpreter.

So why were they speaking English?

Chapter Six

Lucy said, 'I don't know.' She sounded worried; frightened, even.

'Now,' said Fung's voice, heavily accented but definite. 'Now is the time.'

There were two or three other voices speaking in Cantonese. Lucy and Fung seemed to be speaking English so as not to be understood. An argument seemed to break out. It sounded as if there were twenty people jammed into the container.

Jenkins clung to the ladder for the space of two rolls of the ship. He could hear Mrs Nairn's voice in his head, mocking him. *I won't say I told you so.*

All this time, Lucy had been using him.

He put his head in at the curtain. The container was full of people and luggage. He saw Lucy's face turn slack with horror, the surprise on Fung's. And Jer.

A new Jer. A Jer with the skin of his face not yellow, but the colour of old ivory; and his eyeballs not jaundiced gamboge, but clear and white. And in his right hand, tapping against the left, a long, square-ended knife.

Jenkins saw again the severed hand and the cleaver orbiting each other against the clear sky.

Jer nodded and smiled, a familiar, friendly smile, and said, 'Good day, captain.' Jenkins looked at him because he could not bear to look at Lucy.

I fell for it, he thought. Hook, line and sinker.

He said, 'What are you doing?'

Lucy's face was in her hands. She does care, he thought.

'It is time to go,' said Fung.

Behind Jenkins in the courtyard there was shouting and the thump of bodies on containers.

Then something grabbed his leg. Jenkins looked down.

He saw a hand gripping his ankle. He saw another hand, holding a sharpened iron bar whose point rested on the tendon behind his right knee. There were two other men in the courtyard, each holding one of the Filipino bodyguards with his face to the wall.

The man with the knife jerked his head.

Slowly, Jenkins climbed down.

The man grabbed his left arm, the bad one, and held it behind his back with a firmness that was not painful, yet.

Jer's head appeared round the red-checked tablecloth. His eyes were snapping, as if he was very excited. He looked at Jenkins, and spoke rapidly. The man with the knife said, 'You cabin. Give me key. You go first.'

Jenkins gave him the key, and started walking. The man came round behind him, keeping the point of the knife over his right kidney. There were other men there too; Jenkins could hear their feet on the hollow iron. Run, thought Jenkins. Shout, get help.

But he was too weak to run, and there were too many people to run away from.

Jer had not had liver cancer. Jer had had yellow grease-paint, and yellow contact lenses. There had been yellow make-up on the boiler suit Jenkins had found with the sliced thieves. Lucy had depended on her visibility to keep her safe. A visible Jer would not have lasted five minutes in the hurly-burly of the ferry or the hold. An isolated invalid was invisible. So to give himself freedom of movement, Jer had made himself an invalid.

Chang had his enforcers. Lucy had her enforcers too, so she could look after her friends.

Jenkins closed his eyes. The other way Lucy had protected her friends had been by making herself pleasant to the captain. Keeping him happy and out of the way. The captain had been her ally. She must have known that the witnesses to Ho's fall had been unreliable. So she had told Jer to follow him around, make sure he stayed alive for her to work on. She and Jer had always been a team. Jer the muscle; Lucy

284

the mind, operating to blind the captain to what was going on in the cargo. Lucy, the interpreter as spin doctor.

No wonder Lee had tried to drown them on the ferry.

They drove him up the steel stairs outside the accommodation. They let him into his cabin and motioned him to sit down in the heavy steel desk chair. The cabin seemed full of people. A man pulled a set of handcuffs from his pocket and snapped one bracelet on to Jenkins' bad wrist and the other on to the arm of the chair. Then he wrenched the telephone cable out of the wall. He bowed, impassive. 'Sorry,' he said. He went out of the door, and locked it behind him.

He pulled experimentally at the handcuffs. His shoulder hurt like hell. The chair was too heavy for him.

Bitch.

He said it to himself again. He could not make himself feel angry. Sad, yes. Face it, thought Jenkins. There was no reason for her to trust you. If you were her, you would probably have done the same.

There was more shouting in the accommodation. He could hear Pete's voice, and a hoarse yowling that sounded like Mrs Nairn.

The *Glory of Saipan* lifted by the bow, and came down into the trough of a wave with a crash that made her shudder. The wind was going up. Why had these people chained him in his cabin?

A key rattled in the lock. Lucy came in. She opened her mouth to say something, but no sound came out. She had been crying.

Now that he could see her it was not so easy to be objective. He said, 'What are you doing?'

She still did not look at him. She said, 'The engines are at slow ahead. The ship is on autopilot. The crew are in the paint locker and the officers are in their cabins. Pete has been given some sleeping pills. When he wakes up he will release you.'

Jenkins said, 'Why?'

'We are leaving. We'll take the lifeboat.' She shrugged, as if she wanted to say more, but there was no more that could usefully be said.

Jenkins said, 'You can't launch the lifeboat in a sea like this. You'll be killed.'

She smiled. 'You have to say that.'

'It's true. Listen. I was on my way to tell you. We can go all the way. I'll take you –'.

'Excuse me,' said Lucy. 'I must be quick. All I can say is that I and my friends would rather die than go aboard those tuna boats.'

He said, 'That's what I wanted to tell you. I won't put you on the tuna boats.'

She smiled at him. There was regret in it, tenderness. She said, 'Maybe that's true. But there are too many of us for me to take the chance.'

The *Glory* crashed into a new trough. A gust screamed in the aerials.

Jenkins said, 'Assuming you drop the lifeboat into the sea, you'll never get aboard it. And even if you did get aboard it, it wouldn't do you any good. You're five hundred miles from land, and there's a gale warning.'

Lucy did not seem to be listening. She said, 'You may not believe this. But I am sorry I lied to you.'

He looked at her. He thought she was beautiful. He said, 'It wasn't necessary. Not at the end.'

She said, 'Maybe.' She sounded uncertain.

He said, 'Who are you?'

'An ordinary person,' she said. 'I heard that Mr Chang was arranging this ship. I became one of his, well, recruiting agents. I recruited some people I knew, who were stuck in China, not allowed to leave legally because of politics, not rich enough to leave illegally. Jer is an old friend, a fighting instructor. He came to protect me, and to fight against Ho and Lee. On the ferry Fung lost his temper and told one of Chang's spies what I was doing. So the spy told Lee, and Lee tried to kill us.' She bowed her head. 'And you saved us.'

'And all that stuff about credit card forgery?'

'I thought then that it was the kind of explanation you would want to hear. An economic explanation, you know? Some people only understand that kind.' The green eyes were avoiding his. 'Ho was Chang's policeman, and so was

Lee, and Lee wanted to kill me because I looked like running counter to his boss's interests.'

'And all the rest was lies.'

'Lies.' She shrugged. 'But now I must take these people on the last part of this trip, or it's the Venus Mountain.'

'Lucy Moses,' said Jenkins. 'Not your real name.'

She smiled. 'No.'

'You're leading them out of captivity to the promised land?'

'That's right.'

'Was it true about your daughter?'

'Yes.'

Thank God, thought Jenkins. He said, 'Lucy, I love you.'

She took his face between her palms and kissed him. Her lips were soft and warm and slightly salty from the tears. Real tears. She said, 'I am sorry about the lies. And about Ho. So is Jer. Neither of us want you hurt.'

He said, 'Nor I you. And I promise you, if you go over the side, you will die.'

The door slammed. The key rattled in the lock. She was gone.

He saw what followed through the porthole.

They came up from the containers in a procession, carrying their old suitcases and their bundles. There were fifty-four of them – the Christians and some others, the whole of the Lucy faction, according to plan. They crowded on to the steel postage-stamp of the boat deck, wearing lifejackets, big orange slabs of cloth-coloured cork that made frames for their cream-coloured faces.

Jer seemed to be in charge of operations. He jammed the door from the alleyway and posted sentries at the heads of the steel stairs leading from the other decks. Then he attacked the lifeboat.

He was a big, fit man, but on a ship he was lost. It was obvious that he had had no previous dealings with davits. To launch the lifeboat (the manual said) a trigger mechanism was activated. This allowed the two cradles carrying the lifeboat to slide down their tracks, initially at thirty degrees to the horizontal, then steepening to the vertical, at which point the lifeboat swung clear of the cradles, which were now vertical, and hung suspended from the miniature cranes of the davits, well clear of the ship's side. It was at this point that the operator was to activate the hand-cranked winch, lowering the boat gently into the waters below.

This was not what happened when Jer tried to launch the lifeboat from the boat deck of the *Glory of Saipan*.

He stood at the front of the crowd and looked at the machinery. He saw a series of drums, on which lay coils of greasy black cable. The cable snaked away overhead, bartaut, round various pulleys whose function he did not fully understand. He could feel the pressure of the fifty-odd people and their luggage on the lurching deck, their eyes on his back, the effort it was costing them not to shout advice. If Ho was still on the ship and came up there would be a massacre. The sentries on the stairways might be desperate, but there was a limit to what a desperate university professor could do against Ho.

So Jer did not think things out properly. He grabbed the winch handle, and knocked off the ratchet, and let go a few turns. The cables slackened, but the boat did not move. He stood up and shoved it. He might as well have shoved the Great Wall of China.

Think, he told himself. Calm. He was sweating. He had exercised as best he could in his cabin, but his outings had been too brief and furtive to give him true calm in an emergency. The crowd was beginning to talk. Its yammer made him nervous. Spray whacked into his face. There must, he realized, be some sort of safety catch, or trigger. He followed the cables now, and found a lever of white-painted steel, leprous with rust. He tugged it with both hands. It would not budge. Of course, he thought, with the winch cables slack, the full weight of the lifeboat would be on the mechanism.

Frustration was blurring his thoughts. Quick, he thought. *Quick*. He shouted, 'Wind the handle back up!' And although he knew it was no use yet, he tugged at the trigger.

It was at that moment that a cross sea, a jagged reef of water twenty feet high, slammed into the *Glory*'s starboard side, the side where the boat was, and the crowd, and Jer. And things happened very quickly.

The surge of water shot up the ship's side and slammed

into the bottom of the lifeboat, forcing it three important inches back up the track, taking the load off the trigger mechanism. Jer felt the lever in his hand disengage. And suddenly the crowd was yelling, because as the wave receded the lifeboat had begun to slide, slowly at first, then faster, until the cradles tipped and the crane-jibs lurched outboard.

'Ratchet's on!' yelled the man at the winch, sweating into the collar of his lifejacket.

The boat dropped away, taking up the slack of the falls as the *Glory* rolled to starboard. It reached the end of the steel wires with a bang that shook the accommodation block. 'Wind!' yelled Jer.

The man on the winch tried, and failed. 'Jammed!' he yelled.

Jer knew nothing about the sea or ships.

As the next wave piled up to starboard, he thought he saw what was going to happen. The fat steel boat hung suspended, swung outwards by the ship's starboard roll. It was going to swing back in and smash against the ship's side. Someone had to get on board, let go the quick-release shackles he thought he could see connecting the falls to the lifeboat, drop it into the sea.

Jer looked at the next wave on the starboard bow. It was a long, grey slope of water with a dirty little topknot of foam, moving slow and easy seventy yards away. Plenty of time, he thought. I'll jump on to the boat and trip the shackles. They'll all climb down the ladder. They won't like it, but they'll have to.

He climbed light-footed over the rail. The lifeboat hung six feet below him, big as a swimming pool.

He jumped.

He missed.

It was a quirk of the sea, the merest wriggle of the *Glory* as the previous wave cleared her stern. It was enough to make Jer lose his footing and jump nine inches short, into the gap between the lifeboat and the ship's side.

He knew it was wrong as soon as he started falling. His mouth opened, and he put out his hands, square, flat martial-artist's hands still with traces of yellow greasepaint, and hooked his fingers over the lifeboat's gunwale.

The fingers caught. He hung there. Above and behind the rail, the crowd in its orange lifejackets moaned with relief.

The next wave came under just as Jer was pulling himself up and over the lifeboat's side. The *Glory* rolled to port. The lifeboat swung against her side like a two-ton hammer hitting a seven-thousand-ton gong.

Jer was between the hammer and the gong.

His ribs went through his heart and met his backbone on the way out of his chest. He dropped into the grey sea and sank like a stone.

The crowd stood stunned in its orange lifejackets. The next six waves beat the lifeboat to iron filings against the ship's side.

The *Glory of Saipan* only carried the one.

Then the people on the boat deck heard an odd sound. They looked up at the superstructure, the pylon aerials of the monkey island reeling against the whizzing grey cloud. Below the aerials, elbows on the rail, was a man in a white boiler suit. The man was laughing heartily, if somewhat theatrically. The people on the boat deck looked at him dully until he went away.

The man was Ho.

Chapter Seven

Lucy's cabin felt cold and neat and uninhabited. The straw hat was gone from the wall. She sat in the corner, grey-faced. She did not look up as Jenkins came in.

He said, 'I am going to take you right to San Francisco. I will land you somewhere where you can step off the ship and catch the bus.'

She raised her eyes. They were red with tears.

'Trust me,' he said. 'No tuna boats.'

She said, 'Jer is dead. Ho was watching. He was laughing.'

Jenkins said, 'I'm sorry about Jer.' He wanted to make her understand. 'He was a brave man. But he was . . . out of his depth. Listen. I'm going to take you ashore. All of you. No tuna boats. Right up the beach.'

She said, 'Why should I believe you?'

He said, 'Because I'm no bloody good at telling lies. And I want you to come with me.'

She smiled, a far-off, wintry smile. She took his hand in her cold fingers. She said, 'Thank you. Please, now. I need to be on my own?'

Jenkins said, 'Will you come?'

She squeezed his hand. This time, the pressure was warmer. He felt an answering warmth. 'Don't worry,' he said, and left the cabin.

He could hear the phones in the ship's office ringing as he walked up to the bridge. Pete was up there, looking groggy and dull-eyed. The windscreen wipers were whining like dogs. Beyond the windows were the white, ghostly crests of breaking waves. 'Jesus,' he said, when he saw Jenkins. 'Feel like I was mugged.'

Jenkins ignored him. 'Ho's alive,' he said. 'You said you couldn't find him.'

'I couldn't,' said Pete. 'But I'm not surprised he's still on board. You try looking for someone in that lot.'

Looking at him, Jenkins saw only injured innocence. What else did you expect?

'Get some coffee,' said Jenkins. 'Have a shower. Get woke up.'

Pete nodded, the sulky nod of the unjustly bollocked. Jenkins rang Rodriguez. 'Come up to the bridge,' he said.

Rodriguez arrived, bug-eyed. 'Was locked up,' he said. 'In paint locker. Also Mrs Nairn and chief. Very angry.' He grinned. 'But they're happy. They say, ten hours to rendez-vous, then we get rid of all these peoples.'

The telephone rang. Mrs Nairn's voice said, 'I've just been locked up for four hours. What the bloody hell –'

Jenkins said, 'Some of the passengers tried to go over-board. I've got the situation under control.'

'You have?' She sounded surprised. 'Congratulations.'

Jenkins rang off. He said to Rodriguez, 'Get me someone who can paint.'

'Paint?'

'With a brush.'

'Unh-hunh,' said Rodriguez. 'Graceland, here I come.'

It was not a nice job. It did not please Ramos the second engineer, who had to run leads off the generator and hitch them up in the hissing rain to a banana-bunch of inspection lights. But it was not nearly as bad for Ramos as it was for Eduardo, who was a deckhand. In fact, Rodriguez had to promise Eduardo four bottles of Fundador to get him to do it.

So now Eduardo was hanging over the stern of the *Glory of Saipan*, with the rain rattling on his hard-hat and his bony arse strapped into a bosun's chair, and a pot of black paint lashed to his leg. By the yellow glare of the inspection lamps he was painting out some of the letters in GLORY OF SAIPAN with a big brush, while the white wake tore at the black seas five feet under his boots.

When he had finished with the black, his mate on deck

lowered him a can of white and a new brush. He worked for another half-hour. Then he said, through chattering teeth, 'Done.'

They winched him up. Rodriguez leaned over the stern, inspecting his work. '*Mabuti*,' he said, bellowing over the noise of the generator. 'Good.'

Eduardo stood shivering and dripping on the afterdeck. He said, 'So give me one of the bottles.'

'Bottles?' said Rodriguez, the inspection lights glinting from his gold teeth. 'You crazy? First you finish.'

So Eduardo took his paintpots up to the bow, poor devil. And while the *Glory* turned tail-to-sea and went slow ahead, he slapped on the paint. An hour later the brush had fallen out of his numb hands, and the paint was mixed with sea-water, and he was half dead with cold. But the job was done.

The ship sailed on towards the rendezvous point with a black patch of paint under the flare of each bow, masking the name *Glory of Saipan*. But on her transom, blotchy with more new paint, were the words: YOOFUS – LIBERIA. As good as Jenkins could manage in the time allowed, and possibly enough to confuse a tuna boat skipper looking for a ship of a different name.

He had taken the big step. For the sake of Lucy and her Israelites, he had done the right thing, whether they were grateful or not.

It was not a comfortable feeling. Those tuna boats repre-sented safety and security. Beyond them, he was outside the law of Chang, and the law of the USA, and the law of the sea.

On your own. You and Lucy, and three hundred and sev-enty others. Leading with your chin.

The Nairns were in their cabin. Pete was asleep. The crew did not know what was happening.

Nobody except Jenkins knew what was happening.

How can they stop us now?

The bridge filled with a shrill warble. The satellite phone was ringing.

Raymond Chang was frowning through the window of the chauffeur-driven Mercedes at the huge neo-Stalinist build-ings flowing past on the margins of the boulevard.

This morning, after a week in galleries and libraries, he and Rachel had been ready to depart for the ceramic galleries of the Beijing Gugung when his father had called to instruct him to visit a Mr Lim in the Ministry of Culture, to discuss the decorations of some hotel on Hainan Island. It was not that Hainan Island was unimportant; the making of money was a topic dear to Raymond's heart, and the Hainan project was going to produce a lot of it. Nor was it entirely that Mr Lim was a windbag who substituted a vast appetite for flattery for influence or taste. What really irritated Raymond was that being with Lim meant he could not be with Rachel, who had therefore left for the museum with Mr Pei the major-domo, despite her protests that if she could not go with Raymond, she preferred to go by herself.

The Mercedes whispered to a halt at the foot of the grey-green cliff of masonry. Raymond stepped out, and was conducted into the presence of Mr Lim, a small, buck-toothed man who reeked of ancient cigarettes. 'Ah, Mr Chang,' said Mr Lim. 'Let us talk about wallpaper.'

Raymond sat down on a hard chair and smiled a mechanical smile. His father had said that Mr Lim needed placating. If he wanted to talk about wallpaper, wallpaper was what they were going to talk about.

Rachel, in the Beijing Gugung, was not having a good morning either. Pei had stuck to her side like glue. His smile did not falter, but he kept looking at the watch on his thick, hairless wrist, and sucking air through his teeth. After she had been there half an hour, he was still interfering with her concentration. She said, in Mandarin, 'Why don't you go home? I'll take a taxi.'

He said, 'I am your translator.'

'But I speak Mandarin.'

'Everybody needs a translator.' A telephone twittered in his pocket. Honestly, thought Rachel, with a surge of irritation. Telephones in the Gugung are too much. She started to walk away. Behind her, she heard Pei terminate the call, and his footsteps. 'That was Mr Raymond,' he said.

'Oh?' She was surprised that Raymond would have called her at the museum. But she was in the sort of state in which the mere mention of his name made her feel happy. 'Why didn't you let me talk to him?'

'No need,' said Pei. 'He's found something interesting. He wants to show you.'

'What?'

'Surprise,' said Pei, with horrid coyness. 'Come.'

She went. They left the museum, and climbed into the other Chang Mercedes – his and hers, she thought of them as; she was sometimes shocked at how easy it was to get used to all this Mercedes stuff. Pei said something to the driver that she did not catch. The car pulled away. It moved fast. It shot through the late-morning cloud of bicycles and dived on to a succession of back roads, turning off the last one at a pair of high steel gates in a wall topped with barbed wire. The gates opened at the final moment. The car roared through and into a concrete yard, and stopped with a screech of brakes.

It was a big courtyard, perhaps fifty yards square. The wall in which the gate was set closed off one side of it. The other three sides were formed by a high building. There were perhaps ten storeys of windows – small windows, Rachel observed with puzzlement. Not only small, but barred. It looked like a prison. She said, 'What is this place?'

'Surprise,' said Pei, not smiling any more. 'We get out.'

Rachel found herself standing in the yard, her puzzlement cooling into something like fear. There was a revolting smell, composed of sweat and latrines. Pei said, 'Over there.' Over there was a door. It seemed to be made of steel, painted green. As Rachel watched, a slot the size of a letterbox opened at eye level and closed again. 'Come,' said Pei, gripping her arm above the elbow.

And at that moment Rachel knew that this was a prison.

'Welcome to the Residence of Right-Line Thought,' said Pei.

Her knees were weak with terror. She kept her face straight. She looked Pei in his soulless black eyes, and said, 'Get your hands off me.'

He held on. His fingers were like joinery cramps. The green steel door yawned wide.

Panic flowed through her like squid's ink in water. Raymond, she thought. *Raymond! Help!*

No help came.

Two small men in large peaked caps came out of the door and dragged her in. The door clanged shut.

Mr Pei climbed into the Mercedes and told the driver to take him home.

On the bridge of the *Glory of Saipan*, now the *Yoofus* of Liberia, Jenkins picked up the satellite phone.

A Chinese voice he did not recognize said, 'Captain Jenkins? Call for you.' There was the sound of scuffling. Then another voice. Rachel's. 'Who's that?' she said.

'Me.'

Rachel said, 'I'm in prison.'

The deck under Jenkins' feet seemed to vanish, suspending him in mid-air. He said, 'Prison?'

'Mr Chang arranged it,' said Rachel. 'I think the governor is on his payroll. They made me ring you.' Her voice was squeezed tight, only just under control.

The handset was slippery in Jenkins' palm. Calm, he thought. He said, 'Who are they and what do they want?'

'You have to make a delivery. Once you have made the delivery, I will be released.' Her voice wavered. 'What is this delivery?'

Jenkins tried to think of an answer. None came. Instead, he said, 'Tell them that I will do exactly what they want me to do.'

'Oh, Daddy,' said Rachel.

The connection broke.

Jenkins stared at the screen.

Deliver Lucy.

Or lose Rachel.

Christ.

After three-quarters of an hour on wallpaper, Mr Lim had moved on to chandeliers. 'Yes, indeed,' said Mr Lim, darting a covert glance at his watch. 'There are also the types of chandeliers made of metal. There are the type made of bronze, the type made of steel, the type made of polished brass, even, it occurs to me, ormolu –'

'Excuse me,' said Raymond. 'I am experiencing personal

inconvenience.' Politeness was one thing. But this was intolerable. Raymond wanted to get back to Rachel. 'A small infirmity I picked up in Xian.'

Mr Lim smiled understandingly and bowed.

Raymond got up, squeezing his buttocks like a man caught short. 'Thank you for your enlightening discourse,' he said, and ran for his life past the lavatory door and down into the Mercedes.

The car rolled through the gates of the Chang house. Raymond jumped out and walked into the huge, warm interior. 'Rachel!' he shouted.

Pei materialized at his side. 'She is not here,' he said.

'Where did she go?'

'Elsewhere. On your father's orders.'

Raymond felt as if someone had let off a shotgun in his face. 'What do you mean?' he said.

'Your father thought that she might get into trouble,' said Mr Pei. 'She is in a safe place.'

Raymond smiled. Behind the smile, he was furious. How dare his father dispose of Rachel as if she were some sort of toy he was no longer to be allowed? His hands itched to pick up Mr Pei, bounce him off some walls –

Think carefully.

If his father was displeased, Rachel was on a razor's edge. Only Rachel; because in his father's world the interests of the son were identical with the wishes of the father. It was not a world in which love played any part.

Raymond found that he was frightened.

He said, casually, 'Where did you take her?'

Pei knew that naturally there was complete confidence between Raymond and old Mr Chang. He also knew that those who crossed the Chang family did not generally live very long. And lurking in the back of Pei's mind was the notion that Mr Chang was fifteen years older than him, and, though lucky, not immortal. Pei saw himself less as Mr Chang's employee than as a Chang family retainer. Who would in time, if he played his cards right, become an old retainer.

So Pei did not hesitate. He said, 'People's Prison Number Five.'

There seemed to be a thunderstorm operating between Raymond's ears. But he smiled quietly, and yawned. 'Oh, dear,' he said. 'I think I'll have a spot of lunch.'

Lunch appeared. He made himself sit down and eat it. Then, languidly but with a shaking hand, he collected a handful of papers from his office, put them in his briefcase, and called his car.

The car took him to the prison. He climbed out, walked in at the administrator's entrance, and demanded to see the governor. The governor was a round-faced man from the north. He found Raymond's suit impressive, and his haircut, and the air of negligent authority he brought with him into the fluorescent-lit office with the hard chairs and the chipped enamel desk.

Raymond said, 'You are holding a gweilo, Rachel Jenkins, on the orders of my father.'

The governor waited.

'This was a temporary arrangement,' said Raymond.

The governor ducked his head. 'The state is always at the service of the enterprising individual.'

'My father has instructed me to take delivery of this woman.'

The governor squirmed in his hard chair. 'You understand . . . how to say this?' He was pale with embarrassment. 'Your authority?'

Raymond forced his eyes to maintain light, face-saving contact with the eyes across the desk. He pulled out his passport; the Hong Kong passport, not the British.

The governor read the passport, slowly. This young man was certainly who he said he was. But the governor was in a bind. If he checked with the father, and the father had indeed given the son authority to receive the woman, he would not only have lost face, but implicitly criticized the dutifulness of the Chang family. If he did not check with the father, and released the girl contrary to his wishes, he would have made an enemy. But prison governors have as many enemies as prisoners. And at least he would have acted legally, and in an emergency would be able to invoke the law.

The governor smiled. He picked up a telephone, and

barked an order. Studying his fingernails on the other side of the desk, Raymond felt the sweat of relief flow over his body.

Rachel was brought in five minutes later, pale and haggard. When she saw Raymond, her face flooded with colour; pink and gold, like a peach, thought Raymond.

Raymond said, 'So this is the woman.'

Rachel thought, He looks so worried, poor darling. Don't cry. Hang on.

'Come with me,' said Raymond, stony-faced.

Her knees were trembling so badly that she thought she would not be able to walk. Somehow she stayed upright as the governor showed them down the stairs in person. She climbed into the Mercedes. Raymond said punctilious farewells to the governor and climbed in after her. He found her hand. It felt nearly as cold and frightened as his.

'Drive,' he said to the chauffeur.

Rachel looked at him. The tears were pouring down her face. She said, 'Thank you.'

He shook his head. She saw that he was crying too. She held his dark head against her breast. He said, 'I can smell that prison on you. I am sorry.' He was still crying. 'He betrayed you. He betrayed me. Stupid old man.' Rachel could feel him shaking. 'How dare he?' he said.

'Quiet,' said Rachel. 'It's all right.'

Raymond said, 'If you think it's all right, you don't understand what he did.' He was grinning through the tears, a ghastly, stretched-looking grin. 'He thought you loved me. But he thought that my duty to him would be stronger than my love for you. He did not believe I could love you. So all he had to do was get you out of the way. And then he could whistle me in to heel. Like a dog.'

Rachel said, 'It's not just you. It's my father –'

He was not listening. 'Like a dog,' he said. 'He is getting old. He can't imagine how people think any more. So now he is going to find out that a dog can bite.' He leaned forward and opened the glass partition. 'Take us to the airport,' he said.

Rachel picked up the telephone and dialled. There was a long wait. Then she heard her father's voice, distant, in the middle of the sea.

'It's me,' she said. 'I am out of there.' She listened. 'And I am on my way out of Beijing.' She took a deep breath and squeezed Raymond's hand. 'Now perhaps you could tell me just exactly what has been going on?'

Raymond watched her as she listened. I will not be mixed up with my father's dirty little games any more. I will make my own life –

'Goodness,' said Rachel, with that inscrutable mildness Raymond found so hard to penetrate. 'Well for God's sake get on with it.' Another pause. 'I can look after myself,' she said. 'You worry about those people. Where's a hotel in San Francisco?'

'Four Seasons,' said Raymond.

'Dad,' said Rachel. 'See you at the Four Seasons Hotel in San Francisco. Date?'

'Date,' said Jenkins' voice, tinny across the dark miles of sea.

She rang off. She smiled, brightly. 'Well,' she said. 'It's you and me against them.'

'Thank God,' said Raymond.

Chapter Eight

Beyond the bridge windows of the *Glory of Saipan*, the world was beginning to change with the dawn. The black sea had become grey, heaving under a sky like corrugated iron. Where the sea met the sky, a line of grubby orange had briefly come into being.

The ARPA range was set at twenty-five miles. Dead ahead, range eleven miles, were ten little green dots. Jenkins hit the button that projected the ARPA's vectors thirty minutes into the future, then an hour, two hours. The blips on the screen grew long green tails that converged. An alarm beeped. Up in the top right-hand corner, a message appeared: *TCA 1 hour 07 mins.*

The VHF said in a harsh Chinese-American voice, '*Iron Hotel, Iron Hotel, this is Catcher.*'

Jenkins was alone on the bridge. The doors were locked. He was nervous. Everyone on the *Glory of Saipan* was nervous.

There was a knock on the bridge door. 'Rodriguez,' said a voice. Jenkins let him in.

'Everything OK?' said Rodriguez.

'No.'

'No?' Rodriguez looked shocked. 'Problem?'

Jenkins pointed at the fading orange stripe where the blips on the radar lay in wait. 'Those guys,' he said.

'Uh-huh,' said Rodriguez, squinting at the ARPA. 'We hand over passengers.'

'No.'

The heavy eyebrows met the oily black hairline. 'No?'

Jenkins said, 'That's not the boats we were meant to meet. That's coastguard spies.'

'Jesus Maria,' said Rodriguez.

'So we go on,' said Jenkins. 'Turn off the VHFs, right?'

'Sure,' said Rodriguez. He ran down the bridge windows, clicking off the sets as if they were going to bite him. 'So what we do?'

'What we're being paid for,' said Jenkins. He walked over to the chart room.

Rodriguez nodded enthusiastically enough to dislodge his forelock. Jenkins dug San Francisco Bay and Approaches out of the chart chest. Twenty-four hours, he reckoned; perhaps thirty, depending on the weather. He set the autopilot to the new course. The ship's nose turned northward.

'Navtex,' said Rodriguez.

The paper tongue said gale northwesterly force eight, backing westerly, nine to ten.

On the ARPA the tuna boats were still in a bunch. They had noticed his change of course, and were heading up to meet the *Glory*. They would be alongside in twenty minutes, or so they thought. Jenkins looked out of the windows. Down where they ought to be, a black cloud was dragging a skirt of rain across the sea. Jenkins felt anxious and jumpy. You'll see them soon enough, he told himself.

The bridge door clattered as someone shook it from the outside. Mrs Nairn's voice said, 'Who's there?' Rodriguez was standing by the wheel, close to the door. Jenkins could see the thought forming in his mind. Mrs Nairn is not someone you lock doors against. One of us. Captain didn't mean her, when he said lock doors.

And before Jenkins could even open his mouth to tell him different, Rodriguez had unlocked the door and let her in. 'Morning, Mrs Nairn,' said Rodriguez, grinning from ear to ear. 'Stormy weather.'

Jenkins' finger found the off button for the ARPA, and pressed it. The screen died to a green point and became blank. Mrs Nairn did not take her eyes off his face. Her tongue came out and wetted her dry lips. She said, 'Should be just about on the rendezvous.'

Jenkins said, 'Not yet.'

She said, 'Any minute now.'

'Twelve hours, easy,' said Jenkins.

At that moment, Rodriguez said, 'There,' and pointed.

Jenkins saw Mrs Nairn's eyes follow the brown finger with the silver class ring. He followed it with his own.

The black rain squall had blown away. Under the grey roof of cloud the sea heaved slow and turgid, like unset concrete agitated from below. Balanced on the swell four hundred yards off the starboard bow were a clump of fat, dirty fishing boats, sentry-box wheelhouses in front of long working decks.

'Whole bloody ocean to muck around in, and they choose here,' said Jenkins from a dry throat. 'Take the wheel, Rodriguez. Port ten.'

'Port ten,' said Rodriguez.

'What are they doing out here?' said Mrs Nairn. She looked confused, but not yet suspicious.

'Fishing, I suppose,' he said. They were heading across the *Glory*'s bows. Well, thought Jenkins, if they want to play collisions, they've got more to lose than us.

'Aren't you going to slow down?' said Mrs Nairn.

'Fuel consumption,' said Jenkins.

The rain had started again. The wipers were whining on the windscreen. The fishing boats were close enough for the watchers on the bridge to see down on to their decks.

'How do you know that that's not the fleet for the cargo?' said Mrs Nairn.

'Sorry?'

'The pickup,' said Mrs Nairn. 'The pickup fleet.' Her voice was becoming shrill. Her grey cheeks had turned pink.

Jenkins said, 'They would have made radio contact.'

Mrs Nairn looked down at the radios. She said, 'They're not switched on.'

Jenkins said, 'Excuse me, no time to chat. Don't want to hit one of these fellas.'

The windscreen wiper cleared its quadrant of glass. Through it, Jenkins saw one of the fishing boats, plump as a bath toy, thirty feet from the *Glory*'s starboard bow. The hatch-covers were off, ready to receive cargo. A man had burst out on to the deck beside the wheelhouse. His face was clearly visible: a Chinese face, slack-jawed with amazement, tilted up at the patch of fresh paint on the *Glory*'s bow. And a finger, pointed, stabbing the air between its owner and the high, rusty bridge of the container ship.

'Wonder what he wants?' said Jenkins.

And then the fishing boat had slid astern, and the *Glory* was ploughing on into the empty sea. A blast of wind wailed in the aerials above the monkey island.

Mrs Nairn looked at Jenkins with a face that seemed actually mottled. Her eyes moved up to the GPS. The screen said 40°N 135°W. She stumped off the bridge.

'Temper,' said Rodriguez, and giggled.

Jenkins said, 'Lock that door.' He picked up the telephone and dialled Lucy's cabin.

She answered quickly. It sounded as if there were several people with her. Her voice was thin and tired. He said, 'Mrs Nairn's on her way down. We've just sailed past your tuna boats. I want to keep her away from radios, even portable radios.'

She said, 'Of course.' She started to say something else, but he put the telephone down.

Mrs Nairn walked quickly down the stairs. She did not know what that bastard on the bridge thought he was doing, but he was not going to get away with it, not while she breathed. She had worked up to her armpits in blood for her money, and she intended to get it. In her mind was the mobile home by the garbage dump, Edwin passed out on the steps in a cloud of flies, her knitting the same beermat over and over again. That was hell. Rally the forces, she thought. We may even get Jenkins' share as well.

When she arrived in the alleyway at the bottom of the stairs, she could hear the pop of a can from their cabin. Let him not be pissed, she thought. Please. She went in.

The can was Seven-Up, thank God. He raised the can, said, 'Health.' She looked at his bony face. You poor old bastard. Not fair at your age. Let us go carefully, and we can have things really nice again, like in the old days.

She said, 'We're at the rendezvous. Jenkins sailed straight past the pickup fleet.'

Nairn frowned at her. 'Past?'

'That yellow tart got to him,' she said. 'I think he's taking the ship up the fucking beach.'

'Not true.'

Chang said, 'Whatever this woman has promised you to make you behave in this way, you won't get it.'

Jenkins was surprised. 'This woman?'

'Lucy Ng is her name. I believe they call her Lucy Moses. She recruited some passengers for me. She thinks she is leading them out of captivity to the promised land.'

'And you arranged to have her killed by Lee.'

'At first. Then I . . . repealed her sentence, to preserve order.' Chang sighed. 'I underestimated her, it seems. I had failed to take into account that her friends had no intention of paying their full fares. Which of course is why she has put herself out to influence you. I expect she spoke about freedom. Her reasons were financial, I can assure you.'

Jenkins said, 'She hasn't influenced me.'

Chang laughed. He said, 'Mr Jenkins, it is not too late to change your mind. You undertook this work because you needed money to support your wife; I know this. What has Lucy Moses promised you to make you throw this away?'

Jenkins said, 'You wouldn't understand.'

'Try me.'

'I did what I thought was right.'

There was a silence, full of the soothing hiss of the ether. 'So at Zamboanga,' said Chang, finally. 'You did that from conscience, not a desire for revenge.'

'That's right.'

Chang said, 'Mr Jenkins, it is true that I misjudged you.'

The line went dead.

The *Glory*'s anchors slammed into her plating as she dived into a trough. With each wave it felt as if she ended up lower, as if she wanted to nod her way out of the grey turmoil of the surface and into the quiet black deeps. Onward and downward, thought Jenkins, in the hum of the ship; nice and quiet, nothing happening.

Like falling. Nothing happens until you splatter on the concrete. Chang would not admit a mistake to a man he planned to allow to live.

The telephone rang. Ship's internal. Pick it up.

Lucy's voice. Thin again. Feeling the strain. But the sound

of it warmed his heart. 'Please,' she said. 'Come here. Tell me your plan.' Pause. 'I need you.' *What has she promised you?* Chang had said.

Nothing, he had replied.

Not quite true. There was love, affection, a small fire in a cold desert. Possibly even a future.

He stood up. His shoulder was aching, and he felt weak and chilled. Twenty-four hours from now, it would all be over.

But of course it would not be over. What had Lucy promised him that went beyond the *Glory of Saipan*'s arrival on the shores of America?

The bodyguards were still outside the bridge door. Wearily, he shuffled down the stairs; one flight, two, three. He turned into the alleyway where Lucy's cabin was. There was a smell of fried blood from the galley. Jer's door was hooked back. The cabin was empty, as if it had never been tenanted. He stopped outside Lucy's door.

He knocked.

The door opened.

He stood there, looking in.

There were two people in the cabin. One of them was on the bunk, tied up with lashings of blue polypropylene rope. The other one had opened the door with his left hand. In the other hand he held a long, flat-ended cleaver.

The one on the bunk was Lucy, her eyes rolling above the rope tied into her mouth and round the back of her head.

The other one, the one who reached out and grabbed Jenkins' jersey and yanked him back into the cabin, was Ho.

Chapter Nine

Jenkins hit the bulkhead with his bad shoulder. He distinctly felt stitches pop. The pain gave the cabin a nauseating spin. He must have moaned aloud, because Ho said, 'Shut mouth.'

When he looked up, Ho was standing flat-footed, cleaver in hand, like a butcher sizing up a carcass. Jenkins said, between lips numb with fear at what he knew was going to happen, 'What the hell are you doing in this lady's cabin?'

Ho's white boiler suit was smeared with black oil. He swung the cleaver. A chip of plywood flew off the leeboard of the bunk. 'End coming,' he said.

Jenkins said, 'Do you want to die?'

Ho grinned.

Jenkins said, 'This ship is going to sail into a big storm. If I am not on the bridge it will sink, and everybody on board will die. You need a captain, Ho.' What might have been an uncertain blankness passed over Ho's face. 'Go up to the bridge,' said Jenkins. 'Ask the mate on watch.'

Ho stared. Jenkins realized with a sinking heart that the blankness was just blankness, not uncertainty. He was not buying it. We were nearly there, thought Jenkins. But now he is going to slice us into julienne strips.

Ho took a step forward. Jenkins could smell him, sweat and oil and some sort of sickly scent. It smelt like the soap at the tennis club all that time ago, when he had thought then that there was no further to fall.

He said to Lucy, 'I love you.' Man in front of firing squad makes statement, lights last cigarette. It seemed a ridiculously small thing to say; too small to contain everything he wanted to tell her, about freedom and honesty and all the rest of it. Still, he meant it.

Ho moved.

The cleaver flashed. Jenkins was too weak to duck, even if he had been fast enough. He felt the blade whack him on the back of the neck, left-hand side. He felt a big, solid concussion. His head came off and flew across the cabin, thumping hollow on the side of the bunk. A door slammed.

The ceiling was dirty, lit by a fly-specked fluorescent tube. Jenkins blinked at it. Then he realized that severed heads could not blink. Besides, somewhere beyond the pain in his neck there was a pain in his shoulder. And a leg, folded nastily against a chair. Without thinking, he moved the leg. He saw it move. That was good, too. Severed heads cannot move legs.

He rolled. Bees were loose in his skull, and his tongue flopped in his mouth. There were things he should be remembering, but he could not remember what they were. He clambered up to his knees. With banana fingers he untied the knot at the back of Lucy's head. She spat out the onion that had been keeping her from talking. She looked furious.

He tried to say, 'He hit me with the blunt side.' But it came out as a sort of gargling. Anyway, Lucy was already on the telephone, yelling in Chinese. Ho had forgotten about the telephone.

He had after all gone to ask the mate on watch whether it was true that Jenkins was essential. He would be back. Bolt the door, before he comes back.

He was already back.

There were feet in the alleyway now, a lot of feet. And Ho's voice. Ho was yelling. Someone out there was yelling back. The door burst open. Ho came in. He slammed it behind him and shot the bolt. He did not have his cleaver. His eyes were rolling in a way that reminded Jenkins of a frightened horse. Feet and fists were hammering on the door. When he looked at Jenkins the massive calm had gone. In its place was a short, chunky man, scared witless. 'Captain. Please.'

The battering on the door was confusing Jenkins. He wished it would stop, so he could think straight about what to do with this bastard who wanted help. Help him, he thought, above the bells of Notre Dame in his ears. You have to help people, cargo, bastards, whoever they are. Otherwise you are Chang and Soares and Ho.

This was Ho.

Too complicated. He started to move, slowly, he hoped helpfully.

The thumping on the door changed. It was not feet and fists any more. It was something harder and more metallic. Two more wallops, and the bolt went. Into the fog in Jenkins' head there burst a doorway full of Chinese men, yelling. In the background a white fountain seemed to be playing. Ah, yes, thought Jenkins, his mind at last finding something it could get hold of. Those metallic crashes. Someone had used the fire extinguisher on the lock.

The cabin was full of people shouting in Cantonese. Jenkins was on his feet, wobbling. A shoulder crashed into him and he sprawled on to the bunk beside Lucy. The crowd surged away. The cabin was suddenly empty, the splintered door swaying on its hinges to the *Glory*'s roll. The babble of voices in the alleyway surged to a peak.

There was a new sound, a terrible squealing yell. It sounded as if a big animal was being killed out there.

Jenkins got up and walked the five miles to the door. The squealing turned to a gurgle and stopped. He put his head into the passageway. It was blocked with a knot of people. Above the people, the fire extinguisher was still fountaining foam. But now the foam was shot with pink, like Christmas cake icing.

'Christ,' said Jenkins.

The knot of people convulsed. The door at the end of the alleyway opened. There was a blast of salty wind, the roar of a breaking wave. The door slid shut again. The alleyway was empty except for Jenkins and the foam on the deck, and the blood that had come out of Ho when the crowd had cut him into slabs.

Jenkins went back to Lucy's cabin and untied the knots on her legs. She held on to him. She was shaking. She said, 'It was revenge for Jer.'

Jenkins nodded. They were supposed to be Christians, liberal academics, non-violent.

But they had also been cargo. Like Mrs Nairn said. Cargo is cargo.

And they who live by the bloody great knife will die by the bloody great knife.

The tuna boats moved purposefully into the fringes of the storm and stopped. They came head-to-wind, the monstrous seas sweeping up and under their high bows, the gusts moaning in their flying bridges. The lead boat stopped alongside something floating in the water.

A couple of men looked over the side. One of them lashed a tuna gaff to the fall of the derrick they used for unloading the catch and lowered it at the thing in the sea. At the third attempt, the hook bit. The other man pressed a button, and the derrick motor whined.

As the thing came up out of the sea, the derrick man saw it transformed into a white boiler suit, slashed with the deep cuts of sharp knives. Inside the boiler suit was what had once been Ho.

'Down,' said the hook man. The derrick operator lowered the body to the deck. It lay there, streaming water, but not blood; all the blood had gone. The hook man bent and frisked the boiler-suit pockets. In the leg pocket, he found what he had been looking for: a black box, with a stubby aerial and a trigger, similar to an emergency position-indicating radio beacon, but transmitting not on a distress frequency, but on a frequency listened to only by Mr Chang's tuna boats.

'Shit,' said the hook man. He switched off the beacon and slid it into his pocket. Waste not, want not. Then he made a circular movement with his finger.

The derrick lifted the corpse of Ho from the deck and swung it over the side. The hook man pulled out a sheath knife, leaned overboard and cut the body free. It slid away into the landscape of shifting grey hills, became a white speck that came and went, and then was gone.

The tuna fleet grew white moustaches. The boats turned west, with a little south in it, and started for home.

★

Jenkins sat on the edge of Lucy's bunk and listened to the bells ringing in his ears. She was pale. Her hair was sticking out like a doll's. She smoothed it, without much result.

They sat there in silence, shivering. It felt like a funeral. She said, 'So what now?'

Jenkins told her.

She said, 'You'd do that?'

'It hasn't happened yet.' Jenkins liked the way she smiled at him. He remembered what Chang had said. *What has she promised you?*

This was enough.

She said softly, 'And when we land? What will you do then?'

He said, 'I'd like you to come with me to meet someone at the Four Seasons Hotel.' That was as far ahead as he had thought. It sounded ridiculous. He said, quickly, back on familiar ground, 'I want you to get everyone out of the containers and into the hold. We're in for some weather.'

He left without looking back.

He went out and into the cold alleyway. His shoulder felt as if it was bleeding. He could not move his head, and the shivering had become a sort of spastic tremor. At the top of the stairs he met Pete, puffy-eyed, struggling into a jersey outside his cabin.

'Chrissakes,' said Pete. 'What's happening? What was all that noise?'

'The passengers killed Ho,' said Jenkins. What do I tell Pete? he thought. As little as possible. But he was a seaman, and he was going to find out. 'We've got a gale,' he said. 'Which is a bastard, because we can't stay at sea.'

Pete frowned. 'Why not?'

'We missed the bloody tuna boats. We've got a bearing running hot in the engine. We can't hang around out here.'

'Missed them?' The *Glory* lurched. The anchors slammed back into the hawse pipes with a sound like giant hammers. He said, 'We're going to lose containers, this rate,' remotely, doing the first mate's job, looking after the cargo. 'So what about the passengers?'

'I talked to mission control,' said Jenkins. The lies came easily to the faraway voice that was doing the talking for him.

'They want us to take them ashore in San Francisco.'

'Ashore?' said Pete, and let his mouth hang open.

'That's what the man said.' He won't buy it, thought Jenkins. He's not crazy.

'Jesus,' said Pete, his opaque plum-coloured eyes widening a fraction. 'That's a bit illegal.'

'The money's good,' said Jenkins.

'Yeah,' said Pete, apparently comforted. He yawned. 'Oh, well. Snacktime, I reckon.' He shuffled off towards the messroom. Jenkins went on up to the bridge.

Pete did not go into the messroom. When he heard the bridge door slam behind Jenkins, he walked quickly to the door of the Nairns' cabin, and knocked hard. From inside came an odd moaning. He tried the handle. It was locked. He ran down to the paint locker and came back with a fire axe. He walloped the door twice, over the lock. It swung inwards.

Mr and Mrs Nairn had fallen off the bunk, and formed an incoherent mass of white flesh trussed with gaffer tape. Pete stood for a moment with his hands in his pockets, laughing. Then he pulled out a knife and cut the tape. Mrs Nairn hid her nakedness with a bathrobe. She said, 'Where's that fucking –'

'Shut up,' said Pete, in a new, sharp voice that stopped her dead. 'You hurt?'

'No.'

'Chief?'

'No.'

'So get some clothes on,' said Pete. 'Mrs Nairn, tell me what happened.'

The Nairns did as they were told. Something about Pete had changed, as if before he had been running on idle, and now he was going full steam ahead. 'Right,' said Pete. 'Mrs Nairn, you stay here. Chief, get down to the engine room and do as you are told.'

'Do what?' said Nairn, weaving a little.

'Do this,' said Pete. 'And you stand a little tiny chance of getting your money.'

Mrs Nairn was not stupid. She noticed the change. She also noticed that Pete had not said 'we'. He had said 'you'.

★

Ramos was in the engine room, sitting at the control panel. He had no idea what was going on up there, except that, judging by the movement of the foam chair in which he was sitting, they were steaming into some weather. This was nearly finished. Money soon. He was wondering if he could trust Juan his brother-in-law to weed sweetcorn during the summers. He could see Juan now, asleep between the rows, lazy bastard –

Out on the console, a light was blinking. Oil cleaner warning light, probably a malfunction in the warning system. Dirty old ship, nothing worked.

Another red light started to blink next to the first.

This was very unusual. Ramos's eyes flicked across to the oil pressure meters. Two needles out of four had sunk to zero. As he watched, a third went down, and another light came on. His mouth hung open. His heart walloped his ribs. He grabbed a pair of ear defenders and ran out of the control room.

As his boots hit the diamond-pattern steel outside the door, they started to slide. He crashed to the deck, and slid on, noticing with astonishment and disbelief that the deck was an inch deep in hot black oil. His slide took him to the door of the oil cleaner room. This time his mouth hung open wide enough for him to get oil in it and cough and spit and still be astonished.

There was a black man in the oil cleaner room. He seemed to be naked except for a pair of black boxer shorts. His black arms rose and fell. In the black hands was a fire axe that had once been red and was now black. The fire axe was chopping pipes, skilfully, so the scalding jets of oil squirted away from his vulnerable body and into the bilges.

Ramos opened his mouth further, to shout. But more oil got in, and he changed his mind. He began to scrabble his way back to the control room. The figure among the oil cleaners sensed the movement and turned its head. Ramos caught the blaze of yellow-red eyes in an oil-black face, and was terrified. He went on, slithering. He lurched in at the door, fell heavily, reached up and hit the alarm button with the flat of his hand. As the dull clang of bells spread through the ship, he dialled the bridge.

A cool voice answered. Mr Pelly, he thought; fat face, hard man. He said, 'Oil. No oil.'

'Ah,' said Pelly, calm, stupid, like all American, British, Australian. 'Stop engines.' The telegraph buzzed.

Ramos went to the fuel-supply handle, and pulled it all the way towards him. The *Glory*'s engine slowed. Man with axe loco-loco, crazy, thought Ramos, the sweat pouring off him. Bearings may be OK. Hope I stop engine in time.

Hope not fulfilled.

Deprived of oil, the bottom-end bearing of number three piston had run dry. Being dry, it was red-hot even as Ramos stopped the engine. The last few rotations brought it to white heat, vaporized the oil in the sump, and ignited the vapour. There was a dull *whump*, and a sheet of orange-blue flame blazed across the engine room.

Ramos yelled to nobody in particular, 'Fire!' Then he went out of the door furthest from the flames and bolted like a rabbit through the airtight doors, the last of which he managed to lock behind him.

He stood on the stern of the ship, shivering, taking great gulps of raw, salty air. He thought about the eyes he had seen three minutes ago.

They had been the eyes of the chief engineer.

Then Ramos recalled he was standing on top of two hundred tons of bunker crude which would soon be approaching its flashpoint. So he began to pick his way forward, as far away from it as possible.

As he came to the side of the containers, he saw against the humped back of a huge grey wave a spidery black figure picking its way down the side-deck towards the accommodation. Sweet Lord, thought Ramos, just let me live, and I will never go to sea again.

Jenkins had been watching the big grey seas coming up from astern, lifting the *Glory*'s back end so her nose went down and for a moment the bridge windows were looking into the long, shining valley of the trough. Then they passed under, creaming knee-deep along the narrow walkway beside the containers, dropping the stern into the next trough, leaving the iron box of the ship stalled until the next wave picked up her back end and it all began again.

The wind was going westerly. The swell was northwesterly.

Thirty miles to go, maybe. The containers were breaking loose. You have to admit, Jenkins had been telling himself, that there is a bit of a sea out here. In fact there is a bloody enormous sea out there.

For a second, the deck lost its tremor and went completely quiet. Then the bridge was deafening with alarm bells. Engine stopped. Out of the window he could see from the waves that the ship was yawing, that the waves which had been marching under the ship from stern to bow were moving on to the beam. Soon she would be lying in the troughs, rolling her rotten guts out.

Jenkins cranked the engine-room telegraph. There was no answering buzz to signify that the engine room had got the message. He picked up the telephone and dialled. There was not even a ringing tone.

He went and looked aft, through the chart-room windows.

Back there by the funnel, volumes of oily black smoke were rolling. But not from the funnel itself; from somewhere alongside. Jenkins thought of the hold, the watertight doors that people usually forgot to close, and choking black smoke billowing down the Burma Road. His heart was suddenly beating with uncomfortable speed.

He dialled Pete Pelly. He said, 'Fire party. And get down there and round up the passengers.' The bees were still loud in his head, but fear was louder. 'Get them into the accommodation. Shut the watertight doors. Flood the engine room if necessary, but only for Chrissakes if necessary.'

'Yeah,' said Pete, so relaxed he seemed nearly to be yawning.

'And don't let the bloody generator go out.'

'Right.' The phone went down.

It was encouraging to have at least one officer you could trust.

Next, thought Jenkins. Damage report. Extent of damage unknown. Engine failure, unlikely to be rectified. On the plus account, the waves were big enough to interfere with coastguard radar. The clouds were thick enough to interfere with satellite pictures. The breeze was blowing the *Glory* in the general direction of San Francisco at near enough three

317

knots, improvable to five. San Francisco was a lee shore, but it was definitely San Francisco.

The bridge door slammed. Mrs Nairn came in. Her hair had burst its moorings and her eyes were wild. She said in a flat, cracked voice, 'What do you think you're doing?'

Jenkins said, 'The engine has stopped.'

'The arrangement was this,' said Mrs Nairn, without apparently having heard. 'We hand over to the tuna boats. We deliver to Oakland. We get our money.' She chewed the inside of her grey lips. 'You didn't stop for the tuna boats. So Edwin's stopped the ship for you.'

Jenkins leaned against the windows for support. He said, 'The tuna boats won't come now.'

Her face had caved in on itself. She was an old and hunted animal, shrivelled and vicious in a corner. She put her face close to his. She smelt of sweat. She said, 'I want the fucking cargo put on those tuna boats.'

The *Glory* took a huge, looping roll. The coffee jar fell off its ledge, slid to the far end of the bridge, and burst like a bomb against the door.

'I told you,' said Jenkins. 'There are no tuna boats.' He switched on the ARPA, maximum range.

The land was a bright line twenty-five miles ahead. Otherwise the screen was blank.

'Get on the radio,' said Mrs Nairn. 'This is the provident fund. It's what we get, after all this time. Just because you're shagging your bit of yellow velvet . . . Christ.' She shook her head. 'How can I make you see, you stupid drongo? You're a white man. And you're dropping us in it, me and Edwin? We've worked all our lives. You can't do this. You just can't do this.'

For some reason, Jenkins found he was thinking of the tennis courts at the Stanley Club; the little wire cages in which free people, identically dressed, lunged after balls, following sets of rules.

'We're all here because we choose to be,' said Mrs Nairn. 'If these people die, it's their bloody lookout. I don't care how many of 'em go. *I want my fucking money.*'

Jenkins looked at her face, vaguely illuminated by the green ARPA. Mrs Nairn the doctor had gone. Instead there

318

was a crone, sharp and weaselly, with eyes like slate pebbles. He said, 'We'll get them ashore.'

She started to cry. A smell of bunker crude arrived on the bridge. A voice said, 'What you done to her?'

Jenkins looked up. It was Nairn, naked, his ribs sticking out over his oil-smeared pot belly, his eyes red and yellow and grey in his blackened face. Jenkins said, 'She did it to herself.' The *Glory* lurched again, a long, horrible roll. There were crashes and clangings from aft. More containers loose. He could smell drink on Nairn. He said, 'Engines stopped.'

'Smashed 'em,' said Nairn. 'They're burning.'

Jenkins said, 'Too late.'

'Oh, no, it's not,' said Nairn. 'I'm assuming command here.'

'I'm in command,' said Jenkins. 'I'm putting her ashore.'

Nairn's teeth showed black and yellow. His skeletal arm swung at Jenkins, slowly, hopelessly. Jenkins stepped back from the oily fist. Nairn fell forwards on to the deck. He stayed there on his hands and knees, his head weaving. Mrs Nairn took his hand. 'Edwin,' she said. 'Get up.' She pulled his arm. He clambered to his feet. He seemed to be crying.

They stood there side by side, Nairn the oil-smeared skeleton and Mrs Nairn, square as a rugby forward, streaked with oil from her husband's body. Black smoke was billowing from the ship's stern, and the waves rolled under like grey hills.

'I hope you're happy,' said Mrs Nairn, and led her husband away.

Jenkins thumbed the transmit button on his radio, called Pete, and said, 'I want to get rid of some containers. From the back end.'

'Why?' said Pete.

Jenkins felt sick and light-headed at the same time. He said, 'We're going sailing.'

Pete said, 'What –'

'And you'd better flood the engine room. We could lose the generator any minute now.'

'Oh, good,' said Pete. 'Will you tell me what the fuck is going on?'

319

Jenkins said, 'We are trying not to drown,' and switched off the radio.

At Beijing airport, Raymond and Rachel went through the departure gate quickly, looking neither right nor left. They passed security and fought their way on to the plane. They looked like proper coach passengers, harassed and bedraggled. The plane took off. Raymond ordered white wine.

Rachel lay back in her seat and thought of China rolling below, a great trap covered in people. She took Raymond's hand. 'California, here we come,' she said.

Raymond said, 'What will we do in California?'

'Be,' said Rachel. 'It's what Californians do.'

'Do be do be do,' said Raymond.

Chapter Ten

The hours passed. The generator kept going. The containers, unlashed, floated off the hatch-covers. Pushed by the gale on her accommodation, the *Glory of Saipan* drifted towards America.

Johnny was at the wheel. Jenkins was leaning on the ARPA handles as if it was a Zimmer frame. It was quiet up here, the noise of the passengers crammed into the accommodation a distant, starling-roost rumour.

Pete came on to the bridge. His skin was grey, his face a flabby moon. 'Done,' he said. 'Now perhaps you will tell me what the fuck you are playing at.'

'Wind's behind us,' said Jenkins. 'Blowing us ashore.'

Pete's grey tongue came out and wet his lips. The *Glory*'s nose plunged into a wave, and white water boomed on the windows.

'Sailing lesson,' said Jenkins, gazing upon the screen. 'We have disposed of the aft containers. So our windage is up the front end of the ship. So we are a sailing boat now, and as long as we've got a generator for the steering gear we can steer to and fro, aim ourselves, within reason.'

'Within reason?' said Pelly. 'What are you talking about?'

Jenkins fought the temptation to lay his forehead on the cool glass of the ARPA. When he punched the buttons at the side of the screen, it showed two headlands jutting at each other across an expanse of open water spanned by a green, hammock-like structure. The Golden Gate Bridge.

The green line of the *Glory*'s course led towards the southern side of the gap.

Before Nairn had wrecked the engines, they could have

321

ignored port control, sailed under the bridge, turned right and taken their chances.

Not any more.

Not without an engine.

From the aft windows, the *Glory*'s stern looked lower than before. The black smoke had ceased to billow. The generator was still there. Jenkins saw a wave come up from astern, black in the deck-lights, rise, inundate the transom and the base of the funnel, and pass forward, sluicing off the hatch-covers. Sooner or later they were going to get a couple of gallons of water in the generator air intake. Then there would be no more lights, no more steering.

Pete said, 'What are you going to do when you lose the generator?'

'We'll blow ashore nose first. The stern'll come round. The ship'll make a lee. They can go up the beach in the life rafts.'

'Just like that,' said Pete.

Jenkins said, 'Perhaps you'd like to call lifeboats and helicopters.'

Pete's eyes slid away. He said, 'You're barmy.'

Jenkins thought, He's right. It was the thing that he had been trained to be frightened of all his life. He saw the *Glory* lodged in hard brown sand, with the waves smashing in on her. He could see her rusty bottom as she rolled, the little bodies scoured out of her, struggling for a tiny moment, then limp in the black water.

He went across to the telephone and dialled Lucy's cabin. The starling-roost roared in the background. He said, 'Going ashore could be dangerous. I could call the coastguard. Helicopters.'

'Please not,' she said. 'How long?'

'Four hours.'

'Good.'

He hung up. He leaned on the ledge under the bridge windows.

The nose went down. It went deep, as a big wave, bigger than the rest, began to lift the stern. Jenkins looked over his shoulder up the hatch-covers, saw the black swell of it in the deck-lights, saw the silver gleam of its crest; a breaking crest.

He saw it hang over the squat black bulk of the generator for what felt like an hour. He saw it curl, towering over the generator, and begin to fall –

The lights went out.

The *Glory* shuddered, streaming water as she unburied herself. From the wheel, Johnny said, 'No steering, sah.' A wail of fear rose from the crowds in the accommodation.

Jenkins said to Johnny, 'Leave that. Ask the chief to get the generator going again.'

'Sah.' The door opened and closed, and he was gone. Fool's errand, thought Jenkins. Got to try, though.

Jenkins went to the windows along the forward side of the bridge. The *Glory* was still pitching; still sailing. But there was north in the wind again. Without a rudder she would be blown southwards, away from the entrance, and on to the beach.

Could be worse, said a minute, ludicrous voice in Jenkins' mind.

He looked out of the window, at the blackness that was all there was. White water flowered under the *Glory*'s bow. She came up again. The night ahead became black again.

Not all black.

Out there in the inky darkness there came into being a tiny ruby. It vanished as soon as it had arrived, then came again and again, and vanished again.

Five seconds later it was back, in the same place.

It was a buoy: the first marker buoy for the southern limit of the San Francisco Channel.

Chapter Eleven

Jenkins said, 'Pass the word for Lucy.' There was a murmuring. The bridge door opened and closed. Then Lucy's voice said in the dark, 'Yes?' He could feel the warmth of her beside him.

'We're going ashore,' he said. 'On to the beach. I want to tell you exactly what will happen, so you can tell everyone else.'

Lucy said, 'Is it safe?'

'If everyone does as they're told. I'm going to run the ship's nose on to the sand. The back end will slew round, so the hull will be parallel to the beach, like a wall. It will give you shelter from the waves. What I'm going to do is send some men ashore with lines. Ropes. Then we can get the women and children down the side and into life rafts, and the men on the beach can pull them ashore. I want you to find me the men. Men with families, who'll wait for their wives and kids, not just fade into the trees.'

Lucy said, 'I see.' She sounded doubtful.

'And I want you to make sure that everyone on board has a lifejacket. Rodriguez will hand them out. Can you explain?'

'Yes,' said Lucy. Jenkins felt her hand squeeze his. 'It is easy to forget that there are honest people in the world.'

Jenkins felt tired. 'Not honest,' he said. 'After a while you just can't be bothered with all the nonsense.' The tennis cages were in his mind again. Inside, points were being scored and ritual dances danced. Outside there were no points, no set steps. But there was freedom.

He felt her hair on his cheek, her fingers on his face, the

324

softness of her lips. 'Thank you.' After she had gone, the bridge door opened and closed again.

Jenkins said, 'Who's there?'

'Pete,' said a voice. 'With Ramos.'

Jenkins said, 'Can you get me emergency power for the satcom and the ARPA?'

'Can do,' said Ramos. 'Er . . . captain, what is your plan?'

'Beach the ship. Land the passengers and ourselves. Walk into town,' said Jenkins.

'No, no,' said Ramos. 'Money plan.'

'You'll be paid from the ship's safe.'

'Ah,' said Ramos, as if that made everything all right, and there were no twenty-foot seas surging under the *Glory*'s hull, and no lee shore. 'Fine. I fix power for satcom.'

'Pete,' said Jenkins. 'You there?'

'Here,' said Pete.

'I'm afraid it hasn't worked out the way you expected.'

'No,' said Pete in a flat, hostile voice. His face was flat, too. Jenkins had never seen him look so Chinese, the Oriental eyes narrow and unreadable. 'It hasn't.'

'Get ready with scramble nets and life rafts. And see what you can dig up in the way of long lines.'

'Yeah,' said Pete. 'OK, then.' There was a pause. 'You meant to do this all along, right?'

'You got some money,' said Jenkins. 'Now move it.' The bridge door slammed.

Jenkins stood sweating in the dark. He had expected Pete to be worse.

A red light glowed on the satcom console. Ramos came back on the bridge. 'Connected up,' he said. 'Don't know how much power.'

Jenkins looked at his watch. The luminous hands said one a.m. It would all be over by daylight. He pressed the on switch of the ARPA. The coast was a green wall, two and a half hours away. The wind had gone northwest. They were going to hit the beach a couple of miles south of the Golden Gate.

The satellite phone was ringing. He picked it up.

The voice on the other end was Rachel's. She said, 'Where are you?'

325

He did not want to worry her. He said, 'A couple of hours from San Francisco.'

'Us too.'

'Us?'

'Me and Raymond. We've just landed. We're going to the Four Seasons.'

Jenkins lay back in the chair and let the relief cover him like bathwater. Then he thought of the line of big waves thundering on the beach. He said, 'We're not in yet.'

'Where are you coming in?'

'Just across from Chinatown.' He grinned at the telephone. 'See you on TV.'

'Dad . . .'

'I've got a lot to do. Must go.'

'Be careful.'

Jenkins' heart was light and happy. He blew her a silent kiss, and switched the datacom to fax mode. At the top of the screen, he typed PRESS RELEASE. Below the heading, he typed HUGH CHANG IN WHITE SLAVE RACKET. EMBARGOED TILL 0900 WESTERN STANDARD TIME. Then he wedged himself against the ship's looping corkscrew and began to type.

He typed for half an hour, stacked up a list of names and numbers, and transmitted the release. The rustling chatter outside the door was growing. The passengers were getting restless.

They would not be the only ones.

Mr Chang was in the house on the Peak. He had just got back from dinner with some of his contacts on the Hainan project. As usual at this hour he was in his study, to deal with the calls from parts of the planet where it was now early morning.

But the first call was not from the far side of the planet. It was on his personal private line, from Mr Soong, his best contact at the New China News Agency. Mr Soong sounded oddly reserved. He said, 'I have just received a most peculiar press release. Your comments would be appreciated.'

Chang said, 'One minute.' He put Soong on hold, and pressed the intercom for his secretary. 'Gladys. Have we issued a press release?'

Gladys Yip said, 'Not exactly.'

Mr Chang permitted himself a frown. He said, 'Not exactly?'

'Something has just arrived. From a ship at sea. Should I bring it in?'

'If you think it right,' said Chang, with reptilian patience.

Miss Yip thought it right.

Chang read the paper she brought in. Then he said, in his voice like the rustle of a snake in dead leaves, 'Get me the captain of the *Glory of Saipan*.'

Five minutes later, Jenkins was on the line.

Chang said, 'What is this slander?'

Jenkins said, 'Say what you've got to say. I'm busy.'

'I merely wanted to ask if this is how you repay favours.'

'Blackmail and white slavery, you mean?'

'I could make you extremely rich,' said Chang.

'Don't you worry about that,' said Jenkins. 'You could think about the chief engineer and his wife, of course, and Pete Pelly. They'd be up for hush money. But you'd have to pay them more than the New China News Agency will, or the *Eastern Express*, or *Star News*, or the *San Francisco Examiner*. I sent them all press releases.'

There was a silence. Then Chang said, 'All this to pay your wife's debts?'

'Excuse me,' said Jenkins, 'must go now.' The line went dead.

Chang pressed the Gladys button. 'No calls,' he said.

'Very good.'

Chang began to gather papers together. Six million dollars was a lot of money. But the damage was worse than that. He could rubbish the story; but when a ship went ashore somewhere on the West Coast, questions would be asked. And there had been ugly noises coming from the capital, lately. Anti-corruption noises. Nobody was bullet-proof, nowadays.

And there was Raymond.

Chang pressed his hands to his temples and breathed deeply. This man Jenkins had robbed him of his money, and robbed him of his son, and robbed him of his good name. In short, Jenkins had robbed him of the things that were dearest to him.

So it was only fair that he should reciprocate.

Chang said to Gladys, 'Ask them to get the plane ready. I shall be leaving for Beijing in an hour.'

But before he left his office he made one last call, to his old friend Tommy Wong.

It was the usual sort of evening at the Yacht Club. Diana had sat there and made conversation with a business contact of Jeremy's while Jeremy talked race organization and essential maintenance with the secretary. There had been a few gins, nothing out of the ordinary, and the contact, Wayne, an American, had been talking about playing golf in the Philippines, how it was real irritating when kids stole your ball off the fairway and tried to sell it back to you, and how he personally was not in favour of shooting them, though the caddies did, sometimes. Actually Wayne was quite boring, so Diana had tried it on with him a bit, a hand on the knee here, a flash of boob there. It was just so great to be, well, free. Anyway, Wayne's face had begun to get that blurred, doggy look. But unfortunately Jeremy had noticed. So Jeremy had come over from the bar like a shot from a gun, which had tickled Diana. And Wayne had said, to make him feel OK because really his eyes had gone quite violent, that he could have the contract to guard some old office building or other. So Jeremy had ordered more drinks, and at eleven o'clock, early for them, they had all gone out of the Yacht Club and into the car park, and Jeremy had put Wayne into a taxi and shouted the name of his hotel at the driver, and slapped the roof, and the taxi had gone.

'Brilliant,' Jeremy had said to her, fondling her breast through the silk. 'My little geisha, eh?'

Diana had sort of giggled, not getting the point, and looked up at him. He was so nice looking. So young looking. She liked the way his hair curled over his ears, and his eyes were that mixture of bright and, well, cruel. You could never tell what he was thinking. That was what was so sexy about him. She had a faint memory of Dave. Dave's face moved too much, and his eyes had a sort of edgy look. That had been the trouble with Dave. He was either straight-down-the-line, or getting worked up about things. Not sexy at *all*.

She took Jeremy's arm and stroked it, feeling the hard swell of bicep. His teeth flashed white in the lights. He pulled her in behind the stub end of a wall. She smelled the Rothmans and gin on him and felt his tongue in her mouth and his thing shoving hard against the crotch of her silk Versace slacks, and she felt the tingle, felt herself go all loose and gooey, so she wanted him now –

Someone behind him shouted. Diana let go of him, and stood there patting her hair into place, frowning as two men came across the car park: Chinese men, not well dressed.

They seemed to have come out of a BMW at the far end of the car park. The light in the BMW went on long enough for them to see a Chinese inside it. Jeremy said, 'Tommy Wong.'

Diana thought there was something a tiny bit sinister about the two men. Then she saw that both of them were holding things in their hands: long, shiny things. Carving knives. And suddenly she was frightened. She held out her handbag to the man on the left. 'There,' she said. 'Have it. Honestly.'

But the Chinese man was looking at her eyes, not her handbag. Next to her, there was a *whock* sound, and Jeremy screamed. Then another blow, and a heavy splashing, and something round rolled away across the car park. Something with black hair and a smile. Jeremy's smile.

Diana opened her mouth to scream.

The thing in the Chinese man's hand flashed in the car park lights, and there was a huge, numbing pain, and everything went dark, for ever.

Tommy Wong was out of the car park before the bodies hit the ground. He could have told Mr Chang right at the beginning.

This Jenkins business had been a mistake.

Jenkins was sitting in the ship's office. The candle on the desk in front of him cast yellow lights in the sweat on the faces of Johnny and the engineers, and deep shadow over the piles of banknotes in front of him. 'Rodriguez on deck,' said someone.

'Tell him to come and see me,' said Jenkins.

The men picked up the envelopes and signed for them. White Filipino teeth flashed in the gloom. The deck was heaving underfoot, but the sound of the wind in the aerials was only a moan now, not the wild shrieking of an hour ago.

'OK,' he said, closing the ship's ledger. 'Go, please.'

They went. He divided the remaining banknotes into piles of a thousand dollars. Get-out money. He breathed deeply, pressed his fingers to his eyes. He was very tired, and there was an ominous heat and pulsation in his shoulder. He put the money into four envelopes, pocketed one, and picked his way through the crowd on the alleyway floor to the chief's cabin.

The door was locked. 'Let me in,' said Jenkins. Silence. 'I've got your money.'

The door opened. He couldn't see the face, but there was no smell of drink, so he assumed it was Mrs Nairn. Her voice said, 'What money?'

'It'll buy you a plane ticket.'

'Fucking great,' said Mrs Nairn.

'Thank you for your help.'

'Stick it up your arse,' said Mrs Nairn, grabbing the envelopes out of his hand.

Jenkins went up to the bridge. There was nobody in the wheelhouse. The ARPA was out; insufficient power. Beyond the side door, Jenkins could see a figure silhouetted against the lighter sky. Pete. He went out on to the wing of the bridge, walking quietly, so tired he felt he was wading through viscous water. The air smelt of fog.

Pete had his back to him. He was hunched over sideways, holding something to his ear. A portable VHF set, the volume turned down. He was saying something into the transponder. Orders to the deck crew preparing for beaching, thought Jenkins.

Then he realized that something was wrong.

Pete was talking Chinese.

Chapter Twelve

Overhead, the clouds had cracked open, and the rifts were blue-black voids of stars. Ahead and to starboard was a long mound of diamonds under a nimbus of grubby red light. San Francisco.

The VHF clicked off. Pete turned to face him, his face red and grey in the lights of the city. The *Glory*'s bow plunged into a trough. The lights dimmed. Fog, thought Jenkins. San Francisco fog.

He said, 'Who are you talking Chinese to?'

'Chinese?' Pete was moving towards him, sociably, it seemed. Jenkins tried to get his brain round the problem. But all problems had vanished in the big problem that was half an hour away. 'Nah, mate.'

'Then who were you talking to?'

'I wasn't.' Pete's voice was light and irritating.

Jenkins leaned against the steel bulkhead of the bridge wing. Why would Pete, who did not speak Chinese, be speaking Chinese on a radio half an hour before the *Glory of Saipan* hit the beach?

None of the passengers had radios.

So Pete had been talking to someone else. Someone in that frieze of lights beyond the fog bank. Someone who would be waiting: not an Anglo-American, because Anglo-Americans spoke English. A Chinese American.

The *Glory* plunged again. A hand came suddenly out of the dark. Hard fingers dug into Jenkins' windpipe. He felt himself picked up and slammed against the metal bulkhead. Splinters of fire twisted in his cut shoulder. He tried to shout, but the fingers kept the sound pinned in his chest.

'I have really been looking forward to this,' said Pete's voice in his ear.

To what? thought Jenkins, dazed.

'I am going to fucking kill you,' said Pete's voice. 'But first there are a couple of things I would like you to know. Such as that you being a nice kind wanker has been very, very useful to me, because I was having some little problems myself about Mr Chang and his tuna boats, because Mr Chang was getting all these people to hisself. We would have bought some of them off him, of course. But we hate expense. What I am arranging now is for us to be met. And the people I want off this ship, which is the pretty ones like your friend Lucy, I will take away and they can bloody come and work for my people or be sent back to China. So,' he said, 'you've really made things very easy for us. Mr Chang will think it's you who's ballsed up his plans. So that is less work for us. Well, none, really.'

The fingers had relaxed enough for Jenkins to say, 'I don't understand.'

'My employers,' said Pete, 'are the 14K. A Triad, old boy. I am employed as Hung Kwan, Red Pole. You would probably call me a head of field operations, something like that. I paid that nice Mr Soares to hire me. I paid off Ho, too, and Lee. Not so they were working for me, but so they gave me . . . freedom of movement. The only one who really got in the way was you. You can pay anyone to do anything, in this life, except a fucking Boy Scout. So regrettably and all that, this is ta-ra, captain.'

The fingers closed again. The blood in Jenkins' head wanted to blow his skull apart. Prat, he thought. You told Pete to find evidence that Ho had gone overboard. You left Pete in control of the facts because he was white, not yellow or brown. You deserve this.

A new voice said, 'Captain? You there?' There was a roaring silence. Then the voice said, 'Hey! He got my money.'

Pete's voice said, 'If he's got your money, your money's going overboard.'

The other voice began to protest.

Pete said, 'Who's going to stop me?' The hands on Jenkins' throat lifted. Jenkins knew he was being hoisted on

332

to the rail. The hands pushed him outboard, so he could hear the hungry roar of the sea forty feet below. He plucked at Pete's arms, ineffectual as a baby. The other voice was shouting. It sounded like Rodriguez.

Then Jenkins felt an odd lurching, and Pete's voice said, 'Urgh.' The fingers on Jenkins' throat slackened, and new hands grabbed him by the shirt and dragged him off the rail and on to the deck. Against the sky Pete's pearly shape took two steps backwards, then two more, until he was leaning against the ship's rail. There was something wrong with the shape of him: as if he were inflatable, and someone had taken his plug out. His arms waved against the grey of the fog bank. He bent double over the ship's rail, head outwards, his body heaving. Jenkins saw him hang there for a moment. Then Rodriguez stepped forward and gave him a shove, and his feet went up, and he was gone.

Man overboard, thought Jenkins stupidly. He levered himself upright and staggered to the rail. The water was a turbulent black, edged with fog. Naturally there was no body. Man bloody overboard.

'Stick knife in him,' said Rodriguez, matter-of-factly. 'So he no kill you.' He cleared his throat. 'You got my money?'

Jenkins fumbled in his pocket for the envelope, and handed it over. 'I count it,' said Rodriguez. He went into the wheelhouse and started flicking a lighter. 'Is good,' he called, after two minutes.

Jenkins stayed on the bridge wing, numb, the blood still roaring in his ears –

Not the blood.

The roaring was nothing to do with blood.

It was breakers.

The wind was dropping: no more than force five now. The *Glory* moved towards the beach at a couple of knots, trailing her flooded aft compartments like an animal with a severed spine dragging its hind legs. The beach was a huge red glow.

The motion of the waves was changing. They were steeper now, lifting the stern and dipping the nose until from the bridge windows Jenkins found himself looking at the ink-black wall of the next wave. At those times, he could feel the weight of the ship – seven thousand tons of iron, four hundred pasts, all hoping for futures.

Then the wave would pass under, and the ship would hang stalled, stern down, nose up, and a wail of fear would rise from the jam-packed cabins and alleyways of the accommodation. And Jenkins would wait, watching the luminous card of the magnetic compass, the only light left on the bridge now that the gyro was out, watching for the swing of the card that would mean that the wind on the super-structure was not strong enough to keep the *Glory* tail-to-sea, the swing that meant she had broached, to lie side-on in the troughs, to roll so the black water would flood into the accommodation and all of them would drown –

But the card did not swing, and the stern rose, and the nose went down again. The *Glory* could almost have been stationary. Blackness had swamped the blink of the channel buoys. But ahead the roaring was louder, and in front of the glow in the sky was a thicker mass crossed by a line of ghostly white.

Land, and surf.

Any minute now, thought Jenkins. He walked out on to the wing of the bridge.

The wind was still dropping. Keep going, he told it. It fluttered and eddied round his head, fell flat for a moment. And in that moment he heard louder than ever before the roar of the breakers; and over the clamminess of the night he smelled a warm smell, marram and pines and car exhaust and frying onions. The smell of the land.

Below him, the next wave steepened and ran forward along the hull. His eyes stayed on it. Instead of rolling on into the black, it changed. Its crest grew higher and thinner, knife-blade thin, and a hundred yards in front of the *Glory*'s nose it plunged down on itself, smooth-backed, reflecting the red glow. Jenkins could not see the white water of its break, because he was behind it. But he heard the thunder of its collapse add itself to the general thunder of the surf. Any minute now, he thought.

He went back into the bridge and yelled down the dark stairs, 'Hold on!' He heard Lucy's voice shrill above the murmur as she translated.

Another wave passed under, and another. On the third, he felt a plucking sensation at his feet. His tongue rasped on his lips. Stern touched, he thought. This is as it should be.

The next wave came. In the trough, the stern touched again. The roar of the surf was all around, and the air was wet with spray. The waves were breaking halfway along the *Glory*'s hull. Ahead and abeam, the water was white; fifteen-foot walls of it, toppling and crashing.

But the *Glory* was still afloat by the bow.

The stern touched again, harder this time. A wail of alarm rose from the people in the dark, Lucy's voice yelling a reassuring descant.

Another wave. The stern hit with a crash. The crest took the bow up, dragged it forward, and dropped it. This time the bow hit too, a boom like an earthquake. The bridge windows smashed with a huge jangle of broken glass and the wheelhouse was full of turbulent air. The passengers were screaming.

Another wave. The stern lifted. The bow lifted. Another huge crash, and the groan of tortured welds and beams as the ship tried to twist, accommodating itself to the seas. The fog shredded and blew away. Through the empty sockets of the windows, the water was all white. But it ended fifty yards away. Fifty yards away was the pale glimmer of a beach.

Fifty yards.

The *Glory* lifted again, sluggishly, slammed down. The slam was not so loud this time, because the waves were moving her in so she was aground all along her length.

Now, thought Jenkins. Please.

The next wave did not lift her bow at all, because it was hard aground. But her stern was a hundred yards to seaward, in deeper water. The wave picked it up and slewed it to port. The next wave slewed it a little more.

After a year or two that lasted perhaps five minutes, the *Glory of Saipan* lay almost parallel to the beach, hard aground.

Fung had been sitting on his suitcase in the dark, holding his daughter's hand. The first time the *Glory* had touched, she had not noticed. The second time, she had jumped

335

convulsively. Then the noise had started, a loud lamentation like the crying of souls in hell. Her hand had become hot and sticky. 'All right,' Fung had said, soothingly. 'All right.' Under his suitcase, the deck had performed terrifying evolutions. People had been flung to and fro in the black alleyway. Fung held on to his daughter, expecting at any minute the doors to burst in and a cold black hammer of salty water to come in and squash the breath from them all.

That was not what happened. What happened was that after sundry crashes and shakings, the ship came to rest, its deck tilted at an angle that made it hard for Fung to keep his footing. But it was at least still, with a stillness that seemed to Fung to have much to do with dry land, except when a wave burst against its side, causing it to shudder and groan. He began to feel the first threads of hope.

After ten minutes, Lucy's voice came down the companionway. 'Silence!' she said. 'The captain announces that the ship is safely on the beach.'

Fung squeezed his daughter's hand, and patted her on her lifejacket. He said, 'I have to do a small amount of work. Mrs Chen will look after you.' And before he could start crying, he got up and picked his way through the crowd to the yellow beam of the flashlight.

'OK?' said the mate Rodriguez, flashing the light in his eyes. 'Eight men? Lifejackets on? We go.'

He opened the door.

Wind blasted in, and a cloud of salt spray. Fung found himself pushed through the door, out on to the little deck where in former times the cooks had set up their cauldrons.

The men crowded out. Rodriguez and half a dozen deckhands closed the door. Rodriguez said, 'Need one, two men ashore with little rope to pull big rope. Wind blowing on beach. Tide going out now, so waves not big. Very good, eh?'

It did not look good to Fung.

The *Glory* was lying parallel to the shore, listing towards the beach. Every time a wave hit her raised starboard side, the hull shuddered and a cloud of white spray rose in the wind and thundered across her hatch-covers. The Hapag Lloyd container where Fung had lived had gone. So had most of the others.

'So,' said Rodriguez. 'Man needed.' Against the white burst of the sea, Fung saw that he was holding up something that could have been a rope.

All the men had families. Bigger families than Fung. Fung sighed. Resignation, he thought. He was the only English speaker. He said, in Chinese, 'I'll go.'

Nobody argued.

Rodriguez showed him down on to the hatch-covers and tied the rope round his waist. 'Careful,' he said, and giggled. 'Get away from ship, quick.'

The ship's port rail was almost at sea level. Fung stepped gingerly downhill, towing rope. He stood with his eyes closed, praying, feeling the ship shudder under the impact of a new wave. When he opened his eyes, the hundred and fifty feet of thundering water had become a silver road to the beach and the city lights beyond: the kind of road, he thought, that you could walk on.

He stepped on to it.

He had been wrong about walking.

It was like stepping into a washing machine. Fung was dragged down and backwards, under the ship, and slammed into the plating so his head rang like a temple gong. He opened his mouth to say that this was not what he had expected. Salt water rushed in. He had no breath. He struggled, panicky, tangling his legs in the rope. He could not tell which way up he was.

Then, suddenly, the lifejacket dragged his head up into the air. He rose on a wave, expecting to hit the ship's side again. But he caught a glimpse of a star-studded sky, and something long and black against it, on which the waves sent up clouds of spray. The ship, he thought, and struck out away from it, to the lights behind the beach.

Some time later, he felt something touch his foot. Sand. He tried to walk, but his legs were tangled. He lay in the water and let the surf wash him in, leave him high and dry, stranded on the firm American sand.

As he untangled his legs, he was crying. He walked up the beach. Two figures rose from the sand. '*Wo*,' said one of them. 'Who *you*?' They were muscular, with big moustaches. They exuded a strong smell of marijuana.

337

Fung dried his eyes. 'Person from sea,' he said. 'Now please to help me pull in this string?'

From the bridge wing Jenkins had watched with his Steiners the black dot of Fung's head struggle through the waves. There were people on the beach. Not police. Not yet. Down on the container tops, he saw the sudden blooming of inflating life rafts – three of them, thirty people each. He watched the figures on the beach haul in the inch-and-a-half -thick rope attached to Fung's thin rope, and make it fast to what looked like a dead pine tree half buried in the sand. He watched them launch the first life raft, saw the people pile in pell-mell. He thought, We've been lucky. The ebb tide was taking the sting out of the sea, and the wind was dropping. And the *Glory*'s hull made a good lee.

The life raft pushed off. The men on the beach would be hauling, now. The waves would do most of the work; the men's job was only to steer. The life raft hit the beach. The people spilled out. They had taken two more ropes ashore. Now there were three life rafts in operation, shuttling to and fro. Won't be long, thought Jenkins.

An arm went round his waist, Lucy's arm. She said, 'Thank you for everything.'

'Luck,' he said. He had the dim notion that what she had said sounded final, as if she were saying goodbye. 'You'd better get going.'

'What about you?'

'I'll see you on the beach.'

'The captain gets off last.'

'That sort of thing. If I miss you, my daughter's at the Four Seasons. I'm meeting her there.'

She said, 'We were lucky to find a real captain.' Her life-jacket scraped his as she kissed him on the mouth. Then she was gone. We were lucky, she had said. Again the finality.

But just now, there were other things to worry about.

Chiu the prostitute was cold, and wet, and frightened. She probably had cystitis, she thought. She was a quarter of a mile from the soft beds of San Francisco. But how the hell was she expected to work with cystitis?

338

'Get in,' said the voice beside her.

The raft was just in front of her. She jumped into it. It dropped away at the last minute. She winded herself as she landed. Someone landed on top of her, a man, stinking of whiskey. Well, she thought, it's not the first time.

''Scuse I,' said the voice of the chief engineer.

'Edwin,' said his wife. 'You drinking?'

'Me?' said Nairn.

Chiu felt something loose sliding in the bottom of the raft. It was a bottle, a half-bottle. Chiu did not usually drink. But she was wet, with only half her luggage, right in the middle of being shipwrecked, and she had no idea where she was going to go, or what she was going to do. There were times when a girl needed a drink. She swigged. The raft started for the beach.

Jenkins walked slowly down the steps to the deck. The crowd down there was smaller now. He wondered if Lucy had gone ashore yet. He hoped she had. It would be good to have someone waiting for you on the beach.

He pulled the flashlight out of his pocket and went through the accommodation, top to bottom, looking for people. It was empty; a squalid steel box, discarded clothes underfoot, overflowing lavatories and doors hanging open, trembling like winter beech leaves under the concussions of the seas. She would be OK till the tide turned in a couple of hours. Then she would start to break up.

Someone will have some fun with the salvage, thought Jenkins, flicking his torch into his cabin, the last cabin he checked. Not me.

The beam caught something shiny on the deck. It was Rachel's tropical snowstorm. It must have fallen. The base had come away from the plastic dome, and the snow and water had leaked out. It was just the debris of a tawdry knick-knack, made in Hong Kong. It had served its purpose, thought Jenkins. We all serve our purposes, and move on to the next phase.

He went on deck.

There were forty people left, plus Rodriguez and a couple of deckhands. The rest were ashore. A life raft was alongside.

On the beach, dark specks migrated upwards, into the strip of darkness before the lights began. Soon the police would come.

'Go on,' said Jenkins to Rodriguez. 'I'll follow on with anyone who's left.'

'Sah,' said Rodriguez, his teeth white in the darkness. It had started to rain. In an hour or so, it would be dawn.

Rodriguez left. The last half-dozen people were standing around, hesitant, without orders. 'Pull that rope,' said Jenkins. 'Hard.' He showed them how. The life raft on the beach began to inch its way out through the waves.

It came alongside, a dim yellow disc, heaving and flapping. The people jumped in, clumsily, sprawling over bundles and each other in the grey-black pre-dawn. Jenkins looked at his watch. They had been aground for thirty minutes; no more. He looked left and right, along the flat hatch-covers of the *Glory*. This was the way all voyages ended. It did not matter what you stepped on to. It was stepping off the ship that ended the voyage.

He waited for the boom and tremor of one more wave, the lift of the life raft on the surge. Then he stepped aboard.

The rope was hard in his hands. He hauled. Other people on the raft hauled too, raggedly. The raft spun and tipped in the breakers. People screamed. Icy water thumped inboard. But they stayed upright, they and their goods, on the yellow disc. And in not more than three minutes the bottom of the raft hit hard sand, and a wave kicked them on and receded, so that underfoot the world was a dizzying sheet of rushing foam.

'Out!' said Jenkins. He lifted a child in one hand and a bundle in the other, and stepped over the side and on to sand so hard and unmoving after the ship and the raft that it made him stumble. But he put the child above high-water mark, and went back to where the black figures were struggling through the last fringes of the surf, dragging them up the beach until they were standing on loose, powdery sand unwetted by the night's sea. They assembled into their little groups and vanished up the beach. Then, it seemed suddenly, he was standing on a slope of sand that was lightening with the dawn, in the rain. The slope of sand was empty, except for footprints, hundreds of them, making a dark stream that disappeared into the dunes.

Jenkins was alone.

He strained his eyes into the half-darkness.

No Lucy.

He was horribly tired. Lifting each foot as if it were an anvil, he plodded up the rain-wet sand and into the trees. He did not look back. He knew there was a ship out there, the Pacific, and beyond the Pacific, Diana. But all that was the past, and none of it needed looking at.

He found a flight of wooden steps and plodded up and through some trees. And suddenly he was in a street, lined with sprawling houses. The houses made him think about baths, hot water. As he thought about hot water, he realized he was cold. Being cold made him think about luggage. He had left his luggage on the ship, all those miles away, light years away, in the Pacific. When he shoved his hands into his pockets, his fingers closed on the envelope of getaway money.

It was like being born again. No luggage. Just a thousand dollars, and the future.

He walked on quickly, moving through a maze of small, tree-lined streets. There were sirens away and behind him. A cab rolled by. He put up his hand.

'Four Seasons,' he said to the driver.

The driver nodded, turned up the radio and moved off. In the growing light, half a dozen Chinese were walking under a line of Monterey pines. 'Bring me your poor, your huddled fucking masses,' said the driver.

Jenkins sat back and watched the houses get closer together and join up, the neon signs start to sprout at the intersections. He got some change from the driver, made him stop at a payphone, and called the Four Seasons.

Rachel answered. She sounded sleepy. The sleep disappeared when she heard his voice. 'Where are you?' she said.

'Ashore. Round the corner.'

'Fantastic. Come here. Now. Quick. What are we going to do?'

'Something or other,' said Jenkins. 'Has a Chinese woman rung?'

341

'No.'

She would be there, thought Jenkins. 'See you in ten minutes,' he said.

Lucy had stepped ashore and dried the drips from her suitcase. She had found Fung, who had waited for her. She had walked with him through the dunes, and on to the road that led inland, towards the lights. The sky overhead had been a pale, rainy grey. She had advised Fung to take a different route from the others, as crowds would excite suspicion. She had kissed Lin goodbye. Then she had turned across a park that had appeared on the left.

When she could no longer hear the sea, she stepped into some bushes and changed into a double-breasted pinstriped business suit with a skirt to just above the knee. She checked her handbag for the false passport. The sky was light, now; a drizzle was falling. She painted her mouth red, fixed her mascara and stepped out on to the blacktop road. It was six o'clock. There were joggers, and from the direction of the sea the sound of sirens.

She flagged down a taxi and told the driver to take her to the airport. As they drove along the shore, she kept her eyes inland, not looking at the sea, or the little groups of Chinese, who might have been out for a morning stroll. She did not want to be reminded of Jer. Or of Jenkins. Particularly not of Jenkins. Jenkins was starting a new life, whether she was there or not. The *Glory of Saipan* had been her first ship, but it could not be the last.

The lobby of the Four Seasons was beige and soothing, quiet as a funeral parlour. Jenkins looked for Lucy among the soft lights and the deep carpets. She was not there. He walked to the desk, hearing the squelch of seawater in his shoes. He asked for Rachel.

The receptionist's name was Gloria. She smiled a radiant white smile. 'Captain Jenkins?' she said. 'Your daughter is in the Grosvenor Suite.'

Rachel had briefed her, thought Jenkins with affection. 'Any other messages?'

'No, sir.' She scrutinized his face. 'I'm sorry, sir.'

Jenkins waded slowly across the deep carpet towards the elevators. She would come, he thought. Surely she would come. But second by second, the certainty was becoming merely a possibility. There in the lobby in the early San Francisco morning, a terrible thought took shape in his mind. Perhaps it had always been merely a possibility.

The elevator blinked down towards him. The door opened.

Behind him, the receptionist said, 'Sir?'

Jenkins' heart walloped in his chest.

'Phone call,' she said. 'Will you take it in the suite?'

'I'll take it here,' said Jenkins, dry-mouthed. He squelched to a bank of house phones, and picked one up. Lucy's voice said, 'You arrived.'

Jenkins said, 'Where are you?'

'At the airport.'

Jesus, thought Jenkins. No. He said, 'What are you doing there?'

'I'm going back.'

'Back?'

'To China.'

Silence rolled between them as wide as the Pacific. Eventually, Jenkins croaked, 'Why?'

She said, 'You know why.' More silence. 'It was you who showed me how to do it.'

'No,' said Jenkins, becoming frantic. 'I didn't do anything –'

'You were going to go halfway,' she said. 'But you couldn't. You went the distance, did what was right. You gave me a . . . demonstration of how to do it.' She laughed, a laugh full of pain. 'So now I've got to do what's right. And what's right is to go back.'

'Lucy,' he said. 'For God's sake. I love you.'

She sounded weary. 'I love you too. But you're the one who showed me that there are things that are more important than love.' Like freedom, thought Jenkins. But freedom was an idea, and Lucy was a woman, flesh and blood . . .

'You can stop me if you want,' she said. 'You can get me pulled off the flight. But I'm counting on you to understand.'

343

He had taken the *Glory of Saipan* and her cargo away from Chang, in the teeth of what could have happened to Rachel. He understood, all right. Not that it helped.

'You could wish me luck,' she said.

'Good luck.'

'Thank you.'

She was crying. Jenkins was sure of it. He said, 'Lucy –'

'They're calling the flight,' she said. 'Goodbye.'

Definitely crying.

The telephone went down.

The elevator was still there. Jenkins climbed aboard, and let it carry him up through the concrete layers and into the future.